Tom Swift Omnibus #3

Victor Appleton

Tom Swift Omnibus #3

Tom Swift Among the Diamond Makers
(Or the Secret of Phantom Mountain)

Tom Swift in the Caves of Ice
(Or the Wreck of the Airship)

Tom Swift and His Sky Racer
(Or the Quickest Flight on Record)

Tom Swift Among the Diamond Makers
or The Secret of Phantom Mountain

TABLE OF CONTENTS:

A Suspicious Jeweler

"Well, Tom Swift, I don't believe you will make any mistake if you buy that diamond," said the jeweler to a young man who was inspecting a tray of pins, set with the sparkling stones. "It is of the first water, and without a flaw."

"It certainly seems so, Mr. Track. I don't know much about diamonds, and I'm depending on you. But this one looks to be all right."

"Is it for yourself, Tom?"

"Er—no—that is, not exactly," and Tom Swift, the young inventor of airships and submarines, blushed slightly.

"Ah, I see. It's for your housekeeper, Mrs. Baggert. Well, I think she would like a pin of this sort. True, it's rather expensive, but—"

"No, it isn't for Mrs. Baggert, Mr. Track," and Tom seemed a bit embarrassed.

"No? Well, then, Tom—of course it's none of my affair, except to sell you a good stone, But if this brooch is for a young lady, I can't recommend anything nicer. Do you think you will take this; or do you prefer to look at some others?"

"Oh, I think this will do, Mr. Track. I guess I'll take—"

Tom's Words were interrupted by a sudden action on the part of the jeweler. Mr. Track ran from behind the showcase and hastened toward the front door.

"Did you see him, Tom?" he cried. "I wonder which way he went?"

"Who?" asked the lad, following the shopkeeper.

"That man. He's been walking up and down in front of my place for the last ten minutes—ever since you've been in here, in fact, and I don't like his looks."

"What did he do?"

"Nothing much, except to stare in here as if he was sizing my place up."

"Sizing it up?"

"Yes. Getting the lay of the land, so he or some confederate could commit a robbery, maybe."

"A robbery? Do you think that man was a thief?"

"I don't know that he was, Tom, and yet a jeweler has to be always on the watch, and that isn't a joke, either, Tom Swift. Swindlers and thieves are always on the alert for a chance to rob a jewelry store, and they work many games."

"I didn't notice any particular man looking in here," said Tom, who still held the diamond brooch in his hand.

"Well I did," went on the jeweler. "I happened to glance out of the window when you were looking at the pins, and I saw his eyes staring in here in a suspicious manner. He may have a confederate with him, and, when you're gone, one may come in, and pretend to want to look at some diamonds. Then, when I'm showing him some, the other man will enter, engage my attention, and the first man will slip out with a diamond ring or pin. It's often done."

"You seem to have it all worked out, Mr. Track," observed the lad, with a smile. "How do you know but what I'm in with a gang of thieves, and that I'm only pretending to want to buy a diamond pin?"

"Oh, I guess I haven't known you, Tom Swift, ever since you were big enough to toddle, not to be sure about what you're up to. But I certainly didn't like the looks of that man. However, let's forget about him. He seems to have gone down the street, and, after all, perhaps I was mistaken. Just wait until I show you a few more styles before you decide. The young lady may like one of these," and the jeweler went to another showcase and took out some more trays of brooches.

"What makes you think she's a young lady, Mr. Track?" asked the lad.

"Oh, it's easy guessing, Tom. We jewelers are good readers of character. I can size up a young fellow coming in here to buy an engagement or a wedding ring, as soon as he enters the door. I suppose you'll soon be in the market for one of those, Tom, if all the reports I hear about you are true—you and a certain Mary Nestor."

"I—er—I think I don't care for any of these pins," spoke Tom, quickly, with a blush. "I like the first lot best. I think I'll take the one I had in my hand when that man alarmed you. Ha! That's odd! What did I do with it?"

Tom looked about on the showcase, and glanced down on the floor. He had mislaid the brooch, but the jeweler, with a laugh, lifted it out of a tray a moment later.

"I saw you lay it down," he said. "We jewelers have to be on the watch. Here it is. I'll just put it in a box, and—"

With an exclamation, Mr. Track gave a hasty glance toward his big show window. Tom looked up, and saw a man's face peering in. At the sight of it, he, too, uttered a cry of surprise.

The next instant the man outside knocked on the glass, apparently with a piece of metal, making a sharp sound. As soon as he heard it, the jeweler once more sprang from behind the showcase, and leaped for the door crying:

"There's the thief! He's trying to cut a hole through my show window and reach in and get something! It's an old trick. I'll get the police! Tom, you stay here on guard!" and before the lad could utter a protest, the jeweler had opened the door, and was speeding down the street in the gathering darkness.

Tom stared about him in some bewilderment. He was left alone in charge of a very valuable stock of jewelry, the owner of which was racing after a supposed thief, crying:

"Police! Help! Thieves! Stop him, somebody!"

"This is a queer go," mused Tom. "I wonder who that man was? He looked like somebody I know, and yet I can't seem to place his face. I wonder if he was trying to rob the placer Maybe there's another one—a confederate—around here."

This thought rather alarmed Tom, so he went to the door, and looked up and down the street. He could see no suspicious characters, but in the direction in which the jeweler was running there was a little throng of people, following Mr. Track after the man who had knocked on the window.

"I wish I was there, instead of here," mused the lad. "Still I can't leave, or a thief might come in. Perhaps that was the game, and one of the gang is hanging around, hoping the store will be deserted, so he can enter and take what he likes."

Tom had read of such cases, and he at once resolved that he would not only remain in the jewelry shop, but that he would lock the door, which he at once proceeded to do. Then he breathed easier.

The town of Shopton, in the outskirts of which Tom lived with his father, and where the scene above narrated took place, was none too well lighted at night, and the lad had his doubts about the jeweler catching the oddly-acting man, especially as the latter had a good start.

"But some one may head him off," reasoned Tom. "Though if they do catch him, I don't see what they can prove against him. Hello, here I am carrying this diamond pin around. I might lose it. Guess I'll put it back on the tray."

He replaced in the proper receptacle one of the pins he bad been examining when the excitement occurred.

"I wonder if Mary will like that?" he said, softly. "I hope she does. Perhaps it would be better if she could come here herself and pick out one—"

Tom's musing was suddenly interrupted by a sharp tattoo on the glass door of the jewelry shop. With a start, he looked up, to see staring in on him the face of the man who had been there before—the man of whom the jeweler was even then in chase.

"Why—why—" stammered Tom.

The man knocked again.

"Tom—Tom Swift!" he called. "Don't you know me?"

"Know you—you?" repeated the lad.

"Yes— don't you remember Earthquake Island—how we were nearly killed there—don't you remember Mr. Jenks?"

"Mr. Jenks?"

Tom was so startled that he could only repeat words after the strange man, who was talking to him from outside the glass door.

"Yes, Mr. Jenks," was the reply. "Mr. Barcoe Jenks, who makes diamonds. I saw you in the store about to buy a diamond—I wanted to tell you not to—I'll give you a better diamond than you can buy—I just arrived in this place—I must have a private talk with you—Come out—I'll share a wonderful secret with you."

A flood of memory came to Tom. He did recall the very strange man who walked around Earthquake Island—where Tom and some friends had been marooned recently—walked about with a pocketful of what he said were diamonds. Now Barcoe Jenks was here.

"I must see you privately, Tom Swift," went on Mr. Jenks, as he once more tapped on the glass. "Don't waste money buying diamonds, when you and I can make better ones. Where can I have a talk with you? I—" Mr. Jenks suddenly looked down the dimly- lighted street. "They're coming back!" he cried. "I don't want to be seen. I'll call at your house later to-night—be on the watch for me—until then—good-by!"

He waved his hand, and was gone in an instant. Tom stood staring at the glass door. He hardly knew whether to believe it or not—perhaps it was all a dream.

He pinched himself to make sure that he was awake. Very substantial flesh met his thumb and finger, and he felt the pain.

"I'm awake all right," he murmured. "But Barcoe Jenks here—and still talking that nonsense about his manufactured diamonds. I think he must be crazy. I wonder—"

Once more the lad's musing was interrupted. He heard a murmur of excited voices outside the store, on the street. Then the door of the jewelry shop was tried. Mr. Track's face was pressed against the glass.

"Open the door! Let me in, Tom!" he called. "I've caught the thief," and as the lad unlocked the portal he saw that the jeweler held by the arm a ragged lad. "Ah; you scoundrel! I've caught you!" cried the diamond merchant, shaking the small chap, while Tom looked on, more mystified than ever.

A Midnight Visit

While Mr. Track, the jeweler, and several citizens, attracted by the chase after the supposed thief, are crowded into the store, anxious to hear explanations of the strange affair, I will take the opportunity to tell you something of Tom Swift, the lad who is to figure in this story.

Many of you have already made his acquaintance, when he has been speeding about in his airship or fast electric runabout, and to others we will state that our hero first made his bow to the public in the book called "Tom Swift and His Motor-Cycle," the initial volume of this series.

In that story there was related how Tom made the acquaintance of an odd individual, named Mr. Wakefield Damon, who was continually blessing himself, some part of his anatomy, or his possessions. Mr. Damon was riding a motor-cycle, and it started to climb a tree, to his pain and fright. Afterward Tom purchased the machine, and had many adventures on it, including a chase after a gang of men who had stolen a valuable patent model belonging to Mr. Swift.

Mr. Swift, and his son were both inventors. They lived together in a fine house in the suburbs of Shopton, New York, and with them dwelt Mrs. Baggert, the housekeeper (for Tom's mother was dead), and also Garret Jackson, an expert engineer, who aided the young inventor and his father in perfecting many machines.

There was also another semi-member of the household, to wit, Eradicate Sampson, an eccentric colored man, who owned a mule called Boomerang. Eradicate did odd jobs around the place, and the mule assisted his owner—that is when the mule felt like it.

In the second volume of the series, entitled "Tom Swift and His Motor-Boat," there was related the incidents following a pursuit after a gang of unprincipled men, who sought to get Possession of some of Mr. Swift's patents, and it was while in this boat that Tom, his father, and a friend, Ned Newton, rescued from Lake Carlopa a Mr. John Sharp, who fell from his burning balloon. Mr. Sharp was a skilled aeronaut, and after his recovery he joined Tom in building a big airship, called the *Red Cloud*. Tom's adventures in this craft are set down in detail in the third volume of the series, called "Tom Swift and His Airship." Not only did he and Mr. Sharp and Mr. Damon make a great trip, but they captured some bank robbers, and incidentally cleared themselves from the imputation of having looted the vault of seventy-five thousand dollars, which charge was fostered by a certain Mr. Foger, and his son Andy, who was Tom's enemy.

Not satisfied with having conquered the air, Tom and his father set to work to gain a victory over the ocean. They built a boat that could navigate under water, and, in the fourth book of the series, called "Tom Swift and His Submarine Boat," you will find an account of how they went under the ocean to secure a sunken treasure, and the fight they had with their enemies who sought to get it away from them. They went through many perils, not the least of which was capture by a foreign warship.

In the fifth book, entitled "Tom Swift and His Electric Runabout," there was told the story of a wonderfully speedy electric automobile the young inventor constructed, and how he made a great race in it, and saved from ruin a bank, in which his father and Mr. Damon were interested.

Tom's ability as an inventor had, by this time, become well known. One day, as related in a volume called "Tom Swift and His Wireless Message," he received a letter from a Mr. Hosmer Fenwick, of Philadelphia, asking his aid in perfecting an airship which the resident of the Quaker City had built, but which would not work. In his small monoplane, the *Butterfly*, Tom and Mr. Damon went to Philadelphia, as Mr. Damon was acquainted with Mr. Fenwick.

Tom carefully inspected the *Whizzer* which was the name of Mr. Fenwick's airship, and, after some difficulties, succeeded in getting the electric craft in shape to make a flight.

Tom, Mr. Damon and Mr. Fenwick started to make a trip to Cape May in the *Whizzer*, but were caught in a terrific storm, and blown out to sea. The wind became a hurricane, the airship was disabled, and wrecked in mid-air. When it fell to earth it landed on one of the small West Indian islands, but what was the terror of the three castaways to find that the island was subject to earthquake shocks.

But the earth-tremors were not the only surprise in store for Tom and his two friends, On the island they found five men and two ladies, who, by strange chance, had been stranded there when the yacht *Resolute*, owned by Mr. George Hosbrook, was wrecked in the same storm that disabled the airship. Mr. Hosbrook, a millionaire, was taking a party of friends to the West Indies.

When the castaways (among whom were Mr. and Mrs. Amos Nestor, parents of Mary Nestor, a girl of whom Tom was very fond) found that there was danger of the island being destroyed in an earthquake, they were in despair. There seemed no way of being rescued, as the island was out of the line of regular ship travel.

Tom, however, was resourceful. With the electrical apparatus from the wrecked airship, he built a wireless plant, and sent messages for help, broadcast over the ocean.

They were finally heard, and answered, by an operator on board the steamer *Camberanian*, which came on under forced drought, and rescued Tom and his friends. It was only just in time, for, no sooner had they gotten aboard the steamer in lifeboats, than the whole island was destroyed by an earthquake shock.

But Tom, the parents of Mary Nestor, Mr. Damon, Mr. Fenwick, and all the others, got safely home. Among the survivors from the yacht *Resolute* was a Mr. Barcoe Jenks, who now, most unexpectedly, had confronted Tom through the glass window of the jewelry store. Mr. Jenks was a peculiar man. Tom discovered this on Earthquake Island. Mr. Jenks carried with him some stones which he said were diamonds. He asserted that he had made them, but Tom did not know whether or not to believe this.

When it seemed that the castaways would not be saved Mr. Jenks offered Tom a large sum in these same diamonds for some plan whereby he might escape the earthquakes. Mr. Jenks said there was a certain secret in connection with the manufactured diamonds that he had to solve—that he had been defrauded of his rights— and that a certain Phantom Mountain figured in it. But Tom, at that time, paid little attention to Mr. Jenks' talk. The time was to come, however, when he would attach much importance to it.

When this story opens, Tom was more interested in Mr. Barcoe Jenks than in any one else, and was wondering what he wanted to see him about. The young inventor could not quite understand how Mr. Track, the jeweler, could come back with a lad he suspected of being a thief, when the person who had acted so suspiciously, and who had knocked on the glass, was the queer man, Mr. Jenks.

"Yes, Tom I caught him," the jeweler went on. "I chased after him, and nabbed him. It was hard work, too, for I'm not a good runner. Now, you little rascal, tell me why you tried to rob my store?" and the diamond merchant shook the lad roughly.

"I—I didn't try to rob your store," was the timid answer.

"Well, perhaps you didn't, exactly, but your confederates did. Why did you rap on the glass, and why were you staring in so intently?"

"I wasn't lookin' in."

"Well, if it wasn't you, it was some one just like you. But why did you run when I raced down the street?"

"I—I don't know," and the lad began to snivel. "I—I jest ran—that's all—'cause I see everybody else runnin', an' I thought there was a fire."

"Ha! That's a likely story! You ran because you are guilty! I'm going to hand you over to the police."

"Did he get anything, Mr. Track?" asked one of the men who had joined the jeweler in the chase.

"No, I can't say that he did. He didn't get a chance. Tom Swift was in here at the time. But this fellow was only waiting for a chance to steal, or else to aid his confederates."

"But, if he didn't take anything, I don't see how you can have him arrested," went on the man.

"On suspicion; that's how!" asserted Mr. Track. "Will some one get me a constable?"

"I wouldn't call a constable," said Tom, quietly.

"Why not?"

"Because that isn't the person who looked in your window."

"How do you know, Tom?"

"Because that person came back while you were out. I saw him."

"You saw him? Did he try to steal any of my diamonds, Tom?"

"No, I guess he doesn't need any."

"Why not?" There was wonder in the jeweler's tone.

"Why, he claims he can make all he wants."

"Make diamonds?"

"So he says."

"Why, he must be crazy!" and Mr. Track laughed.

"Perhaps he is," admitted Tom, "I'm only telling you what he says. He's the person who acted so suspiciously. He came back here, I'm telling you, while you were running down the street, and spoke to me."

"Oh, then you know him?" The jeweler's voice was suspicious.

"I didn't at first," admitted Tom. "But when he said he was Mr. Barcoe Jenks, I remembered that I had met him when I was cast away on Earthquake Island."

"And he says he can make diamonds?" asked Mr. Track.

"What did he want of you?" and the jeweler looked at Tom, quizzically.

"He wanted to have a talk with me," replied the lad, "and when he saw me in your store, he tried to attract my attention by knocking on the glass."

"That's a queer way to do," declared Mr. Track. "What did he want?"

"I don't know exactly," answered Tom, not caring to go into details just then. "But I'm sure, Mr. Track, that you've got the wrong person there. That lad never looked in the window, nor knocked on the glass."

"That's right—I didn't," asserted the captive.

The jeweler looked doubtful.

"Why did you run?" he asked.

"I told you, I thought there was a fire."

"That's right, I don't believe he's the fellow you want," put in another man. "I was standing on the corner, near White's grocery store, and I noticed this lad. That was before I heard you yelling, and saw you coming, and then I joined in the chase. I guess the man you were after got away, Track."

"He did," asserted Tom. "He came back here, a little while ago, and he ran away just now, as he heard you coming."

"Where did he go?" asked the jeweler, eagerly.

"I don't know," answered Tom. "Only you've got the wrong lad here."

"Well, perhaps I have," admitted the diamond merchant. "You can go, youngster, but next time, don't run if you're not guilty."

"I thought there was a fire," repeated the lad, as he hurriedly slipped through the crowd in the store, and disappeared down the dark street.

"Well, I guess the excitement's all over, and, anyhow, you weren't robbed, Track," said a stout man, as he left the store. The others soon followed, and Tom and the jeweler were once more alone in the shop.

"Can you tell me something about this man, Tom?" asked Mr. Track, eagerly. "So he really makes diamonds. Who is he?"

"I'd rather not tell—just now," replied the young inventor. "I don't take much stock in him, myself. I think he's visionary. He may think he has made diamonds, and he may have made some stones that look like them. I'm very skeptical."

"If you could bring me some, Tom, I could soon tell whether they were real or not. Can you?"

The lad shook his head.

"I don't expect to see Mr. Jenks again," he said. "He talked rather wildly about waiting to meet me, but that man is odd— crazy, perhaps—and I don't imagine I'll see him. He's harmless, but he's eccentric. Well, there was quite some excitement for a time."

"I should say there was. I thought it was a plan to rob me," and the jeweler began putting away the diamond pins. In fact, the excitement so filled the minds of himself and Tom that neither of them thought any more of the object of the lad's visit, and the young inventor departed without purchasing the pin he had come after.

It was not until he was out on the street, walking toward his home, that the matter came back to his mind.

"I declare!" he exclaimed. "I didn't get that pin for Mary, after all! Well, never mind, I have a week until her birthday, and I can get it tomorrow."

He walked rapidly toward home, for the weather looked threatening, and Tom had no umbrella. He was musing on the happenings of the evening when he reached his house. His father was out, as was Garret Jackson, the engineer; and Mrs. Baggert, the housekeeper, was entertaining a lady in the sitting-room, so, as Tom was rather tired, he went directly to his own room, and, a little later got into bed.

It was shortly after midnight when he was awakened by hearing a rattling on the window of his room. The reason he was able to fix the time so accurately was because as soon as he awakened he pressed a little electric button, and it illuminated the face of a small clock on his bureau. The hands pointed to five minutes past twelve.

"Humph! That sounds like hail!" exclaimed Tom, as he arose, and looked out of the casement. "I wonder if any of the skylights of the airship shed are open? There might be some damage. Guess I'd better go out and take a look."

He had mentally reasoned this far before he had looked out, and when he saw that the moon was brightly shining in a clear sky, he was a bit surprised.

"Why—that wasn't hail," he murmured. "It isn't even raining. I wonder what it was?"

He was answered a moment later, for a shower of fine gravel from the walk flew up and clattered against the glass. With a start, Tom looked down, and saw a dark figure standing under an apple tree.

"Hello! Who's there?" called the lad, after he had raised the sash.

"It's I—Mr. Jenks," was the surprising answer.

"Mr. Jenks?" repeated Tom.

"Yes—Barcoe Jenks, of Earthquake Island."

"You here? What do you want?"

"Can you come down?"

"What for?"

"Tom Swift, I've something very important to tell you," was the answer in a low voice, yet which carried to Tom's ears perfectly. "Do you want to make a fortune for yourself—and for me?"

"How?" Tom was beginning to think more and more that Mr. Jenks was crazy.

"How? By helping me to discover the secret of Phantom Mountain, where the diamonds are made! Will you?"

"Wait a minute—I'll come down," answered Tom, and he began to grope for his clothes in the dim light of the little electric lamp.

What was the secret of Phantom Mountain? What did Mr. Jenks really want? Could he make diamonds? Tom asked himself these questions as he hastily dressed to go down to his midnight visitor.

A STRANGE STORY

"Well, Mr. Jenks," began Tom, when he had descended to the garden, and greeted the man who had acted so strangely on Earthquake Island, "this is rather an odd time for a visit."

"I realize that, Tom Swift," was the answer, and the lad noticed that the man spoke much more calmly than he had that evening at the jewelry shop. "I realize that, but I have to be cautious in my movements."

"Why?"

"Because there are enemies on my track. If they thought I was seeking aid to discover the secret of Phantom Mountain, my life might pay the forfeit."

"Are you in earnest, Mr. Jenks?"

"I certainly am, and, while I must apologize for awakening you at this unseemly hour, and for the mysterious nature of my visit, if you will let me tell my story, you will see the need of secrecy."

"Oh, I don't mind being awakened," answered Tom, good-naturedly, "but I will be frank with you, Mr. Jenks. I hardly can believe what you have stated to me several times—that you know how diamonds can be made."

"I can prove it to you," was the quiet answer.

"Yes, I know. For centuries men have tried to discover the secret of transmuting base metals into gold, and how to make diamonds by chemical means. But they have all been failures."

"All except this process—the process used at Phantom Mountain," insisted the queer man. "Do you want to hear my story?"

"I have no objections."

"Then let me warn you," went on Mr. Jenks, "that if you do hear it, you will be so fascinated by it that I am sure you will want to cast your lot in with mine, and aid me to get my rights, and solve the mystery. And I also want to warn you that if you do, there is a certain amount of danger connected with it."

"I'm used to danger," answered Tom, quietly. "Let me hear your story. But first explain how you came to come here, and why you acted so strangely at the jewelry store."

"Willingly. I tried to attract your attention at the store, because I saw that you were going to buy a diamond, and I didn't want you to."

"Why not?"

"Because I want to present you with a beautiful stone, that will answer your purpose as well or better, than any one you could buy. That will prove my story better than any amount of words or argument. But I could not attract your attention without also attracting that of the jeweler. He became suspicious, gave chase, and I thought it best to vanish. I hope no one was made to suffer for what may have been my imprudence."

"No, the lad whom Mr. Track caught was let go. But how did you happen to come to Shopton?"

"To see you. I got your address from the owner of the yacht *Resolute*. I knew that if there was one person who could aid me to recover my rights, it would be you, Tom Swift. Will you help me? Will you come with me to discover the secret of Phantom Mountain? If we go, it will have to be in an airship, for in no other way, I think, can we come upon the place, as it is closely guarded. Will you come? I will pay you well."

"Perhaps I had better hear your story," said the young inventor. "But first let me suggest that we move farther away from the house. My father, or Mr. Jackson, or the housekeeper, may hear us talking, and it may disturb them. Come with me to my private shop," and Tom led the way to a small building where he did experimental work. He unlocked the door with a key he carried, turned on the lights, which were run by a storage battery, and motioned Mr. Jenks to a seat.

"Now I'll hear your story," said Tom.

"I'll make it as short as possible," went on the queer man. "To begin with, it is now several years ago since a poorly dressed stranger applied to me one night for money enough to get a meal and a bed to sleep in. I was living in New York City at the time, and this was midnight, as I was returning home from my club.

"I was touched by the man's appearance, and gave him some money. He asked for my card, saying he would repay me some day. I gave it to him, little thinking I would hear from the man again. But I did. He called at my apartments about a week later, saying he had secured work as an expert setter of diamonds, and wanted to repay me. I did not want to take his money, but the fact that such a sorry looking specimen of manhood as he had been when I aided him, was an expert handler of gems interested me. I talked with the man, and he made a curious statement.

"This man, who gave his name as Enos Folwell, said he knew a place where diamonds could be made, partly in a scientific manner, and partly by the forces of nature. I laughed at him, but he told me so many details that I began to believe him. He said he and some other friends of his, who were diamond cutters, had a plant in the midst of the Rocky Mountains, where they had succeeded in making several small, but very perfect diamonds. They had come to the end of their rope, though, so to speak, because they could not afford to buy the materials needed. Folwell said that he and his companions had temporarily separated, had left the mountain where they made diamonds, and agreed to meet there later when they had more money with which to purchase materials. They had all agreed to go out into civilization, and work for enough funds to enable them to go on with their diamond making.

"I hardly knew whether to believe the man or not, but he offered proof. He had several small, but very perfect diamonds with him, and he gave them to me, to have tested in any way I desired.

"I promised to look into the matter, and, as I was quite wealthy, as, in fact I am now, and if I found that the stones he gave me were real, I said I might invest some money in the plant."

"Were the diamonds good?" asked Tom, who was beginning to be interested.

"They were—stones of the first water, though small. An expert gem merchant, to whom I took them, said he had never seen any diamonds like them, and he wanted to know where I got them. Of course I did not tell him.

"To make a long story short, I saw Folwell again, told him to communicate with his companions, and to tell them that I would agree to supply the cash needed, if I could share in the diamond making. To this they agreed, and, after some weeks spent in preparation, a party of us set out for Phantom Mountain."

"Phantom Mountain?" interrupted Tom. "Where is it?"

"I don't know, exactly—it's somewhere in the Rockies, but the exact location is a mystery. That is why I need your help. You will soon understand the reason. Well, as I said, myself, Folwell and the others, who were not exactly prepossessing sort of men, started west. When we got to a small town, called Indian Ridge, near Leadville, Colorado, the men insisted that I must now proceed in secret, and consent to be blindfolded, as they were not yet ready to reveal the secret of the place where they made the diamonds.

"I did not want to agree to this, but they insisted, and I gave in, foolishly perhaps. At any rate I was blindfolded one night, placed in a wagon, and we drove off into the mountains. After traveling for some distance I was led, still blindfolded, up a steep trail.

"When the bandage was taken off my eyes I saw that I was in a large cave. The men were with me, and they apologized for the necessity that caused them to blindfold me. They said they were ready to proceed with the making of diamonds, but I must promise not to seek to discover the secret until they gave me permission, nor was I to attempt to leave the cave. I had to agree.

"Next they demanded that I give them a large sum, which I had promised when they showed me, conclusively, that they could make diamonds. I refused to do this until I had seen some of the precious stones, and they agreed that this was fair, but said I would have to wait a few days.

"Well, I waited, and, all that while, I was virtually a prisoner in the cave. All I could learn was that it was in the midst of a great range, near the top, and that one of the peaks was called Phantom Mountain. Why, I did not learn until later.

"At last one night, during a terrific thunder storm, the leader of the diamond makers—Folwell—announced that I could now see the stones made. The men had been preparing their chemicals for some days previous. I was taken into a small chamber of the cave, and there saw quite a complicated apparatus. Part of it was a great steel box, with a lever on it.

"We will let you make some diamonds for yourself," Folwell said to me, and he directed me to pull the lever of the box, at a certain signal. The signal came, just as a terrific crash of thunder shook the very mountain inside of which we were. The box of steel got red-hot, and when it cooled off it was opened, and was given a handful of white stones."

"Were they diamonds?" asked Tom, eagerly.

Mr. Jenks held out one hand. In the palm glittered a large stone—ostensibly a diamond. In the rays of the moon it showed all the colors of the rainbow—a beautiful gem. "That is one of the stones I made—or rather that I supposed I had made," went on Mr. Jenks. "It is one of several I have, but they have not all been cut and polished as has this one.

"Naturally I was much impressed by what I saw, and, after I had made certain tests which convinced me that the stones in the steel box were diamonds, I paid over the money as I had promised. That was my undoing."

"How?"

"As soon as the men got the cash, they had no further use for me. The next I remember is eating a rude meal, while we discussed the future of making diamonds. I knew nothing more until I found myself back in the small hotel at Indian Ridge, whence I had gone some time previous, with the men, to the cave in the mountain."

"What happened?" asked Tom, much surprised by the unexpected outcome of the affair. "I had been tricked, that was all! As soon as the men had my money they had no further use for me. They did not want me to learn the secret of their diamond making, and they drugged me, carried me away from the cave, and left me in the hotel."

"Didn't you try to find the cave again?"

"I did, but without avail. I spent some time in the Rockies, but no one could tell where Phantom Mountain was; in fact, few had heard of it, and I was nearly lost searching for it.

"I came back East, determined to get even. I had given the men a very large sum of money, and, in exchange, they had given me several diamonds. Probably the stones are worth nearly as much as the money I invested, but I was cheated, for I was promised an equal share in the profits. These were denied me, and I was tricked. I determined to be revenged, or at least to discover the secret of making diamonds. It is my right."

"I agree with you," spoke Tom.

"But, up to the time I met you on Earthquake Island, I could form no plan for discovering Phantom Mountain, and learning the secret of the diamond makers," went on Mr. Jenks. "I carried the gems about with me, as you doubtless saw when we were on the island. But I knew I needed an airship in which to fly over the mountains, and pick out the location of the cave where the diamonds are made."

"But how can you locate it, if you were blindfolded when you were taken there, Mr. Jenks?"

"I forgot to tell you that, on our journey into the mountains, and just before I was carried into the cave, I managed to raise one corner of the bandage. I caught a glimpse of a very peculiarly shaped cliff—it is like a great head, standing out in bold relief against the moonlight, when I saw it. That head of rock is near the cave. It may be the landmark by which we can locate Phantom Mountain."

"Perhaps," admitted the young inventor.

"What I want to know is this," went on Mr. Jenks. "Will you go with me on this quest—go in your airship to discover the secret of the diamond makers? If you will, I will share with you whatever diamonds we can discover, or make; besides paying all expenses. Will you go, Tom Swift?"

The young inventor did not know what to answer. How far was Mr. Jenks to be trusted? Were the stones he had real diamonds? Was his story, fantastical as it sounded—true? Would it be safe for Tom to go?

The lad asked himself these questions. Mr. Jenks saw his hesitation.

"Here," said the strange man, "I will prove what I say. Take this diamond. I intended it for you, anyhow, for what you did for me on Earthquake Island. Take it, and—and give it to the person for whom you were about to purchase a diamond to-night. But, first of all, take it to a gem expert, and get his opinion. That will prove the truth of what I say, Tom Swift, and I feel sure that you will cast your lot in with mine, and help me to discover the secret of Phantom Mountain, and aid me to get my rights from the diamond makers!"

Andy Foger Gets a Fright

Tom Swift considered a few minutes. On the face of it, the proposition appealed to him. He had been home some time now after his adventures on Earthquake Island, and he was beginning to long for more excitement. The search for the mysterious mountain, and the cave of the diamond makers, might offer a new field for him. But there came to him a certain distrust of Mr. Jenks.

"I don't like to doubt your word," began Tom, slowly, "but you know, Mr. Jenks, that some of the greatest chemists have tried in vain to make diamonds; or, at best, they have made only tiny ones. To think that any man, or set of men, made real diamonds as large as the ones you have, doesn't seem—well—" and Tom hesitated.

"You mean you can hardly believe me?" asked Mr. Jenks.

"I guess that's it," assented Tom.

"I don't blame you a bit!" exclaimed the odd man. "In fact, I didn't believe it when they told me they could make diamonds. But they proved it to me. I'm ready now to prove it to you."

"I'll tell you what I'll do. Here's this one stone, cut ready for setting. Here's another, uncut," and Mr. Jenks drew from his pocket what looked like a piece of crystal. "Take them to any jeweler," he resumed—"to the one in whose place I saw you to- night. I'll abide by the verdict you get, and I'll come here tomorrow night, and hear what you have to say."

"Why do you come at night?" asked Tom, thinking there was something suspicious in that.

"Because my life might be in danger if I was seen talking to you, and showing you diamonds in the daytime—especially just now."

"Why at this particular time?"

"For the reason that the diamond makers are on my trail. As long as I remained quiet, after their shabby treatment of me, and did not try to discover their secret, they were all right. But, after I realized that I had been cheated out of my rights, and when I began to make an investigation, with a view to discovering their secret whereabouts, I received mysterious and anonymous warnings to stop."

"But I did not. I came East, and tried to get help to discover the cave of the diamond makers, but I was unsuccessful. I needed an airship, as I—said, and no person who could operate one, would agree to go with me on the quest. Again I received a warning to drop all search for the diamond makers, but I persisted, and about a week ago I found I was being shadowed."

"Shadowed; by whom?" asked Tom.

"By a man I never remember seeing, but who, I have no doubt, is one of the diamond-making gang."

"Do you think he means you harm?"

"I'm sure of it. That is the reason I have to act so in secret, and come to see you at night. I don't want those scoundrels to find out what I am about to do. On my return from Earthquake Island, I again endeavored to interest an airship man in my plan, but he evidently thought me insane. Then I thought of you, as I had done before, but I was afraid you, too, would laugh at my proposition. However, I decided to come here, and I did. It seemed almost providential that my first view of you was in a jewelry shop, looking at diamonds. I took it as a good omen. Now it remains with you. May I call here to-morrow night, and get your answer?"

Tom Swift made up his mind quickly. After all it would be easy enough to find out if the diamonds were real. If they were, he could then decide whether or not to go with Mr. Jenks on the mysterious quest. So he answered:

"I'll consider the matter, Mr. Jenks. I'll meet you here tomorrow night. In the meanwhile, for my own satisfaction, I'll let an expert look at these stones."

"Get the greatest diamond expert in the world, and he'll pronounce them perfect!" predicted the odd man. "Now I'll bid you goodnight, and be going. I'll be here at this time tomorrow."

As Mr. Jenks turned aside there was a movement among the trees in the orchard, and a shadowy figure was seen hurrying away.

"Who's that?" asked the diamond man, in a hoarse whisper. "Did you see that, Tom Swift? Some one was here—listening to what I said! Perhaps it was the man who has been shadowing me!"

"I think not. I guess it was Eradicate Sampson, a colored man who does work for us," said Tom. "Is that you, Rad?" he called.

"Yais, sah, Massa Tom, heah I is!" answered the voice of the negro, but it came from an entirely different direction than that in which the shadowy figure had been seen.

"Where are you, Rad?" called the young inventor.

"Right heah," was the reply, and the colored man came from the direction of the stable. "I were jest out seein' if mah mule Boomerang were all right. Sometimes he's restless, an' don't sleep laik he oughter."

"Then that wasn't you over in the orchard?" asked Tom, in some uneasiness.

"No, sah, I ain't been in de orchard. I were sleepin' in mah shack, till jest a few minutes ago, when I got up, an' went in t' see Boomerang. I had a dream dat some coon were tryin t' steal him, an' it sort ob 'sturbed me, laik."

"If it wasn't your man, it was some one else," said Mr. Jenks, decidedly.

"We'll have a look!" exclaimed Tom. "Here, Rad, come over and scurry among those trees. We just saw some one sneaking around."

"I'll sure do dat!" cried the colored man. "Mebby it were somebody arter Boomerang! I'll find 'em."

"I don't believe it was any one after the mule," murmured Mr. Jenks, "but it certainly was some one—more likely some one after me."

The three made a hasty search among the trees, but the intruder had vanished, leaving no trace. They went out into the road, which the moon threw into bold relief along its white stretch, but there was no figure scurrying away.

"Whoever it was, is gone," spoke Tom. "You can go back to bed, Rad," for the colored man, of late, had been sleeping in a shack on the Swift premises.

"And I guess it's time for me to go, too," added Mr. Jenks. "I'll be here to-morrow night, Tom, and I hope your answer will be favorable."

Tom did not sleep well the remainder of the night, for his fitful slumbers were disturbed by dreams of enormous caves, filled with diamonds, with dark, shadowy figures trying to put him into a red-hot steel box. Once he awakened with a start, and put his hand under his pillow to feel if the two stones Mr. Jenks had given him, were still there. They had not been disturbed.

Tom made up his mind to find out if the stones were really diamonds, before saying anything to his father about the chance of going to seek Phantom Mountain. And the young inventor wished to get the opinion of some other jeweler than Mr. Track—at least, at first.

"Though if this one proves to be a good gem, I'll have Mr. Track set it in a brooch, and give it to Mary for her birthday," decided the young inventor. "Guess I'll take a run over to Chester in the *Butterfly*, and see what one of the jewelers there has to say."

In addition to his big airship, *Red Cloud*, Tom owned a small, swift monoplane, which he called *Butterfly*. This had been damaged by Andy Foger just before Tom left on the trip that ended at Earthquake Island, but the monoplane had been repaired, and Andy had left town, not having returned since.

Telling his father that he was going off on a little business trip, which he often did in his aeroplane, Tom, with the aid of Mr. Jackson, the engineer, wheeled the *Butterfly* out of its shed.

Adjusting the mechanism, and seeing that it was in good shape, Tom took his place in one of the two seats, for the monoplane would carry two. Mr. Jackson then spun the propellers, and, with a crackle and roar the motor started. Over the ground ran the dainty, little aeroplane, until, having momentum enough, Tom tilted the wing planes and the machine sailed up into the air.

Rising about a thousand feet, and circling about several times to test the wind currents, Tom headed his craft toward Chester, a city about fifty miles from Shopton. In his pocket, snugly tucked away, were the two stones Mr. Jenks had given him.

It was not long before Tom saw, looming up in the distance the church spires and towering factory chimneys of Chester, for his machine was a speedy one, and could make ninety miles an hour when driven. But now a slower speed satisfied our hero.

"I'll just drop down outside of the city," he reasoned, "for too much of a crowd gathers when I land in the street. Besides I might frighten horses, and then, too, it's hard to get a good start from the street. I'll leave it in some barn until I want to go back."

Tom sent his craft down, in order to pick out a safe place for a landing. He was then over the suburbs of the city, and was following the line of a straight country road.

"Looks like a good place there," he murmured. "I'll shut off the motor, and vol-plane down."

Suiting the action to the word, Tom shut off his power. The little craft dipped toward the ground, but the lad threw up the forward planes, and caught a current of air that sent him skimming along horizontally.

As he got nearer to the ground, he saw the figure of a lad riding a bicycle along the country highway. Something about the figure struck Tom as being familiar, and he recognized the cyclist a moment later.

"It's Andy Foger!" said Tom, in a whisper. "I wondered where he had been keeping himself since he damaged the *Butterfly*. Evidently he doesn't dare venture back to Shopton. Well, here's where I give him a scare."

Tom's monoplane was making no more noise, now, than a soaring bird. He was gliding swiftly toward the earth, and, with the plan in his mind of administering some sort of punishment to the bully, he aimed the machine directly at him.

Nearer and nearer shot the monoplane, as quietly as a sheet of paper might fall. Andy pedaled on, never looking up nor behind him, A moment later, as Tom threw up his headplanes, to make his landing more easy, and just as he swooped down at one side of the cyclist, our hero let out a most alarming yell, right into Andy's ear.

"Now I've got you!" he shouted. "I'll teach you to slash my aeroplane! Come with me!"

Andy gave one look at the white bird-like apparatus that had flown up beside him so noiselessly, and, being too frightened to recognize Tom's voice, must have thought that he had been overtaken by some supernatural visitor.

Andy gave a yell like an Indian, about to do a stage scalping act, and fairly dived over the handlebars of his bicycle, sprawling in a heap on the dusty road.

"I guess that will hold you for a while," observed Tom, grimly, as he put on the ground-brake and brought his monoplane to a stop not far from the fallen rider.

A MYSTERIOUS MAN

For several minutes Andy Foger did not arise. He remained prostrate in the dust, and Tom, observing him, thought perhaps the bully might have been seriously injured. But, a little later, Andy cautiously raised his head, and inquired in a frightened voice:

"Is it—is it gone?"

"Is what gone?" asked Tom, grimly.

At the sound of his voice, Andy looked up. "Was that you, Tom Swift?" he demanded. "Did you knock me off my wheel?"

"My monoplane and I together did," was the reply; "or, rather, we didn't. It was the nervous reaction caused by your fright, and the knowledge that you had done wrong, that made you jump over the handlebars. That's the scientific explanation."

"You—you did it!" stammered Andy, getting to his feet. He wasn't hurt much, Tom thought.

"Have it your own way," resumed our hero. "Did you think it was a hobgoblin in a chariot of fire after you, Andy?"

"Huh! Never mind what I thought! I'll have you arrested for this!"

"Will you? Delighted, as the boys say. Hop in my airship and I'll take you right into town. And when I get you there I'll make a charge of malicious mischief against you, for breaking the propeller of the *Butterfly* and slashing her wings. I've mended her up, however, so she goes better than ever, and I can take you to the police station in jig time. Want to come, Andy?"

This was too much for the bully. He knew that Tom would have a clear case against him, and he did not dare answer. Instead he shuffled over to where his wheel lay, picked it up, and rode slowly off.

"Good riddance," murmured Tom. He looked about, and saw that he was near a house, in the rear of which was a good-sized barn. "Guess I'll ask if I can leave the *Butterfly* there," he murmured, and, ringing the doorbell, he was greeted by a man.

"I'll pay you if you'll let me store my machine in the barn a little while, until I go into the city, and return," spoke the lad.

"Indeed, you're welcome to leave it there without pay," was the answer. "I'm interested in airships, and, I'll consider it a favor if you'll let me look yours over while it's here."

Tom readily agreed, and a few minutes later he had caught a trolley going into the city. He was soon in one of the largest jewelry stores of Chester.

"I'd like to get an expert opinion as to whether or not those stones are diamonds," spoke Tom, to the polite clerk who came up to wait on him, and our hero handed over the two gems which Mr. Jenks had given him. "I'm willing to pay for the appraisement, of course," the young inventor added, as he saw the clerk looking rather doubtfully at him, for Tom had on a rough suit, which he always donned when he flew in his monoplane.

"I'll turn them over to our Mr. Porter, a gem expert," said the clerk. "Please be seated."

The young man disappeared into a private office with the stones, and Tom waited. He wondered if he was going to have his trouble for his pains. Presently two elderly gentlemen came from the little room, on the glass door of which appeared the word "Diamonds."

"Who brought these stones in?" asked one of the men, evidently the proprietor, from the deference paid him by the clerk. The latter motioned to Tom.

"Will you kindly step inside here?" requested the elderly man. When the door was closed, Tom found himself in a room which was mostly taken up with a bench for the display of precious stones, a few chairs, and some lights arranged peculiarly; while various scales and instruments stood on a table.

"You wished an opinion on—on these?" queried the proprietor of the place. Tom noticed at once that the word "diamonds" was not used.

"I wanted to find out if they were of any value," he said. "Are they diamonds?"

"Would you mind stating where you got them?" asked the other of the two men.

"Is that necessary?" inquired the lad. "I came by them in a legitimate manner, if that's what you mean, and I can satisfy you on that point. I am willing to pay for any information you may give me as to their value."

"Oh, it isn't that," the proprietor hastened to assure him. "But these are diamonds of such a peculiar kind, so perfect and without a flaw, that I wondered from what part of the world they came."

"Then they are diamonds?" asked Tom, eagerly.

"The finest I have ever tested!" declared the other man, evidently Mr. Porter, the gem expert. "They are a joy to look at, Mr. Roberts," he went on, turning to the proprietor. "If it is possible to get a supply of them you would be justified in asking half as much again as we charge for African or Indian diamonds. The Kimberly products are not to be compared to these," and he looked at the two stones in his hand—the one cut, and sparkling brilliantly, the other in a rough state.

"Do you care to state where these diamonds came from?" asked Mr. Roberts, looking critically at Tom.

"I had rather not," answered the lad. "It is enough for me to know that they are diamonds. How much is your charge?"

"Nothing," was the unexpected answer. "We are very glad to have had the opportunity of seeing such stones. Is there any chance of getting any more?"

"Perhaps," answered Tom, as he accepted the gems which the expert held out to him.

"Then might we speak for a supply?" went on Mr. Roberts, eagerly. "We will pay you the full market price."

"What is the value of these stones?" asked Tom.

Mr. Roberts looked at his gem expert.

"It is difficult to say," was the answer of the man who had handed Tom the gems. "They are so far superior to the usual run of diamonds, that I feel justified in saying that the cut one would bring fifteen hundred dollars, anywhere. In fact, I would offer that for it. The other is larger, though what it would lose in cutting would be hard to say. I should say it was worth two thousand dollars as it is now."

"Thirty-five hundred dollars for these two stones!" exclaimed Tom.

"They are worth every cent of it," declared Mr. Roberts. "Do you want to sell?"

Tom shook his head. He could scarcely believe the good news. Mr. Jenks had told the truth. Now the young inventor could go with him to seek the diamond makers.

"Can you get any more of these?" went on Mr. Roberts.

"I think so—that is I don't know—I am going to try," answered the lad.

"Then if you succeed I wish you would sell us some," fairly begged the proprietor of the store.

"I will," promised Tom, but he little knew what lay before him, or perhaps he would not have made that promise. He thanked the diamond merchant for his kindness, and arranged to have the cut stone set in a pin for Miss Nestor. The uncut gem Tom took away with him.

Thinking of many things, and wondering how best to start in his airship *Red Cloud* for the mysterious Phantom Mountain, Tom hurried back to where he had left the monoplane, wheeled it out, and was soon soaring through the air toward Shopton.

"I think I'll go with Mr. Jenks," he decided, as he prepared for a landing in the open space near his aeroplane shed. "It will be a risky trip, perhaps, but I've taken risks before. When Mr. Jenks comes to-night I'll tell him I'll help him to get his rights, and discover the secret of the diamond makers."

As Tom was wheeling the *Butterfly* into the shed, Eradicate came out to help him.

"Dere's a gen'man here to see yo', Massa Tom," said the colored man.

"Who is it?"

"I dunno. He keep askin' ef yo' de lad what done bust up Earthquake Island, an' send lightnin' flashes up to de sky, an' all sech questions laik dat."

"It isn't Mr. Damon; is it, Rad? He hasn't been around in some time."

"No, Massa Tom, it ain't him. I knows dat blessin' man good an' proper. I jest wish he'd bless mah mule Boomerang some day, an' take some oh de temper out ob him. No, sah, it ain't Massa Damon. De gen'man's in de airship shed waitin' fo' you."

"In the airship shed! No strangers are allowed in there, Rad."

"I knows it, Massa Tom, but he done persisted his se'f inter it, an' he wouldn't come out when I told him; an' your pa an' Mr. Jackson ain't home."

"I'll see about this," exclaimed Tom, striding to the large shed, where the *Red Cloud* was kept. As he entered it he saw a man looking over the wonderful craft.

"Did you want to see me?" asked Tom, sharply, for he did not like strangers prowling around.

"I did, and I apologize for entering here, but I am interested in airships, and I thought you might want to hire a pilot. I am in need of employment, and I have had considerable to do with balloons and aeroplanes, but never with an airship like this, which combines the two features. Do you wish to hire any one."

"No, I don't!" replied Tom, sharply, for he did not like the looks of the man.

"I was told that you did," was the rather surprising answer.

"Who told you?"

The man looked all around the shed, before replying, as if fearful of being overheard. Then, stepping close to Tom, he whispered:

"Mr. Jenks told me!"

"Mr. Jenks?" Tom could not conceal his astonishment.

"Yes. Mr. Barcoe Jenks. But I did not come here to merely ask you for employment. I would like to hire out to you, but the real object of my visit was to say this to you."

The man approached still closer to Tom, and, in a lower voice, and one that could scarcely be heard, he fairly hissed:

"Don't go with Barcoe Jenks to seek the diamond makers!"

Then, before Tom could put out a hand to detain him, had the lad so wished, the man turned suddenly, and fairly ran from the shed.

Mr. Damon Is on Hand

The young inventor stood almost spellbound for a few moments. Then recovering himself he made a dash for the door through which the mysterious man had disappeared. Tom saw him sprinting down the road, and was half-minded to take after him, but a cooler thought warned him that he had better not.

"He may be one of those men who are on Mr. Jenks' trail," reasoned Tom, in which case it might not be altogether safe to attempt to stop him, and make him explain. Or he may be a lunatic, and in that case it wouldn't be altogether healthy to interfere with him.

"I'll just let him go, and tell Mr. Jenks about him when he comes to-night. But I must warn Rad never to let him in here again. He might damage the airship."

Calling to the colored man, Tom pointed to the stranger, who was almost out of sight down the road, and said earnestly:

"Rad, do you see that fellow?"

"I sho do, Massa Tom, but I sorter has t' strain my eyes t' do it. He's goin' laik my mule Boomerang does when he's comm' home t' dinnah."

"That's right, Rad. Well, never let that man set foot inside our fence again! If he comes, and I'm home, call me. If I'm away, call dad or Mr. Jackson, and if you're here alone, drive him away, somehow."

"I will, Massa Tom!" exclaimed the colored man, earnestly, "an' if I can't do it alone, I'll get Boomerang t' help. Once let dat ar' mule git his heels on a pusson, an' dat pusson ain't goin' t' come bodderin' around any mo'—that is, not right away."

"I believe you, Rad. Well, keep a lookout for him, and don't let him in," and with that Tom entered the house to think over matters. They were beginning to assume an aspect he did not altogether like. Not that Tom was afraid of danger, but he preferred to meet it in the open, and the warning, or threat, of the mysterious man disquieted him.

When Mr. Swift came home, a little later, his son told him of the midnight interview with Mr. Jenks, for, up to this time, the aged inventor was unaware of it, and Tom also gave an account of the diamonds, speaking of their value.

"And do you propose to go to Phantom Mountain, in search of the makers of these gems, Tom?" asked Mr. Swift.

"I had about decided to do so, dad."

"And you're going in the *Red Cloud?*"

"Yes."

"Who are going with you?"

"Well, Mr. Jenks will go, of course, and I've no doubt but that if I mention the prospective trip to Mr. Damon, that he'll bless his skating cap, or something like that, and come along."

"I suppose so, Tom, and I'd like to have you take him. But I think you'll need some one else."

"Because, from what you have told me, you are going out to a dangerous part of the country, and you may have to deal with unscrupulous men. Three of you are hardly enough to cope with them. You ought to have at least another member of your party. If I was not busy on my invention of a new wireless motor I would go along, but I can't leave. You might take Mr. Jackson."

"No, you need him here to help you, dad."

"How about Eradicate?"

Tom smiled.

"Rad would get homesick for his mule Boomerang, and I'd have to bring him back just when we'd found the diamonds," replied the young inventor. "No, we'll have to think of some one else. I'll ask Mr. Damon, and then I'll consider matters further. I expect to see Mr. Jenks to-night, and he may have some one in mind."

"Perhaps that will be a good plan. Well, Tom, I trust you will take good care of yourself, and not run into unnecessary danger. Is the *Red Cloud* in good shape for the voyage?"

"It needs looking over. I'm going to get right at it."

"It's a pretty indefinite sort of a quest you're going on, Tom, my son. How do you expect to find Phantom Mountain?"

"Well, it's going to be quite a task. In the first place we'll head for Leadville, Colorado, and then we'll go to Indian Ridge and make some inquiries. We may get on the track of the place that way. If we don't, why I'll take the airship up as high as is necessary and sort of prospect until we see that big cliff that's shaped like a head. That will give us something to go by."

"Well, do the best you can. If you can discover the secret of making diamonds it will be a valuable one."

"I guess it will, dad; and Mr. Jenks is entitled to know it, for he paid his good money to that end. He has promised to go halves with me, as payment for the use of the airship, and I must say the two diamonds he gave me last night have proved very valuable."

"Two diamonds, Tom? You only showed me one, an uncut gem"; and Mr. Swift looked at his son.

"Oh, the other—er—the other is—I left it with a jeweler," and Tom blushed a trifle, as he thought of the present he contemplated making to Mary Nestor.

That afternoon, as Tom was out in the shed of the *Red Cloud* looking over the airship, to see what would be necessary to do to it in order to get it in shape for a long trip, he heard voices outside.

"Yes—yes, I know the way in perfectly well," he caught. "You needn't bother to come, my good fellow. Just step this way, and I'll show you something worth seeing."

"I wonder if it's that mysterious man coming back?" thought Tom. He dropped the tool he was using, and hurried to the door. As he approached it he heard the voice continue.

"Why bless my shoe laces, Mr. Parker! You'll see a wonderful airship, I promise you. Wonderful! Bless my hatband, but I hope Tom is here!"

"Mr. Damon!" exclaimed our hero, as he recognized the tones of his eccentric friend. "But who is with him?"

A moment later he caught sight of the gentleman who was always blessing himself, or something. Behind him stood another man, whose features Tom could not see plainly.

"Hello, Tom Swift!" called Mr. Damon. "Looking over the *Red Cloud*, eh? Does that mean you're off on another trip?"

"I guess it does," answered the lad.

"Where to this time? if I may ask."

"I'm thinking of going off to the mountains to find a band of men engaged in making diamonds," replied Tom.

"Making diamonds! Bless my finger ring! Making diamonds! A trip to the mountains! Bless my disposition! but do you know I'd like to go with you!"

"I was thinking of asking you, Mr. Damon."

"Were you? Bless my heart, I'm glad you thought of me. You don't by any possible chance want another person; do you?"

"We were thinking of having four in the party, Mr. Damon," and Tom wondered who was with his eccentric friend.

"Then bless my election ticket! This is the very chance for you, Mr. Parker!" cried Mr. Damon. "Will you go with us? It will be just what you need," and Mr. Damon stepped aside, revealing to Tom the features of Mr. Ralph Parker, the scientist who had correctly predicted the destruction of Earthquake Island.

Mr. Parker Predicts

Tom Swift was a most generous lad, but when he saw that Mr. Damon had with him Mr. Parker, the gloomy scientist, who seemed to take delight in predicting disasters, our hero's spirits were not exactly of the best. He would have much preferred not to take Mr. Parker on the quest for the diamond makers, but, since Mr. Damon had mentioned it, he did not see how he could very well refuse.

"But perhaps he won't care to go," thought Tom.

He was undeceived a moment later, however, for the scientist remarked:

I am very glad to meet you once more, Mr. Swift. I have scarcely thanked you enough for what you did for us in erecting your wireless station on Earthquake Island, which, as you recall, I predicted would sink into the sea. It did, I am glad to say, not because I like to see islands destroyed, but because science has been vindicated. Now I have just heard you remark that you are about to set off to the mountains in search of some men who are making diamonds. I need hardly state that this is utterly useless, for no diamonds, commercially valuable, can be made by men. But the trip may be valuable in that it will permit me to demonstrate some scientific facts.

"Therefore, if you will permit me, I will be very glad to accompany you and Mr. Damon. I shall be delighted, in short, and I can start as soon as you are ready."

"There's no hope for it!" thought Tom, dismally. "I suppose he'll wake up every morning, and predict that before night the world will come to an end, or he'll prophesy that the airship will blow up, and vanish, when about seven miles above the clouds. Well, there's no way out of it, so here goes."

Thereupon Tom welcomed the scientist as cordially as he could, and invited him to form one of the party that would set off in the airship to search for Phantom Mountain.

"Bless my jewelry box!" exclaimed Mr. Damon. when this formality was over. "Tell me more about it, Tom."

Which our hero did, stating the need of maintaining secrecy on account of the danger to Mr. Jenks. Mr. Damon and Mr. Parker both agreed to say nothing about the matter, and then the scientist became much interested in the *Red Cloud*, which he closely examined. He even complimented Tom on the skill shown in making it, and, contrary to our hero's expectation, did not predict that it would blow up the next time it was used.

"How did you happen to arrive just at this time, Mr. Damon?" asked Tom.

"It was partly due to Mr. Parker," was the answer. "I had not seen him since we were rescued from the island, until a few days ago he called on me at my home. I happened to mention that you lived near here, and suggested that he might like to see some of your inventions. He agreed, and we came over in my auto. And now, bless my liver-pin! I find you about to start off on another trip."

"And have you fully decided to go with me?" asked Tom. "There may be danger, and I don't like the way that mysterious man behaved."

"Oh, bless my revolver!" cried Mr. Damon. "I'm used to danger by this time. Of course I'm going, and so is Mr. Parker. Do you know," and the man, who was always blessing something, came closer to the lad, and whispered: "Do you know, Tom, Mr. Parker is a very peculiar individual."

"I'm sure of it," answered the young inventor, looking at the gentleman in question, who was then inside the airship cabin.

"But he's all right, even if he is predicting unpleasant things," went on Mr. Damon. "I think we'll get better acquainted with him after a bit."

"I hope so," agreed Tom, but he did not realize then how close his companionship with Mr. Parker was to be, nor what dangers they were to share later.

The friends talked at considerable length of the prospective trip, and Tom, by this time, had ascertained what needed to be done to the airship to get it in shape to travel. It would take about a week, and, in the meanwhile, Mr. Damon would go home and get his affairs in order for the voyage. Tom's father was introduced to Mr. Parker, and, the former, finding that the scientist held some views in common with him, invited the gloomy predictor to remain at the Swift home until the *Red Cloud* was ready to sail. Tom could not repress a groan at this, but he decided he would have to make the best of it.

Mr. Damon left for home that afternoon, promising to be on hand at the time set to start for Phantom Mountain.

Tom was up waiting for Mr. Jenks at twelve o'clock that night. Shortly after the hour he saw a dark figure steal into the orchard. At first he feared lest it might be one of the spies who were, he was now convinced, on the trail of the man who was seeking to discover the secret of the diamond makers. But a whistle, which came to the lad's ear a moment later (that being a signal Mr. Jenks had agreed to sound), told Tom that it was none other than the visitor he expected.

"All right, Mr. Jenks, I'm here," called Tom, cautiously. "Come over this way," and he went out from the shadow of the house, where he had been waiting, and met the men. "We'll go into my private work-shop," the youth added, leading the way.

"Have you decided to go with me?" asked Mr. Jenks, in an anxious whisper. "Did you find the diamonds to be real ones?"

"I did; and I'm going," spoke Tom.

"Good! That relieves my mind. But we are still in danger. I was followed by my shadower to-day, and only succeeded in shaking him off just before coming here. I don't believe he knows what I am about to do."

"Oh, yes he does," said Tom.

"He does? How?"

"Because he was here, and warned me against you!"

"You don't mean it! Well, they are getting desperate! We must be on our guard. What sort of a man was he?"

Tom described the fellow, and Mr. Jenks stated that this tallied with the appearance of the person who had been shadowing him.

"But we'll fool them yet!" cried Tom, who had now fully entered into the spirit of the affair. "If they can follow us in the *Red Cloud* they're welcome to. I think we'll get ahead of them."

He then told of Mr. Damon and Mr. Parker, and Mr. Jenks agreed that it would add to the strength of the party to take these two gentlemen along.

"Though I can't say I care so much for Mr. Parker," he added. "But now as to ways and means. When can we start?"

Thereupon he and Tom talked over details in the seclusion of the little office, and arranged to leave Shopton in about a week. In the meanwhile the airship would be overhauled, stocked with supplies and provisions, and be made ready for a swift dash to the mountains.

"And now I must be going," said Mr. Jenks. "I have a great deal to do before I can start on this trip, and I hope I am not prevented by any of those men who seem to be trailing me."

"How could they prevent you?" Tom wanted to know.

"Oh, there are any number of ways," was the answer. "But I'm glad you found that my diamonds were real. We'll soon have plenty, if all goes well."

As Mr. Jenks left the shop, he started back, in some alarm.

"What's the matter?" asked Tom.

"Over there—I thought I saw a figure sneaking along under the trees—that man—perhaps—"

"That's Eradicate, our colored helper," replied Tom, with a laugh. "I posted him there to see that no strangers came into the orchard. Everything all right, Rad?" he asked, raising his voice.

"Yais, sah, Massa Tom. Nobody been around yeah this night."

"That's good. You can go to bed now," and Eradicate, yawning loudly, went to his shack. A little later Tom sought his own room, Mr. Jenks having hurried off to town, where he was boarding.

The next few days saw Tom busily engaged on the airship, making some changes and a few repairs that were needed. His father, Eradicate and Mr. Jackson helped him. As for Mr. Parker, the scientist, he went about the place, being much interested in the various machines which Tom or Mr. Swift had patented.

At other times the scientist would stroll about the extensive grounds, making what he said were "observations." One afternoon Tom saw him, apparently much excited, kneeling down back of a shed, with his ear to the ground.

"What is the matter?" asked the lad, thinking perhaps Mr. Parker might be ill.

"Have you ever had any earthquakes here, Tom Swift?" asked the scientist, quietly.

"Earthquakes? No. We had enough of them on the island."

"And you are going to have one here, in about two minutes!" cried Mr. Parker. "I predict that this place will be shaken by a tremendous shock very soon. We had all better get away from the vicinity of buildings."

"What makes you think there will be an earthquake?" asked Tom.

"Because I can hear the rumbling beneath the ground at this very minute. It is increasing in volume, showing that the tremors are working this way. There will soon be a great subterranean upheaval! Listen for yourself."

Tom cast himself down on the grass. Placing his ear close to the ground he did hear a series of dull thuds. He arose, not a little alarmed. There had never been any earthquakes in Shopton, yet he had great respect for Mr. Parker's scientific attainments.

Just then Eradicate Sampson came along. He saw Tom and Mr. Parker lying flat on the ground, and surprise showed on his honest, black face.

"Fo' de land sakes!" cried Eradicate. "What am de mattah now, Massa Tom?"

"Earthquake coming," answered Tom, briefly. "Better get away from the buildings, Rad. They might fall!" Tom's face showed the alarm he felt. What would happen to all of his valuable machines—to the *Red Cloud*?

"Earthquake?" murmured Eradicat— and he, too, cast himself down to listen. A moment later he arose with a laugh.

"What's the matter?" cried Tom.

"Why, dat ain't no earthquake!" declared the colored man.

"No. Then perhaps you know what it is," said Mr. Parker, somewhat sharply.

"Course I knows what it am," answered Eradicate, with dignity. "Dat noise am my mule Boomerang, kickin' in his stable, on account oh me not feedin' him yet. Dat's what it am. I'se gwine right now t' gib him his oats, and den yo' see dat de noise stop. Boomerang allers kick dat way when he's hungry. I show yo'!"

And, sure enough, when Eradicate had gone to the mule's stable, which was near where Mr. Parker had heard the mysterious sounds, they immediately ceased.

"Dat mule was all de earthquake dere was around here," said the colored man as he came out.

Mr. Parker walked away, saying nothing, and Tom did not make any comments—just then.

OFF FOR THE WEST

It was a great relief to Tom, to find that there was no danger from an earth tremor. Now that he had made up his mind to go in search of the diamond makers, he wanted nothing to interfere with it. Lest the feelings of Mr. Parker might be hurt by the mistake he had made, the young inventor cautioned Eradicate not to say anything more about the matter.

"'Deed an' I won't," the colored man promised. "I'se only too glad dere wa'n't no earthquake, dat's what I is."

As for Mr. Parker, he did not appear much put out by his error in predicting.

"I am sure that what I heard was a tremor, due to some distant earthquake shock," he said. "The mule's kicking was only a coincidence."

And Tom let him have his way about it. The week was drawing to a close, and the *Red Cloud* was nearly in shape for the voyage. At almost the last minute Tom found that he needed some electrical apparatus for the airship, and as he had to go to Chester for it, he decided he would make the trip in his monoplane, and, while in the city, would also get the diamond pin he was having made for Mary Nestor.

He started off early one morning, in the swift little craft *Butterfly*, and soon had reached Chester. The diamond brooch was ready for him.

"It is one of the most beautiful stones we have ever set," the diamond merchant told him. "Don't forget, if you find any more, Mr. Swift, to let us have a chance to bid on them."

"I may," Tom promised, rather indefinitely. Then, having purchased his electrical supplies, he made a quick trip to Shopton, stopping on the way to call on Miss Nestor.

"Why Tom, I'm delighted to see you!" cried the girl, blushing prettily. "Did you come for some apple turnovers?" and she laughed, as she referred to a call Tom had once paid, when a new cook had been engaged, and when the pastry formed a feature of the meal.

"No turnovers this time," said the young inventor. "I came to wish you many happy returns of the day."

"Oh, you remembered my birthday! How nice of you!"

"And here is something else," added our hero, rather awkwardly, as he handed her the diamond pin.

"Oh, Tom! This for me! Oh, it's too lovely—it's far too much!"

"It isn't half enough!" he declared, warmly. "Oh, what a large diamond!" Mary cried as she saw the sparkling stone. "I never saw one so large and beautiful!"

"It's just as easy to make them large as small," explained Tom.

"Make them?" she looked the surprise she felt.

"Yes, I'm about to start for the place where diamonds are made."

"Oh, Tom! But isn't it dangerous? I mean won't you have to go to some far country—like Africa—to get to where diamonds are made?"

"Well, we are going on quite a trip, but not as far as that. And as for the danger—well, we'll have to take what comes," and he told her something of the proposed quest.

"Oh, it sounds—sounds scary!" Mary exclaimed, when she had heard of Mr. Jenks' experience. Do be careful, Tom!"

"I will," he promised, and, somehow he was glad that she had cautioned him thus—and in such tones as she had used. For Mary Nestor was a girl that any young chap would have been glad to have manifest an interest in him.

"Well, I guess I'll have to say good-by," spoke Tom, at length. "We expect to start in a couple of days, and I may not get another chance to see you."

"Oh, I—I hope you come back safely," faltered Mary, and then she held out her hand, and Tom—well, it's none of our affair what Tom did after that, except to say that he hurried out, fairly jumped into his monoplane, and completed the trip home.

As the *Red Cloud* has been fully described in the volume entitled "Tom Swift and His Airship," we will not go into details about it now. Sufficient to say that it was a combination of a biplane and dirigible balloon. It could be used either as one or the other, and the gas-bag feature was of value when the wind was too great to allow the use of the planes, or when the motive power, for some reason stopped. In that event the airship could remain suspended far above the clouds if necessary. There was provision for manufacturing the gas on board.

The *Red Cloud* was fitted up to accommodate about ten persons, though it was seldom that this number was carried. Two persons could successfully operate the machinery. There were sleeping berths, and in the main cabin a sitting-room, a dining-room, and a kitchen. There was also the motor compartment, and a steering tower, from which the engines could be controlled.

It was in this craft that the seekers after the diamond makers proposed undertaking the trip. Mr. Damon came on from his home in Waterfield about two days before the date set to leave, and Mr. Jenks, had, three days before this, taken up his abode at the Swift home. Mr. Parker, as has been stated, was already there, and he had put in his time making a number of scientific observations, though he had made no more predictions.

Nothing more had been seen of the mysterious man who had warned Tom, and the young inventor and Mr. Jenks began to hope that they had thrown their enemies off the track.

"Though I don't imagine they'll give up altogether," said Mr. Jenks. "They're too desperate for that. We'll have trouble with them yet."

"Well, it can't be helped," decided Tom. "We'll try and be ready for it, when it comes," and then, dismissing the matter from his mind, he busied himself about the airship.

The food and supplies had all been put aboard, and they expected to start the next morning. In order to make sure that any stones which they might succeed in getting from the diamond makers were real gems, a set of testing apparatus was taken along. Mr. Parker had had some experience in this line, and, in spite of the fact that he might make direful predictions, Tom was rather glad, after all, that the scientist was going to accompany them.

"But what is worrying me," said Mr. Damon, "is what we are going to do after we get to Phantom Mountain. What are your plans, Mr. Jenks? Will you go in, and demand your share of the diamond-making business?"

"I have a right to it, as I invested a large sum in it, and I am entitled to more than a half-share. But, of course, I can't say what I'll do until I get there. We may have to act very secretly."

"I'm inclined to think we will," said Tom. "My plan would be to gain access to the cave, if possible, and watch them at work. We might be able to discover the secret of making diamonds, and, after all, that's what you want, isn't it, Mr. Jenks?"

"Yes, I paid my money for the secret, and I ought to have it. If I can get it quietly, so much the better. If not, I'll fight for my rights!" and he looked very determined.

"Bless my powder horn!" cried Mr. Damon. "That's the way to talk! And so we're to go cruising about in the air, looking for a mountain shaped like a man's head."

"That's it," a greed Mr. Jenks, "and when we find it we will be near Phantom Mountain, and the diamond makers."

The final details were completed that night. The last of the supplies had been put aboard, the larder was well stocked, the diamond testing apparatus was stored safely away, and all that remained was for the adventurers to board the *Red Cloud* in the morning, and soar away.

That night Tom was uneasy. Several times he got up, and looked toward the shed where the airship was stored. He could not rid himself of the idea that the men to whose interest it was that the diamond-making secret remain undiscovered, might attempt to wreck the airship before the start. Consequently both Eradicate Sampson and Engineer Jackson were on guard. Tom looked from his window, to the shed where the *Red Cloud* was housed. He saw nothing to cause him any uneasiness.

"I guess I'm just nervous," he mused. "But, all the same, I'll be glad when we've started

They were all up early the next morning, Mr. Damon beginning the day by blessing the sunrise, and many other things that struck his fancy. The airship was wheeled out of the shed, and Tom gave her a final inspection.

"It's all right," he declared. "All aboard!"

"Now, do be careful," begged Mr. Swift. "Don't take too many chances, Tom."

"I'll not."

The adventurers were in the forward part of the ship, and Tom had taken his place at the wheels and levers in the pilot house. As he was about to start the motor he looked toward the road, and saw a horse and carriage. In the vehicle was a girlish figure, at the sight of which Tom blushed and smiled. He waved his hand.

"I came to wish you good luck!" cried Mary Nester, for it was she in the carriage.

"Thanks!" cried Tom, leaning from the window of the pilot house. "It was good of you to get up so early."

"Oh. I'm always up early," she informed him.

"Look out that the motor doesn't scare your horse," Tom warned her.

"Old Dobbin doesn't mind anything," was her answer. "I'll see that he doesn't run away with me, as long as you're not on earth to rescue me. Good-by, Tom!"

"Good-by!" he called, and then he pulled the lever that set in motion the motor, and whirled the great propellers about. They whizzed around with a roar, and the *Red Cloud*, shivering and trembling with the vibration, rose in the air like some great bird.

"We're off for the West and Phantom Mountain!" called Tom to his companions.

As the airship soared upward, Eradicate Sampson ran forward from where he had been standing near his mule Boomerang. He waved his hands, and shouted something.

"Bless my hatband! What does he want?" asked Mr. Damon, watching him curiously.

"It sounds as if he were calling to us to come back," spoke Mr. Parker.

"It's too late now," decided Tom. "Maybe he forgot to tell us good-by," but, he felt a vague wonder at Eradicate's odd motions; for the colored man was pointing toward the stern of the airship, as if there was something wrong there. But the *Red Cloud* soared on.

A Warning by Wireless

Rapidly the airship ascended, and, when it was high over the town of Shopton, Tom headed the craft due west. Looking down he tried to descry Mary Nestor, in her carriage, but the trees were in the way, their interlocking branches hiding the girl. Tom did see crowds of other persons, though, thronging the streets of Shopton, for, though the young inventor had made many flights, there was always a novelty about them, that brought out the curious.

"A good start, Tom Swift," complimented Mr. Parker. "Is it always as easy as this?"

"Starting always is," was the answer, "though, as the Irishman said, coming down isn't sometimes quite so comfortable."

"Bless my gizzard! That's so," cried the eccentric Mr. Damon. "Can we vol-plane to earth in the *Red Cloud*, Tom?"

"Yes, but not as easily as in the *Butterfly*. However I hope we will not have to. Now, Mr. Damon, if you will just take charge of the steering apparatus for a minute, I want to go aft."

"What for?"

"I wish to see if everything is all right. I can't imagine why Eradicate was making those queer motions."

Mr. Damon, who knew how to operate the *Red Cloud*, was soon guiding her on the course, while Tom made his way to the rear compartments, through the motor room, where the stores of supplies and food were kept. He made a careful examination, looking from an after window, and even going out on a small, open platform, but could discover nothing wrong.

"I guess Rad was just capering about without any special object," mused Tom, but it was not long after this that they learned to their dismay, that the colored man had had a method in his madness.

On his way back through the motor room Tom looked to the machinery, and adjusted some of the auxiliary oil feeders. The various pieces of apparatus were working well, though the engine had not yet been speeded up to its limit. Tom wanted it to "warm- up" first.

"Everything all right?" asked Mr. Damon, as Tom rejoined them in the pilot house, which was just forward of the living room in the main cabin.

"Yes, I can't imagine what made Rad act that way. But I'll set the automatic steering gear now, Mr. Damon, and then you will be relieved."

Mr. Jenks was gazing off toward the west—to where he hoped to discover the secret of Phantom Mountain.

"How do you like it?" asked Tom.

"It's great," replied the diamond man. "I've never been in an airship before, and it's different than what I expected; but it's great! It's the only craft that will serve our purpose among the towering mountain peaks, where the diamond makers are hidden. I hope we can find them."

In a little while the *Red Cloud* was skimming along at faster speed, guided by the automatic rudders, so that no one was needed in the pilot house, since there was no danger of collisions. Airships are not quite numerous enough for that, yet, though they may soon become so.

Tom and the others devoted several hours to arranging their staterooms and bunks, and getting their clothing stowed away, and when this was done Mr. Parker and Mr. Jenks sat gazing off into space.

"It's hard to realize that we are really in an airship," observed the diamond man. "At first I thought I would be frightened, but I'm not a bit. It doesn't seem as if anything could happen."

"Something is likely to happen soon," said Mr. Parker, suddenly, as he gazed at some weather instruments on the cabin wall.

"Bless my soul! Don't say that!" cried Mr. Damon. "What is it?"

"I think, from my observations, that we will soon have a hurricane," said the scientific man. "There is every indication of it'"; and he seemed quite delighted at the prospect of his prediction coming true.

"A hurricane!" cried Mr. Damon. "I hope it isn't like the one that blew us to Earthquake Island."

"Oh, I think there will be no danger," spoke Tom. "If it comes on to blow we will ascend or descend out of the path of the storm. This craft is not like the ill-fated *Whizzer*. I can more easily handle the *Red Cloud*; even in a bad storm."

"I'm glad to hear that," remarked Mr. Jenks. "It would be too bad to be wrecked before we got to Phantom Mountain."

"Well, I predict that we will have a bad storm," insisted Mr. Parker, and Tom could not help wishing that the scientist would keep his gloomy forebodings to himself.

However the storm had not developed up to noon, when Tom, with Mr. Damon's help, served a fine meal in the dining-room. In the afternoon the speed of the ship was increased, and by night they had covered several hundred miles. Through the darkness the *Red Cloud* kept on, making good time. Tom got up, occasionally, to look to the machinery, but it was all automatically controlled, and an alarm bell would sound in his stateroom when anything went wrong.

"Bless my napkin!" exclaimed Mr. Damon the next morning, as they sat down to a breakfast of fruit, ham and eggs and fragrant coffee, "this is living as well as in a hotel, and yet we are— how far are we above the earth, Tom?" he asked, turning to the young inventor.

"About two miles now. I just sent her up, as I thought I detected that storm Mr. Parker spoke of."

"I told you it would come," declared the scientist, and there was a small hurricane below them that morning, but only the lower edge of it caught the

Red Cloud, and when Tom sent her up still higher she found a comparatively quiet zone, where she slid along at good speed.

That afternoon Tom busied himself about some wires and a number of complicated pieces of apparatus which were in one corner of the main cabin.

"What are you doing now?" asked Mr. Jenks, who had been talking with Mr. Parker, and showing that scientist some of the manufactured diamonds.

"Getting our wireless apparatus in shape," answered the lad. "I should have done it before, but I had so much to do that I couldn't get at it. I'm going to send off some messages. Dad will want to know how we are doing."

As he worked away, he also made up his mind to send another message, in care of his father, for there was a receiving station in the Swift home. And to whom this message was addressed Tom did not say, but we fancy some of our readers can guess.

Finally, after several hours of work, the wireless was in shape to send and receive messages. Tom pulled over the lever, and a crackling sound was heard, as the electricity leaped from the transmitters into space. Then he clamped the receiver on his ear.

"All ready," he announced. "Has anybody any messages they wish sent?" For, with the courtesy of a true host he was ready to serve his guests before he forwarded his own wireless notes.

"Just tell my wife that I'm enjoying myself," requested Mr. Damon. "Bless my footstool! But this is great! We're off the earth yet, connected with it."

Mr. Jenks had no one to whom he wanted to send any word, but Mr. Parker wish to wire to a fellow scientist the result of some observations made in the upper air.

Tom noted all the messages down, and then, when all was in readiness he began to call his home station. He knew that either his father or Mr. Jackson, the engineer, could receive the wireless.

But, no sooner had the young inventor sent off the first few dots and dashes representing "S. I."—his home station call—than he started and a look of surprise came over his face.

"They're calling us!" he exclaimed.

"Who is?" asked Mr. Jenks.

"My house—my father. He—he's been trying to get us ever since we started, but I didn't have the wireless in shape to receive messages. Oh, I hope it's not too late!"

"Too late! Bless my soul, too late for what?" gasped Mr. Damon, somewhat alarmed by Tom's manner.

The lad did not answer at once. He was intently listening to a series of dots and dashes that clicked in the telephone receiver clamped to his left ear. On his face there was a look of worriment.

"Father has just sent me a message," he said. "It's a warning flashed through space! He's been trying to get it to me since yesterday!"

"What is it?" asked Mr. Jenks, rising from his seat.

"The mysterious man is aboard the airship—hidden away!" cried Tom. "That's what Eradicate was trying to call to our attention as we started off. Eradicate saw his face at a rear window, and tried to warn us! The mysterious man is a stowaway on board!"

DROPPING THE STOWAWAY

Tom's excited announcement startled Mr. Damon and the others as much as if the young inventor had informed them that the airship had exploded and was about to dash with them to the earth. The men leaped to their feet, and stared at the lad.

"A stowaway on board!" cried Mr. Damon. "Bless my soul! How did he—"

"Are you sure that message is straight?" asked Mr. Jenks. "Did Eradicate see the man?"

"He says he did," answered Tom. "The man is hidden away on board now—probably among the stores and supplies."

"Bless my tomato sauce!" exploded Mr. Damon. "I hope he doesn't eat them all up!"

"We must get him out at once!" declared Mr. Jenks.

"I knew something would happen on this voyage," came from Mr. Parker. "I predicted it from the first!"

Tom thought considerable, but he did not answer the scientist just then. Another communication was coming to him by wireless. He listened intently.

"Father says," the lad told his companions "that Eradicate only had a glimpse of the man at the last moment. He was looking from the rear storeroom window—he's the same man who called on me that time—Rad remembers him very well."

"Bless my shoes! What's to be done?" inquired Mr. Damon, looking around helplessly.

"We must get him out, that's all," decided Mr. Jenks; with vigor. "Get him out and drop him overboard!"

"Drop him overboard!" cried Mr. Parker, in horror.

"Not exactly, but get rid of him," proceeded the diamond seeker. "That man is one of my enemies. He has been sent by the band of diamond makers hidden among the mountains, to spy on me, and, if possible, prevent me from seeking to discover their secret. He tried to work on Tom's Swift's fears, and frighten him from using his airship on this quest. Then, when he failed, the man must have sneaked into the shed, and hidden himself in the ship. We must get rid of him, or he may wreck the *Red Cloud!*"

"That's so!" cried Tom. "We must try to capture him. I think we had better—" the lad paused, and again listened to the wireless message. "Father says Eradicate saw the man have a gun, so we must be careful," the young inventor translated the dots and dashes.

"Bless my powder horn!" exploded Mr. Damon.

"We shall have to proceed cautiously then," spoke Mr. Jenks. "If he is like any others in the gang he is a desperate man."

"Better sneak up on him then, if we can," proposed Mr. Parker. "There are enough of us to cope with one man, even if he is armed. You have weapons aboard, haven't you?" he inquired of Tom.

"Yes," was the hesitating answer, "but I don't want to use them if I can help it. Not only because of the danger, and a dislike of shedding blood, but because a stray bullet might pierce the gas bag and damage the ship."

"That's so," agreed Mr. Jenks. "Well, I guess if we go at it the right way we can capture him without any shooting. But we must talk more quietly—we ought to have whispered —he may have heard us."

"I don't think so," replied Tom. "The storeroom is far enough off so that he couldn't hear us. Besides, the motor makes such a racket that he couldn't distinguish what we were talking about, even if he heard our voices. So, unless he heard the wireless working, and suspects something from that, he probably doesn't know that we are aware of his presence aboard."

"But why do you think he has remained quiet all this while, Tom?" asked Mr. Damon.

"Probably he wants to wait until the ship is farther out west," suggested Mr. Jenks. "Then he will be nearer his friends, and can get help, if he needs it."

"And do you really believe he would destroy the *Red Cloud*?" asked Mr. Parker.

"I think that all he is waiting for is a favorable chance," declared the diamond seeker. "He would destroy the craft, and us too, if he could prevent us from discovering the secret of Phantom Mountain, I believe."

"Then we must get ahead of him," decided Tom, quietly. "I have just flashed to dad a message, telling him that we will heed his warning. Now to capture the stowaway!"

"And while we're about it, give him a good scare when we do get him," suggested Mr. Jenks.

"How?" asked Tom.

"Threaten to drop him overboard. Perhaps that will make him tell how he happened to get in our ship, and what are the plans of the gang of diamond makers. We may get valuable information that way."

"I don't believe you can scare such fellows much," was Tom's opinion, but it was agreed to try.

"How are you going to capture him?" asked Mr. Parker. "If he has a gun it won't be any too easy to go in the storeroom, and drag him out."

"We'll have to use a little strategy," decided Tom, and then they discussed several plans. The one finally adopted was that Tom and Mr. Damon should enter the storeroom, casually, as if in search of food to cook for supper. They would discuss various dishes, and Mr. Damon was to express a preference for something in the food line, the box containing which, was well hack in the room. This would give the two a chance to penetrate to the far end of the apartment, without arousing the suspicions of the hidden man, who, doubtless, would be listening to the conversation.

"And as soon as we get sight of him, you and I will jump right at him, Mr. Damon," said Tom. "Jump before he has a chance to use his gun. Mr. Jenks and Mr. Parker will be waiting outside the room, to catch him if he gets away from us. I'll have some ropes ready, and we'll tie him up, and—well, we'll decide later what to do with him."

"All right. I'm ready as soon as you are, Tom," said the eccentric man. "Come ahead."

They went softly to the storeroom, and listened at the door. There was no sound heard save that made by the machinery.

"I wonder if he's really here?" whispered Mr. Damon.

"We'll soon find out," answered Tom. "Let's go in."

They entered, and, in pursuance of their plan, Tom and his friend talked of various foods.

"I think I'd like some of that canned lobster, with French dressing on," spoke the eccentric man.

"That's away in the back end of the room," said Tom, in a loud voice. "It's under a lot of boxes."

"Then I'll help you get it out! Bless my frying pan! but I am very fond of lobster!" exclaimed Mr. Damon, in as natural tones as was possible under the circumstances.

He and Tom moved cautiously back among the boxes and barrels. They were glancing about with eager eyes. Tom switched on an electric light, and, the instant he did so, he was aware of a movement in a little space formed by one box which was placed on top, of two others. The lad saw a dark figure moving, as if to get farther out of sight.

"I've got him!" cried Tom, making a dive for the shadow.

A moment later the young inventor was bowled over, as a dark figure leaped over his head.

"Catch him, Mr. Damon!" he cried.

"Bless my hatband! I—I—" Mr. Damon's voice ended in a grunt. He, too, had been knocked down by the fleeing man.

"Look out, Mr. Jenks!" cried Tom, to warn those on guard at the door of the storeroom.

There was the report of a gun, some excited shouts, and when Tom could scramble to his feet, and rush out, he beheld Mr. Parker calmly sitting on a struggling man, while Mr. Jenks held a gun, that was still smoking.

"We caught him!" cried the scientist.

"Anybody hurt?" asked Tom, anxiously.

"No, I knocked up his gun as he fired," explained Mr. Jenks. "Where are the ropes, Tom?"

The cords were produced and the man, who had now ceased to struggle, was tightly bound. He uttered not a word, but he smiled grimly when Mr. Damon remarked:

"I guess I'll go back in the storeroom, Tom, and see how much food he ate."

"Oh, I guess he didn't take much," declared the lad. "He wasn't there long enough."

"Well, Farley Munson, so it's you, is it?" asked Mr. Jenks, as he surveyed the prisoner.

"Do you know him?" asked Tom, in some surprise.

"He was in with the diamond makers," said Mr. Jenks. "He was one of those who took me to the secret cave. But it will be the last time he ever goes there. How high up are we, Tom?"

"About two miles. Why?"

"I guess that will be far enough to let him fall," went on the diamond seeker. "Come on, Mr. Damon, help me throw him overboard!"

"You—you're not going to throw me over—with the airship two miles high; are you?" gasped the man.

"Will you tell us what we want to know, if we don't?" asked Mr. Jenks.

"What do you want to know?"

"How you got aboard, and what your object was in coming."

"That's easy enough. I had been hanging around the shed for several days, watching a chance to get in. Finally I saw it, when that colored man went to feed his mule, and I slipped in, and hid in the airship. The stores were all in then, and I stowed myself away among the boxes. I had food and water, so I didn't touch any of yours," and he looked at Mr. Damon, who seemed much relieved.

"And what was your object?" demanded Mr. Jenks.

"I wanted to prevent you from going to Phantom Mountain."

"How?"

"By destroying the airship if need be. But I hoped to accomplish it by other means. I would have stopped at nothing, though, to prevent you. You must keep away from there!"

"And if we refuse?" asked Tom.

"Then you'll have to take what comes!"

"But not from you!" exclaimed Mr. Jenks. "We're going to get rid of you."

The man's face showed the alarm he felt.

"Oh, don't worry," said Mr. Jenks, quickly, "we're not going to toss you overboard. We're not as desperate as your crowd. But we're going to get rid of you, and then go on before you can send any word to your confederates. We'll put you off in the most lonesome spot we can find, and I guess you'll be some time getting back to civilization. By that time we'll have the secret of the diamonds."

"You never will!" declared the man, firmly. And he would say nothing more, though by threats and promises Mr. Jenks tried to get from him something about the men in with him, and where the cave of the diamonds was located.

Heavily bound with ropes the man was locked in a small closet, to be kept there until a favorable spot was reached for letting him go. Mr. Jenks' plan, of dropping him down in some place where he would have difficulty in sending on word to his confederates was considered a good one.

Three days later, in crossing over a lonely region, near the Nebraska National Forest, Farley Munson, which was one of the names the spy went by, was dropped off the airship, when it was sent down to within a few feet of the earth.

"It will take you some time to get to a telegraph office," said Mr. Jenks, as a package of food, and a flask of water was tossed down to the stowaway. He shook his fist at those in the airship, and shouted after them:

"You'll never discover the secret of Phantom Mountain!"

"Yes, we will," declared Tom, as he sent the *Red Cloud* high into the air again.

A Weary Search

During the three days when the stowaway had been kept a prisoner, the *Red Cloud* had made good time on her western trip. She was now about two hundred and fifty miles from Leadville, Colorado, and Tom knew he could accomplish that distance in a short time. It was necessary, therefore, since they were so close to the place where the real search would begin, to make some more definite plans.

"We will need to replenish our supply of gasoline," said Tom, shortly after the stowaway had been dropped, and when the young inventor had made a general inspection of the airship.

"Is it all gone?" inquired Mr. Damon.

"Not all, but we will soon be in the wildest part of the Rocky Mountains, and gasoline is difficult to procure there. So I want to fill all our reserve tanks. But I would rather do that before we get far into Colorado."

"Why?" inquired Mr. Parker.

"Because airships are not so common but what the appearance of one attracts attention. Ours is sure to be talked about, and commented on. In that case, in spite of our precaution in putting Munson off in this lonely place, word of the *Red Cloud* being in the vicinity of Leadville may reach the diamond makers, and put them on their guard. We want to take them unawares if we can."

"That's so," agreed Mr. Jenks. "We had better get our gasoline at the first stopping place, then, and proceed with our search. Our first object ought to be to look for the landmark—the head of stone. Then we can begin to prospect about a bit."

"My idea, exactly," declared Tom. "Well, then, I'll go down at the first place we cross, where we can get gasoline, and then we'll be in a position to hover in the air for a long time, without descending."

The airship kept on her way, traveling slowly the remainder of that day, and at dusk, when there was less chance of big crowds seeing them, the *Red Cloud* was sent down on the outskirts of a large village. Tom and Mr. Damon went to a supply store, and arranged to have a sufficient quantity of the gasoline taken out to the airship. It was delivered after dark, and little talk was occasioned by the few who were aware of the presence of the craft. Then, once more, they went aloft, and Tom sent several wireless messages to Shopton, including one to Miss Nestor.

"Please tell my wife that I am well, and that I have a good appetite," said Mr. Damon.

Mr. Parker also sent a message to a scientific friend of his, stating that he made some observations among the mountains, of the region in which the airship then was, and that the indications were that a great landslide would soon take place.

"That won't worry us," spoke Tom, "for we'll be far above it."

"I hope we will be near enough to enable me to observe it, and make some scientific notes," came from Mr. Parker. "I am positive that one of these mountain peaks that we saw to-day will disappear in a landslide within a few days. I have an instrument somewhat like the one that records earthquakes, and it has been acting strangely of late."

Tom wondered what enjoyment Mr. Parker got out of life, when he was always looking for some calamity to happen, but the scientist seemed to take as much pleasure in his gloomy forebodings now, as he had on Earthquake Island.

They reached the vicinity of Leadville the next day, but took care to keep high above the city, so that the airship could not be observed. With powerful glasses they examined the mountainous country, looking for the little settlement of Indian Ridge.

"There it is!" exclaimed Mr. Jenks, just as dusk was settling down. I can make out the hotel I stopped at. Now we can really begin our search. The next thing is to find the stone head, and then, I think, I will have my bearings."

"We'll begin the hunt for that landmark in the morning," said Tom.

High in the air hovered the *Red Cloud*. At that distance above the earth she must have looked like some great bird, and the adventurers thought it unlikely that any one in the vicinity of Leadville would observe them.

The quest for the great mountain peak, that looked like a stone head, was under way. Back and forth sailed the airship. Sometimes she was enveloped in fog, and no sight could be had of the earth below. At other times there were rain storms, which likewise prevented a view. Mr. Parker was on the lookout for his predicted mountain landslide, but it did not occur, and he was much disappointed.

"It's queer I can't pick out that landmark," said Mr. Jenks after two days of weary searching, when their eyes were strained from long peering through telescopes. "I'm sure it was around Indian Ridge, yet we've covered almost all the ground in this neighborhood, and I haven't had a glimpse of it."

"Perhaps it was destroyed in a landslide, or some cataclysm of nature," suggested Mr. Parker. "That is very possible."

"If that's the case we're going to have a hard time to locate the cave of the diamond makers," answered Mr. Jenks, "but I hope it isn't so."

They continued the search for another day, and then Tom, as they sat in the comfortable cabin of the airship that night, hovering almost motionless (for the motor had been shut down) made a proposition.

"Why not descend in some secluded place," he suggested, "and wander around on foot, making inquiries of the miners. They may know where the stone head is, or they may even know about Phantom Mountain."

"Good idea," spoke Mr. Jenks. "We'll do it."

Accordingly, the next morning, the *Red Cloud* was lowered in a good but lonely landing place, and securely moored. It was in a valley, well screened from observation, and the craft was not likely to be seen, but, to guard against any damage being done to it by passing hunters or miners, Mr. Parker and Mr. Damon agreed to remain on guard in it, while Tom and Mr. Jenks spent a day or two traveling around, making inquiries.

The young inventor and his companion proceeded on foot to a small settlement, where they hired horses on which to make their way about. They were to be gone two days, and in that time they hoped to get on the right trail.

THE GREAT STONE HEAD

It was a wild and desolate country in which Tom Swift and Mr. Jenks were traveling. Villages were far apart, and they were at best but small settlements. In their journeys from place to place they met few travelers.

But of these few they made cautious inquiries as to the location of Phantom Mountain, or the landmark known as the great stone head. Prospectors, miners and hunters, whom they asked, shook their heads.

"I've heard of Phantom Mountain," said one grizzled miner, "but I couldn't say where it is. Maybe it's only a fish story—the place may not even exist."

"Oh, it does, for I've been there!" exclaimed Mr. Jenks.

"Then why don't you go back to it?" asked the miner.

"Because I can't locate it again," was the reply.

"Humph! Mighty queer if you've seen a place once, and can't get to it again," and the man looked as if he thought there was something strange about Tom and his companion. Mr. Jenks did not want to say that he had been taken to the mountain blindfolded, for that would have caused too much talk.

"I think if we spent to-night in a place where the miners congregate, listened to their talk, and put a few casual questions to them, more as if we were only asking out of idle curiosity, we might learn something," suggested Tom.

"Very well, we'll try that scheme."

Accordingly, after they had left the suspicious miner the two proceeded to a small milling town, not far from Indian Ridge. There they engaged rooms for the night at the only hotel, and, after supper they sat around the combined dance hall and gambling place.

There were wild, rough scenes, which were distasteful to Tom, and to Mr. Jenks, but they felt that this was their only chance to get on the right trail, and so they stayed. As strangers in a western mining settlement they were made roughly welcome, and in response to their inquiries about the country, they were told many tales, some of which were evidently gotten up for the benefit of the "tenderfeet."

"Is there a place around here called Phantom Mountain?" asked Tom, at length, as quietly as he could.

"Never heard of it, stranger," replied a miner who had done most of the talking. "I never heard of it, and what Bill Slatterly don't know ain't worth knowin'. I'm Bill Slatterly," he added, lest there be some doubt on that score.

"Isn't there some sort of a landmark around here shaped like a great stone head?" went on Tom, after some unimportant questions. "Seems to me I've heard of that."

"Nary a one," answered Mr. Slatterly. "No stone heads, and no Phantom Mountains—nary a one.

"Who says there ain't no Phantom Mountains?" demanded an elderly miner, who had been dozing in one corner of the room, but who was awakened by Slatterly's loud voice. "Who says so?"

"I do," answered the one who claimed to know everything.

"Then you're wrong!" Tom's heart commenced beating faster than usual.

"Do you mean to say you've seen Phantom Mountain, Jed Nugg?" demanded Slatterly.

"No, I ain't exactly seen it, an' I don't want to, but there is such a place, about sixty mile from here. Folks says it's haunted, and them sort of places I steer clear from."

"Can you tell me about it?" asked Mr. Jenks. eagerly. "I am interested in such things."

"I can't tell you much about it," was the reply, "and I wouldn't git too interested, if I was you. It might not be healthy. All I know is that one time my partner and I were in hard luck. We got grub-staked, and went out prospectin'. We strayed into a wild part of the country about sixty mile from here, and one night we camped on a mountain—a wild, desolate place it was too."

The miner stopped, and began leisurely filling his pipe.

"Well?" asked Tom, trying not to let his voice sound too eager.

"Well, that was Phantom Mountain."

The miner seemed to have finished his story.

"Is that all?" asked Mr. Jenks. "How did you know it was Phantom Mountain?"

"'Cause we seen the ghost—my partner and I—that's why!" exclaimed the man, puffing on his pipe. "As I said, we was campin' there, and 'long about midnight we seen somethin' tall and white, and all shimmerin', with a sort of yellow fire, slidin' down the side of the mountain It made straight for our camp."

"Huh! Guess you run, didn't you, Jed?" asked Bill Slatterly.

"Course we did. You'd a run too, if you seen a ghost comm' at you, an' firm' a gun."

"Ghosts can't fire guns!" declared Bill. "I guess you dreamed it, Jed."

"Ghosts can't fire guns, eh? That's all you know about it. This one did, and to prove I didn't dream it, there was a bullet hole in my hat next mornin'. I could prove it, too, only I ain't got that hat any more. But that was Phantom Mountain, strangers, an' my advice to you is to keep away from it. I was on it but I didn't exactly see it, 'cause it was dark at the time."

"Was it near a peak that looked like a stone head?" asked Tom.

"It were, stranger, but I didn't take much notice of it. Me and my partner got out of them diggin's next day, and I never went back. I ain't never said much about this place, but it's called Phantom Mountain all right, and I ain't the only one that's seen a ghost there. Other grub-stakers has had the same experience."

"Why ain't I never heard about it?" demanded Bill, suspiciously.

"'Cause as why you're allers so busy talkin' that you don't never listen to nothin' I reckon," was Jed's answer, amid laughter.

"Can you tell us what trail to take to get there?" asked Tom, of the miner.

"Yes, it's called the old silver trail, and you. strike it by goin' to a place called Black Gulch, about forty mile from here. Then it's twenty mile farther on. But take my advice and don't go."

"Can it be reached by way of Indian Ridge?" asked Mr. Jenks, wondering how he had been taken to the cave of the diamond makers. He did not remember Black Gulch.

"Yes, you can git there by Indian Ridge way, but it's more dangerous. You're likely to lose your way, for that's a trail that's seldom traveled." Mr. Jenks thought that, perhaps, was the reason the gang had taken him that way. "It's easier to get to the stone head and Phantom Mountain by Black Gulch, but it ain't healthy to go there, strangers, take my advice on that," concluded the miner, as he prepared to go to sleep again.

Tom could scarcely contain the exultation he felt. At last, it seemed, they were on the trail. He motioned to Mr. Jenks, and they slipped quietly from the place, just as another dance was beginning.

"Now for Black Gulch!" cried Tom. "We must hurry back to the airship, and tell the good news.

"It's too late to-night," decided Mr. Jenks, and so they waited until morning, when they made an early start.

They found Mr. Damon and Mr. Parker anxiously awaiting their return. Mr. Damon blessed so many things that he was nearly out of breath, and Mr. Parker related something of the observations he had made.

"I think I have discovered traces of a dormant volcano," he said. "I am in hopes that it will have an eruption while we are here."

"I'm not," spoke Tom, decidedly. "We'll start for Black Gulch as soon as possible."

The airship once more rose in the air, and, following the directions the miner had given him, Tom pointed his craft for the depression in the mountains which had been given the name Black Gulch. It was reached in a short time, and then, making a turn up a long valley the airship proceeded at reduced speed.

"We ought to see that stone head soon now," spoke Tom, as he peered from the windows of the pilot house.

"It's queer we didn't notice it when we were up in the air," remarked Mr. Jenks. "We've been over this place before, I'm sure of it."

The next moment Mr. Damon uttered a cry. "Bless my watch- chain!" he exclaimed. "Look at that!"

He pointed off to the left. There, jutting out from the side of a steep mountain peak was a mass of stone—black stone—which, as the airship slowly approached, took the form and shape of a giant's head.

"That's it! That's it!" cried Tom. "The great stone head!"

"And now for Phantom Mountain and the diamonds!" shouted Mr. Jenks, as Tom let the airship slowly settle to the bottom of the valley.

ON PHANTOM MOUNTAIN

Out from the *Red Cloud* piled Tom and the others. They made a rush for the irregular mass of rock which bore so strong a resemblance to the head of some gigantic man.

"That's the one! That's the thing I saw when they were taking me along here blindfolded!" exclaimed Mr. Jenks. "I'm sure we're on the right trail, now!"

"But what gets me, though," remarked Mr. Damon, "is why we couldn't see that landmark when we were up in the air. We had a fine view, and ought to have been able to pick it out with the telescopes."

The adventurers saw the reason a few seconds later. The image was visible only from one place, and that was directly looking up the valley. If one went too far to the right or left the head disappeared from view behind jutting crags, and it was impossible to see it from overhead, because the head was almost under a great spur of a mighty mountain.

"We might have hunted for it a week in the airship, and been directly over it," said Tom, "and yet we would never have seen it."

"Yes, but we never would have gotten here in such good shape if it hadn't been for your wonderful craft," declared Mr. Jenks. "It brought us here safely and quickly, and enabled us to elude the men who tried to keep us back. We're here in spite of them. If we had traveled by train they might have interfered with us in a dozen ways."

"That's so," agreed Mr. Damon. "Well, now we're here, what's to be done? Which way do we start to reach the cave where the diamonds are manufactured, Mr. Jenks?"

"That I can't say. As you know, I only had a momentary glimpse of this stone head as they wore taking me along the trail. Then one the men noticed that the bandage had slipped and he pulled it into place. So I really can't say which direction to take now, in order to discover the secret."

"How long after you saw the head before you reached the cave?" asked Tom. "In that way we may be able to tell how far away it is."

"Well, I should say it was about two or three hours after I saw the head, before we got to the halting place, and I was carried into the cave. That would make it several miles from here, for we went in a wagon."

"Yes, and they might have driven in a round-about way, in order to deceive you," suggested Mr. Damon. "At best we have but a faint idea where the diamond cave is, but we must search for it; eh, Tom?"

"Certainly. We'll start right in. And as the airship will be of but little service to us now, I suggest that we leave it in this valley. It is very much secluded, and no one will harm it, I think. We can then start off prospecting, for I have a large portable tent, and we can carry enough food with us, with what game we can shoot, to enable us to live. I have a regular camping outfit on board."

"Fine!" cried Mr. Parker, "and that will give me a chance to make some observations among the mountains, and perhaps I can predict when a landslide, or an eruption of some dormant volcano, may occur."

"Bless my stars!" cried Mr. Damon. "I don't wish you any bad luck, Mr. Parker, but I sincerely hope nothing of the sort happens! We had enough of that on Earthquake Island!"

"One can not halt the forces of nature," said the scientist, solemnly. "There are many towering peaks around here which may contain old volcanoes. And I notice the presence of iron ore all about. This must be a wonderful place in a thunder and lightning storm."

"Why?" asked Tom, curiously.

"Because lightning would be powerfully attracted here by the presence of the metal. In fact there is evidence that many of the peaks have been struck by lightning," and the scientist showed curious, livid scars on the stone faces of the peaks within sight.

"Then this is a good place to stay away from in a storm," observed Mr. Damon. "However, we won't worry about that now. If this is the landmark Mr. Jenks was searching for, then we must be in the vicinity of Phantom Mountain."

"I think we are," declared the diamond seeker. "Probably it is within sight now, but there are so many peaks, and this is such a wild and desolate part of the country that we may have trouble in locating it."

"We've got to make a beginning, anyhow," decided Tom, "and the sooner the better. Come, we'll make up our camping kits, and start out."

It was something to know that they were on the right trail, and it was a relief to be able to busy oneself, and not be aimlessly searching for a mysterious landmark. They all felt this, and soon the airship was taken to a secluded part of the valley, where it was well hidden from sight in a grove of trees.

Tom and Mr. Damon then served a good meal, and preparations were made to start on their search among the mountains—a search which they hoped would lead them to Phantom Mountain, and the cave of the diamond makers.

The tent which would afford them shelter was in sections, and could be laced together. They carried food, compressed into small packages, coffee, a few cooking utensils; and each one had a gun, Tom carrying a combination rifle and shotgun, for game.

"We can't live very high while we're on the trail," said the young inventor, "but it won't be much worse than it was on Earthquake Island. Are we all ready?"

"I guess so," answered Mr. Damon. "How long are we going to be away?"

"Until we find the diamond makers!" declared Tom, firmly.

Shouldering their packs, the adventurers started off. Tom turned for a last look at his airship, dimly seen amid the trees. Would he ever come back to the

Red Cloud? Would she be there when he did return? Would their quest be successful? These questions the lad asked himself, as he followed his companions along the rocky trail.

"Perhaps we can find the road by which these men go in and out of the cave," suggested Mr. Damon, when they had gone on for several miles.

"I fancy not," replied Mr. Jenks. "They probably take great pains to hide it. I think though, that our best plan will be to go here and there, looking for the entrance to the cave. I believe I would remember the place."

"But why can't you follow the directions given by the miner who told you about Phantom Mountain?" asked Mr. Damon.

"Because his talk was too indefinite," answered Mr. Jenks. "He was so frightened by seeing what he believed to be a ghost, that he didn't take much notice of the location of the place. All he knows is that Phantom Mountain is somewhere around here."

"And we've got to hunt until we find it; is that the idea?" asked Mr. Parker.

"Or until we see the phantom" added Tom, in a low voice.

"Bless my topknot!" exclaimed Mr. Damon. "You don't mean to say you expect to see that ghost; do you Tom?"

"Perhaps," answered the young inventor, and he did not add something else of which he was thinking. For Tom had a curious theory regarding the phantom.

They tramped about the remainder of that day. Toward evening Tom shot some birds, which made a welcome addition to their supper. Then the tent was put together, some spruce and hemlock boughs were cut to make a soft bed, and on these, while the light of a campfire gleamed in on them, the adventurers slept.

Their experience the following day was similar to the first. They saw no evidence of a large cave such as Mr. Jenks had described, nor were there any traces of men having gone back and forth among the mountains, as might have been expected of the diamond makers, for, as Mr. Jenks had said, they made frequent journeys to the settlement for food, and other supplies.

"Well, I haven't begun to give up yet," announced Tom, on the third day, when their quest was still unsuccessful. "But I think we are making one mistake."

"What is that?" inquired Mr. Jenks.

"I think we should go up higher. In my opinion the cave is near the top of some peak; isn't it, Mr. Jenks?"

"I have that impression, though, as you know, I never saw the outside of it. Still, it might not be a bad idea to ascend some of these peaks."

Following this suggestion, they laid their trail more toward the sky, and that night found them encamped several thousand feet above the sea-level. It was quite cool, and the campfire was a big one about which they sat after supper, talking of many things.

Tom did not sleep well that night. He tossed from side to side on the bed of boughs, and once or twice got up to replenish the fire, which had burned low. His companions were in deep slumber.

"I wonder what time it is?" mused Tom, when he had been up the third time to throw wood on the blaze. "Must be near morning." He looked at his watch, and was somewhat startled to see that it was only a little after twelve. Somehow it seemed much later.

As he was putting the timepiece back into his pocket the lad looked around at the dark and gloomy mountains, amid which they were encamped. As his gaze wandered toward the peak of the one on the side of which the tent was pitched, he gave a start of surprise.

For, coming down a place where, that afternoon, Tom had noticed a sort of indefinite trail. was a figure in white. A tall, waving figure, which swayed this way and that—a figure which halted and then came on again.

"I wonder—I wonder if that can be a wisp of fog?" mused the young inventor. He rubbed his eyes, thinking it might be a swirling of the night mist or a defect of vision. Then, as he saw more plainly, he noticed the thing in white rushing toward him.

"It's the phantom—the phantom!" cried Tom, aloud. "It's the thing the miner saw! We're on Phantom Mountain now!"

WARNED BACK

Tom's cries awakened the sleepers in the tent. Mr. Damon was the first to rush out.

"Bless my nightcap, Tom!" he cried. "What is it? What has happened? Are we attacked by a mountain lion?"

For answer the young inventor pointed up the mountain, to where, in the dim light from a crescent moon, there stood boldly revealed, the figure in white.

"Bless—bless my very existence!" cried the odd man. "What is it, Tom?"

"The phantom," was the quiet answer. "Watch it, and see what it does."

By this time Mr. Jenks and Mr. Parker had joined Tom and Mr. Damon. The four diamond seekers stood gazing at the apparition. And, as they looked, the thing in white, seemingly too tall for any human being, slid slowly forward, with a gliding motion. Then it raised its long, white arms, and waved them threateningly at the adventurers.

"It's motioning us to go back," said Mr. Parker in an awed whisper. "It doesn't want us to go any farther."

"Very likely," agreed Tom, coolly. "But we're not going to be frightened by anything like that; are we?"

"Not much!" exclaimed Mr. Jenks. "I expected this. A ghost can't drive me back from getting my rights from those scoundrels!"

"Suppose it uses a revolver to back up its demand?" asked the scientist.

"Wait until it does," answered Mr. Jenks. But the figure in white evidently had no such intentions. It came on a little distance farther, still waving the long arms threateningly, and then it suddenly disappeared, seeming to dissolve in the misty shadows of the night.

"Bless my suspenders!" cried Mr. Damon." "That's a very strange proceeding! Very strange! What do you make of it, Tom?"

"It is evidently some man dressed up in a sheet," declared Mr. Jenks. "I expected as much."

"The work of those diamond makers; do you think?" continued Mr. Damon.

"I believe so," answered Tom, slowly, for he was trying to think it out. "I believe they are the cause of the phantom, though I don't know that it's a man dressed in a sheet."

"Why isn't it?" demanded Mr. Jenks.

"Because it was too tall for a man, unless he's a giant."

"He may have been on stilts," suggested Mr. Parker.

"No man on stilts could walk along that way," declared Tom, confidently. "He glided along too easily. I am inclined to think it may be some sort of a light."

"A light?" queried Mr. Damon.

"Yes, the diamond makers may be hidden in some small cave near here, and they may have some sort of a magic lantern or a similar arrangement, for throwing a shadow picture. They could arrange it to move as they liked, and could cause it to disappear at will. That, I think, is the ghost we have just seen."

"But the diamond makers have only been in this mountain recently," objected Mr. Jenks, "and the phantom was here before them. In fact, that was what gave the place its name."

"That may be," admitted the lad. "There are many places that have the name of being haunted, but no one ever sees the ghost. It is always some one else, who has heard of some one who has seen it. That may have been the case here. I grant that this place may have been called 'Phantom Mountain' for a number of years, due to the superstitious tales of miners. The diamond makers came along, found the conditions just right for their work, and adopted the ghost, so to speak. As there wasn't any real spirit they made one, and they use it to scare people away. I think that's what we've just seen, though I may be wrong in my theory as to what the phantom is."

"Well, it's gone now, at any rate," said Mr. Jenks, "and I think we'd better get back inside the tent. It's cold out here."

"Aren't some of us going to stand guard?" demanded Mr. Damon.

"What for?" asked Mr. Jenks.

"Why—er—bless my key-ring! Suppose that ghost takes a notion to come down here, and use his gun, as he did on the miners?"

"I don't believe that will happen," remarked Tom. "The diamond makers, if the white thing had anything to do with them, have given us a warning, and I think they'll at least wait until morning to see how we heed it."

"We aren't going to heed it!" burst out Mr. Jenks. "I'm going to go right ahead and find that cave where they make diamonds!"

"And we're with you!" exclaimed Tom. "We'll have a good fire going the rest of the night, and that may keep intruders away. In the morning we'll begin our search, and we'll go up the trail where we saw the white figure."

A big pile of wood had been collected for the fire, and Tom now piled some logs and branches on the blaze. It would last for some time now, and the adventurers, still talking of the "ghost" went back into the tent. It was over an hour before they all got to sleep again, and Mr. Jenks and Mr. Damon took turns in getting up once or twice during the remainder of the night to replenish the fire.

Morning dawned without anything further having occurred to disturb them, and, after a hearty breakfast, to which Tom added some fish he caught in a nearby mountain stream, they set off up the trail on Phantom Mountain.

They had left their tent standing, as they proposed making that spot their headquarters until they located the cave they were seeking. What their course would be after that would depend on the circumstances.

If they had expected to have an easy task locating the cavern in which Mr. Jenks had seen diamonds made, the adventurers were disappointed. All that day they tramped up and down the mountain, looking for some secret entrance, but none was disclosed. The higher they went up the great peak, the fainter became the trail, until, at length it vanished completely.

But this was not to be wondered at, since it was on solid rock, in which no footsteps would leave an impression.

"They never brought you up here in a wagon, Mr. Jenks," decided Tom, when he saw how steep the place was.

"I'm inclined to think so myself," admitted the diamond man. "They must have reached the cave from some other way. As a matter of fact, I walked some distance after getting out of the vehicle, before we got to the cavern. But, even at that, I don't believe we came this way."

"Yet the phantom was here," persisted Tom, "and I'm convinced that the cave is in this neighborhood. It's up to us to find it!"

But they searched the remainder of that day in vain, and as night was coming on, they made their way back to the camp. As Tom, who was in the lead, approached the tent, he saw something black fastened to the entrance.

"Hello!" he cried. "Some one's been here. That wasn't on the tent when he left this morning."

"What is it?" asked Mr. Damon.

"A black piece of paper, written on with white ink," replied the lad. He was reading it, and, as he perused it a look of surprise came over his face.

"Listen to this!" called Tom. "It's evidently from the diamond makers."

Holding up the black paper, on which the white writing stood out in bold relief Tom read aloud:

"Be warned in time! Go back before it is too late! You are near to death! Go back!"

"Bless my shoelaces!" cried Mr. Damon. "This is getting serious."

THE LANDSLIDE

Gathered about the young inventor, the three men looked at the warning. The writing was poor, and it was evident that an attempt had been made to disguise it. But there was no misspelling of words, and there were no rudely drawn daggers, or bloody hands or anything of that sort. In fact, it was a very business-like sort of warning.

"Rather odd," commented Mr. Jenks. "Black paper and white ink."

"White ink is easy enough to make," stated Mr. Parker. "I fancy they wanted it as conspicuous as possible."

"Yes," agreed Tom, "and this warning, together with the antics of the thing in white last night, shows that they are aware of our presence here, and perhaps know who we are. We will have to be on our guard."

"Do you think that fellow Munson, whom we left in the forest, could have gotten here and warned them?" asked Mr. Damon.

"It's possible," admitted Tom, "but now let's see if the person who pinned this warning on our tent took any of our things."

A hasty examination, however, showed that nothing had been disturbed, and Tom and Mr. Damon were soon getting supper ready, everyone talking, during the progress of the meal, about the events of the day, and the rather weird culmination of it.

"Well, we haven't had a great deal of success—so far," admitted Tom, as they sat about the fire, in the fast gathering dusk. "I think, perhaps, we'd better try on the other side of the mountain to-morrow. We've explored this side pretty thoroughly."

"Good idea," commented Mr. Jenks. "We'll do it, and move our camp. I only hope those fellows don't find our airship and destroy it. We'll have a hard time getting back to civilization again, if we have to walk all the way."

This contingency caused Tom some uneasiness. He did not like to think that the unscrupulous men might damage the *Red Cloud*, that had been built only after hard labor. But he knew he could accomplish nothing by worrying, and he tried to dismiss the matter from his mind.

They rather expected to see the thing in white again that night, but it did not appear, and morning came without anything having disturbed their heavy sleep, for they were tired from the day's tramp.

It took them the greater part of the day to make a circuit of the base of Phantom Mountain in order to get to a place where a sort of trail led upward.

"It's too late to do anything to-night," decided Tom, as they set up the tent. "We'll rest, and start the first thing in the morning."

"And the ghost isn't likely to find us here," added Mr. Damon. "Where are you going, Mr. Parker?" he asked, as he saw the scientist tramping a little way up the side of the mountain.

"I am going to make some observations," was the answer, and no one paid any more attention to him for some time. Supper was nearly ready when Mr. Parker returned. His face wore a rather serious air, and Mr. Damon, noting it, asked laughingly:

"Well, did you discover any volcanoes, that may erupt during the night, and scare us to death?"

"No," replied Mr. Parker, calmly, "but there is every indication that we will soon have a terrific electrical storm. From a high peak I caught a glimpse of one working this way across the mountains."

"Then we'd better fasten the tent well down," called Tom. "We don't want it to blow away."

"There will not be much danger from wind," was Mr. Parker's opinion.

"From what then?" asked Mr. Jenks.

"From the discharges of lightning among these mountain peaks, which contain so much iron ore. We will be in grave danger."

The fact that the scientist had not always made correct predictions was not now considered by his hearers, and Tom and the two men gazed at Mr. Parker in some alarm.

"Is there anything we can do to avoid it?" asked Mr. Jenks.

"The only thing to do would be to leave the mountain," was the answer, "and, as the iron ore extends for miles, we can not get out of the danger zone before the storm will reach us. It will be here in less than half an hour."

"Then we'd better have supper," remarked Tom, practically, "and get ready for it. Perhaps it may not be as bad as Mr. Parker fears."

"It will be bad enough," declared the gloomy scientist, and he seemed to find pleasure in his announcement.

The meal was soon over, and Tom busied himself in looking to the guy ropes of the tent, for he feared lest there might be wind with the storm. That it was coming was evident, for now low mutterings of thunder could be heard off toward the west.

Black clouds rapidly obscured the heavens, and the sound of thunder increased. Fitful flashes of lightning could be seen forking across the sky in jagged chains of purple light.

"It's going to be a heavy storm," Tom admitted to himself. "I hope lightning doesn't strike around here."

The storm came on rapidly, but there was a curious quietness in the air that was more alarming than if a wind had blown. The campfire burned steadily, and there was a certain oppressiveness in the atmosphere.

It was now quite dark, save when the fitful lightning flashes came, and they illuminated the scene brilliantly for a few seconds. Then, by contrast, it was blacker than ever.

Suddenly, as Tom was gazing up toward the peak of Phantom Mountain, he saw something that caused him to cry out in alarm. He pointed upward, and whispered hoarsely:

"The ghost again! There's our friend in white!"

The others looked, and saw the same weird figure that had menaced them when they were encamped on the other side of the peak.

"They must have followed us," said Mr. Jenks, in a low voice.

Slowly the figure advanced, It waved the long white arms, as if in warning. At times it would be only dimly visible in the blackness, then, suddenly it would stand out in bold relief as a great flash of fire split the clouds.

The thunder, meanwhile, had been growing louder and sharper, indicating the nearer approach of the storm. Each lightning flash was followed in a second or two, by a terrific clap. Still there was no wind nor rain, and the campfire burned steadily.

All at once there was a crash as if the very mountain had split asunder, and the adventurers saw a great ball of purple-bluish fire shoot down, as if from some cloud, and strike against the side of the crag, not a hundred feet from where stood the ghostly figure in white.

"That was a bad one," cried Mr. Damon, shouting so as to be heard above the echoes of the thunderclap.

Almost as he spoke there came another explosion, even louder than the one preceding. A great ball of fire, pear shaped, leaped for the same spot in the mountain.

"There's a mass of iron ore there!" yelled Mr. Parker. "The lightning is attracted to it!"

His voice was swallowed up in the terrific crash that followed, and, as there came another flash of the celestial fire, the figure in white could be seen hurrying back up the mountain trail. Evidently the electrical storm, with lightning bolts discharging so close, was too much for the "ghost."

In another instant it looked as if the whole place about where the diamond seekers stood, was a mass of fire. Great forked tongues of lightning leaped from the clouds, and seemed to lick the ground. There was a rattle and bang of thunder, like the firing of a battery of guns. Tom and the others felt themselves tingling all over, as if they had hold of an electrical battery, and there was a strong smell of sulphur in the air.

"We are in the midst of the storm!" cried Mr. Parker. "We are standing on a mass of iron ore! Any minute may be our last!"

But fate had not intended the adventurers for death by lightning. Almost as suddenly as it had begun, the discharge of the tongues of fire ceased in the immediate vicinity of our friends. They stood still—awed—not knowing what to do.

Then, once more, came a terrific clap! A great mass of fire, like some red-hot ingot from a foundry, was hurled through the air, straight at the face of the mountain, and at the spot where the figure in white had stood but a few minutes before.

Instantly the earth trembled, as it had at Earthquake Island, but it was not the same. It was over in a few seconds. Then, as the diamond seekers looked, they saw in the glare of a score of lightning flashes that followed the one great clap, the whole side of the mountain slip away, and go crashing into the valley below.

"A landslide!" cried Mr. Parker. "That is the landslide which I predicted! The lightning bolt has split Phantom Mountain!"

THE VAST CAVERN

For a time the roiling, slipping, sliding and tumbling of the mass of earth and stones, down the side of the mountain, effectually drowned all other sounds. Even the thunder was stilled, and though Tom and his companions called to one another in terror, their voices could not rise above that terrific tumult.

Finally, when they found that the direction of the slide was away from their tent, and that they were not likely to be engulfed, they grew more calm.

Gradually the noise subsided. The great boulders had rolled to the bottom of the valley, and now only a mass of earth and stones was sliding down. Even this stopped in about five minutes, and, as though satisfied with what it had done, the electrical storm passed. Not a drop of rain had fallen.

"Bless my shirt studs!" exclaimed Mr. Damon, who was the first to speak after the din had quieted. "Bless my soul! But that was awful!"

"It was just what I expected," said Mr. Parker, calmly. "I knew, from my observations, that we were in a region where landslides and terrific electrical storms may be expected at any time. I fully looked for this."

"Well," remarked Mr. Jenks, rather sarcastically, "I hope it came up to your expectations, Mr. Parker."

"Oh, fully," was the answer, "though I wish it could have happened in daylight, so that I could better have observed certain phenomena regarding the landslide. They are very interesting."

"At a distance," admitted Tom, with a laugh of relief. "Well, I'm glad it's over, though we'll have to wait until morning to see what damage has been done. Lucky we weren't struck by lightning. I never saw such bolts!"

"Me, either!" declared Mr. Damon. "This mountain seems to attract them."

"It is like a magnet," said Mr. Parker. "I think I shall be able to make some fine observations here."

"If we live through it," murmured Mr. Jenks.

They watched the play of lightning about a distant bank of clouds, but the storm was now far away, only a faint rumbling of thunder being heard.

"I'm wondering what happened to the phantom," said Tom, after a pause. "Seems to me he was right in that track of the storm."

"Do you think it was a 'he'?" asked Mr. Jenks.

"I think we'll find that it's some sort of a man," answered the young inventor. "We may find out very soon, now. I've changed my theory about the ghost being reflections of light."

"How's that?" Mr. Damon wanted to know.

"Well, I think we are on the side of Phantom Mountain where the diamond cave is," went on the lad. "The fact that the phantom appeared here, soon after we arrived, shows that the men kept close track of our movements. It also shows, I think, that the phantom did not have to travel far to be on the spot, whereas we had to make quite a trip to get around the base of the mountain. I think the cave is up there," and Tom pointed toward the spot where the weird figure had been last seen, before the storm drove it back.

"There may be two phantoms," suggested Mr. Jenks. "They may keep one on this side of the mountain, and one on the other, to warn intruders away.

"It's possible," admitted Tom. "Well, we'll see how things look in the morning, when we'll take up our march again, and go up the mountain. We'll reach the top, if possible, which we couldn't do from the other side, as it was too steep."

"I hope we shall be able to go forward in the morning," came from Mr. Jenks.

"What do you mean?" asked the lad, struck by a peculiar significance in the diamond man's tones.

"Why, that landslide may have opened a great gully in the side of Phantom Mountain, which will prevent us from passing. It was a terrific lot of earth and stones that slid away," answered Mr. Jenks.

"It certainly was," agreed Mr. Parker. "I would not be surprised if the mountain was half destroyed, and it may be that the diamond cave no longer exists."

"Not very cheerful, to say the least," murmured Mr. Jenks to Tom, and, as it was getting quite chilly, following the storm, they went inside the tent.

Tom could hardly wait for daylight, to get up and see what havoc the landslide had wrought. As soon as the first faint flush of dawn showed over the eastern peaks, he hurried from the tent. Mr. Damon heard him arise, and followed.

A curious scene met their eyes. All about were great rocks rent and torn by the awful power of the lightning. The fronts of the stone cliffs were scarred and burned by the electrical fire, and fantastic markings, grotesque faces, and leering animals seemed to have been drawn by some gigantic artist who used a bolt from heaven for his brush.

But the eyes of Tom and Mr. Damon took all this in at a glance, and then their gaze went forward to where the avalanche had torn away a great part of the mountain.

"Whew! I should say it was a landslide!" cried Tom.

"Bless my wishbone, yes!" agreed Mr. Damon.

Below them, in the valley, lay piled immense masses of earth and stones. Boulders were heaped up on boulders, and rocks upon rocks, being tossed about in heaps, strung about in long ridges, and swirled about in curves, as though some cyclone had toyed with them after the lightning flash had tossed them there.

"But the mountain isn't half gone," said Tom, as his eyes took in what was left of the phantom berg. "I guess it will take a few more bolts like that one, to put this hill out of business."

Though the landslide had been a great one, the larger part of the mountain still stood. An immense slice had been taken from one side, but the summit was untouched.

"And there's where the diamond cave is!" cried Tom, pointing to it.

"I think so myself," agreed Mr. Jenks, who came from the tent at that moment, and joined the lad and Mr. Damon. "I think we shall find the cave somewhere up there. We must start for it, as soon as we have eaten, and we may reach it by night."

The three stood gazing up toward the summit of the great mountain. Suddenly, as the sun rose higher in the heavens, it sent a shaft of rosy light on the face of the berg that had been scarred by the landslide. Tom Swift uttered an exclamation, and pointed at something.

"See!" he cried. "Look where the trail is—the trail down which the phantom must have come. It is on the edge of a cliff now!"

They looked, and saw that this was so. The increasing light had just revealed it to them. When the lightning bolt had torn away a great portion of the mountain it had cut sheer down for a great depth and when the earth and stones fell away they left a narrow pathway, winding around the mountain, but so near the edge of a great chasm, that there was room but for one person at a time to walk on that footway. The uncertain trail up Phantom Mountain had all but been destroyed.

"The way up to the peak is by that path, now," spoke Tom, in a low voice.

"Bless my soul!" cried Mr. Damon. "It's as much as a man's life is worth to attempt it. If he got dizzy, he'd topple over, and fall a thousand feet. Dare we risk it?"

"It's the only way to get up," went on Tom. "It's either that way, or not at all. We've tried the other side without success. We must go up this way—or turn back."

"Then we'll go up!" cried Mr. Jenks. "It may not be as dangerous as it looks from here."

But it was even more dangerous than it appeared, when they went part way up it after a hasty breakfast. The trail was a mere ledge of rock now, and in some places, to get around a projecting edge of the mountain, they had to stand with their backs to the dizzy depths at their feet, and with both arms outstretched work their way around to where the trail was wider.

"Shall we risk it?" asked Tom, when they had tried the way, and found it so dangerous. "We can't take anything with us—even our guns, for we couldn't carry them, and if we reach the month of the cave, and find those men there—"

He paused significantly. The adventurers looked at one another. The search for the diamond makers was becoming more and more dangerous.

"I say let's go on!" decided Mr. Damon, suddenly. "We want to locate that cave, first of all. Perhaps, when we do find it, we may see some easier way of getting to it than this. And if those diamond makers do attack us—well, I don't believe they'll shoot defenseless men, and they may listen to reason, and give Mr. Jenks his rights—tell him how to make diamonds in return for the money he gave them."

"I don't believe those scoundrels will listen to reason," replied the diamond man, "but I agree with Mr. Damon that we ought to go on. We may find some other means of reaching the cave—if we can discover it, and we'll take a chance with the men."

"Forward it is, then!" cried Tom. "I have a revolver, and I can supply one of you gentlemen with another. They may come in useful in an emergency. Let's go back to camp, take a little lunch in our pockets, and try to scale the mountain."

They were soon on their way up the dizzy path once more, and, as they advanced, they found it growing more and more dangerous. In some places they found it almost impossible to get around certain corners, where there was barely room for their feet. As Tom remarked grimly, a fat man never could have done it. Fortunately they were all comparatively thin, for their hard work, and not too abundant food, since they had left the airship, had reduced their weight.

Up and up they went, higher and higher, sometimes finding the path wide enough for two to walk abreast, and again seeing it narrow almost to a ribbon. They hardly dared look down into the chasm at their left—a chasm filled, in part, with the rocks and boulders tossed into it by the lightning bolt.

Tom was in the lead, and had just made a dangerous turn around a shoulder of rock—one of those places where he had to extend both arms, and fairly hug the cliff before he could get around.

But, when he had made it, and found himself on a broad pathway, cut in the living rock, he gave a great shout—a shout that caused his companions to hasten to his side. They found the young inventor pointing to a clump of bushes and small trees.

But it was not the shrubbery that Tom desired to call to their attention. They saw that in an instant, for, dimly seen through the leaves, was something black, and, as they looked more closely, they saw that it was a great hole in the side of the mountain—a vast cavern, opening like a tunnel.

"The cave! The cave!" cried Tom. "The diamond makers' cave

Hardly had he spoken than two men, each one carrying a gun, showed themselves in the mouth of the cavern, and, instant later they both ran toward the little party of adventurers.

The Phantom Captured

Surprise held Tom and his friends almost spellbound for the moment. The young inventor's hand went toward the pocket where he carried his revolver. Mr. Jenks, who had the only other weapon, sought to draw it, but he was stopped by a gesture of one of the two men with guns.

"Hold on, strangers!" the man cried. "I know what you're up to! Better not try to draw anything—it might not be healthy. Now, then, who are you, and what do you want?"

The question came rather as a surprise, at least to Tom and Mr. Jenks. They had taken it for granted that these men—if they were the diamond makers—would know Mr. Jenks, and guess at his errand in coming back to Phantom Mountain. But, it seemed, that they took them all for casual strangers.

No one answered for a moment. Tom caught the eye of Mr. Jenks, and there was a look of hope in it. If ever there was a time for strategy, it was now. Evidently Munson, the stowaway on the airship, had not yet been able to send a warning to his confederates. And neither of the two men recognized Mr. Jenks as the man who had been defrauded of his rights. It might be possible to conceal the real object of the adventurers until they had time to formulate a plan of action.

"Well," exclaimed the man with the gun, impatiently, "I ask you folks a question. What do you want?"

Fortunately, neither Mr. Damon nor Mr. Parker replied. The former because he deferred to Tom and Mr. Jenks, and the scientist because he was busy inspecting some curious rocks he picked up. As it turned out this was the luckiest thing he could have done. It lent color to what Mr. Jenks said a moment later.

"What are you doing up here?" demanded the man again. "Don't you know this is private property?"

"We—we were just looking around," answered Mr. Jenks, which was true enough; as far as it went.

"Prospecting," added Tom.

"After gold?" demanded the second man, suspiciously.

"We'd be glad to find some," retorted the lad. At that moment Mr. Parker began breaking off bits of rock with a small geologist's hammer which he carried. The men with the guns looked at him.

"So you think you'll find gold up here?" asked the one who had first spoken.

"Is there any?" inquired Tom, trying to make his voice sound eager.

"Nary a bit, strangers," was the answer, and the two men laughed heartily. "Now, we don't want to seem harsh," went on the man who seemed to be the spokesman, "but you'd better get away from here. This is private ground, and dangerous too—how'd you ever get up the trail—we heard it was destroyed."

"There is still a narrow path," said Mr. Jenks. "We came up that—the lightning and landslide haven't left much of it, though."

Mr. Parker looked quickly up from the rocks at which he was tapping with his small hammer. "You have terrific lightning up here," he said. "I am much interested in it, from a scientific standpoint. I predict that some day the entire mountain will be destroyed by a blast from the sky."

"I hope it won't be right away," spoke one of the men. "Now I guess you folks had better be leaving while there's a path left to go down by."

"Might I ask," broke in Mr. Parker, as calmly as though he was lecturing to a class of students, "might I ask if you have noticed any peculiar effect of the lightning up here on the summit of the mountain? Does it fuse and melt rocks, so to speak?"

"What's that?" cried the spokesman, with a sudden flash of anger. The two men looked at each other.

"I wanted to know, merely for scientific reasons, whether the lightning up here ever melted rocks?" repeated Mr. Jenks.

"Well, whether it's for scientific reasons or for any other, I'm not going to answer you!" snapped the man. "It's none of your affair what the lightning does up here. Now you'd all better 'vamoose'—clear out!"

"All right—we'll go," said Tom, quickly, at the same time motioning to Mr. Jenks to agree with him. The eyes of the young inventor were roving about. He saw what looked like a second trail, leading down the mountain, from the far side of the cave. He was convinced now that there was another way to get to it. Possibly they might find it. At any rate nothing more could be done now. They must go back, for the cavern was too well guarded to attempt to enter it by force—at least just yet.

"Yes, we'll go back," assented Mr. Jenks.

Mr. Parker was tapping away at the rocks. He looked toward the black mouth of the big cave. On what corresponded to the roof of it, some distance back from the entrance, he saw a slender metal rod sticking up into the air.

"May I ask if that's a lightning rod?" he inquired innocently. "If it is, I should like to ask about its action in a mountain that is so impregnated with iron ore.

"You may ask until you get tired!" cried the spokesman, again showing unreasoning anger, "but you'll get no answer from us. Now get away from here before we do something desperate. You're on private ground and you're not wanted. Clear out while you have the chance."

There was no help for it. Slowly our friends turned and began to go down the dangerous trail. They were soon out of sight of the two men who stood before the cave, with their guns ready, but neither Tom nor any of his companions spoke for some time.

When they had rounded one of the most dangerous turns the young inventor sat down to rest, an example followed by the others.

"Well," asked Tom, "do you think those are some of the diamond makers, Mr. Jenks?"

"I certainly do, though I never saw those two men before. If I could once get inside the cave, I could tell whether or not it was the one where I was practically held a prisoner. But I'm sure it is. I know some of the men used to go off every day with guns, and not come back until night. I have no doubt they were on guard, just as these two are. And, also, I think I heard them speak of a second entrance to the cavern. The one we just saw may not be the main one, through which I was taken."

"I believe we are on the right track," ventured Mr. Damon, "but we will either have to go up there after dark, which will be risky, on account of the narrow trail, or else we will have to find some other path."

"The last would be better," spoke Tom.

"That rod of metal sticking up on top of the cave interested me," said the scientist. "Did you hear anything of that when you were here before, Mr. Jenks?"

"No. Probably that is only a lightning rod, or it may be a staff for a signal flag. But what surprises me is that those men didn't suspect that we were seeking to discover their secret. They took us for ordinary prospectors."

"So much the better," remarked Tom. "We have a chance now of getting inside that cave. But we will have to go back to camp, and make other plans. And we must hurry, or it will be dark before we get there."

They hastened their steps, pausing only briefly to eat some of the lunch they had brought along, and to drink from a spring that bubbled from the side of the mountain. It was getting dusk when they got back to their tent. They found nothing disturbed.

"I wonder if we'll see that phantom again to-night?" ventured Tom, as they were sitting about the campfire a little later.

"Probably not," remarked Mr. Jenks. "I don't believe the ghost will venture down the dangerous trail after dark, and the gang may think that the warning given us by the two men on guard at the cave will be sufficient. But if we don't leave here by to-morrow I think we will have another visit from the thing in white."

It was about an hour after this when Tom was collecting some wood in a pile nearer the fire, so as to have it ready to throw on, in case there was any alarm in the night, that he happened to look up toward the summit of the mountain. A slight noise, as of loose stones rolling down, attracted his attention, and, at first, he feared lest another landslide was beginning, but a moment later he saw what caused it.

There, advancing down the steep and dangerous trail was the figure in white—the phantom. Instantly a daring plan came into Tom's head. Dropping the wood softly, he moved back out of the glare of the fire.

"Mr. Jenks!" he called in a whisper.

The diamond man, who was behind the tent, came toward Tom.

"What is it?" he asked. Then, as he saw the ghostly visitor, he added: "Oh—the phantom again! What's it up to?"

"The same thing," replied Tom, "but it won't do it long, if my plan succeeds."

"What plan is that, Tom?"

"I'm going to try to capture that—that man—or whatever it is. Will you help?"

"Surely!"

"Then let's work around behind it, while Mr. Damon and Mr. Parker come up from in front. We'll solve this part of the mystery, anyhow, if it's possible!"

The two other men were soon told of the plan. Meanwhile the thing in white had advanced slowly, until within a few hundred feet of the camp. They could see now that it was no shaft of light, but some white body, shaped like a tall, thin man, draped in a white garment. The long arms waved to and fro. There was no semblance of a head.

"You and Mr. Parker go right toward it, slowly, Mr. Damon," advised Tom. "Mr. Jenks and I will make a circle, and get in back. Then, if it's anything alive we'll have it."

The "ghost" continued to advance. Tom and the diamond man stole off to one side, their buckskin moccasins making no sound. Mr. Damon and the scientist went boldly forward.

This movement appeared to disconcert the spirit. It halted, waved the arms with greater vigor than before, and seemed to indicate to the adventurers that it was dangerous to advance. But Mr. Damon and Mr. Parker kept on. They wanted to give Tom and Mr. Jenks time enough to make the circuit.

Suddenly the stillness of the night was broken by a low whistle. It was Tom's signal that he and Mr. Jenks were ready.

"Come on! Run!" cried Mr. Damon.

The scientist and the eccentric man leaped forward.

The "ghost" heard the whistle, and heard the spoken words. The thing in white hesitated a moment, and then raised one arm. There was a flash of lire, and a loud report.

"He's firing in the air!" cried Tom. "Come on, we have him now!"

Undaunted by the display of firearms, Mr. Damon and Mr. Parker kept on. They could hear Tom and Mr. Jenks running up in back of the figure. The latter also heard this, and suddenly turned. Caught between the two forces of our friends, the "ghost" was at a loss what to do.

The next instant Tom, who had distanced Mr. Jenks, made a flying tackle for the figure in white, and caught it around the legs. Very substantial legs they were, too, Tom felt—the legs of a man.

"Wow!" yelled the "ghost," as he went down in a heap, the revolver falling from his hand.

"Come on!" cried Tom. "I have him!"

His friends rushed to his aid. There was a confused mass of dark bodies, arms and legs mingled with something tall and thin, all in white. Suddenly the moon came from behind a cloud and they could see what they had captured—for captured the phantom was.

It proved to be a rather small man, who wore upon his shoulders a framework of wood, over which some white cloth was draped. It had fallen off him when Tom made that tackle.

"Well," remarked the young inventor, as he sat on the struggling man's chest. "I guess we've got you."

"I rather guess you have, stranger," was the cool reply.

BILL RENSHAW WILL HELP

They were all panting from the exertion of the run up the mountain and the contest with the phantom—a phantom no longer— though, truth to tell, the struggle was not nearly so fierce as Tom had expected. He thought the "ghost" would put up a stiff fight.

"Got any ropes to tie him with?" asked Mr. Damon, who was helping Tom hold the man down.

"Ropes? You aren't going to tie me up are you, strangers?" asked the captive.

"That's what we are!" exclaimed Mr. Jenks. "We've had trouble enough in this matter, and if I've got one of the gang, perhaps I can get some of the others, and have my rights. So tie him up, Tom, and we'll take him to camp.

"Oh, you needn't go to all that trouble, strangers," went on the man, calmly. "If one of you will get off my chest, and the other gentleman ease up on my stomach a bit, I'll walk wherever you want me, and not make any trouble. I haven't got a gun."

"Bless my gloves! But you're a cool one," commented Mr. Damon, as he complied with the man's request, and got up from his stomach. "But look out for him, Tom. He had a gun, for he fired it in the air."

"He hasn't it now," answered the young inventor. "I knocked it from his hand when I leaped for him."

"That's what you did," assented the man, as he got up, while Tom kept a tight hold of him, as did Mr. Jenks. "What kind of a grizzly bear hug do you call that, anyhow, that you gave me?"

"That was a football tackle," explained Tom.

"I allers heard that was a dangerous game!" remarked the former phantom simply. "Well, now you've got me, what are you going to do with me?"

"Take you where we can have a good look at you," replied Mr. Jenks, as he kicked aside the wooden framework, and the sheet which had made the "ghost" appear so tall. "So this is how you worked it; eh?"

"Yep. That was the 'haunt' stranger. I made it myself, and it worked all right until you folks come along. I rather suspicioned from the first, when I played the trick over on 'tother side of the mountain, that you wouldn't be so easy to fool as most prospectors are."

"Oh, so you're the only ghost then?" asked Tom.

"I'm the only one."

By this time they had reached the camp. Tom threw some light logs on the fire, which blazed up brightly. As the flames illuminated the face of their captive, Mr. Jenks looked at him, and cried out:

"Why it's Bill Renshaw!"

"That's me," admitted the man who had played the part of the phantom, "and thunder-turtles! if it ain't Mr. Jenks who was once in the diamond cave with us. Whatever happened to you? I never heard. The others said you got tired and went away."

"They took me away—defrauded me of my rights!" declared Mr. Jenks, bitterly. "But I'll get them back! To think of Bill Renshaw playing the part of a ghost!"

"They made me do it," went on the man, somewhat dejectedly. "I wanted to be at work in the cave, but they wouldn't let me."

"Is this man one of the diamond makers?" asked Tom, in great surprise.

"He is—one of the helpers, though I don't believe he knows the secret of making the gems," explained Mr. Jenks. "He was one of the men in the cave when I was there before, and he and I struck up quite a friendship; didn't we, Renshaw?"

"That's what, and there ain't no reason why we can't be friends now; that is unless you hold a grudge against me for firing at you. But I only shot in the air, to scare you away. Them's my instructions. I'm supposed to be on guard, and scare away strangers. I'm tired of the work, too, for I don't get my share, and those other fellows, in the cave, get all the money from the diamonds."

Tom Swift uttered an exclamation. A sudden plan had come to him. Quickly he whispered to Mr. Jenks:

"Make a friend of this man if possible. He evidently is dissatisfied. Offer him a sum to show us another way into the cave, and we may yet discover the secret of the diamond makers."

"I will," declared Mr. Jenks, quietly. Then, turning to Renshaw, he added:

"Bill, come over here. I want to have a talk with you. Perhaps it will be to our mutual advantage."

He led the former phantom to one side, and for some time conversed earnestly with him. Mr. Jenks told the story of how he had been deceived by Folwell and the others who were at the head of the gang of diamond makers. The rich man related how they had taken his money, and, after promising to disclose the secret process to him, had broken faith, and had drugged him, afterward taking him out of the cave.

"I want only my rights, and that for which I paid," concluded Mr. Jenks. "Now, I gather that these men haven't treated you altogether fairly, Bill."

"Indeed they haven't. I helped 'em to the best of my ability, and all I get out of it is to stay out on this lonely side of the mountain, and play ghost. They owe me money, too, and they won't pay me, either, though they have lots, for they sold some diamonds lately."

"Then they are still making diamonds?" asked Mr. Jenks, eagerly. "Have you seen them? Do you know the secret?"

"No, I don't know it, for they won't let me in on it. I'm always sent out of the cave just before they make the gems. But I know they've made some lately, and have sold 'em. I want my share."

"Look here!" exclaimed Mr. Jenks, quickly, wishing to strike while the iron was hot. "I'll make you a proposition. Show us how to get into that cave, unknown to the diamond makers, and I'll pay you twice what they agreed to. Is it a bargain?"

Bill Renshaw considered a moment. Then he thrust out his hand, clasped that of Mr. Jenks, and exclaimed:

"It is. I'll take you into the cave by an entrance that's seldom used. There are four ways to get in. The one where the two men drove you back is the rear one. The front one is on the other side of the mountain, but it's so well concealed that you'd never find it. But I can take you to one where you can get in, and those fellows will never know it. And, what's more, I'll help you if it comes to a fight!"

"Good!" exclaimed Mr. Jenks. "I think we'll discover the secret of the diamond makers this time," and he went to tell the others of the success of his talk. Bill Renshaw had been converted from an enemy into a friend, and the former phantom was now ready to lead Tom and the others into the secret cave.

"We'll start in the morning," decided Mr. Jenks, who, after many disappointments, at last saw success ahead of him.

IN THE SECRET CAVE

Tom Swift was up at break of day, and the others were not far behind him.

"Now for the secret cave!" cried the young inventor as he gazed up the mountain, in the interior of which the mysterious band of men were making the diamonds.

"Have you made any plans, Bill?" asked Mr. Jenks of the former phantom, who had cast his lot in with the adventurers. "What will be the best course for us to follow?"

"You just leave it to me, Mr. Jenks," was the answer. "I'll get you into the cave, and those fellows, who, I believe, are trying to do me out of my rights, as they did you out of yours, will never know a thing about it."

"Bless my finger-nails!" cried Mr. Damon. "That will be great!" We can get in the cave, and watch them make the diamonds at our leisure."

"They don't make them every day," explained Renshaw. "It seems they have to wait for certain occasions. Mostly they make the diamonds when there's a big storm."

"A big storm" asked the scientist with a sudden show of interest. "Do you mean one of those electrical storms, such as we had the other night?"

"That's it, Mr. Parker, though why they wait until there's a storm is more than I can tell."

"Perhaps they know that on such occasions no one will venture up the mountain," spoke Mr. Damon.

"No, it isn't that," declared the scientist. "I think I am on the track of a great scientific discovery, and I will soon be able to make observations that will confirm it."

"Well, I'm going to make an observation right now," said Tom, with a laugh. "I'm going to see what there is for breakfast."

"And that reminds me," came from Mr. Jenks, "shall we move our camp, Bill, and take the tent with us to the cave?"

"I hardly think so," was the answer. "I think the best plan would be to conceal the tent somewhere around here, in case you might need it again. You can also store what food you have left."

"But, bless my appetite, we don't want to starve in that diamond cave!" objected Mr. Damon.

"I'll see that you don't," declared Bill Renshaw. "I'll take you in there, unbeknownst to those fellows, and I'll provide you with plenty of food and water. You see the cave is so big that there are some parts they never visit."

"And we can stay in one of those parts, and eat?" asked Tom.

"Sure," answered Bill.

"And watch the diamond makers at work?" asked Mr. Jenks.

"That's it," replied the former phantom.

"Then the sooner we get started the better," remarked Mr. Damon. Mr. Parker said nothing. He appeared to be thinking deeply, and was tapping at some rocks with his little hammer.

The advice of Bill Renshaw was followed, and the tent, and what food remained, was concealed in the bushes, with rocks piled over to keep away prowling animals. Then they started for the secret cave.

The man who played the part of a ghost picked up the framework and white cloth that had formed his disguise.

"I'll still have to use this," he explained, "for I don't want those fellows to know that I'm helping you. I'll continue to play the spirit of the mountain, but there won't be much need of it. I don't think any more people will come prospecting out here."

"Have you heard of the arrival of Farley Munson?" asked Tom, as he related the facts about the stowaway.

"He hadn't arrived up to a day or so ago," answered Bill. "I guess he's still traveling. Farley is one of the heads of the gang," he added, "and a dangerous man."

As Bill led the way toward the cave, taking a route that the adventurers had never suspected led to it, he explained that the cavern was a large one, capable of holding an army.

"But there's only a small part of it used by the diamond makers," he added. "They work in a small recess, near the summit of the mountain. The little cave, where I'm going to take you, opens off from it by a long passage. And, except that you'll be pretty much in the dark, you'll be quite comfortable. There are tables, chairs, and some bunks in the place. I can get you some lights, and plenty of food."

"But, if you are seen taking away food, won't the others suspect something?" asked Tom.

"I do pretty much as I please," said Bill. "I go and come when I like. All I'm supposed to do is to watch my two sides of the mountain, play the ghost, and give warning when any one is coming. Sometimes I leave black and white messages, like the one I put on your tent. Those fellows fix 'em up for me. I've told 'em about you, though I didn't know who you were, and they think you have gone, for the two men on guard at the rear entrance so reported. Sometimes I stay out on the mountain for a couple of days at a time, when the weather's good, and don't go back to the cave. Those times I take food with me, and so if they see me making off with some supplies they'll think I'm going to camp out."

"It doesn't look as though we'd ever get into a cave near the top of the mountain, going this way," said Tom, as they marched along. "We're going down, instead of up."

"That's the secret of this trail," explained Bill. "We go down in a sort of valley, and then go up a pretty stiff place, and then we're on a direct trail to the entrance I told you about. It's a steep road to climb, but I guess we can manage it."

And a hard climb the adventurers did find it. The road was almost as bad as the one along the edge of the chasm, but they managed to negotiate it, and finally found themselves on a fairly good trail.

"We'll soon be there," Bill assured them. "After you get in the little cave, where I'm going to hide you, I'll have to leave you for a spell, until I get my ghost rigging fixed up again. But I'll see that you have plenty of food and drink."

A little later their guide came to a sudden halt, and peered around anxiously.

"What's the matter?" asked Tom.

"I was just looking to see if any of the men were about," he answered. "But I guess not—it looks all right. The entrance is right here."

They were on a side of the mountain, near the summit. Below stretched a magnificent scene. A great valley lay at their feet, and they could look off to many distant peaks. The main trail to Leadville, and the one to the settlement of Indian Ridge, was in sight.

Suddenly Tom, who had been using a small but powerful telescope, uttered an exclamation, and focussed the instrument on a speck that seemed moving along on the trail below.

"A man—coming up the mountain," cried Tom. "And—it can't be— yet it is—it's Farley Munson—the stowaway!" he cried. "He's coming here!"

"Let me look!" begged Mr. Jenks, taking the glass from Tom. An instant later the diamond man exclaimed: "Yes, it's Munson!"

"Then in here with you—quick!" cried Renshaw. "He can't see us yet, and we'll be out of sight in another minute."

The former spirit pulled aside some thick bushes, and pointed to a hole which was disclosed.

"The entrance to the secret cave," he announced. "Slip in all of you."

Tom, after another glance at the man toiling his way up the mountain, entered the cavern. He was followed by the others. Bill was the last to enter, and he replaced the bushes over the entrance.

"At last!" exclaimed Mr. Jenks, as he gazed up at the roof of the dimly-lighted vault in which they found themselves.

"Yes, we're in the diamond makers' secret cave," added Tom. "Now to catch them at work!"

"Come on," advised Bill, in a low tone, "We're not safe yet," and he produced a lantern from some hidden recess, lighted the wick, and led the way. As the others followed they were aware of a subdued noise in the great cavern.

MAKING THE DIAMONDS

"What's that noise?" asked Tom, as their guide flashed the lantern to show them the way.

"That's the men getting ready to make diamonds, I guess," was the answer. "You see it takes quite a while to get the stuff ready. I don't know what they use—they never tell me any of their secrets."

"Oh, I know the ingredients well enough," said Mr. Jenks, "but I don't know the secret of how they apply the terrific heat and pressure necessary to fuse the materials into diamonds."

"Well, you'll soon know," declared Bill Renshaw. "Of course it isn't always successful. I've known 'em to try half a dozen times before they got any diamonds big enough to satisfy 'em. They gave me some of the small ones when I asked for my wages.

"How did you come to get in with these men?" asked Tom, curious to understand how a person seemingly as honest as Renshaw appeared to be had cast his lot in with the men who had broken faith with Mr. Jenks.

"Oh, I've lived around these parts all my life," was the answer. "I knew of this cave before these diamond fellers came to it. In fact, I showed it to 'em. It was several years ago that a party of men who were prospecting around here came to me and asked if I knew of a small cave near the top of a high mountain, where lightning storms were frequent. I told them about Phantom Mountain, as it was called then, and also of this cave. If there's any place where they have worse lightning storms than here, I'd like to know it. They scare me, sometimes, like the night when that landslide happened, and I'm sort of used to 'em.

"Well, I took these men to the cave, and they hired me as a sort of lookout. Then they began their work, and at first I didn't know what they were up to, but finally I caught on. Then Mr. Jenks came, and disappeared mysteriously, though then I didn't know that they had played a trick on him. I was outside most of the time, pretending I was the ghost. So that's how I came to get in with 'em, and I wish I was out."

"You soon will be, I think," declared Mr. Jenks. "But won't our talking be heard by the men?"

"No danger. There is a thick wall between this part of the cave, and the part where they live and work. I'll soon have you well hid, and then you wait until I come back."

"What about Munson?" asked Tom. "He is evidently on his way here to tell his confederates about us."

"He won't know what has happened to us," said Mr. Jenks, "and he won't see anything of us. I guess we're safe enough."

Through the dark passage they followed Bill Renshaw until he came to a halt in a place that suddenly widened and broadened into a good-sized cave.

"Here's your stopping place," said the former ghost. "Now if you follow that passage, off to the left," and he pointed to it, "you'll come to the larger part of the cave where the diamond makers are. But go cautiously, and don't make any noise. I won't be responsible for what happens."

"We'll take all the risk," interrupted Tom.

"All right. Now there's a couple of lanterns around here. I'll light them, and leave you for a while until I can get some grub. I'll be back as soon as I can."

He glided away, after lighting two lanterns, by the gleams of which the adventurers could see that they were in a vaulted cavern that had evidently been fitted up as a living apartment. The sides, roof and floor were of stone. It was clean, and the air was fresh. There were some chairs, a table, and several cots, with pieces of bagging for bedding, though it was warm in the place.

"I guess we can stay here until we discover the secret," spoke Tom.

"Bless my watch! We can if we have something to eat," came from Mr. Damon, with something like a sigh. "I'm hungry!"

"And I want to make some observations," said Mr. Parker. "From what I have seen of this mountain, I would not be surprised if this cave was to be suddenly destroyed by a landslide or a lightning bolt. I will make some further investigations."

"Well, if it's going to cause you to make such gloomy prophecies as that, I'd just as soon you wouldn't look any further," spoke Tom. in a low voice. But Mr. Parker, taking one of the lanterns, set about examining the rock of which the cave consisted.

In a short time Bill Renshaw returned with enough food to last for two days. He said he was going out on the mountain once more to act the part of a lookout, and would visit the adventurers again the next day.

"In the meanwhile you can do just as you please," he said. "Nobody is likely to disturb you here, and you can sneak up and take a look at the men in the other cave whenever you're ready. Only be careful—that's all I've got to say. They're desperate men."

It was not very pleasant, eating in the gloomy cavern, but they made the best of it. They cooked on a small oil-stove they found in the place, and after some hot coffee they felt much better.

"Well," remarked Tom, after a while, "shall we take a chance, and go look at the men at work?"

"I think so," answered Mr. Jenks. "The sooner we discover this mystery, the better. Then we can go back home."

"And recover my airship," added Tom, who was a bit uneasy regarding the safety of the *Red Cloud*.

"Then, bless my finger-rings! let's go and see if we can find the big cave your friend the ghost told us of," suggested Mr. Damon.

Cautiously they made their way along the passage Bill had pointed out. As they went forward the subdued noise became louder, and finally they could feel the vibration of machinery.

"This is the place," whispered Mr. Jenks. "That sound we hear is one of the mixing machines, for grinding the materials—carbon and the other substances—which go to make up the diamonds. I remember hearing that when I was in the cave before."

"Then we must be near the place," observed Tom.

"Yes, but I didn't have much chance to look around when I was here before. They wouldn't let me. I never even knew of the small cave Bill took us to."

"Well, if we're close to it, we'd better go cautiously, and not talk any more than we're obliged to," suggested Mr. Parker, and they agreed that this was good advice.

They walked on softly. Suddenly Tom, who was in the lead, saw a gleam of light.

"We're here," he whispered. "I'll put out our lantern, now," which he did. Then, stealing forward he and the others beheld a curious sight. The tunnel they were in ended at a small hole which opened into a large cavern, and, fortunately, this opening was concealed from the view of those in the main place.

"The diamond makers!" whispered Tom, hoarsely, pointing to several men grouped about a number of strange machines.

"Yes—the very place where I was," answered Mr. Jenks, "and there is the apparatus—the steel box—from which the diamonds are taken —now to see how they make them."

Fascinated, the adventurers looked into the cave. The men there were unaware of the presence of our friends, and were busily engaged. Some attended to the grinding machine, the roar and clatter of which made it possible for Tom and the others to talk and move about without being overheard. Into this machine certain ingredients were put, and they were then pulverized, and taken out in powdery form.

The power to run the mixing machine was a gasoline motor, which chug-chugged away in one corner of the cave.

As the powder was taken out, other men fashioned it into small balls, which were put on pan, and into a sort of oven, that was heated by a gasoline stove.

"Is that how they make the diamonds?" asked Mr. Damon.

"That is evidently the first step," said Mr. Jenks. "Those balls of powdered chemicals are partly baked, and then they are put into the steel box. In some way terrific heat and pressure are applied, and the diamonds are made. But how the heat and pressure are obtained is what we have yet to learn."

He paused to watch the men at work. They were all busy, some attending to the machines, and others coming and going in and out of the cave. In one part a man was apparently getting ready a meal.

Suddenly there rushed into the cave a man who seemed much excited.

"Are you nearly ready with that stuff?" he cried. "There's a good storm gathering on the mountain!"

"Yes, we'll be ready in half an hour," answered one of the men at the mixing machine.

"Good. It will be flashing lightning bolts then, and we can see what luck we have. The last batch was a failure." The man hurried out again. Mr. Parker touched Tom and Mr. Jenks on their shoulders.

"What is it?" asked Tom.

"I know the secret of making the diamonds,~ said the scientist.

"What?" cried Mr. Jenks.

"It is by the awful power of the lightning bolts!" whispered Mr. Parker. "Everything is explained now—the reason why they make diamonds in this lonely place, near the top of the mountain. They need a place where the lightning is powerful. I can understand it now—I suspected it before. They make diamonds by lightning!"

"Are you sure?" cried Mr. Jenks.

"Positive."

"I agree with you," said Tom Swift. "I was just getting on that track myself, when I saw the electric wires running to the steel box. That explains the upright rod on the top of the mountain. The man says a storm is coming —very well; we'll stay here and watch them make diamonds!"

As he spoke there came the mutter of thunder, and the mountain vibrated slightly. The men in the cave redoubled their activity. Tom and his friends felt that the secret process they had so long sought was about to be demonstrated before their eyes.

FLASHING GEMS

Eagerly the adventurers looked through the opening at the end of the passage into the larger cave. The men opened the small oven in which the balls of white chemicals and carbon mixed, had been baked, and a pile of things, that looked like irregularly- shaped marbles, were placed in the steel box.

This box, which was about the size of a trunk, was of massive metal. It was placed in a recess in the solid rock, and all about were layers of asbestos and other substances that were nonconductors of heat.

"That box becomes red hot," exclaimed Mr. Jenks, in a whisper. "When things are in readiness, that lever is pulled and the diamonds are made. I pulled it once, but I did not then know the process involved. I supposed that the lightning had nothing to do with making the diamonds."

"It has—a most important part," said Mr. Parker. The hidden adventurers could talk in perfect safety now, for the men in the large cave were too excited to pay much attention to them. The muttering of the thunder grew louder, and at times a particularly loud crash told that a bolt had struck somewhere in the vicinity of the cave.

"But, bless my watch-charm!" exclaimed Mr. Damon, "I didn't know lightning made diamonds."

"It does not—always," went on the scientist. "But great heat and pressure are necessary to create the gems. In nature this was probably obtained by prehistoric volcanic fires, and by the terrific pressure of immense rocks. It is possible to make diamonds in the laboratory of the chemist, but they are so minute as to be practically valueless.

"However, these men seem to have hit upon a new plan. They utilize the terrific heat of lightning, and the pressure which is instantaneously obtained when the bolt strikes. I am anxious to see how it is done. Look, I think they are getting ready to make the gems."

Indeed there seemed to be an air of expectancy among the diamond makers. The mixing machine had now been stopped, and, as it was more quiet in the cave, our friends, in their hiding- place, had to speak in mere whispers. All the men were now gathered about the great steel box.

This receptacle had been closed by a solid metal door, which was screwed and clamped tight. Then one of the men examined a number of heavily insulated electric wires that extended from the box off into the darkness where Tom and his companions could not discern them.

"That's Folwell—the man I befriended, and who got me into this game," whispered Mr. Jenks. "He was also one of the first to turn against me. I think he's one of the leaders."

Folwell came back, after having gone into a dark part of the cave. He went over to an electrical switch on one of the stone walls.

"It's almost time," Tom heard him say to his confederates. "The storm is coming up rapidly."

"Will it be severe enough?" asked one of the helpers. "We had all our work for nothing last time. The flashes weren't heavy enough."

"These will be," asserted Folwell. "The indicator shows nearly a million volts now, and it's increasing."

"A million volts!" exclaimed Tom. "I hope it doesn't strike anywhere around here."

"Oh, it will probably be harmlessly conducted down on the heavy wires," said Mr. Parker. "We are in no danger, at present, though ultimately I expect to see the whole mountain shattered by a lightning bolt."

"Cheerful prospect," murmured Tom.

There was a terrific crash outside. The rocky floor of the cave trembled.

"Here she comes!" cried Folwell. "Get back, everybody! I'm going to throw over the switch now!"

The men retreated well away from the steel box. Folwell threw over the lever—the same one Mr. Jenks remembered pulling. Then the man ran to the electric switch on the wall, and snapped that into place, establishing a connection.

There was a moment's pause, as Folwell ran to join the others in their place of safety. Then from without there came a most nerve-racking and terrifying crash. It seemed as if the very mountain would be rent into fragments.

Watching with eager eyes, the adventurers saw sparks flash from the steel box. Instantly it became red hot, and then glowed white and incandescent. It was almost at the melting point.

Then came comparative quiet, as the echoes of the thunder died away amid the mountain peaks.

"I guess that did the trick!" cried Folwell. "It was a terrific crash all right!"

He and the others ran forward. The steel box was now a cherry red, for it was cooling. Folwell threw back the lever, and another man disconnected the switch. There was a period of waiting until the box was cool enough to open. Then the heavy door was swung back.

With a long iron rod Folwell drew something from the retort. It was the tray which had held the white balls. But they were white no longer, for they had been turned into diamonds. From their hiding-place Tom and the others could see the flashing gems, for, in spite of the fact that the diamonds were uncut, some of them sparkled most brilliantly, due to the peculiar manner in which they were made.

"We have the secret of the diamonds!" whispered Mr. Jenks. "There must be a quart of the gems there!"

The men gathered about Folwell, uttering exclamations of delight. The diamonds were too hot to handle yet.

"That's going some!" exclaimed the chief of the diamond makers. "We have a small fortune here."

The was a sudden commotion at one end of the cave. A man rushed in. At the sight of him Tom stared and uttered an exclamation.

"Munson—the stowaway!" he whispered.

"Hello!" cried Folwell, as he saw his confederate. "I thought you were East, keeping Jenks away from here."

"He got the best of me!" cried Munson, "he and that Tom Swift! I stowed away on their airship, but they found me out by a wireless message, and marooned me in the woods. I've been trying to get here ever since! Didn't you get my messages of warning?"

"No—what warnings?" cried Folwell.

"About Jenks, Tom Swift and the others. They're here—they must be on Phantom Mountain now. In fact, I shouldn't be surprised if they were in this cave. I traced them to their camp, but they're gone. They may be among us now—in some of the secret recesses!"

For an instant Folwell stared at the bearer of these tidings. Then he cried out:

"Scatter men, and find these fellows! We must get them before they discover our secret!"

"It's too late—we know it!" exulted Tom Swift. Then he whispered to the others to hurry to the part of the cave where Bill Renshaw had first hidden them.

PRISONERS

"Do you think there is any danger of them finding us?" asked Mr. Damon, as he hurried along beside Tom.

"I'm afraid so," was the answer. "I've been worried ever since we saw Munson heading this way. But we couldn't do any differently."

"Perhaps Bill Renshaw may be able to conceal us," suggested Mr. Jenks. "Very likely he knows that Munson is on hand. Perhaps we will be safe for a while. I want to make a few more observations as to how they manufacture the diamonds, and then, with what I already know, I'll have the secret."

"And I'd like to make some scientific tests of the sides and bottom rocks of the cave," spoke Mr. Parker. "I think it will bear out my theory that the mountain will soon be destroyed."

"Well, you were right about Earthquake Island, and you may be right about this mountain," said Tom, "but if it is going to be annihilated I hope we get far enough away from it."

We can keep our presence here a secret for a few more days, I think that will be long enough," proceeded Mr. Jenks. "Then we will leave."

"And, in the meanwhile, they'll be searching for us," objected Mr. Damon. "I wish that ghost-chap would come back and tell us what to do. Bless my liver-pin, but we are going to be in considerable danger, I'm afraid! Those men may capture us, and decide to make diamond dust from us."

"Come on—hurry to the little cave," urged Tom. "Then we'll get ready to defend ourselves."

"The main cave is a large one," said Mr. Jenks, "and there are many hiding places in it. In fact, it is so large that it will take those fellows several days to complete a circuit of it. By that time Bill Renshaw may come back, and take us to some place in which they have already searched for us. Then we'll be comparatively safe."

This thought was some consolation to them, as they made their way through the dark passage, dimly illuminated by the lantern they had rekindled, to the place where Bill had hidden them. They found things as they had left them, and proceeded to get a meal, though Tom said it would be best not to cook anything, or even to make coffee, for fear the odors would enable the searchers to trail them.

So they ate cold food, glad to get that. Silently they sat about the dimly-lighted cavern, and discussed the situation. True they might even now retreat, going out of the entrance Bill had showed them, and so escape. But Mr. Jenks felt that his mission was not completed yet, and they all agreed to stay with him.

"For there are several points about making diamonds that are not quite clear to me," he said. "I need to know how that steel box is constructed, how the electrical switches are arranged, what kind of lightning rods they use, and how they regulate the pressure. The other things, and how to mix the ingredients, I already know."

"Then we'll do our best to help you," promised Tom. "But now I think we had better see what sort of a defense we can put up. We have our guns and revolvers, and with these chairs and tables we can build a sort of barricade behind which we can take refuge if those fellows do discover our hiding place."

This was conceded to be a good idea, and soon a rude sort of fort was made, behind which the adventurers could take their stand and fight, if necessary, though they hoped this would not come to pass.

They remained quietly in the cave the remainder of that day, and, when it was night, as they could tell by their timepieces— there was no daylight—they divided the hours into watches, taking turns standing guard.

Morning, at least in point of time, came without any disturbance, and they made a cold breakfast. They hoped that Bill Renshaw would come, but he did not appear.

After sitting in the dark cave until afternoon, Tom said:

"I think we might as well go and take another observation of the big cave. We can tell what the men are doing, then, for they don't seem to have been near us. Maybe they have given up the search for us, and we can see them at work, and Mr. Jenks can gain what further knowledge he needs."

"That will be a good plan," agreed the diamond man. "It's maddening to sit here, doing nothing."

"And it will be comparatively safe to go from here to our former post of observation," added Tom, "for there doesn't seem to be any opening along the tunnel, into the larger cave, except the place where we were."

Accordingly they started off. Cautiously they looked through the opening into the apartment where they had seen the diamonds made.

"There's not a soul here!" exclaimed Tom, in a whisper. The others looked. The place was deserted—the machinery silent. Mr. Jenks peered in for a moment, and then exclaimed:

"I'm going in! Now's my chance to find out all that I wish to know! It may never come again, and then we can soon leave Phantom Mountain!"

It was a daring plan, but it seemed to be the best one to follow. They were all tired of inactivity. Mr. Jenks managed to get through the opening, and dropped into the big cave. The others followed. Mr. Jenks hurried over to the steel box, and began an examination of it. Tom Swift was looking at the electrical switch. He saw how it was constructed. Mr. Damon and Mr. Parker were peering interestedly about.

Suddenly the sound of voices was heard, and the echo of footsteps. Mr. Jenks started.

"They're coming back!" he whispered hoarsely. "Run!"

They all turned and sped toward their hiding place. But they were too late. An instant later Folwell, Munson and the other diamond makers confronted them. Our friends made a bold rush, but were caught before they could go ten feet.

"We have them!" cried Munson. "They walked right into our hands!"

It was true. Tom Swift and the others were the prisoners of the diamond makers.

BROKEN BONDS

"Well," remarked Tom Swift, in mournful tones, "this looks as if we were up against it; doesn't it?"

"Bless my umbrella, it certainly does," agreed Mr. Damon.

"And it's all my fault," said Mr. Jenks. "I shouldn't have gone into the big cave. I might have known those men would come back any time."

The above conversation took place as our friends lay securely bound in a small cave, or recess, opening from the larger cavern, where, about an hour before, they had been captured and made prisoners by the diamond makers. Despite their struggles they had been overpowered and bound, being carried to the cave, where they were laid in a row on some old bags.

"It certainly is a most unpleasant situation, to say the least," observed Mr. Parker.

"And all my fault," repeated Mr. Jenks.

"Oh, no it isn't," declared Tom Swift, quickly. "We were just as ready to follow you into that cave as you were to go. No one could tell that the men would return so soon. It's nobody's fault. It's just our bad luck."

From where he lay, tied hand and foot, the young inventor could look out into the cave where he and the others had been caught. The diamond makers were busily engaged, apparently in getting ready to manufacture another batch of the precious stones. They paid little attention to their captives, save to warn them, when they had first been taken into the little cave, that it was useless to try to escape.

"They needn't have told us that," observed Tom, as he and the others were talking over their situation in low voices. "I don't believe any one could loosen these ropes."

"They certainly are pretty tight," agreed Mr. Damon. "I've been tugging and straining at mine for the last half hour, and all I've succeeded in doing is to make the cords cut into my flesh."

"Better give it up," advised Mr. Jenks.

"We'll just have to wait."

"For what?" the scientist wanted to know.

"To see what they'll do with us. They can't keep us here forever. They'll have to let us go some time." Following their capture, Folwell and Munson, the latter the stowaway of the airship, had been in earnest conversation regarding our friends, but what conclusion they had reached the adventurers could only guess.

"And we didn't have time to examine the diamond-making machinery close enough so that we could duplicate it if necessary," complained Tom, a little later.

"No," agreed Mr. Jenks. "There are certain things about it that are not clear to me. Well, I don't believe I'll have another chance to inspect it. They'll take good care of that, though they seem to be getting ready to make more diamonds."

"Perhaps they're going to manufacture a big batch, and then leave this place," suggested Mr. Damon. "They will probably go to some other secret cave, and leave us here."

"I hope they untie us before they leave, and give us something to eat," remarked the young inventor.

For two hours longer the captives lay there, in most uncomfortable positions. Then Folwell and Munson, leaving the group of diamond makers who were grouped about the machinery, approached the captives.

"Well," remarked Munson, "we got ahead of you after all; didn't we. You thought you had our secret, but it will be a long while before you ever make diamonds."

"What are you going to do with us?" asked Tom.

"Never mind. You came where you had no right to, and you must take the consequences."

"We did have a right to come here!" exclaimed Mr. Jenks. "I am entitled to know how the diamonds are made. I paid for the information, and you tricked me. If ever it's possible I'll have the whole gang arrested for swindling."

"You'll never get the chance!" declared Folwell. "You were given some diamonds for the money you invested, and that makes us square."

"No, it doesn't!" declared Mr. Jenks. "I invested the money to learn how to make diamonds, and you know it! You tricked me, and I had a right to try to discover your secret! I nearly have it, too, and I'll get it completely before I'm done with you!"

"No, you won't!" boasted Folwell. "But we didn't come here to tell you that. We came to give you something to eat. We're not savages and we'll treat you as well as we can in spite of the fact that you are trespassers. We're going to give you some grub, but I warn you that any attempt to escape will mean that some of you will get hurt."

He signaled to some of his confederates. These men unbound the captives' arms, and stood over them while they ate some coarse food that was brought into the small cave. They were given coffee to drink, and then, when the simple meal was over, they were securely bound again, and left to themselves, while the diamond makers went back to their machinery.

It was evident that they were going to attempt a big operation, for an unusually large quantity of the white stuff was prepared. The prisoners watched them idly. They could see some but not all of the operations. In this way several hours passed.

Gloom possessed the hearts of Tom and his friends. Not only had their expedition been almost a failure so far, but the young inventor was worried lest the gang might discover and wreck his airship. This would prove a serious loss. Lying there in the semi-darkness the lad imagined all sorts of unpleasant happenings.

At times he dozed off, as did the others. They had become somewhat used to the pain caused by the bonds, for their nerves were numb from the strain and pressure.

Once, as he was lightly sleeping, Tom was awakened by hearing loud voices in the main cave. He looked out, rolling over slightly to get a better view. He saw the man who, once before had run in to give news of an approaching electrical storm.

"Are you fellows all ready?" asked this same man again.

"Yes. Is there another storm coming?"

"Yes, and it's going to be a corker!" was the reply. "It's one of the worst I've ever seen. It's sweeping right up the valley. It'll be here in an hour."

"That's good. We need a big flash to make all the material we have prepared into diamonds. It's the biggest batch we ever tried. I hope it succeeds, for we're going to leave—" The rest was in so low a tone that Tom could not catch it.

The storm messenger departed. Folwell and Munson busied themselves about the machinery. Tom dozed off again, dimly wondering what had become of Bill Renshaw, and whether the former ghost knew of their plight. The others were asleep, as the young inventor saw by the dim light of a lantern in the cave. Then, he too, shut his eyes.

Tom was suddenly awakened by feeling some one's hands moving about his clothing. At first he thought it was one of the diamond-making gang, who had sneaked in to rob him. "Here! What are you up to?" exclaimed Tom.

"Quiet!" cautioned a voice. "Are you all here?"

"All of us—yes. But who are you?"

"Easy—keep quiet, Tom Swift! I'm Bill Renshaw! I've been searching all over for you, since I got back to your cave and found it empty. Now I'm going to free you. I got in here by a secret entrance. Wait, I'll cut your ropes." There was a slight sound, and an instant later Tom was freed from his bonds.

In Great Peril

The young inventor could scarcely believe the good luck that had so unexpectedly come to him and his companions. No sooner was Tom able to move freely about than Bill Renshaw performed the same service for Mr. Jenks and the others, cautioning them to be quiet as he awakened them, and cut the ropes.

"Bless my circulation!" exclaimed Mr. Damon, in a hoarse whisper. "How did you ever get here. I'd given ourselves up for lost."

"Oh, I came in off the mountain, as there's a big storm due," explained the man. "There was no need of me playing the haunt in daytime, anyhow. I went to the cave, found you and your things gone, and I surmised that you might have walked into some trap."

"We did," admitted Mr. Jenks, grimly.

"Well, I hunted around until I found you," went on Bill. "This mountain is honeycombed with caves, all opening from the large one, I know them better than these fellows do, so I could explore freely, and keep out of their sight. They didn't know that there was a second entrance to this place, but I did, and I made for it, when I couldn't find you in some of the other caves where I looked. And, sure enough, here you were."

"Well, we can't thank you enough," said Mr. Parker. "But you say there is a big storm coming?"

"One of the biggest that's been around these parts in some time," replied Bill.

"Then perhaps the mountain will be destroyed," went on the scientist, as calmly as if he had remarked that it might rain.

"I hope nothing like that happens until we get away," spoke Mr. Damon, fervently.

"What had we better do?" inquired Tom.

"Get away, unless you want to discover some more of their secrets," advised Bill. "Those fellows are planning something, but I can't find out what it is. They are suspicious of me, I think. But they are up to something, and I believe, it would be best for you to leave while you have the chance. It may not be healthy to stay. That's why I did my best to untie you."

"We appreciate what you have done," declared Mr. Jenks, "but I want my rights. I must learn a few more facts about how to make diamonds from lightning flashes, and then I will have the same secret they cheated me out of. I think if we wait a while we may be able to see the parts of the process that are not quite clear to us. What do you say, Tom Swift?"

"Well, I would like to learn the secret," replied the lad, "and if Bill thinks it's safe to stay here a while longer—

"Oh, I guess it will be safe enough," was the reply. "Those fellows won't bother about you now that they are about to make some more diamonds.

Besides, they think you're all tied up. Yes, you can stay here and watch, I reckon. I've got a couple of guns, and—

"Then we'll stay," decided Tom. "We can put up a better fight now."

Silently, in their prison, but which they could now leave whenever they pleased, the adventurers watched the diamond makers once more. The same process they had witnessed before was gone through with. The white balls were put inside the steel box and sealed up. Then they waited for the storm to reach its height.

That this would not be long was evidenced by the mutterings of thunder which every moment grew louder. The outburst of electrical fury was likely to take place momentarily, and that it would be unusually severe was shown by the precautions taken by the diamond makers. They attached a number of extra wires, and brought out some insulated, hard rubber platforms, on which they themselves stood. Tom and Mr. Jenks were much interested in watching this detail of the work, and sought to learn how each part of the process was done.

"I almost think we can make diamonds, Tom, when we get back to civilization," whispered Mr. Jenks.

"I hope we can," answered Tom, "and we can't get back any too soon to suit me. I want to be in my airship again."

"I don't blame you. But look, they are getting ready to adjust the switch."

The adventurers ceased their whispered talk, and eagerly watched the diamond makers. Folwell and Munson were hurrying to and fro in the big cave, attending to the adjustments of the machinery.

"On your insulated plates—all of you," Folwell gave the order. "This is going to be a terrific storm. The gage shows twice the power we have ever used, and it's creeping up every minute! We'll have more diamonds than ever had before!"

"Yes, if the mountain isn't destroyed," added Mr. Parker, in a low voice. "I predict that it will be split from top to bottom!"

"Comforting," thought Tom, grimly.

"I guess we're all ready," said Folwell, in a low tone to Munson. "We'd better get insulated ourselves. I'm going to throw the switch."

He did so. A moment later the man who had before given warning of the storm came dashing in. He was very much excited.

"It's awful!" he cried. "The lightning is striking all over! Big rocks are being split like logs of wood!"

"Well, it can't do any damage in here," said Munson. "We are well protected. Get on one of the plates," and he motioned to one of the hard-rubber platforms that was not occupied. The roar and rumble of the storm outside had given place to short terrific crashes. In their small cave the adventurers could feel the solid ground shake.

A bluish light began dancing about the electrical wires. There was a smell of sulphur in the air. Crash after crash resounded outside. A flash of flame lit up the whole interior of the cave. It came from the copper switch.

"Something's wrong with the insulation!" cried Munson.

"Don't go near it!" yelled Folwell. "If you value your life, stand still!"

Hardly had he spoken than inside the cavern there sounded a report like that of a small cannon. A big ball of fire danced about the middle of the cave and then leaped on top of the steel box.

"This is a fearful storm," cried Munson.

The adventurers in the cave did not know what to say or do. They were in deadly peril.

Suddenly there came a crash louder than any that had preceded it. The whole side of the cave where the switches were was a mass of bluish flame. Then came a ripping, tearing sound, and a tangle of wires and copper connections were thrown to the floor. At the same time the steel box, containing the materials from which diamonds were made, turned blue, and flames shot from it.

"It's all up with us!" cried Munson. "Run for it, everybody! The wires are down, and this place will be an electric furnace in another minute!"

He leaped toward the exit from the cave.

"What about those fellows?" asked Folwell, indicating the place where Tom and the others had been tied.

"They'll have to do the best they can! It's every man for himself, now!" yelled Munson. There was a wild scramble from the cavern.

"Come on!" cried Tom. "We must escape! It's our only chance!"

He leaped into the big cave, followed by the others. Already long tongues of electrical fire were shooting out from the walls and roof as Tom Swift and his companions, evading them as best they could, sought safety in flight.

The Mountain Shattered—Conclusion

"Can't we get some of the diamonds?" cried Mr. Damon, as he raced along behind Tom. "Now's our chance. Those fellows have all gone!" The odd man made a grab for something as he ran.

"It's as much as our lives are worth," declared the young inventor. "We dare not stop! Come on!"

"I'd like to investigate some of the machinery," spoke Mr. Jenks, "but I wouldn't stop, even for that."

"The storm is too dangerous," called Bill Renshaw. "I can show you a shorter way out than the one those fellows have taken. Follow me."

"No way can be too short," said Mr. Parker, solemnly. "This mountain will go to pieces shortly, I think!"

Tom shuddered. He remembered how narrow had been their escape when Earthquake Island sank into the sea. And that some terrific upheaval was now imminent might be judged from the awful reports that sounded more plainly as the adventurers raced toward the opening of the cave. It was like the bombardment of some doomed city.

Mr. Jenks and Tom cast one longing look behind at the complicated and expensive machinery that had been installed in the cave by the diamond makers. They had abandoned it, and in it lay the secret of making precious gems. But there was no time to stop now, and investigate.

"This way," urged Bill Renshaw. "We'll soon be out."

"But won't it be dangerous to go outside?" asked Mr. Damon. "Shan't we be struck by lightning? There is some protection in here."

"None at all," said Mr. Parker, quickly. "This mountain is a natural lightning rod. To stay here in this cave will be sure death when the storm gets directly over it. And that will be very soon. We must get on insulated ground. Is there any part of this mountain that does not contain iron ore?" the scientist asked of the former spirit.

"Yes; the way out by which we are going lands on a dirt hill."

"That's good; then we may be saved."

On they ran. They had no lanterns, but the blue light of the electricity, as it leaped from point to point inside the cave, where there were outcroppings of iron ore, made the place bright enough to see.

"Here we are!" cried Bill Renshaw at length. "Here's the way out!"

Making a sudden turn in the winding passage he showed the adventurers a small opening in the side of the crag. In an instant they had passed through, and found themselves in daylight once more. The sudden glare almost blinded them, for, though the sky was overcast by clouds, from which jagged tongues of lightning played, the outside was much lighter than the dark cave.

"I should say it was a storm!" cried Tom Swift. "See, it is striking every minute, and all around us!"

In fact, lightning bolts were falling on every side of the adventurers. Every time the balls of fire struck, they burst open great stones, or seared a livid scar on the face of some cliff. As for Tom and the others, they stood on a dry dirt hill, in which, fortunately, there was no iron ore. To this fact they undoubtedly owed their lives, though had there been rain, to moisten the ground and make the earth a good conductor of electricity, they probably would have been badly shocked. But the electrical outburst was not accompanied by rain.

Tom looked up. He saw a compact mass of cloud moving toward the summit of the mountain on the slope of which they stood. From this cloud there played shafts of reddish-green fire.

"Look!" called the young inventor to Mr. Parker. The instant the latter saw the cloud, he cried:

"We must get away from here by all means! That is the center of the storm. As soon as it gets over the mountain, where that lightning rod is, all the electrical fluid will be discharged in one bolt at the mountain, and it will be destroyed! We must run, but keep on the dirt places! Run for your lives!"

They needed no second warning. Turning, they fled down the steep side of the mountain, slipping and stumbling, but taking care not to step on any iron ore. Behind them flashed the lightning bolts.

Suddenly there was a most awful crash. It seemed as if the end of the world had come, and the ear drums of Tom and his companion almost burst with the fearful report. The concussion knocked them down, and they lay stunned for a moment.

Following the terrible report there was a low, rumbling sound. Hardly knowing whether he was dead or alive, Tom opened his eyes and looked about him. What he saw caused him to cry out in terror.

The whole mountain seemed bathed in fire. Great blue, red and green flashes played around it. Then the towering cliff seemed to melt and crumble up, and the great peak, the top of it containing the diamond makers' cave, from which they had fled but a few minutes before, the entire summit was toppled over into the valley on the other side, and in the direction opposite to that where the adventurers stood.

Then came a profound silence, and the lightning ceased. The storm was over, and only the rattle of stones and boulders, as they came to rest in the valley below, reached the ears of our friends.

"Phantom Mountain has been destroyed, just as I said it would be," spoke Mr. Parker, solemnly. Once more he had prophesied correctly.

For a few minutes the adventurers hardly knew what to say. They arose awkwardly from the ground where the shock had tossed them. Then Tom remarked, as calmly as possible:

"Well, it's all over. I guess we may as well get back to our airship."

"What became of Munson and the others?" asked Mr. Damon.

Mr. Jenks pointed to the trail, far below. The figures of some men, running madly, could be seen.

"There they go," he said; "I fancy we have seen the last of them." And they had, for some time at least.

There was little use lingering any longer on Phantom Mountain— indeed little of it was left on which to remain. Looking back toward the place where the cave had been, Tom and the others started forward again. The diamond-making machinery had all been destroyed. So, also, had the finished diamonds stored in the cavern and the large supply which had probably been made by the last terrific crash. No one would ever have them now. Tom and Mr. Jenks felt a sense of disappointment, but they were glad to have escaped with their lives. They sought their former camp, but the tent and all their food was buried under tons of earth and rocks.

Three days later, after rather severe hardships, they were near the place where they had left the *Red Cloud*. They had suffered cold and hunger, for they had no food supplies, and, had it not been that Bill Renshaw knew the haunts of some game, of which they managed to snare some, they would have fared badly, for they had left their guns in the cave.

"Well, there are the trees behind which I hope my airship is hidden," announced Tom, as they came to the spot. "Good old *Red Cloud*! Maybe we won't do some eating when we get aboard, eh?"

"Bless my appetite! but we certainly will!" cried Mr. Damon.

"There's somebody walking around the place," spoke Mr. Jenks.

"I hope it's no one who has damaged the ship," came from Tom, apprehensively. He broke into a run, and soon confronted an aged miner, who seemed to have established a rude sort of camp near the airship.

"Is anything the matter?" asked Tom, breathlessly. "Is my airship all right?"

"I guess she's all right, stranger," was the reply. "I don't know much about these contraptions, but I haven't touched her. I knowed she was an airship, for I've seen pictures of 'em, and I've been waiting until the owner came along."

"Why?" asked Tom, wonderingly.

"Because I've got a proposition to make to you," went on the— miner, who said his name was Abe Abercrombie. "I've been a miner for a good many years, and I'm just back from Alaska, prospecting around here. I haven't had any luck, but I know of a gold mine in Alaska that will make us all rich. Only it needs an airship to get to it, and I've been figuring how to hire one. Then I comes along, and I sees this big one, and I makes up my mind to stay here until the owners come back. That's what I've done. Now, if I prove that I'm telling the truth, will you go to Alaska—to the valley of gold with me?"

"I don't know," answered Tom, to whom the proposition was rather sudden. "We've just had some pretty startling adventures, and we're almost starved. Wait until we get something to eat, and we'll talk. Come aboard the *Red Cloud*," and the lad led the way to his craft which was in as good condition as when he left it to go to the diamond cave. Later he listened to the miner's story.

Tom Swift did go to the valley of gold in Alaska, and what happened to him and his companions there will be told of in the next volume of this series, to be called "Tom Swift in the Caves of Ice; or, the Wreck of the Airship."'

It did not take our friends long, after they had eaten a hearty meal, to generate some fresh gas, and start the *Red Cloud* oh her homeward way. Tom wanted to take Bill Renshaw with him, hut the old man said he would rather remain among the mountains where he had been born. So, after paying him well for his services, they said good-by to him. Abercrombie, the miner, also remained behind, but promised to call and see Tom in a few months.

"Well, we didn't make any money out of this trip," observed Mr. Jenks, rather dubiously, as they were nearing Shopton, after an uneventful trip. "I guess I owe you considerable, Tom Swift. I promised to get you a lot of diamonds, but all I have are those I had from my first visit to the cave."

"Oh, that's all right," spoke Tom, easily. "The experience was worth all the trip cost."

"Speaking of diamonds, look here!" exclaimed Mr. Damon, suddenly, and he pulled out a double handful.

"Where did you get them?" cried the others in astonishment.

"I grabbed them up, as we ran from the cave," said the eccentric man; "but, bless my gaiters! I forgot all about them until you spoke. We'll share them."

These diamonds, some of which were large, proved very valuable, though the total sum was far below what Mr. Jenks hoped to make when he started on the remarkable trip. Tom gave Mary Nestor a very fine stone, and it was set in a ring, instead of a pin, this time.

On their arrival in Shopton, where Mr. Swift, the housekeeper, Mr. Jackson and Eradicate Sampson were much alarmed for Tom's safety, an attempt was made to manufacture diamonds, using a powerful electric current instead of lightning. But it was not a success, and so Mr. Jenks concluded to give up his search for the secret which was lost on Phantom Mountain.

And now we will take leave of Tom Swift, to meet him again soon in other adventures he is destined to have in the caves of ice and the valley of gold.

Tom Swift in the Caves of Ice
Or The Wreck of the Airship

TABLE OF CONTENTS:

ERADICATE IN AN AIRSHIP

"Well, Massa Tom, am yo' gwine out in yo' flyin' machine ag'in to-day?"

"Yes, Rad, I think I will take a little flight. Perhaps I'll go over to Waterford, and call on Mr. Damon. I haven't seen very much of him, since we got back from our hunt after the diamond-makers."

"Take a run clear ober t' Waterfield; eh, Massa Tom?"

"Yes, Rad. Now, if you'll help me, I'll get out the *Butterfly*, and see what trim she's in for a speedy flight."

Tom Swift, the young inventor, aided by Eradicate Sampson, the colored helper of the Swift household, walked over toward a small shed.

A few minutes later the two had rolled into view, on its three bicycle wheels, a trim little monoplane—one of the speediest craft of the air that had ever skimmed along beneath the clouds. It was built to carry two, and had a very powerful motor.

"I guess it will work all right," remarked the young inventor, for Torn Swift had not only built this monoplane himself, but was the originator of it, and the craft contained many new features.

"It sho' do look all right, Massa Tom."

"Look here, Rad," spoke the lad, as a sudden idea came to him, "you've never ridden in an airship, have you?"

"No, Massa Tom, an' I ain't gwine to nuther!"

"Why not?"

"Why not? 'Case as how it ain't healthy; that's why!"

"But I go in them frequently, Eradicate. So does my father. You've seen us fly often enough, to know that it's safe. Why, look at the number of times Mr. Damon and I have gone off on trips in this little *Butterfly*. Didn't we always come back safely?"

"Yes, dat's true, but dere might come a time when yo' WOULDN'T come back, an' den where'd Eradicate Sampson be? I axes yo' dat—whar'd I be, Massa Tom?"

"Why, you wouldn't be anywhere if you didn't go, of course," and Tom laughed. "But I'd like to take you for a little spin in this machine, Rad. I want you to get used to them. Sometime I may need you to help me. Come, now. Suppose you get up on this seat here, and I promise not to go too high until you get used to it. Come on, it will do you good, and think of what all your friends will say when they see you riding in an airship."

"Dat's right, Massa Tom. Dey suah will be monstrous envious ob Eradicate Sampson, dat's what dey will."

It was clear that the colored man was being pursuaded somewhat against his will. Though he had been engaged by Tom Swift and his father off and on for several years, Eradicate had never shown any desire to take a trip through the air in one of the several craft Tom owned for this purpose. Nor had he ever evinced a longing for a trip under the ocean in a submarine, and as for riding in Tom's speedy electric car—Eradicate would as soon have sat down with thirteen at the table, or looked at the moon over the wrong shoulder.

But now, somehow, there was a peculiar temptation to take his young employer at his word. Eradicate had seen, many times, the youthful inventor and his friends make trips in the monoplane, as well as in the big biplane and dirigible balloon combined—the *Red Cloud*. Tom and the others had always come back safely, though often they met with accidents which only the skill and daring of the daring aeronaut had brought to a safe conclusion.

"Well, are you coming, Rad?" asked Tom, as he looked to see if the oil and gasoline tanks were filled, and gave a preliminary twirl to the propeller.

"Now does yo' t'ink it am puffickly safe, Massa Tom?" and the colored man looked nervously at the machine.

"Of course, Rad. Otherwise I wouldn't invite you. But I won't take you far. I just want you to get used to it, and, once you have made a flight, you'll want to make another."

"I don't nohow believe I will, Massa Tom, but as long as you have axed me, an' as yo' say some of dem proud, stuck-up darkies in Shopton will be tooken down a peg or two when de sees me, vhy, I will go wif yo', Massa Tom."

"I thought you would. Now take your place in the little seat next to where I'm going to sit. All start the engine and jump in. Now sit perfectly still, and, whatever you do, don't jump out. The ground's pretty hard this morning. There was a frost last night."

"I knows dere was, Massa Tom. Nope, I won't jump. I-I-Oh, golly, Massa Tom! I guess I don't want to go-let me out!"

Eradicate, his heart growing fainter as the time of starting drew nearer, made as if he would leave the monoplane, in which he had taken his seat.

"Sit still!" yelled Tom. At that instant he started the propeller. The motor roared like a salvo of guns, and streaks of fire could be seen shooting from one cylinder to the other, until there was a perfect blast of explosions.

The speed of the propeller increased as the motor warmed up. Tom ran to his seat and opened the gasoline throttle still more, advancing the spark slightly. The roar increased. The lad darted a look at Eradicate. The colored man's face was like chalk, and he was gripping the upright braces at his side as though his salvation depended on them.

"Steady now" spoke Tom, yelling to be heard above the racket. "Here we go."

The Butter-fly was moving slowly across the level stretch of ground which Tom used for starting his airships. The propeller was now a blur of light. The explosions of the motor became a steady roar, the noise from one cylinder being merged into the blast from the others so rapidly that it was a continuous racket.

With a whizz the monoplane shot across the ground. Then, with a quick motion, Tom tilted the lifting planes, and, as gracefully as a bird, the little machine mounted upward on a slant until, coming to a level about two hundred feet above the earth, Tom sent it straight ahead over the roof of his house.

"How's this, Rad?" he cried. "Isn't it great?"

"It—it—er—bur-r-r-r! It's—it's mighty ticklish, Massa Tom-dat's de word—it suah am mighty ticklish!"

Tom Swift laughed and increased the speed. The *Butterfly* darted forward like some hummingbird about to launch itself upon a flower, and, indeed, the revolutions of the propeller were not unlike the vibrations of the wings of that marvelous little creature.

"Now for some corkscrew twists!" cried the young inventor. "Here we go, Rad!"

With that he began a series of intricate evolutions, making figures of eight, spirals, curves, sudden dips and long swings. It was masterwork in handling a monoplane, but Eradicate

Sampson, as he sat crouched in the seat, gripping the uprights until his hands ached, was in no condition to appreciate it. Gradually, however, as he saw that the craft remained up in the air, and showed no signs of falling, the fears of the colored man left him. He sat up straighter.

"Don't you like it, Rad?" cried Tom.

This time the answer came with more decision.

"It suah am great, Massa Tom! I'm—I'm beginnin' t' like it. Whoop! I guess I do like it! Now if some of dem stuck-up coons could see me—"

"They'd think YOU were stuck up; eh, Rad? Stuck up in the air!"

"Dat's right, Massa Tom. Ha! Ha! I suah am stuck up in de air! Ha! Ha!"

By this time Tom had guided the machine away from the village, and they were flying over the fields, some distance from his house. The colored man was beginning to enjoy his experience very much.

Suddenly, just as Tom was trying to get a bit more speed out of the motor, the machine stopped. The cessation of the racket was almost as startling as a loud explosion would have been.

"Just my luck!" cried Tom.

"What's de matter?" asked Eradicate, anxiously.

"Motor's stalled," replied the young inventor.

"An', by golly, we's falling!" yelled the colored man.

Naturally, with the stopping of the propeller, there was no further straight, forward motion to the monoplane, and, following the law of nature, it began to drop toward the earth on a slant.

"We's fallin'! We'll be killed!" yelled the negro.

"It's all right, I'll just vol-plane back to earth," spoke Tom, calmly. "I've often done it before, higher up than this. Sit still, Rad, I'm volplaning back to the ground."

"An' I'll JUMP back to de ground; dat's what I'll do. I ain't goin' t' wait until I falls, no sah! An' I ain't gwine t' do none ob dat ball-playin' yo' speak ob,

Massa Swift. It's no time t' play ball when yo' life am in danger. I'se gwine t' jump."

"Sit still!" cried Tom, for the colored man was about to spring from his seat. "There's no danger! I didn't say anything about playing ball. I said I'd *volplane* back to the earth. We'll be there shortly. I'll take you down safe. Sit still, Rad!"

He spoke so earnestly that the fears of his colored passenger were quelled. With a quick motion Tom threw up the head planes, to check the downward sweep. The *Butterfly* shot forward on a gradual slant. Repeating this maneuver several times, the young inventor finally brought his machine to within a short distance of the earth, and, also, considerably nearer his own home.

"I wonder if we can make it?" he murmured, measuring the distance with his eye. "I think so. I'll shoot her up a bit and then let her down on a long slant. Then, with another upward tilt, I ought to fetch it."

The monoplane tilted upward. Eradicate gave a cry of terror. It was stilled at a look from Tom. Once more the air machine glided forward. Then came another long dip, another upward glide and the *Butterfly* came gently to earth almost on the very spot whence it had flown upward a few minutes before.

Eradicate gave one mad spring from his seat, almost before the bicycle wheels had ceased revolving, as Tom jammed on the earth-brake.

"Here, where are you going, Rad?" cried the lad.

"Whar am I goin'? I'se goin' t' see if mah mule Boomerang am safe. He's de only kind ob an airship I wants arter dis!" and the colored man disappeared into the shack whence came a loud "hee-haw!"

"Oh, pshaw! Wait a minute, Rad. I'll soon have the motor fixed, and we'll make another try. I'll take you over to Mr. Damon's with me."

"No, sah, Massa Tom. Yo' don't catch dis coon in any mo' airships. Mah mule am good enough fo' me!" shouted Eradicate from the safe harbor of the mule's stable.

Tom laughed, and turned to inspect the motor. As he was looking it over, to locate the trouble, the door of the house opened and a pleasant-faced woman stepped out.

"Oh, Tom," she called. "I looked for you a moment ago, and you weren't here!"

"No, Mrs. Baggert," Tom replied, waving his hand in greeting to the housekeeper, "Rad and I just came back—quite suddenly—sooner than we expected to. Why? Did you want me?"

"Here's a letter that came for you," she went on.

Tom tore open the envelope, and rapidly scanned the contents of the missive.

"Hello!" he ejaculated half aloud. "It's from Abe Abercrombie, that miner I met when we were after the diamond-makers! He says he is on his way east to get ready to start on the quest for the Alaskan valley of gold, in the caves of ice. I had almost forgotten that I promised to make the attempt in the big airship. How did this letter come, Mrs. Baggert?" he asked.

"By special delivery. The messenger brought it a few minutes ago."

"Then we may see Abe any day now. Guess I'd better be looking over the RED CLOUD to see if it's in shape for a trip to the Arctic regions."

Tom's attention for the moment was taken off his little monoplane, and his memory went back to the strange scenes in which he and his friends had recently played a part, in searching for the cave of the diamond-makers on Phantom Mountain. He recalled the promise he had made to the old miner.

"I wonder if he expects us to start for Alaska with winter coming on?" thought Tom.

His musings were suddenly interrupted by the entrance into the yard, surrounding the aeroplane shed, of a lad about his own age.

"Hello, Ned Newton!" called Tom, heartily.

"Hello, yourself," responded Ned. "I've got a day off from the bank, and I thought I'd come over and see you. Say, have you heard the latest?"

"No. What is it?"

"Andy Foger is building an airship."

"Andy Foger building an airship?"

"Yes, he says it will beat yours."

"Humph! It will, eh? Well, Andy can do as he pleases as long as he doesn't bother me. I won't be around here much longer, anyhow."

"Why not, Tom?"

"Because I soon expect to start for the far north on a strange quest. Come on in the shed, and I'll tell you about it. We're going to try to locate a valley of gold, and I guess Andy Foger won't follow me there, even if he does build an airship."

Tom and his chum started toward the shed, the young inventor still holding the letter that was to play such an important part in his life within the next few months. And, had he only known it, the building of Andy Foger's airship was destined to be fraught with much danger to our hero.

ANDY FOGER'S TRIPLANE

"Going to look for a valley of gold, eh?" remarked Ned Newton as he and Tom took seats in a little room, fitted up like a den, where the young inventor frequently worked out the details of the problems that confronted him. "Where is this valley, Tom? Anywhere so I could have a chance at it?"

"It's up in Alaska. Just where I don't know, but Abe Abercrombie, the old miner whom we met when out in Colorado this summer, says he can find it if we circle around in the airship. So I'm going to take a chance. I'll tell you all about it."

And, while Tom is doing this, I will take the opportunity to more formally introduce to my new readers our hero and his friends.

Tom Swift was an inventor of no little note, in spite of his youth. He lived with his father, Barton Swift, who was also an inventor, on the outskirts of the village of Shopton, New York State. Tom's mother was dead, and Mrs. Baggert had kept house for him and his father since he was a child. Garret Jackson, an expert machinist, was also a member of the household, and as has been explained, Eradicate Sampson, who took that name because, as he said he "eradicate de dirt," was also a sort of retainer. He lived in a little house on the Swift grounds, and did odd jobs about the place.

In the first book of the series, entitled "Tom Swift and His Motor Cycle," there was related how the lad became possessed of one of those speedy machines, after Mr. Wakefield Damon had come to grief on it. Mr. Damon was an eccentric man, who was always blessing himself, some part of his anatomy, or some of his possessions.

After many adventures on his motor-cycle, Tom Swift went through some surprising happenings with a motor-boat be bought. After that he built an airship, the *Red Cloud*, and later he and his father constructed a submarine, in which they went under the ocean in search of sunken treasure, enduring many perils and much danger.

Tom Swift's electric runabout, which he built after returning home from the submarine trip, proved to be the speediest car on the road. The experience he acquired in making this machine stood him in good stead, when (as told in the sixth volume, "Tom Swift and His Wireless Message") the airship in which he, Mr. Damon and a friend of the latter's (who had built the craft) were wrecked on Earthquake Island. There Tom was marooned with some refugees from a wrecked steam yacht, among whom were Mr. and Mrs. Nestor, father of a girl of whom Tom thought a great deal.

With parts from the wrecked electric airship the youth rigged up a plant, and sent wireless messages from the island. The castaways nearly lost their lives in the earthquake shocks, but a steamer, summoned by Tom's wireless call, arrived in time to save them, just as the island disappeared beneath the sea.

In the seventh book of the series, entitled "Tom Swift Among the Diamond Makers" there was related the adventures of himself and his friends when they tried to solve the mystery of Phantom Mountain.

Among the castaways of Earthquake Island was a Mr. Barcoe Jenks and a Professor Ralph Parker. Mr. Jenks was a strange man, and claimed to have some valuable diamonds, which he said were made by a gang of men hidden in a cave in the Rocky Mountains. Tom did not believe that the diamonds were real, but Mr. Jenks soon proved that they were.

He asked Tom to aid him in searching for the cave of the diamond makers. Mr. Jenks had been there once—in fact, he had been offered a partnership in the diamond-making business, but, after he had paid his money, he had been drugged, and carried secretly from the cave before he had a chance to note its location.

But he, together with Tom, Mr. Damon and the scientist Mr. Parker, who correctly predicted the destruction of Earthquake Island, set out in the *Red Cloud* to find the diamond makers. They did find them, after many hardships, and were captured by the gang. How Tom and his friends escaped from the cave, after they had seen diamonds made by a powerful lightning flash, and how they nearly lost their lives from the destruction of Phantom Mountain, is fully set down in the book.

Sufficient to say now, that, though they had a general idea of how the precious stones were made, by the power of the lightning, the young inventor and his friends were never quite able to accomplish it, and the secret remained a secret. But they had secured some diamonds as they rushed from the cave (Mr. Damon grabbing them up) and these were divided among Tom and the others.

Just as they were ready to come home in the airship, our friends were met by an old miner, Abe Abercrombie, who spoke of a valley of gold in Alaska, which was the story Tom related to Ned Newton, as the two chums sat in the den of the airship shed.

"Then you don't know all the details about the gold valley, Tom?" remarked Ned, as the young inventor showed his chum the letter that had just arrived.

"No, not all of them. At the time this miner met us I was anxious to get back East, for we had been away so long I knew dad would be worried. But I listened to part of Abe's story, and half promised to go in partnership in this quest for gold. He was to furnish information about the hidden valley, and I was to supply the airship. I expect Abe to come along at any time, now, and then I'll hear more particulars."

"Will you go all the way in the airship?"

"Well, I hadn't thought of that. I could ship it to the nearest place by rail, I suppose, and go on from there. That's a detail to be considered later. I'll talk it over with Abe."

"Who are going?"

"I don't know that even. I suppose Mr. Damon would feel slighted if I left him out. And perhaps Mr. Parker, that gloomy scientist, who is always predicting terrible accidents, will be glad to go along. Then Abe may have some friend he wants to take."

"By Jinks! But you certainly do have swell times, Tom Swift!" exclaimed Ned Newton, enviously. "I wish I could go and have a try at that valley of gold!"

"Why don't you come along, Ned?"

"Do you really mean it?"

"Of course."

"But I don't believe I could get away from the bank."

"Oh, dad and Mr. Damon could fix that. They're directors, you know. Come along, I'd be delighted to have you. Will you?"

"I'll think about it. Jinks! But I sure would like to go. Do you think you can find the valley?"

"Well, there's no telling. We generally do succeed in finding what we go after, even if we didn't get the diamond secret. I'm anxious to have Abe come, now, though until I got his letter I had almost forgotten about my promise to him. But, say, what's this you told me about Andy Foger making an airship?"

"It's true, though I haven't seen it. Jake Porter was telling me about it. Andy's built a big shed in his yard, and he and some cronies of his, including Pete Bailey and Sam Snedecker, are working in there night and day. They've hired a couple of machinists, too. Mr. Foger is putting up the cash, I guess. Say, that was quite a scare you gave Andy on your monoplane, one day."

"Yes, the big bully! and I'd like to scare him worse. But say, do you know I'd like to get a look at his airship. I wonder what sort of a craft it is?"

"We can see it easily enough."

"How?"

"Why, the back part of the shed where he and the others are working is close to our fence. There are some holes in our fence and if you come there, maybe you can look in."

"I can't see through the side of the shed, though."

"Yes, you can."

"How?"

"Why, there's a big window, for light, in the back part of it. I happened to notice it the other day. I didn't look in, because I wasn't much interested, but I saw that one could peer over the top of our fence right into the shop where Andy is working. Want to try it?"

Tom hesitated a moment.

"Well, it seems rather an odd thing to do," he said. "But I would like to see what sort of a flying machine Andy is making, just for my own satisfaction. He may be infringing on some of my patents, and if he is, I'll stop him. Once or twice he's been sneaking around my shed here. I don't believe in sneaking, but I know he wouldn't let me in if I asked him, so I guess it's the only way. I'll go with you, Ned."

"All right. We'll see if we can get a glimpse of Andy's queer shebang through the window."

The two chums left Tom's shop, and were soon in the yard of Ned Newton's house. As he had said, the big shed in Andy's premises came close up to the fence, and there was a window through which one might gaze. The casement did not appear to be curtained.

"I'll get a ladder so we can climb up to the top of the fence, and look over," spoke Ned, as he and Tom went out into the yard back of his house. The fence was high up on an embankment.

A little later Tom and his chum were gazing into the shop window from the ladder.

"Why, it's a triplane—a big triplane!" he exclaimed.

"What's a triplane?" asked Ned, who didn't have much time to study the different types of airships.

"It's one that has three sets of planes, one above the other. A biplane has two sets of planes, and a monoplane only one. Triplanes are larger, and, as far as I've been able to learn, not as satisfactory as either the biplanes or monoplanes. But that's not saying Andy's won't be a success. They certainly are busy in there, though! Andy is flying around like a hen scratching for her little chickens!"

"See anything of his cronies?"

"Yes, Pete and Sam are hammering away. There are a couple of men, too."

"Yes, the machinists. Oh, I guess Andy expects great things from his airship."

"Have you heard what he's going to do with it, Ned? Make flights for pleasure, or exhibit it?"

"No, I haven't heard. Look out, Tom, the ladder is slipping!"

As Ned spoke this warning, the window of the airship shed, through which they were looking, was suddenly raised. The ugly face of Andy Foger peered out. He caught sight of Tom and Ned.

"Get away from there, you spies!" he yelled. "Get away from there, Tom Swift! You're trying to steal some of my ideas! Get away or I'll make you. Sam, bring me my gun! Pete, go tell my father to come here! I'll show Ned Newton and Tom Swift they can't bother me!"

Andy was dancing about in a rage. His two cronies crowded behind him to the window just as the ladder on which Tom and Ned were standing slipped along the fence.

"Jump, Ned!" yelled Tom Swift, as he leaped away to escape being entangled in the rungs.

The young inventor came to the ground with a jar that shook him up considerably, while Ned, who had grasped the top board of the fence, remained hanging there by his hands, his feet dangling in the air.

"Whack his fingers, Andy!" yelled Pete Bailey. "Get a long stick and whack Ned's fingers! That will make him drop off!"

Tom Swift heard, and labored desperately to raise the ladder to enable Ned to get down, for his chum seemed to be afraid to drop.

Abe Is Deceived

Raising a ladder alone is rather an awkward job. Tom found this so when he tried to aid his friend Ned. But, being a muscular lad, the young inventor did finally succeed in getting the ladder up against the fence where the bank clerk could reach it.

Whack! Down upon the top board came a, stick wielded by Andy Foger from the rear window of his shop.

"Wow!" cried Ned. for the blow had been close to his fingers. "Hurry up with that ladder, Tom."

"There it is! But why don't you drop?"

"Too far. I can't reach the ladder now!"

"Yes, you can. Stretch a bit!"

"Whack!" Once more the stick descended on the fence, this time still closer to Ned's clinging hands.

"Hit him good, Andy!" cried Sam Snedecker, "Give me a shot at him!"

"I will not. I want to attend to him myself. You go tell my father, and he'll have Tom Swift arrested for trying to sneak in and get some of my airship ideas!"

By this time Ned's wiggling feet had found the topmost rung of the ladder. The next moment he was rapidly descending it, and, when on the ground, he and Tom carried it away, to prevent its use by the enemy.

"Whew!" exclaimed the young inventor. "I had no idea they would kick up such a row!"

"Me either. Did you hurt yourself when you jumped, as the ladder fell?"

"No. Did they hit your hands?"

"Came mighty near it. Well, I s'pose it serves us right, yet if I can't look over my own back fence it's a pity!"

"Of course we can, only I'd just as soon they hadn't seen us. However—hello! there's Andy looking over here, now."

The mean face of the bully now topped the fence. It was evident that he had crawled from the window of his shop.

"What are you trying to get into my place for, Tom Swift?" he demanded.

"I wasn't trying to get in, Andy Foger."

"Well, you were looking in."

"Only doing as you've done over at my shop, several times, Andy. I wanted to see what sort of an airship you were building."

"Trying to get some ideas for your own, I guess," sneered Andy.

Tom did not think it worth while to answer this taunt.

"I could have you arrested for this," went on Andy, who felt bolder now that he was reinforced by Sam and Pete on either side of him as he looked over the fence into Ned's yard.

"Arrested for what?" demanded the bank clerk.

"For trespassing on my father's premises," went on Andy.

"We weren't on your premises," declared Ned. "We were on our side of the fence all the while."

"Well, you were looking over in my yard."

"A cat may look at a king, you know, Andy," Tom reminded the bully.

"Yah! Think you're smart, don't you! Well, you can't steal any of my ideas for an airship. They're all patented, and I'll soon be making longer and higher flights than you ever dreamed of! I'll show you what a real airship is, Tom Swift! Monoplanes and biplanes are out of date. The only thing that's any good is a triplane. If mine works well—and I'm sure it will—I may build a quadruplane!"

"I wish you luck," spoke Tom, with a shrug of his shoulders.

"Well, you won't have any luck if you come around here any more," went on Pete Bailey. "We'll be on the watch for you fellows, now, and we'll cover this window, so you can't see in."

"That's what we will," agreed Andy, and Sam Snedecker shook his head vigorously to indicate that he, too, approved of this.

"Come on," spoke Tom in a low tone to Ned, "I've seen enough."

The two chums moved toward Ned's house, followed by the jeers and mocking laughter of Andy and his cronies.

"Can't you get back at them in some way?" asked Ned, for he did not like to see himself or his friend apparently vanquished by the bully.

"He laughs best who laughs last, Ned."

"What do you mean?"

"I mean that when Andy tries to fly in his triplane it will be our turn to laugh."

"Won't it fly?"

"Never, the way he has it rigged up. It didn't take but one look to tell me that. He's working on altogether the wrong principle. Wait until he tries to go up, and then we'll have some fun with him."

"Then you got a good view of it through the window?"

"I saw all I wanted to. But say, I was about to take a little trip in my monoplane, to see my friend Mr. Damon, when Abe's letter arrived, and you came along with your news. I started to take Eradicate, but he backed out. Don't you want to come?"

"Sure, I'll go along."

Ned had often ridden in the trim *Butterfly*, though the trips had not been so frequent that he was tired of them. A little later, Tom, having adjusted the motor that had stalled before, compelling him to vol-plane back to earth, the two chums were sailing through the air toward Waterford.

"Why, bless my shoe laces!" cried Mr. Damon, as they alighted in the yard of his house, about an hour later. "I didn't expect you, Tom. But I'm glad to see you!"

"And I to meet you again. I guess you know Ned Newton."

"Ah, yes. How d'ye do, Ned? Bless my appetite! but it's quite chilly. We'll soon have winter. Won't you come in and have some hot chocolate?"

The boys were glad to accept the invitation, and as they were drinking the beverage, which Mrs. Damon made for them, Tom told of the receipt of the letter from the old miner, and also his experience in seeing Andy's airship.

"Why, bless my pocketbook!" cried Mr. Damon. "I had no idea we'd ever hear from Abe Abercrombie again. And so he is really coming on, to tell us about the valley of gold?"

"So he says," replied Tom. "I was wondering if you'd like to go, Mr. Damon."

"Go? Why, bless my very topknot! Of course I would. I'll go with you—only—only," and he leaned forward and whispered cautiously, "don't speak so loudly. My wife might hear you!"

"Doesn't she want you to go off in the airship any more?" asked Tom.

"Well, she'd rather I wouldn't. But she's going on a visit to her mother, soon, and then I think will come my opportunity to take another trip with you. A valley of gold in Alaska, eh? Up where the icebergs and caves of ice are. Say, Tom, I know some one else who would be glad to go."

"Who?" inquired the young inventor, though he had an idea to whom his friend referred.

"Mr. Parker! You know he's taken up his residence in Waterford, now, and only the other day he spoke to me about wishing he could go to the far north. He has some new theory—"

"About the destruction of something or other; hasn't he, Mr. Damon?" interrupted Tom, with a smile.

"That's it, exactly, my boy. Bless my coffeepot! But Mr. Parker has an idea that the whole northern part of this continent will soon be buried thousands of feet deep under an icy avalanche, and he wants to be there to see it. I know he'd like to go with us, Tom."

The young inventor made a little gesture of dissent, but as he knew Mr. Damon, who was very eccentric himself, had taken a great liking to the gloomy scientist, Tom did not feel like refusing. So he said:

"All right, Mr. Damon. If we go, and I think we shall, we'll expect you and Mr. Parker. I'll let you know the result of Mr. Abercrombie's visit, and I needn't request you to keep quiet about it. If there is a valley of gold in Alaska, we don't want everyone to know about it."

"No, of course not, Tom Swift. I'll keep silent about it. Bless my liverpin! But I'll be glad to on the move again, even if it is toward the Arctic regions."

After some further talk, Tom and Ned took their departure, making good time back to Shopton in the speedy monoplane.

For several days after that Tom busied himself about his big airship the *Red Cloud*, for it needed quite a few repairs after the long trip to the mountains where the diamond makers had been discovered in their cave.

"And if we're going up amid the ice and snow," reasoned Tom, "I've got to make some different arrangements about the craft, and provide for keeping warmer than we found necessary when we went west."

So it was that Tom had no time to learn anything further about Andy Foger's airship, even had our hero been so inclined, which he was not. He looked for Abe Abercrombie any day now, for though the old miner had given no date as to when he would arrive, he had said, in his letter, that it would be soon.

It was one day, nearly a week after Tom's attempt to make Eradicate like aeroplaning, that there might have been seen, coming along the Shopton road, which led toward Tom's house, the figure of a grizzled old man. His clothes were rather rough, and he carried a valise that had, evidently, seen much service. There was that about him which proclaimed him for a westerner—a cattleman or a miner.

He walked slowly along, murmuring to himself.

"Wa'al, I might better have taken one of them wagons at th' depot," he said, "than t' try t' walk. It's quite a stretch out t' Tom Swift's house. I hope I find him home."

He trudged on, and, a little later, his gaze was attracted by a large shed, in the rear of a white house the pretentious appearance of which indicated that persons of wealth owned it.

"I guess that must be the place," he remarked. "That shed is big enough to hold the airship. Now to present myself."

As he walked up the front path of the house, he was met by one of the gardeners, who was raking up the leaves.

"Is this the airship place?" asked the miner.

"Yes, that's where the young master is making his triplane," answered the man.

"Is he in?"

"Yes, I guess so. You can walk right back to the shed."

The miner did so. Through the open door of the building he had a glimpse of big stretches of wings, propellers, rudders, and some machinery.

"That's it," he murmured, "though it looks some different than I remembered it. However, maybe Tom's changed it about. I wonder where he is?"

As he spoke a lad came from the shed to meet him—a lad on whose face there was a look of suspicion.

"What do you want?" he demanded.

"I'm lookin' for Tom Swift," was the simple reply. "But I take it you're one of his partners in this airship business. I guess he must have told you about me. I'm Abe Abercrombie, the miner, and I've come to show him the way to that valley of gold in Alaska."

At the mention of Tom Swift's name, Andy Foger, for it was he, had started to utter a denial. But, at the next words of the miner, and as Mr. Abercrombie mentioned "gold" and "Alaska," there came a cunning look over Andy's face.

"Tom Swift isn't here just now," he said, wondering how he could turn to advantage the unexpected visit, and the impending information that the guileless old man was about to give under the mistaken idea that Andy was Tom's friend.

"That's all right, I reckon he'll be along presently. You'll do just as well, I reckon. You're in partnership with him, I take it. So this is the place where he makes his airships, eh? It's a big one," and Mr. Abercrombie looked in at the odd triplane of Andy's—for the airship was almost finished.

"But it'll need to be big if we're to go to Alaska in it," went on the miner. "It's quite a journey t' th' valley where th' gold is. No way t' get t' it except by an airship. An' here I be an' ready to start, I've brought th' map of th' place, jest as I promised. Here it is, better take good care of it. Now, let's talk business," and the miner, having guilelessly handed Andy Foger a folded parchment, sat down on a box at the door of the airship shed, and placed his heavy valise on the ground beside him.

"What's this?" asked the bully, wondering whether he had heard aright.

"It's the map of th' valley of gold—directions how t' git there, an' all that. I guess it's plain enough. Now, when can we start?"

Andy did not know what to say. Fate had, most unexpectedly, placed in his hands a valuable paper. The miner had made a mistake. Andy's house was on the same road as was Tom's and, seeing the airship shed, had deceived the aged man. He had not expected to find two airship manufactories in the same village.

"The map of the valley of gold, "murmured Andy, as he put it in his pocket.

"Yes, jest as I told Tom about when I met him out West. I said I'd bring it with me, an' I did. When will Tom be back? He never spoke of you, though I reckoned he'd have to have some help in makin' his airships. Where is he?"

"He—he—" stammered Andy. He did not know what to say.

At that instant Tom Swift himself passed by in the road. He had been over to Shopton on an errand. One look into the yard of Andy's house showed to our hero the old miner sitting at the door of the airship shed.

"Mr. Abercrombie—Abe!" cried Tom, almost, before he thought.

"Hello, Tom! I got here!" cried the miner, heartily. "I was jest talking to your partner."

"My partner!" spoke Tom in amazement

"Yes—partner in th' airship business. I should think you'd need about three partners to build these machines!"

"My partner! Andy Foger isn't my partner!" cried Tom, wondering what would happen next. "I have no partner! If he said he was he deceived you!"

"No partner? Ain't he your partner?" cried Mr. Abercrombie. "Why, I thought he was. I told him about th' valley of gold—I—I—give him the map—"

"The map?"

"Yes, the map t' tell how to get there. He's got it!"

There was a mocking smile on Andy's face.

"Give that map back at once!" cried Tom, sternly, now understanding something of the situation. "Hand it over at once, Andy Foger!"

"I will—when I get ready! He gave it to me!" cried the bully, and then, before either Tom or Abe could stop him, Andy darted into the big shed, and slammed shut the door.

Tom Gets the Map

For a few seconds Tom was so surprised at the sudden action of the bully that he could neither move nor speak. Then, crying out a command to halt, the young inventor took after his enemy.

"The scamp!" he cried. "The nerve he has! To deceive Abe Abercrombie in that fashion! Wait until I get hold of him!"

"What's it all about?" asked the old miner, who, being a slow thinker had not understood all that had happened. "What's up, Tom Swift?"

"Haven't time to tell you now," flung back the running lad over his shoulder. "I've got to catch Andy! Then I'll explain. He's trying to get ahead of us. I guess, but we'll stop him!" Thereupon Tom flung himself against the door of the airship shed. The young inventor found the portal bolted, though it vibrated with the impact of his body.

"Come out of there, Andy Foger!" cried Tom, pounding on the door. "Come out, or I'll get an officer, and have you arrested!"

There was no answer.

"Come out, I say!" repeated Tom.

"Around th' back! Try th' back door!" suggested the miner, who had hastened to Tom's side. "Maybe he's run out that way!"

Tom listened. There was no movement in the shop. Then the young inventor sprinted around the side. He was just in time to see the bully running away over the lots and fields in the rear of his father's premises. Andy had climbed out of the back window of the shed, into which Tom and Ned had peered that day, had climbed the high fence, dropped down on the other side, and was now running away with all the speed he could muster.

"Come back—!" began Tom, and then he realized that his enemy could not hear him. The bully was too far away. At the same time our hero realized that it would be useless to give chase, for Andy had too much of a start. There was nothing to do but to turn back, and Tom knew that his delay in trying to gain an entrance at the front door had given Andy the very opportunity he needed to escape at the rear.

"Well, this is a bad turn of affairs," remarked the lad, as he faced the puzzled miner.

"What is, Tom?"

"Him having that map. It shows the location of the valley of gold, doesn't it, and tells how to get there?"

"That's what it does!"

"How did Andy happen to get it?"

"Jest as I told you. I was on my way t' your house, havin' inquired at th' post-office, an' the man said that at your place there was a big shed, where you kept your airships. I come along, an', of course, when I see this house, an' the shed, an' had a glimpse of th' airship, I, of course, thought it was your place. An', though you'd never told me about it, I thought maybe this lad was in business with you. So, like a blamed young tenderfoot, I blurted out my business afore I thought, an' handed him the map for safe keepin'. He took it, too, that's the worst of it."

"Yes, that's the worst of it," agreed Tom, "But I'll get it back, if I have to cause his arrest, and search his whole house."

"But he runned away, Tom."

"Oh, he'll come back. Was there only one copy of the map of the valley, Abe?" asked Tom, anxiously.

"Yep; only one"

"Could you make another?"

"No, not if you was to pay me a million dollars! You see I ain't no drawer, an' this map, while I made part of it, was mostly made by my old partner, who was with me when we discovered th' valley of gold, an' was druv back by th' savage Eskimos an' Indians, an' by th' terrible cold. My partner made th' best part of th' map, an' he's dead, poor fellow."

"I see. That's too bad! Then you can't make a duplicate map?"

"Nary a one. But can't you do somethin'? It were amazin' stupid of me, old Abe Abercrombie, t' be took in by a boy like him! Can't you do somethin'?"

"I'm going to try," announced Tom determinedly, as he swung on toward the Foger house. "I'll cause his arrest if he doesn't give it up."

A few minutes later Tom Swift and Abe confronted Mr. Foger. The rich man, father of the bully, was rather surprised at the visit from the young inventor, for the two were not friends.

"Well, what can I do for you, Tom Swift?" asked the banker, for he felt a certain coldness toward our hero, since the latter had defeated him in an effort to wreck a financial institution in which Tom and his father were interested.

"Mr. Foger," spoke Tom, sternly, "your son has just stolen a map belonging to this gentleman," and he indicated Abe.

"My son stolen a map!" exclaimed Mr. Foger. "How dare you make such an accusation, Tom Swift?"

"I dare, because it's true! And, unless that map is returned to me at my house to-night I shall swear out a warrant for Andy's arrest."

"You'd never dare do that!"

"Wait and see!" spoke Tom, firmly. "I will give your son, or you, exactly five hours to return that map—if it isn't back in my hands by then, I'll get a warrant!"

"Preposterous! Stuff and nonsense!" blustered Mr. Foger. "My son never stole anything!"

"He stole this map, and there is plenty of evidence," went on Tom, as he detailed the circumstances.

Mr. Foger hemmed and hawed, and affected not to believe that anything of the kind could have happened. But Tom was firm, and Abe Abercrombie backed up his statements, until even the banker began to waver.

"Very well," he announced at length, "I will look into this matter, and if I find that my son has anything of yours, you shall have it back. But I cannot believe it. Perhaps he took it as a joke."

"In which case," spoke Tom grimly, "he will find that he has carried the joke too far," and with that he and the miner left the Foger home.

"It's all my fault," bewailed Abe, as he and our hero trudged on toward the Swift household.

"No, it wasn't, Abe," declared Tom. "Any one would have been deceived by such tactics as Andy used—that is any stranger. And you didn't expect to find two airship sheds so close together."

"No. That's right, I didn't. That's what threw me off th' track."

"Andy only recently began work on his triplane. I don't know what his object is, and I don't care. Just now I'm more concerned about getting back this map."

"I hope we do get it."

"Oh, we will. I'm going to start off on my own hook, to find Andy. But first I'll take you to my house."

The old miner was soon telling his story to Mr. Swift, the housekeeper and Garret Jackson. They expressed their surprise at Andy's daring act. But Tom didn't do much more talking.

"I'm going out to find Andy," he declared, "and when I do—" He didn't finish his sentence, but they all knew what he meant.

But the bully was in none of his usual haunts, though Tom visited them all. Nor was Andy at the homes of either of his cronies.

"Well, if I don't find him, I shall certainly swear out the warrant," decided Tom. "I'll give him until night, and then I'll call on the police."

Still he did not give up, but went to several other places where Andy might be found. He had about given up, as it was getting toward late afternoon, when, as he came out of a billiardroom, where the bully was in the habit of spending much of his time, Tom saw the lad of whom he was in search.

"Hold on there, Andy Foger!" cried the young inventor. "I want to see you!"

"What about?"

"You know very well. Where's that map you stole?"

"I haven't got it."

"Take care!" and Tom, with a quick step was beside the bully, and had grasped him firmly by the arm.

"You let me alone, Tom Swift!" cried Andy.

"Where's that map?" and Tom gave Andy's arm a wrench.

"It's at your house; that's where it is! I just took it back. It was only a joke."

"A joke, eh? And you took it back?"

"Yes, I did. Now you let me go!"

"I will when I find out if you're telling me the truth or not, Andy Foger. You come with me!"

"Where?"

"To my house. I want to see if that map's there."

"Well, you'll find that it is, and you'd better let me go! My father told me to take the map back, and I did. You let me go!"

Andy struggled to get loose, but Tom had too tight a grip. There was something, too, in the manner of our hero that warned Andy not to trifle with him. So, concluding that discretion was the better part of valor, Andy walked sullenly along toward Tom's home, the young inventor never relaxing the grip on his enemy's arm.

They reached the Swift home. Still holding his captive, Tom rang the bell. His father came to the door, followed by Abe Abercrombie.

"Is the map back?" asked the young inventor, anxiously.

"Yes, Andy brought it here a few minutes ago," announced Mr. Swift.

"Is it the right one, Abe?" inquired Tom.

"Yep, Tom. I made sure of that as soon as I laid my eyes on it. It's th' right one."

"Then you can go, Andy Foger," announced our hero, "and if I ever catch you in another trick like this, I'll take the law into my own hands. Clear out, now!"

"You wait! I'll get even with you," muttered the bully, as he fled down the front walk, as though afraid Tom would, even then, put his threat into execution.

"Did he damage the map any?" asked the lad, as he followed his father and Abe into the house.

"Nary a bit," answered the old miner. "It's jest th' same as it was. There it is," and he spread a crinkled sheet of tough parchment in front of Tom. It was covered with a rude drawing, and with names of places scrawled on it.

"So that's the map, eh?" murmured Tom, eagerly scanning it.

"That's it, an' here's th' valley of gold," went on Abe, as he placed one rough finger on a certain spot. "Right there—hello!" he cried, as he peered more closely at the parchment. "That ink spot wasn't there when I had th' map, a few hours ago."

"What ink spot?" asked Tom, anxiously.

"That one," and the miner indicated a small one near the edge of the map. "That was never there!"

"It looks as if it was recently made," added Mr. Swift, who was something of a chemist.

"An ink spot-freshly made," murmured Tom, "Dad—Abe, I can guess what's happened!"

"What?" demanded the miner.

"Andy Foger made a copy of this map while it was in his possession, and now he knows where the valley of gold is as well as we do! He may get there ahead of us!"

GRAVE SUSPICIONS

Tom's announcement took them all by surprise. For a moment no one knew what to say, while the young inventor looked more closely at the parchment map.

"Do you really think he has dared to make a copy of it?" asked Mr. Swift.

"I do," answered his son. "That ink spot wasn't there when Abe gave him the map; was it?"

"No," replied the miner.

"And it couldn't get on in Andy's pocket," went on Tom. "So he must have had it open near where there was ink."

"His fountain pen might have leaked," suggested Mr. Jackson.

"In that case the ink spot would be on the outside of the map, and not on the inside," declared Tom, with the instinct of a detective. "Unless he had the map folded in his pocket with the inside surface on the outside, the ink couldn't have gotten on. Besides, Andy always carries his fountain pen in his upper vest pocket, and that pocket is too small to hold the map. No, I'm almost positive that Andy or his father have sneakingly made a copy of this map!"

"I'm sorry to have to admit that Mr. Foger is capable of such an act," spoke Mr. Swift, "but I believe it is true."

"And here is another thing," went on the young inventor, who was now closely scanning the parchment through a powerful magnifying glass, "do you see those tiny holes here and there, Mr. Jackson?"

"Yes," answered the engineer.

"Were they there before, Abe?" went on Tom, calling the old miner's attention to them.

"Nary a one," was the answer. "It looks as if some one had been sticking pins in th' map."

"Not pins," said Tom, "but the sharp points of a pair of dividers, or compasses, for measuring distances. Andy, or whoever made a copy of the map, used the dividers to take off distances with. This clinches it, in my mind."

"But what can you do?" asked Tom's father.

"I don't know," answered the young inventor. "It would be of little use to go to Andy. Naturally he would deny having made a copy of the map, and his father would, also. Even though I am sure they have a copy, I don't see how I am going to make them give it up. It's a hard case. There's only one thing I see to do."

"What's that?" asked Abe.

"Start for Alaska as soon as possible, and be first on hand at the valley of gold."

"Good!" cried the miner. "That's the way to talk! We'll start off at once. I know my way around that country pretty well, an' even though winter is coming on, I think we can travel in th' airship. That's one reason why I wanted t' go in one of these flyin' machines. Winter is no time to be in Alaska, but if we have an airship we won't mind it, an' it's the best time t' keep other people away, for th' ordinary miner or prospector can't do anythin' in Alaska in winter—that is away up north where we're goin'."

"Exactly where are we going?" asked Tom. "I have been so excited about discovering Andy's trick that I haven't had much time to consider where we're bound for nor what will be the best plan to follow."

"Well, we're goin' to a region about seven hundred an' fifty miles northwest from Sitka," explained the old miner, as he pointed out the location on the map. "We'll head for what they call th' Snow Mountains, an' th' valley of gold is in their midst. It's just over th' Arctic circle, an' pretty cold, let me tell you!"

"You'll be warm enough in Tom's airship, with the electric stoves going," commented Mr. Jackson.

"Well, we'll need t' be," went on the miner. "Th' valley is full of caves of ice, an' it's dangerous for th' ordinary traveler. In fact an airship was the only way I saw out of th' difficulty when I was there."

"Then you have been to the valley of gold?" asked Tom.

"Well, not exactly *to* it," was the reply, "but I was where I could see it. That was in th' summer, though of course the summer there isn't like here. I'll tell you how it was."

The miner settled himself more comfortably in his chair, and resumed his story.

"It was two year ago," he said, "that me an' Jim Mace started to prospect in Alaska. We didn't have much luck, an' we kept on workin' our way farther north until we come to these Snow Mountains. Then our supplies gave out, an' if it hadn't been for some friendly Eskimos I don't know what we would have done. Jim and me we gave 'em some trinkets an' sich, and th' Indians began talkin' of a wonderful valley of gold, where th' stuff lay around in chunks on top of the ground."

"Me and Jim pricked up our ears at that, so to speak, an' we wanted to see th' place. After some delay we was taken to th' top of a big crag, some distance away from where we had been stopping with the friendly Eskimos, or Indians, as I call 'em. There, away down below, was a valley—an' a curious sort of a valley it were. It seemed filled with big bubbles—bubbles made of solid banks of snow or ice, an' we was told, me an' Jim was, that these were caves of ice, an' that th' gold was near these caves."

"Well, of course me an' my partner wanted to go down the worst way, an' try for some gold, but th' Indians wouldn't let us. They said it was dangerous, for th' ice caves were constantly fallin' in, an' smashin' whoever was inside. But to prove what they said about th' gold, they sent one of their number down, while we waited on th' side of th' mountain."

"Did he get any gold?" asked Tom, eagerly.

For answer the old miner pulled from his pocket a few yellow pebbles—little stones of dull, gleaming yellow.

"There's some of th' gold from amid th' caves of ice," he remarked simply. "I kept 'em for a souvenir, hopin' some day I might git back there. Well, Jim an' me watched th' Indian going down into th' valley. He come back in about three hours, havin' only gone to th' nearest cave, an' he had two pockets filled with these little chunks of solid gold. They gave me an' Jim some, but they wouldn't hear of us goin' t' th' valley by ourselves."

"Then a bad storm come up, an' we had t' hit th' trail for home—the Indians' home, I mean—for Jim an' I was far enough away from ours."

"Well, t' make a long story short, Jim an' me tried every way we knowed t' git t' that valley, but we couldn't. It come off colder an' colder, an' th' tribe of Indians with whom we lived was attacked by some of their enemies, an' driven away from their campin' grounds. Jim an' me, we went too, but not before Jim had drawed this map on a piece of dog-skin we found in one of the huts. We had an idea we might get back, some day, an' find the valley, so we'd need a map t' go by. But poor Jim never got back. He got badly frozen when the Indians drove us an' our friends away, an' he never got over it. He died up there in th' ice, an' we buried him. I took th' map, an' when spring come, I made a hike out of that country. From then until now I've been plannin' how t' git t' that valley, an' th' only way I seen was an airship. Then, when I was prospectin' around out in Colorado I saw Tom's machine hidden in th' trees, an' I waited until he come along, which part you know as well as I do," finished Abe.

"And that's the story of the valley of gold," spoke Mr. Swift.

"That's all there is to it," assented Abe, simply.

"Do you think there is much gold there?" asked Tom.

"Plenty of it—for th' pickin' up," replied the miner. "Around th' caves of ice it's full of it, but, of course, it's dangerous. An' th' only way t' git t' it, an' pass th' savage Indians that are all around in th' mountains about th' valley, is t' fly over their heads in th' airship."

"Then that's what we'll do," decided Tom.

"Will you go all the way in the *Red Cloud?*" inquired Mr. Jackson.

"No, I think I'll send the airship on ahead to some point in Washington—say Seattle," replied Tom, "put it together there, and start for the Snow Mountains. In Seattle we can get plenty of supplies and stores. It will be a good point to start from, and will save us a long, and perhaps dangerous, flight across the United States."

"I think that will be the best plan," agreed Mr. Swift. "But what about Andy—do you think he'll try to follow—or try to get ahead of you now that he has a copy of the map?"

"He may," answered Tom. "But I have a little trick I'm going to work on Andy. I will try to learn whether he really has a copy of the map, though I'm practically certain of it. Then I'll decide what's best to do."

"In th' meanwhile, will you be gettin' ready?" asked Abe. "I'd like t' start as soon as we can, for it's awful cold there, the longer you wait, at this time of th' year."

"Yes, I'll start right to work, getting the *Red Cloud* in readiness to be shipped," promised Tom.

ANDY'S AIRSHIP FLIES

"Hello, Tom, have you heard the news?" asked Ned Newton, of the young inventor, a few days later.

"What news, Ned? I declare I've been so busy thinking out the best plan to ship the *Red Cloud* to Seattle that I haven't been over to town. What's going on? Have they decided to build a new church in Shopton, or something like that?"

"Oh, this about Andy Foger's airship."

"Andy's airship, eh? Is he still working on it?"

"It's all done, so Sam Snedecker was telling me last night, and to-day Andy is going to try to fly it."

"You don't mean it!"

"Sure thing. Let's go over and watch him."

"He might make a fuss, same as he did when we looked in the window of his shed."

"He can't make any fuss now. He's got to take his machine out to fly it, and anybody that wants to can look on. Didn't he watch you make flights often enough?"

"That's so. Where is the trial flight going to take place?"

"In the big meadow. Come on over."

"Guess I will. I can't do much more now. I've been getting some boxes and crates made in which to pack the *Red Cloud*. I'll have to take her all apart."

"Then you're really going to hunt for the valley of gold?"

"Sure thing. How about you going, Ned? I spoke to dad about it, and he said he'd see that you could have a leave of absence."

"Yes, that part's all right. The bank president told me today I could take a vacation any time I wanted it. In fact that's what I came over to see you about. I want to thank your father."

"Then you're going?"

"I sure am, Tom! Won't it be great! I hope I can get a little gold for myself! My folks didn't take very much to the notion of me going off in an airship, but I told them how often you'd gone on trips, and come safely back, so they finally gave their consent. When are you going to start?"

"Oh, in about two weeks. Did I tell you about Andy and the map?"

"No. What trick has he been up to now?"

Thereupon Tom related his suspicions concerning the bully, and also hinted to Ned of a certain ruse he intended to work on Andy when he got the chance.

"Well, if you're ready, suppose we go over and see if Andy's airship will really fly," suggested Ned, after a while. "I'm doubtful myself, and I'd just like to see him come to grief, after the many mean things he's done to you."

"Well," spoke Tom slowly, "I don't know as I wish him any bad luck, but I certainly hope he doesn't use his airship to try to beat us out in the hunt for the valley of gold."

"Do you think he might?"

"It's possible. But never mind about that now. Come on, we'll go over to the big meadow."

The two chums walked along together, talking of many things. Tom told of some communication he had had with Mr. Damon, in which letters the eccentric man had inquired as to when the trip for Alaska would be undertaken.

"Then he's going?" asked Ned.

"Oh, yes, it wouldn't seem natural to go without some of Mr. Damon's blessings. But I think he's going to bring a friend with him."

"Who?"

"Mr. Ralph Parker."

"That gloomy scientist, who is always predicting such terrible things going to happen?"

"That's the gentleman. You met him once, I believe Mr. Damon says Mr. Parker wants to do some scientific studying in the far north, so I've already counted on him as one of our party. Well, perhaps he won't do so much predicting this trip."

A little later Tom and Ned came to a big open field. They saw quite a crowd gathered in it, but no sign of an airship.

"Guess Andy hasn't arrived," spoke Tom.

"No; very likely he's found out that something is wrong with his machine, and he isn't going to risk it."

But almost as Ned spoke, there sounded cries of excitement from the crowd, and, a little later, something big and white, with many wing-shaped stretches of canvas sticking out from all sides, was seen turning into the big meadow from the broad highway that led to Andy's house.

"There she is!" cried Ned.

"There's something, at any rate," conceded Tom, as he hastened his steps. "It's a queer-looking aeroplane, though. My! he's got enough wings to it!"

"Yes, it's Andy's sure enough," went on Ned "There he is in front, giving orders like a major-general, and Sam and Pete are helping him. Let's get closer."

They followed the crowd, which was thronging about the airship that Andy Foger had made, Tom had a glimpse of the machine. It was a form of triplane, with three tiers of main wings, and several other sets of planes, some stationary and some capable of being moved. There was no gas-bag feature, but amidships was a small, enclosed cabin, which evidently held the machinery, and was designed to afford living quarters. In some respects the airship was not unlike Tom's, and the young inventor could see that Andy had copied some of his ideas. But Tom cared little about this.

"Do you think it will go up?" asked Ned.

"It looks to me to be too heavy, and his propellers seem too small," answered Tom. "He's got to have a very powerful motor to make all that bulk fly."

The people were crowding in closer around the airship, for the news that Andy was to attempt a flight had spread about town.

"Now keep back—all of you!" ordered the bully, with a show of anger. "If any one damages my airship I'll have him arrested! Keep back, now, or I won't fly!"

"Reminds me of a little kid saying he won't play if he can't have his own way," whispered Ned to Tom.

"Hello, Andy, give us a ride!"

"Going above the clouds?"

"When are you coming back?"

"Bring down a snowstorm!"

"Be careful that you don't fall!"

These were some of the things shouted at Andy, for he had few friends among the town lads, on account of his mean ways.

"Keep quiet—all of you!" he ordered. "Get back. You might get hurt when I start the motor. I'm going to make a flight soon," he added proudly. "Sam, you come over here and hold this end. Pete, you go back to the rear. Simpson, you get inside and help me with the motor. Henderson, you get ready to shove when I tell you."

These last orders were to the two machinists whom Andy had engaged to help him, and the bully gave himself no end of airs and importance as he bustled about

Tom could not help but admit that Andy's machine was a big affair. There was a great stretch of wings and planes, several rudders other appliances for which the young inventor could not exactly fathom a use. He did not think the machine would fly far, if at all. But Andy was hurrying here and there, getting the triplane in place on a level stretch of ground, as if he intended to capture some great prize.

"Are you going to tackle him about stealing a copy of that map?" asked Ned.

"I will if I get a chance," answered Tom, in a low voice.

He got his opportunity a few minutes later. Andy, hurrying here and there, came face to face with the young inventor.

"Hello, Andy," spoke Tom, good-naturedly. "So you're going to make a flight, eh?"

"Yes, I am, and I s'pose you came around to see if you could get any ideas; didn't you?" sneered Andy.

"Of course," admitted Tom, with an easy laugh. "My airship doesn't fly, you know, Andy, and I want to see what's wrong with it."

There was a laugh in the crowd, at this, for Tom's success was well known.

"Are you going to Alaska?" suddenly asked Tom, in a low voice, of the bully.

"To Alaska? I—I don't—I don't know what you mean?" stammered Andy, as he turned aside.

"Yes, you do know what I mean," insisted Tom. "And I want to tell you that the map you have won't be of much use to you. Why, do you think," he went on, "that Abe would carry the real map around with him that way? It's easy to make a copy look like an original, Andy, and also very easy to put false distances and directions on a map that may fall into the hands of an enemy."

The shot told. Andy's face turned first red and then pale.

"A—a false map!" he stammered. "Wrong directions?"

"Yes—on the copy you made of the map you took from Mr. Abercrombie," went on Tom.

"I—I didn't make any—Oh, I'm not going to talk to you!" blustered Andy. "Get out of my way! I'm going to fly my airship."

The bully pushed past Tom, and started toward the triplane. But Tom had found out what he wanted to know. Andy had made a copy of the map. From now on there would be every danger that the bully would make an effort to get to the valley of gold.

But other matters held Andy's attention now. He wanted to try his airship. With the help of his two cronies, and the machinists, the machine was gone over, oiled up, and finally, after several false starts, the motor was set going.

It made a terrific racket, and the whole machine vibrated as though it would shake apart

"He hasn't got if well enough braced," said Tom to Ned.

"Out of the way, now, everybody!" yelled Andy. "Keep away or you'll get hurt! I'm going up!"

He climbed into the cabin of the craft, and took his position at the steering-wheel. The speed of the motor, its racket and its stream of sparks increased.

"Let go!" cried Andy to those who were holding his craft.

They released their hold. The triplane moved slowly across the ground, gathered speed, and, then, under the impulse of the powerful propellers, ran rapidly over the meadow.

"Hurrah! There he goes!" cried Sam.

"Yes! Now he's going to fly," proudly added Pete Bailey, the other crony of the bully.

"He'd better fly soon, then, or he'll be in the ditch," said Tom grimly, for a little, sluggish stream crossed the meadow not far from where Andy had started.

The next instant, thinking he had momentum enough, Andy tilted his elevation plane. The clumsy triplane rose into the air and shot forward.

"There he goes!" cried Sam.

"Hurrah!" yelled the crowd.

Andy had gone up about ten feet, and was making slow progress.

"I guess Tom Swift isn't the only one in Shopton who can build an airship!" sneered Pete Bailey.

"Look! Look!" yelled Ned. "He's coming down!"

Sure enough, Andy's machine had reached the end of her flight. The motor stopped with something between a cough and a wheeze. Down fluttered the aeroplane, like some clumsy bird, down into the ditch, settling on one side, and then coming to rest, tilted over at a sharp angle. Andy was pitched out, but landed on the soft mud, for there had been a thaw. He wasn't hurt much, evidently, for he soon scrambled to his feet as the crowd surged toward him.

"Well, he flew a little way," observed Ned, grimly.

"But he came down mighty soon," added Tom. "I thought he would. His machine is too big and clumsy. I've seen enough. Come on, Ned. We'll get ready to go to Alaska. Andy Foger will never follow us in that machine."

But Tom was soon to find out how much mistaken he was.

READY FOR THE TRIP

Andy Foger stood looking at his tilted airship. His clothes were covered with mud from the ditch, some of the muck had splashed over his face so that he was a pitiable looking object.

"What's the matter?" panted Pete Bailey.

"Are you hurt?" asked Sam Snedecker.

The two cronies had hurried to the side of the bully.

"Matter? Can't you see what's the matter?" demanded Andy wrathfully. "The machine came down, that's what's the matter! Why didn't you fellows fix the motor better?" he shouted at the two machinists as they came running up, followed by the crowd.

"Fix it better? The motor was all right," declared the taller machinist. "Any of them are likely to stop unexpectedly."

"Well, I didn't think mine would," came from Andy. "Now look at my airship! It's all busted!"

"No, it isn't hurt much," said the other man, after critically looking it over. "We can fix it, and you'll fly yet, Andy."

"I hope I do, if only to fool Tom Swift," declared the bully, as he wiped some of the mud from his face. "Come on, now, help me wheel the machine back, and I'll try it again."

Andy made another attempt, but this time the machine did not even rise off the ground, and then, amid the jeers of the crowd, the discomfited lad took his aeroplane back to the shed in the rear of his house.

"I'll fix it yet, and make a long flight," he declared. "I'll show Tom Swift he can't laugh at me!"

"You'll make a long flight eh?" asked one of the machinists. "Where will you go?"

"Never mind," answered Andy, with a knowing wink. "I've got a plan up my sleeve—my father and I are going to do something that will astonish everybody in Shopton," and then Andy, with many nods and winks, went into the shed, where he began giving orders about the airship. He wanted the motor changed, and one of the machinists made some suggestions about the planes, which, he said, would give better results.

As for Tom and Ned, they strolled away, satisfied that in Andy Foger they would not have a very dangerous rival, as far as airships were concerned.

Tom thought matters over during the next few days. He was now satisfied that Andy had a copy of the map, and, as far as he could see, there was no way of getting it from him, for he could not prove to the satisfaction of the legal authorities that the bully actually had it.

"We'll just have to take a chance, that's all," decided the young inventor in talking matters over with his father, Ned, and Abe Abercrombie. "If Andy and some of his crowd trail after us, we'll just have to run away from them and get to the valley first."

"If they do get there, they won't find it very easy traveling I reckon," remarked Abe. "They'll get all they want of the caves of ice. But hadn't we better get a hustle on ourselves, Tom?"

"Yes, we will soon start now. I have the *Red Cloud* all packed up for shipment to Seattle. We will send it on ahead, and then follow, for it will take some time to get there, even though it's going by fast freight."

"What about Mr. Damon?" asked Ned. "When is he coming?"

"There's no telling," responded Tom. "He may be on hand any minute, and, again, he may only show up just as we are starting. I haven't heard from him in the last day or two,"

At that moment there was a knock on the private office in the aeroplane shed, where Tom, Ned and Abe Abercrombie were talking.

"Who's there?" asked Tom.

"It's me," answered a voice recognizable as that of the colored man Eradicate.

"What is it, Rad?" asked Tom.

"Why I jest thought I'd tell you dat de blessin' man am comin' down de road."

"The blessing man?" repeated Tom. "Oh, you mean Mr. Damon."

"Yais, sah, dat's jest who I done mean. An' dere's anodder gen'man wif him."

"Mr. Parker, I expect," spoke Tom. "Well, tell them to come in here, Rad."

"Yais, sah. Dey's comin' up de path now, so dey is."

The next moment Tom and the others heard a voice saying:

"Why, bless my necktie! The *Red Cloud* is gone!" Mr. Damon had peered into the shed, and had not seen the airship, for Tom had it packed up. "I wonder if Tom Swift has gone away? Bless my top-knot, Mr. Parker, I hope We're not too late!"

"Indeed I hope not," added the scientist. "I wish to make a study of the caves of ice. I think perhaps they may be working south, and, in time, this part of the country may be covered deep under a frozen blanket."

"Cheerful, isn't he, Ned?" asked Tom, with a smile. Then, going to the door of the shed he called out: "Here we are, Mr. Damon. Glad to see you, Mr. Parker." This last wasn't exactly true, but Tom wanted to be polite.

"Bless my collar button, Tom! But what has become of the airship?" asked Mr. Damon, as he looked about the shed, and saw only a number of boxes and crates.

"Taken apart, and packed up, ready for the trip to the valley of gold and the caves of ice," replied the young inventor, and then he briefly told of their plans.

"Well, that's a good idea," declared the eccentric man. "Mr. Parker and I are ready to go whenever you are, Tom."

"Then we'll start very soon. I will get all our supplies in Seattle. Now, to discuss details," and, after Mr. Parker and Mr. Damon had been made acquainted with the old miner, who told his story in brief, they began a discussion of the prospective trip.

Mr. Damon and Mr. Parker took up their residence in Tom's house, and while the eccentric man busied himself in helping our hero, Ned and Abe Abercrombie in getting ready for the trip to Alaska, the gloomy scientist went about making "observations" as he called them, with a view to predicting what might happen in the near future.

He was particularly anxious to get up north, among the caves of ice, and, several times he repeated his statement that he believed the mass of ice in Alaska was working down toward the south. But no one paid much attention to him, though Tom recalled, not without a little shudder, that Mr. Parker had correctly predicted the destruction of Earthquake Island, and also the landslide on Phantom Mountain.

The airship was finally sent off, being forwarded to Seattle in sections, where it could easily be put together. The matter of Andy Foger having a duplicate map of the valley of gold was discussed, but it was agreed that nothing could be done about it. So Tom and the others devoted all their energies to getting in shape for their prospective journey.

Mr. Swift was invited to go, but declined on the ground that he had several inventions to perfect, nor could Mr. Jackson go, as he was needed to help his employer. So Tom, Ned, Mr. Damon, Mr. Parker and Abe Abercrombie made up the party. Tom arranged to send wireless messages to his father from the airship once they were started off toward the valley of gold, and over the frozen north.

One evening, when Tom had been to pay a last visit to Mary Nestor, as he was coming past the Foger premises he saw a number of large vans, loaded with big packing cases coming out of the banker's yard.

"Hum! I wonder if they're moving?" mused our hero. "If they are they're taking a queer time for it." He paused a moment to look at the procession of vans. As he did so he heard the voice of Andy Foger.

"Now, I want you men to be careful of everything!" the bully called out arrogantly. "If you break anything I'll sue you for damages!"

"Oh, that cub makes me sick!" exclaimed one of the drivers as he came opposite Tom.

"What are you moving—eggs, that you have to be so careful?" asked the young inventor, in a low voice.

"Eggs? No! But it might just as well be," was the growling answer. "He's shipping an airship, all taken to pieces, and he has nervous prostration for fear it will be broken. I don't believe the old thing's any good, anyhow."

"An airship—Andy Foger sending away his airship?" gasped Tom. "Where to?"

"Some place in Alaska," was the startling reply. "Pitka or Sitka, or some such place like that. It's all in these boxes, G'lang there!" this to his horses.

"Andy sending his airship to Alaska!" murmured Tom in dismay. "Then he surely is going to make a try for that valley of gold!"

He turned away, while the snarling voice of the bully rang out on the night, urging the drivers to be very careful of the boxes and crates on their trucks.

A THIEF IN THE NIGHT

Tom Swift hardly knew what to think. He had scarcely believed, in spite of the fact that he was sure Andy had a copy of the map, that the bully would actually make an effort to go to the valley of gold.

"And in that airship of his, too," mused Tom. "Well, there's one consolation, I don't believe he'll go far in that, though it does sail better than when he made his first attempt. Well, if he's going to try to beat us, it's a good thing I know it We can be prepared for him, now."

Tom, after watching the big vans for a few minutes, turned and kept on toward his home.

There was more than surprise on the part of Mr. Damon and the others when Tom told his news. There was alarm, for there was a feeling that Mr. Foger and his son might adopt unscrupulous tricks.

"But what can we do?" asked Mr. Swift

"Whitewash him!" exclaimed Eradicate Sampson, who had overheard part of the conversation. "Dat's what I'd do t' him an' his father, too! Dat's what I would! Fust I'd let mah mule Boomerang kick him a bit, an' den, when he was all mussed up, I'd whitewash him!" That was the colored man's favorite method of dealing with enemies, but, of course, he could not always carry it out.

However, after considering the matter from all sides, it was decided that nothing could be done for the present.

"Let them go," said Tom, "I don't believe they'll ever find the valley of gold. I fancy I threw a scare into Andy, talking as I did about the map."

"Well, even if the Fogers do get the gold," said Mr. Parker calmly, "they cannot take away the caves of ice, and it is in them that I am most interested. I want to prove some of my new theories."

"And we need the gold," said Tom, in a low voice; "don't we, Abe?"

"That's what we do, Tom," answered the old miner.

Preparations were now practically completed for their trip to Seattle by rail. Tom made some inquiries in the next few days regarding the Fogers, but only learned that the father and son had left town, after superintending the shipment of their airship.

"Well, we start to-day," remarked Tom, as he arose one morning. "In two weeks, at most, we ought to be hovering over the valley, Abe."

"I hope so? Tom. You've got the map put away safely, have you?"

"Sure thing. Are you all ready?"

"Yes."

"Then we'll start for the depot right after breakfast." The adventurers had arranged to take a local train from Shopton, and get on a fast express at one of the more important! stations.

Good-byes were said, Mr. Swift, Mr. Jackson, Mrs. Baggert and Eradicate waving their adieus from the porch as Tom and the others started for the depot. Miss Mary Nestor had bidden our hero farewell the previous night—it being a sort of second good-bye, for Tom was a frequent caller at her house, and, if the truth must be told he rather disliked to leave the young lady.

Tom found a few of his friends at the station, who had gathered there to give him and Ned *bon-voyage.*

"Bring us back some nuggets, Tom," pleaded Arthur Norton.

"Bring me a musk-ox if you can shoot one," suggested one.

"A live bear or a trained Eskimo for mine," exclaimed another.

Tom laughingly promised to do the best he could.

"I'll send you some gold nuggets by wireless," said Ned Newton.

It was almost time for the train to arrive. In the crowd on the platform Tom noticed Pete Bailey.

"He must feel lost without Andy," observed the young inventor to Ned.

"Yes, I wonder what he's hanging around here for?"

They learned a moment later, for they saw Pete going into the telegraph office.

"Must be something important for him to wire about," observed Ned.

Tom did not answer. The window of the office was slightly open, though the day was cool, and he was listening to the clicks of the telegraph instrument, as the operator sent Pete's message. Tom was familiar with the Morse code. What was his surprise to hear the message being sent to Andy Foger at a certain hotel in Chicago. And the message read:

"Tom Swift's party leaving to-day."

"What in the world does that mean?" thought Tom, but he did not tell Ned what he had picked up as it went over the wire. "Why should Andy want to be informed when we leave? That's why Pete was hanging around here! He had been instructed to let Andy know when we left for Seattle. There's something queer back of all this."

Tom was still puzzling over the matter when their train roiled in and he and the others got aboard.

"Well, we're off!" cried Ned.

"Yes; we're off," admitted Tom, and, to himself he added: "No telling what will happen before we get there, though."

The trip to Chicago was without incident, and, on arrival in the Windy City, Tom was on the lookout for Andy or his father, but he did not see them. He made private inquiries at the hotel mentioned in Pete's telegram, but learned that the Fogers had gone on.

"Perhaps I'm worrying too much," thought Tom. But an event that occurred a few nights later, when they were speeding across the continent showed him that there was need of great precaution.

On leaving Chicago, Tom had noticed, among the other passengers traveling in the same coach as themselves, a man who seemed to be closely observing each member of the party of gold-hunters. He was a man with a black mustache, a mustache so black, in fact, that Tom at once concluded that it had been dyed. This, in itself, was not much, but there was a certain air about the man—a "sporty" air—which made Tom suspicious.

"I wouldn't be surprised if that man was a gambler, Ned," he said to his chum, one afternoon, as they were speeding along. The man in question was several seats away from Tom.

"He does look like one," agreed Ned.

"I needn't advise you not to fall in with any of his invitations to play cards, I suppose," went on Tom, after a pause.

"No, indeed, it's something I don't do," answered Ned, with a laugh. "But it might be a good thing to speak to Abe Abercrombie about him. If that man's a sharper perhaps Abe knows him, or has seen him, for Abe has traveled around in the West considerable."

"We'll ask him," agreed Tom, but the miner, when his attention was called to the man, said he had never seen him before.

"He does look like a confidence man," agreed Abe, "but as long as he doesn't approach us we can't do anything, and don't need to worry."

There was little need to call the attention of either Mr. Damon or Mr. Parker to the man, for Mr. Damon was busy watching the scenery, as this trip was a new one to him, and he was continually blessing something he saw or thought of. As for Mr. Parker, he was puzzling over some new theories he had in mind, and he said little to the others.

On the night of the same day on which Tom had called special attention to the man with the black mustache, our hero went to his berth rather late. He had sent some telegrams to his father and one to Miss Nestor, and, when he turned in he saw the "gambler," as he had come to call him, going into the smoking compartment of the coach. Though Tom thought of the man as a gambler, there was no evidence, as yet, that he was one, and he had made no effort to approach any of our friends, though he had observed them closely.

How long Tom had been asleep he did not know, but he was suddenly awakened by feeling his pillow move. At first he thought it was caused by the swaying of the train, and he was about to go to sleep again, when there came a movement that he knew could not have been caused by any unevenness of the roadbed.

Then, like a flash there came to Tom's mind the thought that under his pillow, in a little leather case he had made for it, was the map, showing the location of the valley of gold.

He sat up suddenly, and made a lunge for the pillow. He felt a hand being hurriedly withdrawn. Tom made a grab for it, but the fingers slipped from his grasp.

"Here! Who are you!" cried Tom, endeavoring to peer through the darkness.

"It's all right—mistake," murmured a voice.

Tom leaned suddenly forward and parted the curtains of his berth. There was a dim light burning in the aisle of the car. By the gleam of it the young inventor caught sight of a man hurrying away, and he felt sure the fellow who had put his hand under his pillow was the man with the black mustache. He confirmed this suspicion a moment later, for the man half turned, as if to look back, and the youth saw the mustache.

"He—he was after my map!" thought Tom, with a gasp.

He sat bolt upright. What should he do? To raise an alarm now, he felt, would only bring a denial from the man if he accused him. There might also be a scene, and the man might get very indignant. Then, too, Tom and his friends did not want their object made known, as it would be in the event of Tom raising an outcry and stating what was under his pillow.

He felt for the map case, opened it and saw, in the gleam of the light, that it was safe.

"He didn't get it anyhow," murmured our hero. "I guess I won't say anything until morning, though he did come like a thief in the night to see if he could steal it."

Tom glanced to where his coat and other clothing hung in the little berth-hammock, and a hasty search showed that his money and ticket were safe.

"It was the map he was after all right," mused Tom. "I'll have a talk with Mr. Damon in the morning about what's best to do. That's why the fellow has been keeping such a close watch on us. He wanted to see who had the map."

Then another thought came to Tom.

"If it was the map he was after," he whispered to himself, "he must know what it's about Therefore the Fogers must have told him. I'll wager Andy or his father put this man up to steal the map. Andy's afraid he hasn't got a copy of the right one. This is getting more and more mysterious! We must be on our guard all the while. Well, I'll see what I'll do in the morning."

But in the morning the man with the black mustache was not aboard the train, and on inquiring of the conductor, Tom learned that the mysterious stranger had gotten off at a way station shortly after midnight.

A Vandal's Act

"Bless my penknife!" exclaimed Mr. Daman, the next morning, when he had been told of Tom's experience in the night, "things are coming to a pretty pass when our enemies adopt such tactics as this! What can we do, Tom? Hadn't you better let one of us carry the map?"

"Oh, I guess not," answered the young inventor. "They have had one try at me, and found that I wasn't napping. I don't believe they'll try again. No, I'll carry the map."

Tom concealed it in an old wallet, as he thought it was less likely to attract attention there than in the new case he formerly used. Still he did not relax his vigilance, and his sleep for the next few nights was uneasy, as he awakened several times, thinking he felt a hand under his pillow.

At length Ned suggested that one of them sit up part of the night, and keep an eye on Tom's berth. This was agreed to, and they divided the hours of darkness into watches, each one taking a turn at guarding the precious map. But they might have spared themselves the trouble, for no further attempt was made to get it.

"I'd just like to know what Andy Foger's plans are?" said Tom one afternoon, as they were within a few miles of Seattle. "He certainly must have made up his mind quickly, after he saw the map, about going in search of the gold."

"Maybe his father proposed it," suggested Ned. "I heard, in our bank, that Mr. Foger has lost considerable money lately, and he may need more."

"I shouldn't wonder. Well, if they are going to Sitka, Alaska, to assemble their ship, I think they'll have trouble, for supplies are harder to get there than in Seattle. But we'll soon be on our way ourselves, if nothing happens. I hope all the parts of the *Red Cloud* arrive safely."

They did, as Tom learned a few hours later, when they had taken up their quarters in a Seattle hotel, and he had made inquiries at the railroad office. In the freight depot were all the boxes and crates containing the parts of the big airship, and by comparison with a list he had made, the young inventor found that not a single part was missing.

"We'll soon have her together again," he said to his friends, "and then we'll start for Alaska."

"Where are you going to assemble the airship?" asked Mr. Damon.

"I've got to hire some sort of a big shed," explained Tom. "I heard of one I think I can get. It's out at the fair grounds, and was used some time ago when they had a balloon ascension here. It will be just what I need."

"How long before we can start for the gold valley?" asked the old miner anxiously.

"Oh, in about a week," answered the lad, "that is, if everything goes well."

Tom lost no time in getting to work. He had the different parts of his airship carted to the big shed which he hired. This building was on one edge of the fair grounds, and there was a large, level space which was admirably adapted for trying the big craft, when once more it was put together.

The gold-seekers worked hard, and to such good purpose that in three days most of the ship was together once more, and the *Red Cloud* looked like herself again. Tom hired a couple of machinists to aid him in assembling the motor, and some of the gas appliances and other apparatus.

"Ha! Bless my rubber shoes!" cried Mr. Damon in delight, as he looked at the big craft "This is like old times, Tom!"

"Yes, indeed," agreed our hero.

"Are you going to give it a preliminary tryout?" asked Ned.

"Oh, yes, I think we can do that to-morrow," replied Tom. "I want to know that everything is in good working shape before I trust the ship on the trip to the frozen north. There are several problems I want to work out, too, for I think I will need a different kind of gas up where the temperature is so low."

"It certainly is cold up here," agreed Ned, for they were now much farther north than when they were in Shopton, and, besides, winter was coming on. It was not the best time of the year to journey into Alaska, but they had no choice. To delay, especially now, might mean that their enemies would get ahead of them.

"We'll be warm in the airship, though; won't we?" asked Abe.

"Oh, yes," answered Tom. "We'll be warm, and have plenty to eat. Which reminds me that I must begin to see about our stock of provisions and other supplies, for we'll soon be on our way."

Work on the airship was hastened to such good advantage the next two days that it was in shape for a trial flight, and, one afternoon, the *Red Cloud* was wheeled from the shed out into big field, the gas was generated, and the motor started.

There was a little hitch, due to the fact that some of the machine adjustments were wrong, but Tom soon had that remedied and then, with the big propellers whirling around, the airship was sent scudding across the field.

Another moment and it rose like a great eagle, and sailed through the air, while a small crowd that had daily gathered in the hope of seeing a flight, sent up a cheer.

"Does it work all right?" asked Ned anxiously, as he stood in the pilothouse beside his chum.

"As good as it did in Shopton," answered the young inventor, proudly.

"Bless my pocketbook! but that's lucky," exclaimed Mr. Damon. "Then we can soon start, eh?"

"As soon as we are stocked up," replied the lad.

Tom put the airship through a number of "stunts" to test her stability and the rudder control, much to the delight of the gathering throng. Everything was found to work well, and after ascending to a considerable height, to the no small alarm of the old miner, Tom made a quick descent, with the motor shut off. The *Red Cloud* conducted herself perfectly, and there was nothing else to be desired.

She was sent down to earth and wheeled back into the shed, and not without some difficulty, for the crowd, which was now very large, wanted to get near enough to touch the wonderful craft.

"To-morrow I'll arrange about the supplies and provisions, and we'll stock her up," said Tom to his companions. "Now you folks had better go back to the hotel."

"Aren't you coming?" asked Ned.

I'm going to bunk here in the shed to-night, said the young inventor.

"What for?"

"I can't take any chances now that the *Red Cloud* is in shape for flying. Some of the Foger crowd might be hanging around, and break in here to damage her."

"But the watchman will be on guard," suggested Ned, for since the hiring of the shed, the young inventor had engaged a man to remain on duty all night.

"I know," answered Tom Swift, "but I'm not going to take any chances. I'll stay here with the watchman."

Ned offered to share the vigil with his chum, and, after some objection Tom consented. The others went back to the hotel, promising to return early in the morning.

Tom slept heavily that night, much heavier than he was in the habit of doing. So did Ned, and their deep breathing as they lay in their staterooms, in the cabin of the airship, told of physical weariness, for they had worked hard to re-assemble the *Red Cloud*.

The watchman was seated in a chair just inside the big door of the shed, near a small stove in which was a fire to take off the chill of the big place. The guard had slept all day, and there was no excuse for him nodding in the way that he did.

"Queer, how drowsy I feel," he murmured several times. "It's only a little after midnight, too," he added, looking at his watch, "Guess I'll walk around a bit to rouse myself."

He firmly intended to do this, but he thought he would wait just a few minutes more, and he stretched out his legs and got comfortable in the chair.

Three minutes more and the watchman was asleep—sound asleep, while a strange, sweet, sickish odor seemed to fill the atmosphere about him.

There was a noise at the door of the shed, a door in which there were several cracks. A man outside laid aside something that looked like an air pump. He applied one eye to a crack, and looked in on the sleeping watchman.

"He's off," the man murmured. "I thought he'd never get to sleep! Now to get in and dose those two lads! Then I'll have the place to myself!"

There was a clicking noise about the lock on the shed door. It was not a very secure lock at best, and, under the skilful fingers of the midnight visitor, it quickly gave way. The man entered. He gave one look at the slumbering watchman, listened to his heavy breathing, and then went softly toward the airship, which looked to be immense in the comparatively small shed—taking up nearly all the space.

The intruder peered in through the cabin windows where Ned and Tom were asleep. Once more there was in the atmosphere a sickish odor. The man again worked the instrument which was like a small air pump, taking care not to get his own face too near it. Presently he stopped and listened.

"They're doped," he murmured. He arose, and took from his mouth and nose a handkerchief saturated with some chemical that had rendered him immune to the effects of the sleep-producing that he had generated. "Sound asleep," he added. Then, taking out a long, keen knife, the vandal stole toward where the great wings of the *Red Cloud* stretched out in the dim light like the pinions of a bird. There was a ripping, tearing, rending sound, as the vandal cut and slashed, but Tom, Ned and the watchman slumbered on.

Tom Is Held up

Tom Swift stirred uneasily in his heavy sleep. He dreamed that he was again in his berth in the railroad car, and that the thief was feeling under his pillow for the map. Only, this time, there seemed to be hands feeling about his clothing, trying to locate his inner pockets.

The lad murmured something unintelligible, but he did not awaken. The fumes prevented that. However, his movements showed that the effect of the drug was wearing off. It was intended only for temporary use, and it lasted less time than it would otherwise have done in a warmer, moister climate, for the cold, crisp air that penetrated the shed from outside dispelled the fumes.

"Guess I'd better not chance it," murmured the intruder. "He may not have it on him. and if I go through all his pockets I'll wake him up. Anyhow, I've done what they paid me for. I don't believe they'll sail in this airship."

The vandal gave one glance at the sleeping lads, and stole from the cabin of the craft. He looked at his work of ruin, and then tiptoed past the slumbering watchman. A moment later and he was outside the shed, hurrying away through the night.

Several hours after this Mr. Damon and the old miner were pounding on the door of the shed. Mr. Parker, the scientist, had remained at the hotel, for he said he wanted to work out a few calculations regarding some of his theories.

"I thought we'd find them up by this time," spoke the eccentric man, as he again knocked on the door. "Tom said he had lots to do to-day."

"Maybe they are working inside, and can't hear our knocks," suggested Abe. "Try th' door."

"Bless my heart! I never thought of that," exclaimed Mr. Damon. "I believe I will."

The door swung open as he pushed it, for it had not been locked when the intruder left. The first thing Mr. Damon saw was the watchman, still asleep in his chair.

"Bless my soul!" the old man shouted. "Look at this, Abe!"

"Something's wrong!" cried the miner, sniffing the air. "There's been crooked work here! Where are the boys?"

Mr. Damon was close to the airship. He looked in the cabin window.

"Here they are, and they're both asleep, too!" he called. "And— bless my eyeglasses! Look at the airship! The planes and wings are all cut and slashed! Something has happened! The *Red Cloud* is all but ruined!"

Abe hastened to his side. He looked at the damage done, and a fierce look came over his face.

"The Fogers again!" he murmured. "We'll pay 'em back for this! But first we must see to the boys!"

They needed small attention, however. The opening of the big door had let in a flood of fresh air, and this dispelled the last of the fumes. The watchman was the first to revive. The sleep caused by the chemical, sprayed from the air-pump by the vandal, had been succeeded by a natural slumber, and this was the case with Ned and Tom. They were soon aroused, and looked with wonder, not unmixed with rage, at the work done in the night.

Every one of the principal planes of the airship, each of the rudders, and some of the auxiliary wings had been cut by a sharp knife—some in several places. The canvas hung in shreds and patches, and the trim *Red Cloud* looked like some old tramp airship now. Tom could scarcely repress a groan.

"Who did it?" he gasped.

"And with us here on guard!" added Ned.

"I—I must have fallen asleep," admitted the watchman in confusion.

"You were all asleep," said Mr. Damon. "I couldn't rouse you!"

"And there was th' smell of chloroform, or something like it in th' shed," added the miner.

"But look at the airship!" groaned Tom.

"Is it ruined—can't we go to the valley of gold?" asked Ned.

Tom did not answer for a few minutes. He was walking around looking at his damaged craft. The sleepy feeling was rapidly leaving him, as well as Ned and the watchman.

"Bless my watch chain!" exclaimed Mr. Damon. "What an ugly, mean piece of work. Can you repair it, Tom?"

"I think so," was the hesitating answer. "It is not as bad as I feared at first. Luckily the gas-bag has not been touched, for, if it had, we could hardly have repaired it. I can fix the wings and the rudders. The propellers have not been damaged, nor has the motor been touched. I think they must have made another attempt to take the map off me," he went on, as he looked at several pockets that had been turned inside out.

An examination of the door showed how the lock had been forced, and the adventurers could easily guess the rest. But who the midnight vandal was they could not tell, though Tom and the others were sure it was some one hired by the Fogers.

"They wanted to delay us," said Tom. "They thought this would hold us back, but it won't—for long. We'll get right to work, and make new planes and rudders. Fortunately the framework isn't hurt any."

Once Tom got into action nothing held him back. He hardly wanted to stop for meals. New canvas was ordered, and that very afternoon some of the damaged wings had been repaired. In the meanwhile the stores and provisions that had been ordered were arriving, and, under the direction of the miner and Mr. Damon were put in the *Red Cloud*. Tom and Ned, with the help of a man they hired, worked diligently to replace the damaged planes and rudders. Mr. Parker came out to the airship shed, but he was of little use as a helper, for he was continually stopping to jot down some memoranda about an observation he thought of, or else he would lay aside his tools to go outside, look at the weather, and make predictions.

But Tom and the others labored to such good advantage that in three days they had repaired most of the damage done. Luckily the vandal had cut and slashed in a hurry, and his malicious work was only half accomplished. There was no clue to his identity.

No trace was seen of the Fogers, and Tom hardly expected it, for he thought they were in Sitka by this time. Nor were any suspicious persons seen hanging around the shed. The adventurers left their rooms at the hotel, and took up their quarters in the airship that would soon be their home for many days. They wanted to be where they could watch the craft, and two guards were engaged.

"We'll start to-morrow," Tom announced gaily one evening when, after a hard day's work the last of the damaged planes had been repaired.

"Start fer th' valley of gold?" asked the miner.

"Yes. Everything is in good shape now. I want to go into town, to send some messages home, telling dad we'll soon be on our way, and I also want to get a few things."

"Shall I come?" asked Ned.

"No, I'd rather you'd stay here," spoke Tom, in a low voice. "We can't take any more chances of being delayed, and, as it's pretty well known that we'll sail to-morrow, the Foger crowd may try some more of their tricks. No, I'll go to town alone, Ned. I'll soon be back, however. You stay here."

Both Tom came nearly never coming back. As he was returning from sending the messages, and purchasing a few things he needed for the trip, he passed through a dark street. He was walking along, thinking of what the future might hold for him and his companions, after they reached the caves of ice, when, just as he got to a high board fence, surrounding some vacant lots, he heard some one whisper hoarsely:

"Here he comes!"

The young inventor was on his guard instantly. He jumped back to avoid a moving shadow, but was too late. Something struck him on the back of his head, and he felt his senses leaving him. He struggled against the feeling, and he realized, even in that exciting moment, that the thick collar of his heavy overcoat, which he had turned up because of a cold wind, had, perhaps, saved him from a broken skull.

"Hold him!" commanded another voice. "I'll go through him!"

The packages dropped from Tom's nerveless fingers. He felt himself sinking down, in spite of his fierce determination not to succumb. He felt several hands moving rapidly about his body, and then he struck blindly out at the footpads.

OFF FOR THE FROZEN NORTH

Tom Swift felt as if he was struggling in some dream or nightmare. He felt strong hands holding him and saw evil faces leering at him.

Then gradually his brain cleared. His muscles, that had been weakened by the cowardly blow, grew strong. He felt his fist land heavily on some one's face. He heard a smothered gasp of pain.

Then came the sound of footsteps running—Tom heard the "ping" of a policeman's night-stick on the sidewalk.

"Here come the cops!" he heard one voice exclaim.

"Did you get it?" asked another.

"No, I can't find it. Cut for it now!"

They released the young inventor so suddenly that he staggered about and almost fell.

The next moment Tom was looking into the face of a big policeman, who was half supporting him.

"What's the matter?" asked the officer.

"Hold-up, I guess," mumbled the lad. "There they go!" he pointed toward two dark forms slipping along down the dimly-lighted street.

The officer drew his revolver, and fired two shots in the air, but the fleeing figures did not stop.

"How did it happen?" asked the policeman. "Did they get anything from you?"

"No—I guess not," answered Tom. He saw the packages containing his purchases lying where they had fallen. A touch told him his watch and pocketbook were safe. The precious map was in a belt about his waist, and that had not been removed. "No, they didn't get anything," he assured the officer.

"I came along too quick for 'em, I guess," spoke the bluecoat. "This is a bad neighborhood. There have been several hold-ups here of late, but I was on the job too soon for these fellows. Hello, Mike," as another officer came running up in answer to the shots and the raps of the night-stick. "Couple of strong-arm-men tackled this young fellow just now. I saw something going on as I turned the corner, and I rapped and ran up. They went down that way. I fired at 'em. You take after 'em, Mike, and I'll stay here. Don't believe you can land 'em, but try! I came up too quick to allow 'em to get anything, though."

Tom did not contradict this. He knew, however, that, had the men who attacked him wished to take his watch or money, they could have done it several times before the officer arrived.

"It was the map they were after," thought Tom, "not my watch or money. This is more of the Foger's work. We must get away from here."

The policeman inquired for more particulars from Tom, who related how the hold-up had taken place. The young inventor, however, said nothing about the map he carried, letting the officer think it was an ordinary attempt at robbery, for Tom did not want any reference in the newspapers to his search for the valley of gold.

Presently the other policeman returned, having been unable to get any trace of the daring men. The two bluecoats wanted to accompany Tom back to the airship shed, for his own safety, but he declared there was no more danger, and, after having given his name, so that the affair might be reported at headquarters, he was allowed to go on his way. His head ached from the blow, but otherwise he was unhurt.

"Those fellows have been keeping watch for me," the lad reasoned, as he walked quickly toward the airship shed. "They must have been shadowing me, and they hid there until I came back. Andy Foger and his father must be getting desperate. I think I know why, too. That little dig I gave Andy about his map is bearing fruit. He begins to think it's the wrong map, and he wants to get hold of the right one. Well, they shan't if I can help it. We'll be away from here in the morning."

There was indignation and some alarm among Tom's friends when he told his story a little later that night.

"Bless my walking-stick!" cried Mr. Damon. "You'll need a bodyguard after this."

"I'd just like t' git my hands on them fellers!" exclaimed the old miner. "I'd show 'em!" and a look at his rugged frame and his muscular arms and gnarled hands showed Tom and Ned that in the event of a fight they could count much on Abe Abercrombie.

"I am glad there will be no more delays, and that we will soon be moving northward," spoke Mr. Parker, a little later. "I am anxious to confirm my theory about the advance of the ice crust, I met a man to-day who had just returned from the north of Alaska. He said that a severe winter had already set in up there. So I am anxious to get to the ice caves."

"So am I," added Tom, but it was for a different reason.

They were all up early the next morning, for there were several things to look after before they started on the trip that might bring much of danger to the adventurers. Under Tom's direction, more gas was generated, and forced into the big bag. A last adjustment was made of the planes, wing tips and rudders, and the motor was given a try-out.

"I guess everything is all right," announced the young inventor. "We'll take her out."

The *Red Cloud* was wheeled from the big shed, and placed on the open lot, where she would have room to rush across the ground to acquire momentum enough to rise in the air. Tom, whenever it was practical, always mounted this way, rather than by means of the lifting gas, as, in the event of a wind, he would have better control of the ship, while it was ascending into the upper currents of air, than when it was rising like a balloon.

"All aboard!" cried the lad, as he looked to see that the course was clear. Early as it was, there was quite a crowd on hand to witness the flight, as there had been every day of late, for the population of Seattle was curious regarding the big craft of the air.

"Let her go!" cried Ned Newton, enthusiastically.

Tom took his place in the steering-tower, or pilothouse, which was forward of the main cabin. Ned was in the engine-room, ready to give any assistance if needed. Mr. Damon, Mr. Parker and Abe Abercrombie were in the main cabin, looking out of the windows at the rapidly increasing throng.

"Here we go!" cried the young inventor, as he pulled the lever starting the motor, There was a buzz and a hum. The powerful propellers whirred around like blurs of light. Forward shot the great airship over the ground, gathering speed at every revolution of the blades.

Tom tilted the forward rudder to lift the ship. Suddenly it shot over the heads of the crowd. There was a cheer and some applause.

"Off for the frozen north!" cried Ned, waving his cap.

Tom shifted the rudder, to change the course of the airship. Mr. Damon was gazing on the crowd below.

"Tom! Tom!" he cried suddenly. "There's the man with the black mustache—the man who tried to rob you in the sleeping-car!" He pointed downward to some one in the throng.

"He can't get us now!" exclaimed Tom, as he increased the speed of the *Red Cloud*, and then, taking up a telescope, after setting the automatic steering gear, Tom pointed the glass at the person whom Mr. Damon had indicated.

PELTED BY HAILSTONES

"Yes, that's the man all right," observed the lad. "But if he came here to have another try for the map, he's too late. I hope we don't land now until we are in the valley of gold." Tom passed the telescope to Ned, who confirmed the identification.

"Perhaps he came to see if we started, and then he'll report to Andy Foger or his father by telegraph," suggested Mr. Damon.

"Perhaps," admitted Tom. "Anyhow, we're well rid of our enemies—at least for a time. They can't follow us up in the air." He turned another lever and the *Red Cloud* shot forward at increased speed.

"Maybe Andy will race us," suggested Ned.

"I'm not afraid of anything his airship can do," declared Tom. "I don't believe it will even get up off the ground, though he did make a short flight before he packed up to follow us. It's a wonder he wouldn't think of something himself, instead of trying to pattern after some one else. He tried to beat me in building a speeding automobile, and now he wants to get ahead of me in an airship. Well, let him try. I'll beat him out, just as I've done before."

They were now over the outskirts of Seattle, flying along about a thousand feet high, and they could dimly make out curious crowds gazing up at them. The throng that had been around the airship shed had disappeared from view behind a little hill, and, of course, the man with the black mustache was no longer visible, but Tom felt as if his sinister eyes were still gazing upward, seeking to discern the occupants of the airship.

"We're well on our way now," observed Ned, after a while, during which interval he and Tom had inspected the machinery, and found it working satisfactorily.

"Yes, and the *Red Cloud* is doing better than she ever did before," said Tom. "I think it did her good to take her apart and put her together again. It sort of freshened her up. This machine is my special pride. I hope nothing happens to her on this journey to the caves of ice."

"If my theory is borne out, we will have to be careful not to get caught in the crush of ice, as it makes its way toward the south," spoke Mr. Parker with an air as if he almost wished such a thing to happen, that he might be vindicated.

"Oh, we'll take good care that the *Red Cloud* isn't nipped between two bergs," Tom declared.

But he little knew of the dire fate that was to overtake the *Red Cloud*, and how close a call they were to have for their very lives.

"No matter what care you exercise, you cannot overcome the awful power of the grinding ice," declared the gloomy scientist. "I predict that we will see most wonderful and terrifying sights."

"Bless my hatband!" cried Mr. Damon, "don't say such dreadful things, Parker my dear man! Be more cheerful; can't you?"

"Science cannot be cheerful when foretelling events of a dire nature," was the response. "I would not do my duty if I did not hold to my theories."

"Well, just hold to them a little more closely," suggested Mr. Damon. "Don't tell them to us so often, and have them get on our nerves, Parker, my dear man. Bless my nail-file! be more cheerful. And that reminds me, when are we going to have dinner, Tom?"

"Whenever you want it, Mr. Damon. Are you going to act as cook again?"

"I think I will, and I'll just go to the galley now, and see about getting a meal. It will take my mind off the dreadful things Mr. Parker says."

But if the gloomy scientific man heard this little "dig" he did not respond to it. He was busy jotting down figures on a piece of paper, multiplying and dividing them to get at some result in a complicated problem he was working on, regarding the power of an iceberg in proportion to its size, to exert a lateral pressure when sliding down a grade of fifteen per cent.

Mr. Damon got an early dinner, as they had breakfasted almost at dawn that morning, in order to get a good start. The meal was much enjoyed, and to Abe Abercrombie was quite a novelty, for he had never before partaken of food so high up in the air, the barograph of the *Red Cloud* showing an elevation of a little over twelve thousand feet.

"It's certainly great," the old miner observed, as he looked down toward the earth below them, stretched out like some great relief map. "It sure is wonderful an' some scrumptious! I never thought I'd be ridin' one of these critters. But they're th' only thing t' git t' this hidden valley with. We might prospect around for a year, and be driven back by the Indians and Eskimos a dozen times. But with this we can go over their heads, and get all the gold we want."

"Is there enough to give every one all he wants?" asked Tom, with a quizzical smile. "I don't know that I ever had enough."

"Me either," added Ned Newton.

"Oh, there's lots of gold there," declared the old miner. "The thing to do is to get it and we can sure do that now."

The remainder of the day passed uneventfully, though Tom cast anxious looks at the weather as night set in, and Ned, noting his chum's uneasiness, asked:

"Worrying about anything, Tom?"

"Yes, I am," was the reply. "I think we're in for a hard storm, and I don't know just how the airship will behave up in these northern regions. It's getting much colder, and the gas in the bag is condensing more than I thought it would. I will have to increase our speed to keep us moving along at this elevation."

The motor was adjusted to give more power, and, having set it so that it, as well as the rudders, would be controlled automatically, Tom rejoined his companions in the main cabin, where, as night settled down, they gathered to eat the evening meal.

Through the night the great airship plowed her way. At times Tom arose to look at some of the recording instruments. It was growing colder, and this further reduced the volume of the gas, but as the speed of the ship was sufficient to send her along, sustained by the planes and wings alone, if necessary, the young inventor did not worry much.

Morning broke gray and cheerless. A few flakes of snow fell. There was every indication of a heavy storm. They were high above a desolate and wild country now, hovering over a sparsely settled region where they could see great forests, stretches of snow-covered rocks, and towering mountain crags.

The snow, which had been lazily falling, suddenly ceased. Tom looked out in surprise. A moment later there came a sound as if some giant fingers were beating a tattoo on the roof of the main cabin.

"What's that!" cried Ned.

"Bless my umbrella! has anything happened?" demanded Mr. Damon.

"It's a hail storm!" exclaimed Tom. "We've run into a big hail storm. Look at those frozen stones! They're as big as hens' eggs!"

On a little platform in front of the steering-house could be seen falling immense hailstones. They played a tattoo on the wooden planks.

"A hail storm! Bless my overshoes!" cried Mr. Damon.

"A hail storm!" echoed Mr. Parker. "I expected we would have one. The hailstones will become even larger than this!"

"Cheerful," remarked Tom in a low voice, with an apprehensive look at Ned.

"Is there any danger?" asked his chum.

"Danger? Plenty of it," replied the young inventor. "The frozen particles may rip open the gas bag. "He stopped suddenly and looked at a gage on the wall of the steering-tower—a gage that showed the gas pressure.

"One compartment of the bag has been ripped open!" cried Tom. "The vapor is escaping! The whole bag may soon be torn apart!"

The noise of the pelting hailstones increased. The roar of the storm, the bombardment of the icy globules, and the moaning of the wind struck terror to the hearts of the gold-seekers.

"What's to be done?" yelled Ned.

"We must go up, to get above the storm, or else descend and find some shelter!" answered Tom. "I'll first see if I can send the ship up above the clouds!"

He increased the speed of the motor so that the propellers would aid in taking the ship higher up, while the gas-generating machine was set in operation to pour the lifting vapor into the big bag.

A Frightened Indian

The violence of the hail storm, the clatter of the frozen pellets as they bombarded the airship, the rolling, swaying motion of the craft as Tom endeavored to send it aloft, all combined to throw the passengers of the *Red Cloud* into a state of panic.

"Bless my very existence!" cried Mr. Damon, "this is almost as bad as when we were caught in the hurricane at Earthquake Island!"

"I am sure that this storm is but the forerunner of some dire calamity!" declared Mr. Parker.

"I'm afraid it's all up with us," came from Abe Abercrombie, as he looked about for some way of escape.

"Do you think you can pull us through, Tom?" asked Ned Newton, who, not having had much experience in airships had yet to learn Tom's skill in manipulating them.

The young inventor alone seemed to keep his nerve. Coolly and calmly he stood at his post of duty, shifting the wing planes from moment to moment, managing the elevation rudder, and, at the same time, keeping his eye on the registering dial of the gas-generating machine.

"It's all right," said Tom, more easily than he felt. "We are going up slowly. You might see if you can induce the gas machine to do any better, Mr. Damon. We are wasting some of the vapor because of the leak in the bag, but we can manufacture it faster than it escapes, so I guess we'll be all right."

"Mr. Parker, may I ask you to oil the main motor? You will see the places marked where the oil is to go in. Ned, you help him. Here, Abe, come over here and give me a hand. This wind makes the rudders hard to twist."

The young inventor could not have chosen a better method of relieving the fears of his friends than by giving them something to do to take their minds off their own troubles. They hurried to the tasks he had assigned to them, and, in a few minutes, there were no more doubts expressed.

Not that the *Red Cloud* was out of danger, Far from it. The storm was increasing in violence, and the hailstones seemed to double in number. Then, too, being forced upward as she was, the airship's bag was pelted all the harder, for the speed of the craft, added to the velocity of the falling chunks of hail, made them strike on the surface of the ship with greater violence.

Tom was anxiously watching the barograph, to note their height. The *Red Cloud* was now about two and a half miles high, and slowly mounting upward. The gas machine was working to its fullest capacity, and the fact that they did not rise more quickly told Tom, more plainly than words could have done, that there were several additional leaks in the gas-bag.

"I'll take her up another thousand feet," he announced grimly. "Then, if we're not above the storm it will be useless to go higher."

"Why?" asked Ned, who had come back to stand beside his chum.

"Because we can't possibly get above the storm without tearing the ship to pieces. I had rather descend."

"But won't that be just as bad?"

"Not necessarily. There are often storms in the upper regions which do not get down to the surface of the earth, snow and hail storms particularly. Hail, you know, is supposed to be formed by drops of rain being hurled up and down in a sort of circular, spiral motion through alternate strata of air—first freezing and then warm, which accounts for the onion-like layers seen when a hailstone is cut in half."

"That is right," broke in Mr. Parker, who was listening to the young inventor. "By going down this hail storm may change into a harmless rain storm. But, in spite of that fact, we are in a dangerous climate, where we must expect all sorts of queer happenings."

"Nice, comfortable sort of a companion to have along on a gold-hunting expedition, isn't He?" asked Tom of Ned, making a wry face as Mr. Parker moved away. "But I haven't any time to think of that. Say, this is getting fierce!"

Well might he say so. The wind had further increased in violence, and while the storm of hailstones seemed to be about the same, the missiles had nearly doubled in size.

"Better go down," advised Ned. "We may fall if you don't."

"Guess I will," assented Tom. "There's no use going higher. I doubt if I could, anyhow, with all this wind pressure, and with the gas-bag leaking. Down she is!"

As he spoke he shifted the levers, and changed the valve wheels. In an instant the *Red Cloud* began to shoot toward the earth.

"What's happened? What in th' name of Bloody Gulch are we up ag'in'?" demanded the old miner, springing to his feet.

"We're going down—that's all," answered Tom, calmly, but he was far from feeling that way, and he had grave fears for the safety of himself and his companions.

Down, down, down went the *Red Cloud*, in the midst of the hail storm. But if the gold-seekers had hoped to escape the pelting of the frozen globules they were mistaken. The stones still seemed to increase in size and number. The gas machine register showed a sudden lack of pressure, not due to the shutting off of the apparatus.

"Look!" cried Ned, pointing to the dial.

"Yes—more punctures," said Tom, grimly.

"What's to be done?" asked Mr. Damon, who had finished the task Tom allotted to him. "Bless my handkerchief! what's to be done?"

"Seek shelter if the storm doesn't stop when we get to the earth level," answered Tom.

"Shelter? What sort of shelter? There are no airship sheds in this desolate region."

"I may be able to send the ship under some overhanging mountain crag," answered the young inventor, "and that will keep off the hailstones."

Eagerly Tom and Ned, who stood together in the pilothouse peered forward through the storm.

The wind was less violent now that they were in the lower currents of air, but the hail had not ceased.

Suddenly Tom gave a cry. Ned looked at him anxiously. Had some new calamity befallen them? But Tom's voice sounded more in relief than in alarm. The next instant he called:

"Look ahead there, Ned, and tell me what you see."

"I see something big and black," answered the other lad, after a moment's hesitation. "Why, it's a big black hole!" he added.

"That's what I made it out to be," went on Tom, "but I wanted to be sure. It's the opening to a cave or hole in the side of the mountain. I take it."

"You're right," agreed Ned.

"Then we're safe," declared Tom.

"Safe? How?"

"I'm going to take the *Red Cloud* in there out of the storm."

"Can you do it? Is the opening big enough?"

"Plenty. It's larger than my shed at home, Jove! but I'm glad I saw that in time, or there would have been nothing left of the gas-bag!"

With skilful hands Tom turned the rudders and sent the airship down on a slant toward the earth, aiming for the entrance to the cave, which loomed up in the storm. When the craft was low enough down so that the superstructure would not scrape the top of the cave, Tom sent her ahead on the level. But he need have had no fears, for the hole was large enough to have admitted a craft twice the size of the *Red Cloud*.

A few minutes later the airship slid inside the great cavern, as easily as if coming to rest in the yard of Tom's house. The roof of the cave was high over their heads, and they were safe from the storm. The cessation from the deafening sound of the pelting hailstones seemed curious to them at first.

"Well, bless my shoelaces! if this isn't luck!" cried Mr. Damon, as he opened the door of the cabin, and looked about the cave in which they now found themselves. It was comparatively light, for the entrance was very large, though the rear of the cavern was in gloom.

"Yes, indeed, we got to it just in time,'" agreed Tom. "Now let's see what sort of a place it is. We'll have to explore it."

"There may be a landslide, or the roof may come down on our heads," objected Mr. Parker.

"Oh, my dear Parker! please be a little more cheerful," begged Mr. Damon.

The adventurers followed Tom from the airship, and all but the young inventor gazed curiously at the interior of the cave. His first thought was for his airship. He glanced up at the gas-bag, and noted several bad rents in it.

"I hope we can fix them," Tom thought dubiously.

But the attention of all was suddenly arrested by something that occurred just then. From the dark recess of the cavern there sounded a fearful yell or scream. It was echoed back a thousand-fold by the rocky walls of the cave, Then there dashed past the little group of gold-seekers a dark figure.

"Look out! It's a bear!" shouted Mr. Damon. "A bear! It's an Eskimo Indian!" yelled Abe Abercrombie, "an' he's skeered nigh t' death! Look at him run!"

As they gazed toward the lighted entrance of the cave they saw leaping and running from it an Indian who quickly scudded out into the hail storm.

"An Indian," exclaimed Tom. "An Indian in the cave! If there's one, there may be more. I guess we'd better look to our guns. They may attack us!" and he hurried back into the airship, followed by Ned and the others.

THE RIVAL AIRSHIP

Well armed, the adventurers again ventured out into the cave. But they need not have been alarmed so soon, for there were no signs of any more Indians.

"I guess that one was a stray Eskimo who took shelter in here from the storm," said Abe Abercrombie.

"Are we in the neighborhood of the Alaskan Indians and Eskimos?" inquired Ned.

"Yes, there are lots of Indians in this region," answered the old miner, "but not so many Eskimos. A few come down from th' north, but we'll see more of them, an' fewer of th' pure-blooded Indians as we get nearer th' valley of gold. Though t' my mind th' Indians an' Eskimos are pretty much alike,"

"Well, if we don't have to defend ourselves from an attack of Indians, suppose we look over the airship," proposed Tom.

"It's too dark to see very much," objected Ned. But this was overcome when Tom started up a dynamo, and brought out a portable search-light which was played upon the superstructure of the *Red Cloud*. The gas-bag was the only part of the craft they feared for, as the hailstones could not damage the iron or wooden structure and the planes were made in sections, and in such a manner that rents in them could easily be repaired. So, in fact, could the gas-bag be mended, but it was harder work.

"Well, she's got some bad tears in her," announced Tom as the light flashed over the big bag. "Luckily I have plenty of the material, and some cement, so I think we can mend the rents, though it will take some days. Nothing could have been better for us than this cave. We'll stay here until we're ready to go on."

"Unless the Indians drive us out," said Abe, in a low tone.

"Why, do you think there is any danger of that?" inquired Tom.

"Well, th' brown-skinned beggars aren't any too friendly," responded the old miner. "Th' one that was in here will be sure to tell th' others of some big spirit that flew into th' cave, an' they'll be crowdin' around here when th' storm's over. It may be we can fight 'em off, though."

"Maybe they won't attack us," suggested Ned, hopefully. "Perhaps we can make them believe we are spirits, and that it will be unlucky to interfere with us."

"Perhaps," admitted Abe, "though my experience has been that these Indians are a bad lot. They haven't much respect for spirits of any kind, an' they'll soon find out we're human. But then, we'll wait an' see what happens."

"And, in the meantime, have something to eat," put in Mr. Damon. "Bless my knife and fork! but the hail storm gave me an appetite."

In fact, there were few things which did not give Mr. Damon an appetite, Tom thought with a smile. But the meal idea was considered very timely, and soon the amateur cook was busy in the galley of the airship, whence speedily came savory odors. The electric lights were switched on, and the adventurers were quickly made comfortable in the cave, which so well sheltered the *Red Cloud*. Tom completed his inspection of the craft, and was relieved to find that while there were a number of small rents, none was very large, and all could be mended in time.

Abe Abercrombie took a look outside the cave after the meal had been served. The old miner declared that they had made a good advance on their northern journey for, though he could not tell their exact location, he knew by the character of the landscape that they had passed the boundaries of Alaska.

"A few more days' traveling at the rate we came will bring us to the Snow Mountains and the valley of gold," he said.

"Well, we won't average such speed as we did during the hail storm," said Tom. "The wind of that carried us along at a terrific pace. But we will get there in plenty of time, I think,"

"Why; is there any particular rush?" asked Ned.

"There's no telling when the Fogers may appear," answered the young inventor in a low voice. "But now we must get to work to repair damage."

The hail storm had ceased, and, with the passing of the clouds the cave was made lighter. But Tom did not depend on this, for he set up powerful searchlights, by the gleams of which he and his companions began the repairing of the torn gas-bag.

They worked all the remainder of that day, and were at it again early the next morning, making good progress.

"We can go forward again, in about two days," spoke Tom. "I want to give the cement on the patches plenty of chance to dry."

"Then I will have time to go out and make some observations, will I not?" asked Mr. Parker. "I think this cave is a very old one, and I may be able to find some evidences in it that the sea of ice is slowly working its way down from the polar regions."

"I hope you don't," whispered Ned to Tom, who shook his head dubiously as the gloomy scientist left the cave.

The weather was very cold, but, in the cavern it was hardly noticed. The adventurers were warmly dressed, and when they did get chilly from working over the airship, they had but to go into the well-heated and cozy cabin to warm themselves.

It was on the third day of their habitation in the cave, and work on putting the patches on the gas-bag was almost finished. Mr. Parker had gone out to make further observations, his previous ones not having satisfied him. Tom was on an improvised platform, putting a patch on top of the bag, when he heard a sudden yell, and some one dashed into the cavern.

"They're coming! They're coming!" cried a voice, and Tom, looking down, saw Mr. Parker, apparently in a state of great fear.

"What's coming?" demanded the young inventor, "the icebergs?"

"No—the Indians!" yelled the scientist. "A whole tribe of them is rushing this way!"

"I thought so!" cried Abe Abercrombie. "Where's my gun?" and he dashed into the airship.

Tom slid down off the platform.

"Get ready for a fight!" he gasped. "Where are you, Ned?"

"Here I am. We'd better get to the mouth of the cave, and drive 'em back from there."

"Yes. If I'd only thought, we could have blockaded it in some way. It's as big as a barn now, and they can rush us if they have a mind to. But we'll do our best!"

The adventurers were now all armed, even to Mr. Parker. The scientist had recovered from his first fright, when he spied the Indians coming over the snow, as he was "observing" some natural phenomenon. Tom, even in his excitement, noticed that the professor was curiously examining his gun, evidently more with a view to seeing how it was made, and on which principle it was operated, rather than to discover how to use it.

"If it comes to a fight, just point it at the Indians, pull the trigger, and work that lever," explained the young inventor. "It's an automatic gun."

"I see," answered Mr. Parker. "Very curious. I had no idea they worked this way."

"Oh, if I only had my electric rifle in shape!" sighed Tom, as he dashed forward at the side of Ned.

"Your electric rifle?"

"Yes, I've got a new kind of weapon—very effective. I have it almost finished. It's in the airship, but I can't use it just yet. However, maybe these repeaters will do the work."

By this time they were at the entrance of the cave, and, looking out they saw about a hundred Indians, dressed in furs, striding across the snowy plain that stretched out from the foot of the mountain in which was the cavern.

"They're certainly comin' on," observed Abe, grimly. "Git ready for 'em, boys!"

The gold-seekers lined up at the mouth of the cave, with guns in their hands. At the sight of this small, but formidable force, the Indians halted. They were armed with guns of ancient make, while some had spears, and others bows and arrows. A few had grabbed up stones as weapons.

There appeared to be a consultation going on among them, and, presently, one of the number, evidently a chief or a spokesman, gave his gun to one of his followers, and, holding his hands above his head, while he waved a rag that might have once been white, came forward.

"By Jove!" exclaimed Tom. "It's a flag of truce! He wants to talk with us I believe!"

"Bless my cartridges!" exclaimed Mr. Damon. "Can they speak English?"

"A little," answered Abe Abercrombie. "I can talk some of their lingo, too. Maybe I'd better see what they want."

"I guess it would be a good plan," suggested Tom, and, accordingly the old miner stepped forward. The Indian came on, until Abe motioned for him to halt.

"I reckon that's as far as it'll be healthy for you t' come," spoke Abe, grimly. "Now what do you fellers want?"

Thereupon there ensued a rapid exchange of jargon between the miner and the Indian. Abe seemed much relieved as the talk went on, until there came what seemed like a demand on the part of the dark-hued native.

"No. you don't! None of that!" muttered Abe. "If you had your way you'd take everything we have."

"What is it? What does he want?" asked Tom in a low voice.

"Why, the beggar began fair enough," replied the miner. "He said one of their number had been in the cave when a storm came an' saw a big spirit fly in, with men on its back. He ran away an' now others have come to see what it was. They don't guess it's an airship, for they've never seen one. but they know we're white folks, an' they always want things white folks have got."

"This fellow is a sort of chief, an' he says the white folks?— that's us, you know?—have taken th' Indians' cave. He says he doesn't want t' have any trouble, an' that we can stay here as long as we like, but that we must give him an' his followers a lot of food. Says they hain't got much. Land! Those beggars would eat us out of everything we had if we'd let 'em!"

"What are you going to tell them?" inquired Mr. Damon.

"I'm goin' t' tell 'em t' go t' grass, or words t' that effect," replied Abe. "They haven't any weapons that amount t' anything, an' we can stand 'em off. Besides, we'll soon be goin' away from here; won't we, Tom?"

"Yes, but—"

"Oh, there's no use givin' in to 'em," interrupted Abe. "If you give 'em half a loaf, they want two. Th' only way is t' be firm. I'll tell 'em we can't accommodate 'em."

Thereupon he began once more to talk to the Indians in their own tongue. His words were at first received in silence, and then angry cries came from the natives. The chief made a gesture of protest.

"Well, if you don't like it, you know what you kin do!" declared Abe. "We've got th' best part of our journey before us, an' we can't give away our supplies. Go hunt food if you want it, ye lazy beggars!"

The peaceful demeanor of the Indians now turned to rage. The leader dropped the rag that had served for a flag of truce, and took back his gun.

"Look out! There's going to be trouble!" cried Tom.

"Well, we're ready for 'em!" answered Abe, grimly.

There was a moment of hesitation among the natives. Then they seemed to hold a consultation with the chief. It was over shortly. They broke into a run, and quickly advanced toward the cave. Tom and the others held their guns in readiness.

Suddenly the Indians halted. They gazed upward, and pointed to something in the air above their heads. They gave utterance to cries of fear.

"What is it; another storm coming?" asked Tom.

"Let's look," suggested Ned. He and Tom stepped to the mouth of the cave—they went outside. There was little danger from the natives now, as their attention was fixed on something else.

A moment later Tom and Ned saw what this was.

Floating in the air, almost over the cave, was a great airship—a large craft, nearly the size of the *Red Cloud*. Hardly able to believe the evidence of their eyes, Tom and Ned watched it. Whence had it come? Whither was it going?

"It's a triplane!" murmured Ned.

"A triplane!" repeated Tom. "Yes—it is—and it's the airship of Andy Foger! Our rivals are on our track!"

He continued to gaze upward as the triplane shot forward, the noise of the motor being plainly heard. Then, with howls of fear, the Indians turned and fled. The rival airship had vanquished them.

THE RACE

Astonished and terrified as the Indians had been at the sight of the big-winged craft, high in the air above their heads, Tom and the others were no less surprised, though, of course, their fear was not exactly the same as that of the Alaskan natives.

"Do you really think that is Andy Foger?" asked Ned, as they watched the progress of the triplane.

"I'm almost sure of it," replied Tom. "That craft is built exactly as his was. but I never expected him to have such good luck sailing it."

"It isn't going very fast," objected Ned.

"No, but it can navigate pretty well, and that's something. He must have hustled to get it together and reach this point with it."

"Yes, but he didn't have to travel as far as we did," went on Ned. "He put his ship together at Sitka, and we came from Seattle."

"Bless my memoranda book!" exclaimed Mr. Damon. "The Fogers here! What's to be done about it?"

"Nothing, I guess," answered Tom. "I'd just as soon they wouldn't see us. I don't believe they will. Get back into the cave. We must use strategy now to get ahead of them. There will be a race to the valley of gold."

"Well, he served us one good turn, anyhow, though he didn't mean to," put in Abe Abercrombie.

"How?" asked Mr. Parker, who was still examining his gun, as though trying to understand it.

"He scared away them pesky natives," went on the miner. "Otherwise we might have had a fight, an' while I reckon we could have beat 'em, it's best not to fight if you kin git out of it."

The gold-seekers had withdrawn inside the mouth of the cave, where they could watch the progress of the rival airship without being seen. The Indians had disappeared beyond a snow-covered hill.

The airship of Andy Foger, for such it subsequently proved to be, floated slowly onward. Its progress was not marked with the speed of Tom's craft, though whether or not the occupants of the *Anthony* (as Andy had vain-gloriously named his craft after himself) were speeding up their motor, was a matter of conjecture.

The adventurers held a short consultation, while standing at the mouth of the cave watching the progress of the *Anthony*. It rose in the air, and circled about.

"He certainly IS trying to pick us up," declared Ned.

"Well, we'll start out after him to-morrow," decided Tom. "I think all the patches will hold then."

They resumed work on the *Red Cloud*, and that night Tom announced that they would start in the morning. Meanwhile Andy's craft had disappeared from sight. There was no further evidence of the Indians.

"I don't reckon they'll come back," spoke Abe, grimly. "They think we are sure-enough spirits, now, able to call creatures out of the air whenever we want 'em. But still we must be on our guard."

As Mr. Parker was not of much service in helping on the airship he agreed to be a sort of guard and took his place just outside the cave, where he could make "observations," and, at the same time watch for the reappearance of Indians. They had little fear of an attack at night, for Abe said the Alaskans were not fond of darkness.

The cold seemed to increase, and, even in the sheltered cave the adventurers felt it. There were several heavy flurries of snow that afternoon, and winter seemed setting in with a vengeance. The daylight, too, was not of long duration, for the sun was well south now, and in the far polar regions it was perpetual night.

After a brief inspection of the ship the next morning, following a good night's rest, when they were not disturbed by any visits from the natives, Tom announced that they would set sail. The day was a clear one, but very cold, and the gold-seekers were glad of the shelter of the warm cabin.

The *Red Cloud* was wheeled from the cave, and set on a level place. There was not room enough to make a flying start, and ascend by means of the planes and propellers, so the gas-bag method was used. The generating machine was put in operation, and soon the big red bag that hovered over the craft began to fill. Tom was glad to see that none of the several compartments leaked. The bag had been well repaired.

Suddenly the *Red Cloud* shot up in the air. Up above the towering snow-covered crags it mounted, and then, with a whizz and a roar, the propellers were set going.

"Once more northward bound!" cried Tom, as he took his place in the pilothouse.

"And we'll see if we can beat Andy Foger there," added Ned.

All that morning the *Red Cloud* shot ahead at good speed. The craft had suffered no permanent damage during her fight with the hail storm, and was as good as ever. They ate dinner high in the air, while sailing over a great stretch of whiteness, where the snow lay many feet deep on the level, and where great mountain crags were so covered with the glistening mantle and a coating of ice as to resemble the great bergs that float in the polar sea.

"I wouldn't want to be wrecked here," said Ned, with a shudder, as he looked down. "We'd never get away. Does any one live down there, Abe?"

"Yes, there are scattered tribes of Indians and Alaskan natives. They live by hunting and fishing, and travel around by means of dog sledges. But it's a dreary life. Me an' my partner had all we wanted of it. An airship for mine!"

"I wonder what's become of Andy?" spoke Tom, that afternoon. "I haven't sighted him, and I've been using the powerful telescope. I can't pick him up, though he can't be so very far ahead of us."

"Let me try," suggested Ned. "Put her up a bit, Tom, where I can look down. Andy won't dare go very high. Maybe I can sight him."

The *Red Cloud* shot upward as the young inventor shifted the elevation rudder, and the bank clerk, with the powerful glass to his eye, swept the space below him. For half an hour he looked in vain. Then, with a little start of surprise he handed the glass to his chum.

"See what you make that out to be," suggested Ned. "It looks like a big bird, yet I haven't seen any other birds to-day."

Tom looked. He peered earnestly through the telescope for a minute, and then cried:

"It's Andy's airship! He's ahead of us! We must catch him! Ned, you and Mr. Damon speed up the motor! The race is on!"

In a few minutes the great airship was hurling herself through space, and, in less than ten minutes Andy's craft could be made out plainly with the naked eye. Fifteen minutes more and the *Red Cloud* was almost up to her. Then those aboard the *Anthony* must have caught sight of their pursuers, for there was a sudden increase in speed on the part of the unscrupulous Foger crowd, who sought to steal a march on Tom and his friends.

"The race is on!" repeated the young inventor grimly, as he pulled the speed lever over another notch.

THE FALL OF THE *ANTHONY*

Had it not been for what was at stake, the race between the two big airships would have been an inspiring one to those aboard Tom's craft. As it was they were too anxious to overcome the unfair advantage taken by Andy to look for any of the finer points in the contest of the air.

"There's no denying that he's got a pretty good craft there," conceded Tom, as he watched the progress of his rival. "I never thought Andy Foger could have done it."

"He didn't do very much of it," declared Ned. "He hired the best part of that made. Andy hasn't any inventive ideas. He probably said he wanted an airship, and his dad put up the money and hired men to build it for him. Andy, Sam and Pete only tinkered around on it."

Later Tom and his chum learned that this was so—that Mr. Foger had engaged the services of an expert to make the airship. This man had been taken to Sitka with the Fogers, and had materially aided them in reassembling the craft.

"Do you think he can beat us?" asked Ned, anxiously.

"No!" exclaimed Tom, confidently. "There's only one craft that can beat my *Red Cloud* and that's my monoplane the *Butterfly*. But I have in mind plans for a speedier machine than even the monoplane. However I haven't any fear that Andy can keep up to us in this craft. I haven't begun to fly yet, and I'm pretty sure, from the way his is going, that he has used his limit of speed."

"Then why don't you get ahead of him?" asked Mr. Damon. "Bless my tape-measure! the way to win a race is to beat."

"Not this kind of a race," and the young inventor spoke seriously. "If I got ahead of Andy now, he'd simply trail along and follow us. That's his game. He wants me to be the path-finder, for, since I cast a doubt on the correctness of the map, a copy of which he stole, he isn't sure where he's going. He'd ask nothing better than to follow us."

"Then what are you going to do if you don't get ahead of him?" asked Ned.

"I'm going to press him close until night," answered Tom, "and when it's dark, I'm going to shoot ahead, and, by morning we'll be so far away that he can't catch up to us."

"Good idea! That's th' stuff!" cried Abe with enthusiasm.

"He's a sneak!" burst out Mr. Damon. "I'd like to see him left behind."

Tom carried out his plan. The remainder of the day he hung just on Andy's flank, sometimes shooting high up, almost out of sight, and again coming down, just to show what the *Red Cloud* could do when pressed.

As for those aboard the *Anthony*, they seemed to be trying to increase their speed, but, if that was their object they did not have much success, for the big, clumsy triplane only labored along.

"I wonder who he's got with him?" said Ned, as darkness was closing down. "I can't make out any one by this glass. They stick pretty closely to the cabin."

"Oh, probably Andy's father is there," said "and, perhaps, some of Mr. Foger's acquaintances. I guess Mr. Foger is as anxious to get this gold as Andy is."

"He certainly needs money," admitted Ned. "Jove! but I hope we beat him!"

But alas for Tom's hopes! His plan of waiting until night and then putting on such speed as would leave Andy behind could not be carried out. It was tried, but something went wrong with the main motor, and only half power could be developed. Tom and Ned labored over it nearly all night, to no effect, and through the hours of darkness they could see the lights from the cabin of the *Anthony* gleaming just ahead of them. Evidently the bully's airship could not make enough speed to run away from the *Red Cloud*, or else it was the plan of the Foger crowd to keep in Tom's vicinity.

The direction held by Andy's craft was a general northwestern one, and Tom knew, in time, and that very soon, it would bring the *Anthony* over the valley of gold. Evidently Andy was placing some faith in his copy of the stolen map.

"Once I get this motor in shape I'll soon pull away from him," announced Tom, about four o'clock that morning, while he and Ned, aided by Mr. Damon, were still laboring over the refractory machine.

"What are you going to do?" asked Ned.

"It's too late to carry out my original plan," went on Tom. "We're getting so near the place now that I want to be there ahead of every one else. So as soon as we can, I'm going to push the *Red Cloud* for all she's worth, and get to the valley of gold first. If possession is nine points of the law, I want those nine points."

"That's the way to talk!" cried Abe. "Once we git on th' ground we kin hold our own!"

It was breakfast time before Tom had the motor repaired, and he decided to have a good meal before starting to speed up his craft. He felt better after some hot coffee, for he and the others were weary from their night of labor.

"Now for the test!" he cried, as he went back to the engine-room. "Here's where we give Andy the go-by, and I don't think he can catch us!"

There was an increasing hum to the powerful motor, the great propellers whirled around at twice their former number of revolutions, and the airship suddenly shot ahead.

Those on the ANTHOMY must have been watching for some such move as that, for, no sooner had Tom's craft begun to creep up on his rival than the forward craft also shot ahead.

But the airship was not built that could compete with Tom's. Like a racer overhauling a cart-horse, the *Red Cloud* whizzed through the air. In a spirit of fun the young inventor sent his machine within a few feet of Andy's. He had a double purpose in this, for he wanted to show the bully that he did not fear him, and he wanted to see if he could discover who was aboard.

Tom did catch a glimpse of Andy and his father in the cabin of the *Anthony*, and he also saw a couple of men working frantically over the machinery.

"They're going to try to catch us!" called Tom to Ned.

This was evident a moment later, for, after the *Red Cloud* had forged ahead, her rival made a clumsy attempt to follow. The *Anthony* did show a burst of speed, and, for a moment Tom was apprehensive lest he had underrated his rival's prowess.

Suddenly Ned, who was looking from a projecting side window of the pilothouse, back toward Andy's ship, cried out in alarm.

"What's the matter?" shouted Tom.

"The airship—Andy's—two of the main wings have collapsed!"

Tom looked. It was but too true. The strain under which the *Anthony* had been put when the machinists increased the speed, had been too much for the frame. Two wings broke, and now hung uselessly down, one on either side. The *Anthony* shot toward the snow-covered earth!

"They're falling!" cried Mr. Parker.

"Yes," added Tom, grimly, "the race is over as far as they are concerned."

"Bless my soul! Won't they be killed?" cried Mr. Damon.

"There's not much danger," replied the young inventor. "They can vol-plane back to earth. That's what they're doing," he added a moment later, as he witnessed the maneuver of the crippled craft. "They're in no danger, but I don't believe they'll get to the valley of gold this trip!"

Tom was soon to learn how easily he could be mistaken.

HITTING THE ICE MOUNTAIN

Onward sped the *Red Cloud*. For a moment after the accident to Andy's ship, Tom had slowed up his craft, but he soon went on again, after he had satisfied himself that his enemies were in no danger.

"Don't you think—that is to say—I know they can't expect anything from us," spoke Mr. Damon, "but for humanity's sake, hadn't we better stop and help them, Tom?"

"I hardly think so," replied the young inventor. "In the first place they would hardly thank us for doing so, and, in the second, I don't believe they need help. They are almost safely down now."

"I don't just mean that," went on the odd man. "But they may starve to death. This is a very desolate country over which we are sailing."

"They must have a supply of food in their ship," declared Tom, "and they have brought their plight on themselves."

"They're in no great danger," put in Abe.

"There are plenty of natives around here, an' if the Fogers need food or aid they can git it by payin' for it. Why, for the sake of th' parts of their damaged airship, th' Eskimos would take th' whole party back t' Sitka and feed 'em well on th' trip. Oh, they're all right."

"Very well, if you say so," assented Mr. Damon. He looked back to watch the *Anthony* slowly settling to earth. It came gently down, proving that Tom knew whereof he spoke, when he had said they could vol-plane down. Before the *Red Cloud* was out of sight Tom and his companions saw Andy and his father leave their wrecked craft and venture out on the snow-covered ground. The Fogers gazed enviously after the airship of our hero as they saw him still forging toward the goal.

"I guess Andy's stolen map won't be of much use to him," mused Tom. "Now we can put on all the speed we like, "and with that he shifted the gears and levers until the airship was making exceedingly good time toward the valley of gold.

The remainder of that day saw our adventurers pursuing their way eagerly. At times they were flying high, and again, when Abe suggested that they go down to observe the character of the country over which they were passing, they skimmed along, just above the big mountains, which seemed almost like icebergs, so covered were they with frost and snow.

They were indeed in a wild and desolate country. Below them stretched a seemingly endless waste of snow and ice—great forests interspersed with treeless patches, while now and then they sailed over a frozen lake.

Once in a while they had glimpses of bands of Indians, dressed in furs, hunting. At such times the natives would look up, on hearing the noise made by the motor of the airship, and catching a glimpse of what must have seemed to them like some supernatural object, they would fall down prostrate in amazement and fear.

"Airships are pretty much of a novelty up here," remarked Abe with a grim smile.

The weather was new very cold, and the gold-seekers had to get out their heavy fur garments, of which they had brought along a goodly supply. True, it was warm in the cabin of the airship, but at times, they wanted to venture out on the deck to get fresh air, or to make some adjustments to the wing planes, and, on such occasions the keen, frosty air, as it was driven past them by the motion of the craft, made even the thickest garments seem none too warm. Then, too, it was colder at the elevation at which they flew than down on the ground.

Another day found them in a still wilder and more desolate part of Alaska. There were scarcely any signs of habitation now, and the snow and ice seemed so thick that even a long summer of sunshine could hardly have melted it. The hours of daylight, too, were growing less and less the farther north they went.

"Do you think you can pilot us right to the Snow Mountains, Abe?" asked Tom, on the third day after the accident to Andy's airship. "Let's get out the map, and have another look at it. We must be getting near the place now. We'll look at the map."

The young inventor went to his stateroom where he kept the important document in a small desk, and the others heard him rummaging around. He muttered impatiently, and Ned heard his chum say: "I thought sure I put it in here." Then ensued a further search, and presently Tom came out, his face wearing rather a puzzled and worried look, and he asked: "Say, Abe, I didn't give that map back to you; did I?"

"Nope," answered the miner. "I ain't seen it since just before th' hail storm. We was lookin' at it then."

"That's when I remember it," went on Tom, "and I thought I put it in my desk. I didn't, by any possible chance give it to you; did I, Ned?"

"Me? No, I haven't seen it."

"That's funny," went on Tom. "I'll look once more. Maybe it got under some papers."

They heard him rummaging again in his desk.

"Bless my bank-book!" cried Mr. Damon. "I hope nothing has happened to that map. We can't find the valley of gold without it."

Tom came back again.

"I can't find it." he said, hopelessly.

Then ensued a frantic search. Every possible place in the airship was looked into, but the precious map did not turn up.

"Perhaps the Fogers took it," suggested Mr. Parker, who had helped in the hunt, in a dreamy sort of fashion.

"That's not possible," said Tom. "They haven't been near enough to us since I saw the map last. No, the last time I had it was just before the hail storm, and, in the excitement of repairing the ship, I have mislaid it."

"Maybe it's back there in the big cave," suggested Ned.

"It's possible," admitted the young inventor. "Pshaw! It's very careless of me!"

"If you think it's in the cave, we'd better go back there and have a hunt for it," suggested Mr. Damon. "Otherwise we are on a wild-goose chase."

"Don't go back!" exclaimed old Abe. "I think we can find th' valley of gold without th' map, now that we have come this far. I sort of remember th' marks on that parchment, an' we are in the right neighborhood now, for I kin see some of th' landmarks my partner and I saw. I say, let's keep on! We can cruise around a bit until we strike th' right place. That won't take us so long as it would to go back to the cave. Besides, if we go back, the Fogers may get ahead of us!"

"With their broken airship?" asked Ned

"Can't they repair it?" demanded Abe.

"Hardly—up in this wild country," was Tom's opinion. "But perhaps it WILL be just as well to keep on. I have a hazy remembrance of the distances and directions on the map, and, though it will take longer to hunt out the valley this way, I think we can do it. I can't forgive myself for my carelessness! I should have kept a copy of the map, or given one of you folks one."

But they would not hear of him blaming himself, and said it might have happened to any one. It was decided that the map must be lost in the big cave, and if it was there it was not likely to be found by their enemies.

"We'll jest have t' prospect about a bit," declared Abe, "only we'll do it in th' air instead of on th' ground."

It was dusk when the fruitless search for the map was over, and they sat in the cabin discussing matters. The lights had not yet been switched on, and the *Red Cloud* was skimming along under the influence of the automatic rudders and the propellers.

"Well, suppose we have supper," proposed Mr. Damon, who seemed to think eating a remedy for many ills, mental and bodily. "Bless my dessert-spoon, but I'm hungry!"

He started toward the galley, while Tom went forward to the pilothouse. Hardly had he reached it than there came a terrific crash, and the airship seemed tossed back by some giant hand. Every one was thrown off his feet, and the lights which had been turned on suddenly went out.

"What's the matter?" cried Ned.

"Have we hit anything?" demanded Mr. Damon.

"Hit anything! I should say we had!" yelled Tom. "We've knocked a piece off a big mountain of ice!"

As he spoke the airship began slowly settling toward the earth, for her machinery had been stopped by the terrific impact.

A Fight with Musk Oxen

"Can I help you, Tom? What's to be done?" demanded Ned Newton, as he rushed to where his chum was yanking on various levers and gear wheels.

"Wait a minute!" gasped the young inventor. "I want to throw on the storage battery, and that will give us some light. Then we can see what We are doing." An instant later the whole ship was illuminated, and those aboard her felt calmer. Still the *Red Cloud* continued to sink.

"Can't we do something?" yelled Ned. "Start the propellers, Tom!"

"No, I'll use the gas. I can't see where we're heading for, as the searchlight is out of business. We may be in the midst of a lot of bergs. We were flying too low. Just start the gas generating machine."

Ned hurried to obey this order. He saw Tom's object. With the big bag full of gas the airship would settle gently to earth as easily as though under the command of the propellers and wing planes.

In a few minutes the hissing of the machine told that the vapor was being forced into the bag and a little later the downward motion of the ship was checked. She moved more and more slowly toward the earth, until, with a little jar, she settled down, and came to rest. But she was on such an uneven keel that the cabin was tilted at an unpleasant angle.

"Bless my salt-cellar!" cried Mr. Damon. "We are almost standing on our heads!"

"Better that than not standing at all," replied Tom, grimly. "Now to see what the damage is."

He scrambled from the forward door of the cabin, no easy task considering how it was tilted, and the others followed him. It was too dark to note just how much damage had been inflicted, but Tom was relieved to see, as nearly as he could judge, that it was confined to the forward part of the front platform or deck of the ship. The wooden planking was split, but the extent of the break could not be ascertained until daylight. The searchlight connections had been broken by the collision, and it could not be used.

"Now to take a look at the machinery," suggested the young inventor, when he had walked around his craft. "That is what I am worried about more than about the outside."

But, to their joy, they found only a small break in the motor. That was what caused it to stop, and also put the dynamo out of commission.

"We can easily fix that," Tom declared.

"Bless my coffee-spoon!" cried Mr. Damon, who seemed to be running to table accessories in his blessings. Perhaps it was because it was so near supper time. "Bless my coffee-spoon! But how did it happen?"

"We were running too low," declared Tom. "I had forgotten that we were likely to get among tall mountain peaks at any moment, and I set the elevation rudder too low. It was my fault. I should have been on the lookout.

We must have struck the mountain of ice a glancing blow, or the result would have been worse than it is. We'll come out of it all right, as it is."

"We can't do anything to-night," observed Ned.

"Only eat," put in Mr. Damon, "and we'll have to take our coffee cups half full, for everything is so tilted that it's like topsy-turvey land. It makes me fairly dizzy!"

But he forgot this in the work of getting a meal, and, though it was prepared under considerable difficulties, at last it was ready.

Bright and early the next morning Tom was up making another inspection of his ship. He found that even if the forward deck was not repaired they could go on, as soon as the motor was in shape, but, as they had some spare wood aboard, it was decided to temporarily repair the smashed platform.

It was cold work, even wearing their thick garments; but, after laboring until their fingers were stiff from the frost, Ned hit on the idea of building a big fire of some evergreen trees near where the ship lay.

"Say, that's all right!" declared Tom, as the warmth of the blaze made itself felt. "We can work better, now!"

The *Red Cloud* was tilted on some rough and uneven ground, in among some little hills. On either side arose big peaks, the one in particular that they had hit towering nearly fifteen thousand feet.

Everything was covered with snow and ice, and, in fact, the ice was so thick on the top of the mountains that the crags resembled icebergs rather than stony peaks. The crash of the airship had brought down a great section of this solid rock-ice.

"Do you think we are anywhere near the valley of gold?" asked Mr. Damon that afternoon, when the work was nearly finished.

"It's somewhere in this vicinity." declared Abe. "Me an' my partner passed through jest such a place as this on our way there. I wouldn't wonder but what it wasn't more than a few hundred miles away, now."

"Then we'll soon be there," said Tom. "I'll start in the morning. I could go to-night, but there are a few adjustments I want to make to the motor, and, besides, I think it will be safer, now that we are among these peaks, to navigate in daylight, or at least with the searchlight going. I should have thought of that before."

"Then, if you're not going to start away at once," spoke Mr. Parker, "I think I will walk around a bit, and make some observations. I think we are now in the region where we may expect a movement of the ice. I want to test it, and see if it is traveling in a southerly direction. If it is not now, it will soon be doing that, and the coating of ice may reach even as far as New York."

"Pleasant prospect," murmured Tom. Then he said aloud: "Well if you are going, Mr. Parker, we'll be with you. I'll be glad of the chance to stretch my legs, and what more remains to be done, can be finished in the morning."

Mr. Damon declared that he did not relish a tramp over the ice and snow, and would stay in the warm cabin, but Tom and Ned, with Abe and Mr. Parker started off. The scientist pointed out what he claimed were evidences of the impending movement of the ice, while Abe explained to the lads how the Alaskan Indians of that neighborhood hunted and fished, and how they made huts of blocks of ice.

"We are nearing th' Arctic circle," the old miner said, "and we'll soon be among th' most savage of the Eskimo tribes."

"Is there any hunting around here?" asked Ned.

"Yes, plenty of musk ox" answered Abe.

"I wish I'd brought my gun along and could see one of the big beasts now," went on Ned. He looked anxiously around, but no game was in sight. After a little farther tramp over the icy expanse they all declared that they had seen enough of the dreary landscape, and voted to return to the ship.

As they neared their craft Tom saw several large, shaggy black objects standing in a line on the path the adventurers had come over a little while before. The objects were between the gold-seekers and the *Red Cloud*.

"What in the world are those?" asked the young inventor.

"Look to me like black stones," spoke Ned.

"Stones?" cried Abe. "Look out, boys, those are musk oxen; and big ones, too! There's a lot of 'em! Make for the ship! If they attack us we're goners!"

The boys and Mr. Parker needed no second warning. Turning so as to rush past the shaggy creatures, the four headed toward the ship.

But if our friends expected to reach it unmolested they were disappointed. No sooner had they increased their pace than the oxen, with snorts of rage, darted forward. The animals may have imagined they were about to be attacked, and determined to make the first move.

"Here they come!" yelled Ned.

"Sprint for it!" cried Tom.

"Oh, if I only had my gun!" groaned Abe.

It was hard work running over the ice and snow, hampered as they were with their heavy fur garments. They soon realized this, and the pace was telling on them. They were now near to the ship, but the savage creatures still were between them and the craft.

"Try around the other way!" directed Tom, They changed their direction, but the oxen also shifted their ground, and with loud bellows of rage came on, shaking their shaggy heads and big horns, while the hair, hanging down from their sides and flanks, dragged in the snow.

"Right at 'em! Run and yell!" advised the young inventor. "Maybe we can scare 'em!"

They followed his advice. Yelling like Indians the four rushed straight for the animals. For a moment only the creatures halted. Then, bellowing louder than ever they rushed straight at Tom and the others.

The largest of the oxen, with a sudden swerve, made for Mr. Parker, who was slightly in the lead off to one side. In an instant the scientist was tossed high in the air, falling in a snow bank.

"Mr. Damon! Mr. Damon!" yelled Tom, frantically. "Get a gun and shoot these beasts!"

The young inventor and his two companions had come to a halt. The oxen also stopped momentarily. Suddenly Mr. Damon appeared on the deck of the airship. He held two rifles. Laying one down he aimed the other at the ox which was rushing at the prostrate Mr. Parker. The eccentric man fired. He hit the beast on the flank, and, with a bellow of rage it turned.

"Now's our time!" yelled Tom. "Head for the ship, I'll get my electric gun!"

"We can't leave Mr. Parker!" yelled Abe.

But the scientist had arisen, and was running toward the *Red Cloud*. He did not seem to be much hurt. Mr. Damon fired again, hitting another beast, but not mortally.

Once more the herd of shaggy creatures came on, but the adventurers were now almost at the ship, on the deck of which stood Mr. Damon, firing as fast as he could work the lever and pull the trigger.

THE CAVES OF ICE

"Keep on firing! Hold 'em back a few minutes and I'll soon turn my electric rifle loose on 'em!" yelled Tom Swift as he sprinted forward. "Keep on shooting, Mr. Damon!"

"Bless my powder-horn! I will!" cried the excited man. "I'll fire all the cartridges there are in the rifle!"

Which, at the rate he was discharging the weapon, would not take a long time. But it had the effect of momentarily checking the advance of the creatures.

Not for long, however. Our friends had barely reached the airship, with Mr. Parker stumbling and slipping on the ice and snow, ere the musk oxen came on again, with loud bellows.

"They're going to charge the ship! They'll ram her!" yelled Ned Newton.

"I think I can stop them!" cried Tom, who had leaped toward his stateroom. He came out a moment later, carrying a peculiar-looking gun, The adventurers had seen it before, but never in operation, as Tom had only put some finishing touches on it since undertaking the voyage to the caves of ice.

"What sort of a weapon is that?" cried Abe, as he helped Mr. Parker on board.

"It's my new electric rifle," answered the young inventor. "I don't know how it will work, as it isn't entirely finished, but I'm going to try it."

Putting it to his shoulder he aimed at the leading musk ox, and pulled a small lever. There was no report, no puff of smoke and no fire, yet the big creature, which had been rushing at the ship, suddenly stopped, swayed for a moment, and then fell over in the snow, kicking in his death agony.

"One down!" yelled Tom. "My rifle works all right, even if it isn't finished!"

He aimed at another ox, and that creature was stopped in its tracks. Mr. Damon had exhausted his cartridges, and had ceased firing, but Abe Abercrombie was ready with his rifle, and opened up on the beasts. Tom killed another with his electric gun, and Abe shot two. This stopped the advance, and only just in time, for the foremost animals were already close to the ship, and had they rushed at the frail hull they might have damaged it beyond repair.

"Here goes for the big one!" cried Tom, and, aiming at the largest ox of the herd, the young inventor pulled the lever. The brute fell over dead, and the rest, terror stricken, turned and fled.

"Hurrah! That's the stuff!" cried Ned Newton, capering about on deck. He had hurried to his stateroom and secured his rifle, and, before the musk oxen were out of sight he had killed one, which gave him great delight.

"Mighty lucky we drove them away," declared Abe. "They are terrible savage at times, an' I reckon we struck one of them times. But say, Tom, what sort of a gun is that you got, anyhow?"

"Oh, it fires electric bullets," explained our hero. "But I haven't time to tell you about it now. Let's get out and skin one of those oxen. The fresh meat will come in good, for we've been living on canned stuff since we left Seattle. We've got time enough before it gets dark."

They hurried to where the shaggy creatures lay in the snow, and soon there was enough fresh meat to last a long time, as it would keep well in the intense cold. Tom put away his electric gun, briefly explaining the system of it to his companions. The time was to come, and that not very far off, when that same electric rifle was to save his life in a remarkable manner, in the wilds of Africa where he went to hunt elephants.

In the cozy cabin that night they sat and talked of the day's adventures. The airship had been slightly lifted up by means of the gas bag, and now rested on a level keel, so it was more comfortable for the gold hunters.

"I did not complete my observations about the great snow slide," remarked Professor Parker, "I trust I will have time to go over the ground again to-morrow."

"We leave early in the morning," objected Tom.

"Besides, I don't believe it would be safe to go over that ground again," put in Mr. Damon.

"Bless my gunpowder! But when I saw those savage creatures rushing at you, I thought it was all up with us. Are you hurt, Parker, my dear fellow? I forgot to ask before."

"Not hurt in the least," answered the scientist. "My heavy and thick fur garments saved me from the beasts' horns, and I fell in some soft snow. I was quite startled for a moment. I thought it might be the beginning of the snow movement."

"It was an ox movement," said Ned, in a low voice to Tom.

Morning saw the travelers again under way, with the *Red Cloud* now floating high enough to avoid the lofty peaks. The weather was clear but very cold, and Tom, who was in the pilot-house, could see a long distance ahead, and note many towering crags, which, had the airship been flying low enough, would have interfered with her progress.

"We'll have to keep the searchlight going all night, to avoid a collision," he decided.

"Are we anywhere near the place?" asked Mr. Damon.

"We're in th' right region," declared the old miner. "I think we're on th' right track. I recognize a few more landmarks."

"There wouldn't have been any trouble if I hadn't lost the map." complained Tom, bitterly.

"Never mind about that," insisted Abe. "We'll find th' place anyhow. But look ahead there; is that another hail storm headin' this way, Tom?"

The young inventor glanced to where Abe pointed. There was a mist in the air, and, for a time great apprehension was felt, but, in a few minutes there was a violent flurry of snow and they all breathed easier. For, though the flakes were so numerous as to completely shut off the view, there was no danger to the airship from them. Tom steered by the compass.

The storm lasted several hours, and when it was over the adventurers found themselves several miles nearer their destination—at least they hoped they were nearer it, for they were going it blind.

Abe declared they were now in the region of the gold valley. They cruised about for two days, making vain observations by means of powerful telescopes, but they saw no signs of any depression which corresponded with the place whence Abe had seen the gold taken from. At times they passed over Indian villages, and had glimpses of the skin-clad inhabitants rushing out to point to the strange sight of the airship overhead. Tom was beginning to reproach himself again for his carelessness in losing the map, and it did begin to took as if they were making a fruitless search.

Still they all kept up their good spirits, and Mr. Damon concocted some new dishes from the meat of the musk oxen. It was about a week after the fight with the savage creatures when, one day, as Ned was on duty in the pilothouse, he happened to lock down. What he saw caused him to call to Tom.

"What's the matter?" demanded the young inventor, as he hurried forward.

"Look down there," directed Ned. "It looks as if we were sailing over a lot of immense beehives of the old-fashioned kind."

Tom looked. Below were countless, rounded hummocks of snow or ice. Some were very large—as immense as a great shed in which a dirigible balloon could be housed—while others were as small as the ice huts in which the Eskimos live.

"That's rather strange," remarked Tom. "I wonder—"

But he did not complete his sentence, for Abe Abercrombie, who had come to stand beside him, suddenly yelled out:

"The caves of ice! The caves of ice! Now I know where we are! We're close to the valley of gold! There are the caves of ice, and just beyond is th' place we're lookin' for! We've found it at last!"

In the Gold Valley

The excited cries of the old miner brought Mr. Damon and Mr. Parker to the pilothouse on the run.

"Bless my refrigerator!" exclaimed Mr. Damon. "Are there more of those savage, shaggy creatures down there?"

"No, but we are over th' caves of ice," explained Abe. "That means we are near th' gold."

"You don't say so!" burst out the scientist. "The caves of ice! Now I can begin my real observations! I have a theory that the caves are on top of a strata of ice that is slowly moving down, and will eventually bury the whole of the North American continent. Let me once get down there, and I can prove what I say."

"I'd a good deal rather you wouldn't prove it, if it's going to be anything like it was on Earthquake Island, or out among the diamond makers." said Tom Swift. "But we will go down there, to see what they are like. Perhaps there is a trail from among the ice caves to the valley of gold."

"I don't think so," said Abe, shaking his head.

"I think th' gold valley lies over that high ridge," and he pointed to one. "That's where me an' my partner was," he went on. "I recognize th' place now."

"Well, we'll go down here, anyhow," decided Tom, and he pulled the lever to let some gas out of the bag, and tilted the deflection rudder to send the airship toward the odd caves.

And, curious enough did our friends find them when they had made a landing and got out to walk about them. It was very cold, for on every side was solid ice. They walked on ice, which was like a floor beneath their feet, level save where the ice caves reared themselves. As for the caverns, they, too, were hollowed out of the solid ice. It was exactly as though there had once been a level surface of some liquid. Then by some upheaval of nature, the surface was blown into bubbles, some large and some small. Then the whole thing had frozen solid, and the bubbles became hollow caves. In time part of the sides fell in and made an opening, so that nearly all the caves were capable of being entered.

This method of their formation was advanced as a theory by Mr. Parker, and no one cared to dispute him. The gold-seekers walked about, gazing on the ice caves with wonder showing on their faces.

It was almost like being in some fantastic scene from fairyland, the big ice bubbles representing the houses, the roofs being rounded like the igloos of the Eskimos. Some had no means of entrance, the outer surface showing no break. Others had small openings, like a little doorway, while of still others there remained but a small part of the original cave, some force of nature having crumbled and crushed it.

"Wonderful! Wonderful!" exclaimed Mr. Parker. "It bears out my theory exactly! Now to see how fast the ice is moving."

"How are you going to tell?" asked Tom.

"By taking some mark on this field of ice, and observing a distant peak. Then I will set up a stake, and by noting their relative positions, I can tell just how fast the ice field is moving southward." The scientist hurried into the ship to get a sharpened stake he had prepared for this purpose.

"How fast do you think the ice is moving?" asked Ned.

"Oh, perhaps two or three feet a year." "Two or three feet a year?" gasped Mr. Damon. "Why, Parker, my dear fellow, at that rate it will be some time before the ice gets to New York."

"Oh, yes. I hardly expect it will reach there within two thousand years, but my theory will be proved, just the same!"

"Humph!" exclaimed Abe Abercrombie, "I ain't goin' to worry any more, if it's goin' t' take all that while. I reckoned, to hear him talk, that it was goin' t' happen next summer."

"So did I," agreed Tom, but their remarks were lost on Mr. Parker who was busy making observations. The young inventor and the others walked about among the ice caves.

"Some of these caverns would be big enough to house the *Red Cloud* in case of another hail storm," observed Tom. "That one over there would hold two craft the size of mine," and, in fact, probably three could have gotten in if the opening had been somewhat enlarged, for the ice cave to which our hero pointed was an immense one.

As the adventurers were walking about they were startled by a terrific crashing sound. They started in alarm, for, off to their left, the top of one of the ice caverns had crashed inward, the blocks of frozen water crushing and grinding against one another.

"It's a good thing we weren't in there," remarked Tom, and he could not repress a shudder, "There wouldn't have been much left of the *Red Cloud* if she had been inside."

It was a desolate place, in spite of the wild beauty of it, and beautiful it was when the sun shone on the ice caves, making them sparkle as if they were studded with diamonds. But it was cold and cheerless, and there were no signs that human beings had ever been there. Mr. Parker had completed the setting of his stake, and picked out his landmarks, and was gravely making his "observations," and jotting down some figures in a notebook.

"How fast is it moving, Parker?" called Mr. Damon.

"I can't tell yet," was the response. "It will require observations extending over several days before I will know the rate."

"Then we might as well go on," suggested Tom. "There is nothing to be gained from staying here, and I would like to get to the gold valley. Abe says we are near it."

"Right over that ridge, I take it to be," replied the miner. "An' we can't get there any too soon for me. Those Fogers may git their ship fixed up, an' arrive before we do if we wait much longer."

"Not much danger, I guess," declared Ned.

"Well, we'll go up in the air, and see what we can find," decided Tom, as he turned back toward the ship.

They found the "ridge" as Abe designated it. to be a great plateau, over a hundred miles in extent, and they were the better part of that day crossing it, for they went slowly, so as not to miss the valley which the miner was positive was close at hand. Mr. Parker disliked leaving the ice caves, but Abe said there were more in the valley where they were going, and the scientist could renew his observations.

It was getting dusk when Tom, who was peering through a powerful glass, called out:

"Well, we're at the end of the plateau, and it seems to dip down into a valley just beyond here."

"Then that's the place!" cried Abe, excitedly. "Go slow, Tom."

Our hero needed no such caution. Carefully he sent the airship forward. A few minutes later they were passing over a large Eskimo village, the fur-clad inhabitants of which rushed about wildly excited at the sight of the airship.

"There they are! Them's th' beggars!" cried the old miner. "Them's th' fellows who drove me an' my partner away. But there's th' valley of gold! I know it now! How t' fill our pockets with nuggets!"

"Are you sure this is the place?" asked Mr. Damon.

"Sartin sure of it!" declared Abe. "Put her down, Tom! Put her down!"

"All right," agreed the young inventor, as he shifted the deflection rudder. The airship began her descent into the valley. The edge of the plateau, leading down into the great depression was now black with the Eskimos and Indians, who were capering about, gesticulating wildly.

"It's quite a surprise party to 'em," observed Ned Newton.

"Yes, I hope they don't spring one on us," added Tom.

Down and down went the *Red Cloud* lower and lower into the valley.

"There are ice caves there!" cried Mr. Parker, pointing to the curiously rounded and hollow hummocks. "Lots of them!"

"And larger than the others!" added Mr. Damon.

The airship was now moving slowly, for Tom wanted to pick out a good landing place. He saw a smooth stretch of the ice just ahead of him, in front of an immense ice cave.

"I'll make for that," he told Ned.

A few minutes later the craft had come to rest. Tom shut off the power and hurried from the pilothouse, donning his fur coat as he rushed out. A blast of frigid air met him as he opened the outer door of the cabin. Back on the ridge of the plateau he could see the fringe of Indians.

"Well, we're here in the valley," he said, as his friends gathered about him on the icy ground.

"An' now for th' gold!" cried Abe, "for it's here that th' nuggets are—enough for all of us! Come on an' have a hunt for 'em!"

THE FOGERS ARRIVE

In Spite of the fact that he tried to remain calm, Tom Swift felt a wild exultation as he thought of what lay before him and his friends. To be in a place where gold could be picked up! where they might all become fabulously wealthy! where the ground might be seen covered with the precious yellow metal! this was enough to set the nerves of any one a-tingle!

Tom could hardly realize it at first. After many hardships, no little danger, and after an attempt on the part of their enemies to defeat them, they had at last reached their goal. Now, as Abe had said, they could hunt for the gold.

But if they expected to see the precious yellow nuggets lying about ready to be picked up like so many kernels of corn, they were disappointed. A quick look all about showed them only a vast extent of ice and snow, broken here and there by the big caves of ice. There were not so many of the latter as at the first place they stopped, but the caverns were larger.

"Gold—I don't see any gold," remarked Ned Newton, with a disappointed air. "Where is it?"

"Bless my pocketbook, yes! Where is it?" demanded Mr. Damon.

"Oh, we've got to dig for it," explained Abe. "It's only when there's been a slight thaw that some of th' pebble nuggets kin be seen. They're under th' ice, an' we've got t' dig for 'em."

"Does it ever thaw up here?" asked Mr. Parker. "The ice of the caves seems thick enough to last forever."

"It does thaw an' melt some," went on the miner. "But some of th' caves last all through what they call 'summer' up here, though it's more like winter. We're above th' Arctic circle now, friends."

"Maybe we can keep on to the Pole," suggested Ned.

"Not this trip," spoke Tom, grimly. "We'll try for the gold, first."

"Yes, an' I'm goin' t' begin diggin' right away!" exclaimed Abe, as he turned back into the airship, and came out again with a pick and shovel, a supply of which implements had been brought along. The others followed his example. and soon the ice chips were flying about in a shower, while the sun shining on them gave the appearance of a rainbow.

"Look at those Indians watching us," remarked Ned to Tom, as he paused in his chipping of the frozen surface. The young inventor glanced up toward the distant plateau where a fringe of dark figures stood. The natives were evidently intently watching the gold-seekers.

"Do you think there's any danger from them. Abe?" asked Tom.

"Not much," was the reply. "They made trouble for me an' my partner, but I guess th' airship has scared 'em sufficient, so they won't come snoopin' down here," and Abe fell to at his digging again.

Mr. Damon was also vigorously wielding a pick, but Mr. Parker like the true scientist he was, had renewed his observations. Evidently the gold had no attractions for him, or, if it did, he preferred to wait until he had finished his calculations.

Vigorously the adventurers wielded their implements, making the ice fly, but for an hour or more no gold was discovered. Mr. Damon, after picking lightly at a certain place, would get discouraged, and move on to another. So did Ned, and Tom, after going down quite a way, left off work, and walked over to one of the big ice caves.

"What's up?" asked Ned, resting from his labors.

"I was thinking whether it would be safe to put the *Red Cloud* in this ice cave for a shelter," replied Tom. "There may come up a hail storm at any time, and damage it. The caves would be just the place for it, only I'm afraid the roof might collapse."

"It looks strong," said Ned. "Let's ask Mr. Parker his opinion."

"Good idea," agreed Tom.

The scientist was soon taking measurements of the thickness of the cave roof, noting its formation, and looking at the frozen floor.

"I see no reason why this cave should collapse," he finally announced. "The only danger is the movement of the whole valley of ice, and that is too gradual to cause any immediate harm. Yes, I think the airship could be housed in the ice cave."

"Then I'll run her in, and she'll be safer," decided Tom. "I guess we three can do it, Ned, and leave Mr. Damon and Abe to keep on digging for gold." The airship was so buoyant that it could easily be moved about on the bicycle wheels on which it rested, and soon, after the lower edge of the opening into the ice cave had been smoothed down, the *Red Cloud* was placed in the novel shelter.

"Now to continue the search for the yellow nuggets!" cried Ned, and Tom went with him, even Mr. Parker condescending to take a pick, now. Abe was the only one who dug steadily in one place. The others tried spot after spot.

"You've got t' stick t' one lead until you find somethin', or until it peters out," explained the miner. "You must git down to th' dirt before you'll find any gold, though you may strike a few grains that have worked up into th' ice."

After this advice they all kept to one hole until they had worked down through the ice to the dirt surface below. But even then, Abe, who was the first to achieve this, found no gold, and the old miner went to another location.

All the rest of that day they dug, but with no result. Not even a few grains of yellow dust rewarded their efforts.

"Are you sure this is the right place?" asked Mr. Damon, somewhat fretfully, of Abe. as they ate supper that night in the airship, sheltered as it was in the ice cave.

"I'm positive of it," was the reply. "There's gold here, but it will take some prospectin' t' find it. Maybe th' deposits have been shifted by th' ice movement, as Mr. Parker says. But it's here, an' we'll git it. We'll try ag'in t'-morrow."

They did try, but with small success. Laboring all day in the cold the only result was a few little yellow pebbles that Tom found imbedded in the ice. But they were gold, and the finding of them gave the seekers hope as they wearily began their task the following day. The weather seemed even colder, and there was the indication of a big storm.

They were scattered in different places on the ice, not far away from the big cave, each one picking away vigorously. Suddenly Abe, who had laboriously worked his way down to the dirt, gave an exultant yell.

"I've struck it! Struck it rich!" he shouted, leaping about as he threw down his pick, "Look here, everybody!" He stooped down over the hole. They all ran to his side, and saw him lifting from a little pocket in the dirt, several large, yellow pebbles.

"Gold! Gold!" cried Abe. "We've struck it at last!"

For a moment no one spoke, though there was a wild beating of their hearts. Then, off toward the farther end of the valley there sounded a curious noise. It was a shouting and yelling, mingled with the snapping of whips and the howls and barkings of dogs.

"Bless my handkerchief!" cried Mr. Damon. "What's that?"

They all saw a moment later. Approaching over the frozen snow were several Eskimo sledges, drawn by dog teams, and the native drivers were shouting and cracking their whips of walrus hide.

"The natives are coming to attack us!" cried Ned.

Tom said nothing. He was steadily observing the approaching sleds. They came on rapidly. Abe was holding the golden nuggets in his gloved hands.

"Get the guns! Where's your electric rifle, Tom?" cried Mr. Damon.

"I don't believe we'll need the guns—just yet," answered the young inventor, slowly.

"Bless my cartridge-belt! Why not?" demanded the eccentric man.

"Because those are the Fogers," replied Tom. "They have followed us—Andy and his father! Andy Foger here!" gasped Ned.

Tom nodded grimly. A few minutes later the sleds had come to a halt not far from our friends, and Andy, followed by his father, leaped off his conveyance. The two were clad in heavy fur garments.

"Ha, Tom Swift! You didn't get here much ahead of us!" exulted the bully. "I told you I'd get even with you! Come on, now, dad, we'll get right to work digging for gold!"

Tom and his companions did not know what to say.

JUMPING THE CLAIM

There was a sneering look on Andy's face, and Mr. Foger, too, seemed delighted at having reached the valley of gold almost as soon as had our friends. Tom and the others looked at the means by which the bully had arrived. There were four sleds, each one drawn by seven dogs, and in charge of a dark-skinned native. On the two foremost sleds Andy and his father had ridden, while the other two evidently contained their supplies.

For a moment Andy surveyed Tom's party and then, turning to one of the native drivers, he said:

"We'll camp here. You fellows get to work and make an ice house, and some of you cook a meal—I'm hungry."

"No need build ice house," replied the native, who spoke English brokenly.

"Why not?" demanded Andy.

"Live in ice cave-plenty much ob'em—plenty much room," went on the Eskimo, indicating several of the large caverns.

"Ha! That's a good idea," agreed Mr. Foger, "Andy, my son, we have houses already made for us, and very comfortable they seem, too. We'll take up our quarters in one, and then hunt for the gold."

Mr. Foger seemed to ignore Tom and his friends. Abe Abercrombie strode forward.

"Look here, you Fogers!" he exclaimed without ceremony, "was you calculatin' on stakin' any claims here?"

"If you mean are we going to dig for gold, we certainly are," replied Andy insolently, "and you can't stop us."

"I don't know about that," went on Abe, grimly. "I ain't goin' t' say nothin' now, about th' way you stole th' map from me, an' made a copy, but I am goin t' say this, an' that is it won't be healthy fer any of you t' git in my way, or t' try t' dig on our claims!"

"We'll dig where we please!" cried Andy. "You don't own this valley!"

"We own as much of it as we care to stake out, by right of prior discovery!" declared Tom, firmly.

"And I say we'll dig where we please!" insisted Andy. "Hand me a pick," he went on to another of the natives.

"Wait jest a minute," spoke Abe calmly, as he put his little store of nuggets in the pocket of his fur coat, and drew out a big revolver. "It ain't healthy t' talk that way, Andy Foger, an' th' sooner you find that out th' better. You ain't in Shopton now, an' th' only law here is what we make for ourselves. Tom, maybe you'd better get out th' rifles, an' your electric gun, after all. It seems like we might have trouble," and Abe cooly looked to see if his weapon was loaded.

"Oh, of course we didn't mean to usurp any of your rights, my dear friend!" exclaimed Mr, Foger quickly, and he seemed nervous at the sight of the big revolver, while Andy hastily moved until he was behind the biggest of the sledge drivers. "We don't want to violate any of your rights," went on Mr. Foger. "But this valley is large, and do I understand that you claim all of it?"

"We could if we wanted to," declared Abe stoutly; "but we'll be content with three-quarter of it, seein' we was here fust. If you folks want t' dig fer gold, go over there," and he pointed to a spot some distance away.

"We'll dig where we please!" cried Andy.

"Oh, will you?" and there was an angry light in Abe's eyes. "I guess, Tom, you'd better git—"

"No! No! My son is wrong—he is too hasty," interposed Mr. Foger. "We will go away—certainly we will. The valley is large enough for both of us—just as you say. Come, Andy!"

The bully seemed about to refuse, but a look at Abe's angry face and a sight of Mr. Damon coming from the cave where the airship was, with a rifle, for the eccentric man had hastened to get his weapon— this sight calmed Andy down. Without further words he and his father got back on their sleds, and were soon being driven off to where a large ice cave loomed up, about a mile away.

"Good riddance," muttered the miner, "now we kin go on diggin' wthout bein' bothered by that little scamp."

"I don't know about that," spoke Tom, shaking his head dubiously. "There's always trouble when Andy Foger's within a mile. I'm afraid we haven't seen the last of him."

"He'd better not come around here ag'in," declared Abe. "Queer, how he should turn up, jest when I made a big strike."

"They must have come on all the way from where their airship was wrecked, by means of dog sleds," observed Ned, and the others agreed with him. Later they learned that this was so; that after the accident to the *Anthony*, the crew had refused to proceed farther north, and had gone back. But Mr. Foger had hired the natives with the dog teams, and, by means of the copy of the map and with what knowledge his Eskimos had, had reached the valley of gold.

"We have certainly struck it rich," went on Abe, as he went back to where he had dug the hole. "Now we'd better all begin prospectin' here, for it looks like a big deposit. We'll stake out a large enough claim to take it all in. I guess Mr. Parker can do that, seein' as how he knows about such things."

The scientist agreed to do this part of the work, it being understood that all the gold discovered would be shared equally after the expenses of the trip had been paid.

Feverishly Abe and the others began to dig. They did not come upon such a rich deposit as the miner had found, but there were enough nuggets picked up to prove that the expedition would be very successful.

No more attention was paid to the Fogers, but through the telescope Tom could see that the bully and his father had made a camp in one of the ice caves, and that both were eagerly digging in the frozen surface of the valley.

Before night several thousand dollars' worth of gold had been taken out by our friends. It was stored in the airship, and then, after suppers the craft's searchlight was taken off, and placed in such a position in front of the cave of ice so that the beams would illuminate the claim staked out by Tom and the others.

"We'll stand watch an' watch," suggested Abe, "but I don't think them Fogers will come around here ag'in."

They did not, and the night passed peacefully. The next day our friends were again at work digging for gold. So were the Fogers, as could be observed through the glass, but it was impossible to see whether they got any nuggets.

The gold seemed to be in "pockets," and that day the ones in the vicinity of the strike first made by Abe were cleaned out.

"We'll have to locate some new 'pockets,'" said the miner, and the adventurers scattered over the frozen plain to look for other deposits of the precious metal.

Tom and Ned were digging together not far from one another. Suddenly Ned let out a joyful cry.

"Strike anything?" asked Tom.

"Something rich," answered the bank clerk. He lifted from a hole in the ground a handful of the golden pebbles.

"It's as good as Abe's was!" exclaimed Tom. "We must stake it out at once, or the Fogers may jump it. Come on, we'll go back and tell Abe, and get Mr. Parker and Mr. Damon over here."

The three men were some distance away, and there was no sign of the Fogers. Tom and Ned hurried back to where their friends were, leaving their picks and shovels on the frozen ground.

The good news was soon told, and, with some stakes hastily made from some extra wood carried on the airship, the little party hastened back to where Tom and Ned had made their strike.

As they emerged from behind a big hummock of ice they saw, standing over the holes which the lads had dug, Andy Foger and his father! Each one had a rifle, and there was a smile of triumph on Andy's face!

"What are you doing here?" cried Tom, the hot blood mounting to his cheeks.

"We've just staked out a claim here," answered the bully.

"And you deserted it," put in Mr. Foger smoothly. "I think your mining friend will tell you that we have a right to take up an abandoned claim."

"But we didn't abandon it!" declared Tom. "We only went away to get the stakes."

"The claim was abandoned, and we have 'jumped' it," went on Mr. Foger, and he cocked his rifle. "I need hardly tell you that possession is nine points of the law, and that we intend to remain. Andy, is your gun loaded?"

"Yes, pa."

"I—I guess they've got us—fer th' time bein'," murmured Abe, as he motioned to Tom and the others to come away. "Besides they've got guns, an' we haven't—but wait," added the miner, mysteriously. "I haven't played all my tricks yet."

ATTACKED BY NATIVES

To state that Tom and his friends were angry at the trick the Fogers had played on them would be putting it mildly. There was righteous indignation in their hearts, and, as for the young inventor he felt that much blame was attached to him for his neglect in not remaining on guard at the place of the lucky strike while Ned went to call the others.

"I guess Andy must have been spying on us," spoke Ned, "or he would never have known when to rush up just as he did; as soon as we left."

"Probably," admitted Tom, bitterly.

"But, bless my penholder!" cried Mr. Damon. "Can't we do something, Abe? Won't the law—?"

"There ain't any law out here, except what you make yourself," said the miner. "I guess they've got us for th' time bein'."

"What do you mean by that?" asked Tom, detecting a gleam of hope in Abe's tone.

"Well, I mean that I think we kin git ahead of 'em. Come on back to th' ship, an' we'll talk it over."

They walked away, leaving Andy and his father in possession of the rich deposits of gold, and that it was much richer even then than the hole Abe had first discovered was very evident. The two Fogers were soon at work, digging out the yellow metal with the pick and shovels Tom and Ned had so thoughtlessly dropped.

"What little law there is out here they've got on their side," went on Abe, "an' they've got possession, too, which is more. Of course we could go at 'em in a pitched battle, but I take it you don't want any bloodshed?" and he looked at Tom.

"Of course not," replied the lad quickly, "but I'd like to meet Andy alone, with nothing but my fists for a little while," and Tom's eyes snapped.

"So would I," added Ned.

"Perhaps we can find another pocket of gold better than that one," suggested Mr. Damon.

"We might," admitted Abe, "but that one was ours an' we're entitled to it. This valley is rich in gold deposits, but you can't allers put your hand on 'em. We may have t' hunt around for a week until we strike another. An', meanwhile, them Fogers will be takin' our gold! It's not to be borne! I'll find some way of drivin' 'em out. An' we've got t' do it soon, too."

"You mean if we don't that they'll get all the gold?" asked Mr. Damon.

"No, I mean that soon it will be th' long night up here, an' we can't work. We'll have t' go back, an' I don't want t' go back until I've made my pile."

"Neither do any of us, I guess," spoke Tom, "but there doesn't seem to be any help for it."

They discussed several plans on reaching the ship, but none seemed feasible without resorting to force, and this they did not want to do, as they feared there might be bloodshed. When night closed in they could see the gleam of a campfire, kindled by the Foger party, at the gold-pocket, from bits of the scrubby trees that grew in that frigid clime.

"They're going to stay on guard," announced Tom. "We can't get it away from them to-night."

Though Abe had spoken of some plan to regain the advantage the Fogers had of them, the old miner was not quite ready to propose it. All the next day he seemed very thoughtful, while going about with the others, seeking new deposits of gold. Luck did not seem to be with them. They found two or three places where there were traces of the yellow pebbles, but in no very great quantity.

Meanwhile the Fogers were busy at the pocket Ned had located. They seemed to be taking out much of the precious metal.

"And it all ought to be ours," declared Tom, bitterly.

"Yes, and it shall be, too!" suddenly exclaimed. Abe. "I think I have a plan that will beat 'em."

"What is it?" asked Tom.

"Let's get back to the ship, and I'll tell you," said Abe. "We can't tell when one of their natives might be sneakin' in among these ice caves, an' they understand some English. They might give my scheme away."

In brief Abe's plan, as he unfolded it in the cabin of the *Red Cloud* was this:

They would divide into two parties, one consisting of Ned and Tom, and the other of the three men. The latter, by a circuitous route, would go to the ice caves where the Fogers had established their camp. It was there that the Indians remained during the day, while Andy and his father labored at the gold pocket, for, after the first day when they had had the natives aid them, father and son had worked alone at the hole, probably fearing to trust the Indians. At night, though either Andy or his father remained on guard, with one or two of the dusky-skinned dog drivers.

"But we'll work this trick before night," said Abe. "We three men will get around to where the natives are in the ice cave. We'll pretend to attack them, and raise a great row, firing our guns in the air, and all that sort of thing, an' yellin' t' beat th' band. Th' natives will yell, too, you can depend on that."

"Th' Fogers will imagine we are tryin' t' git away with their sleds an' supplies, an' maybe their gold, if they've got it stored in th' ice cave. Naturally Andy or his father will run here, an' that will leave only one on guard at th' mine. Then Tom an' Ned can sneak up. Th' two of 'em will be a match for even th' old Foger, if he happens t' stay, an' while Tom or Ned comes up in front, t' hold his attention, th' other can come up in back, an' grab his arms, if he tries t' shoot. Likely Andy will remain at th' gold hole, an' you two lads kin handle him, can't you?"

"Well, I guess!" exclaimed Tom and Ned together.

The plan worked like a charm. Abe, Mr. Damon and Mr. Parker raised a great din at the ice cave where the Foger natives were. The sound carried to the hole where Andy and his father were digging out the gold. Mr. Foger at once ran toward the cave, while Andy, catching up his gun, remained on the alert.

Then came the chance of Tom and Ned. The latter coming from his hiding-place, advanced boldly toward the bully, while Tom, making a detour, worked his way up behind.

"Here! You keep away!" cried Andy, catching sight of Ned. "I see what the game is, now! It's a trick!"

"You're a nice one to talk about tricks!" declared Ned, advancing slowly.

"Keep away if you don't want to get hurt!" yelled Andy.

"Oh, you wouldn't hurt me; would you?" mocked Ned, who wanted to give Tom time to sneak up behind the bully.

"Yes, I would! Keep back!" Andy was nervously fingering his weapon. The next instant his gun flew from his grasp, and he went over backward in Tom's strong grip; for the young inventor, in his sealskin shoes had worked up in the rear without a sound. The next moment Andy broke away and was running for his life, leaving Tom and Ned in possession of the gold hole, and that without a shot being fired. A little later the three men, who had hurried away from the cave as Mr. Foger rushed up to see what caused the racket, joined Tom and Ned, and formal possession was taken of their lucky strike.

"We'll guard it well, now," decided Tom, and later that day they moved some supplies near the hole, and for a shelter built an igloo, Eskimo fashion, in which work Abe had had some experience. Then they moved the airship to another ice cave, nearer their "mine" as they called it, and prepared to stand guard.

But there seemed to be no need, for the following day there was no trace of the Fogers. They and their natives had disappeared.

"I guess we were too much for them," spoke Tom. But the sequel was soon to prove differently.

It was three days after our friends had regained their mine, during which time they had dug out considerable gold, that toward evening, as Tom was taking the last of the output of yellow pebbles into the cave where the airship was, he looked across the valley.

"Looks like something coming this way," observed the young inventor. "Natives, I guess."

"It is," agreed Ned, "quite a large party, too!"

"Better tell Abe and the others," went on Tom. "I don't like the looks of this. Maybe the sudden disappearance of the Fogers has something to do with it."

Abe, Mr. Damon and Mr. Parker hurried from the ice cave. They had caught up their guns as they ran out.

"They're still coming on," called Tom, "and are headed this way."

"They're Indians, all right!" exclaimed Abe. "Hark! What's that?"

It was the sound of shouting and singing.

Through the gathering dusk the party advanced. Our friends closely scanned them. There was something familiar about the two leading figures, and it could now be seen that in the rear were a number of dog sleds.

"There's Andy Foger and his father!" cried Ned. "They've gone and got a lot of Eskimos to help them drive us away."

"That's right!" admitted Tom. "I guess we're in for it now!"

With a rush the natives, led by the Fogers, came on. They were yelling now. An instant later they began firing their guns.

"It's a fierce attack!" cried Tom. "Into the ice cave for shelter! We can cover the gold mine from there. I'll get my electric gun!"

THE WRECK OF THE AIRSHIP

Almost before our friends could retreat into the cave which now sheltered the *Red Cloud*, the attacking natives opened fire. Fortunately they only had old-fashioned, muzzle-loading muskets, and, as their aim was none of the best, there was comparatively little danger. The bullets, however, did sing through the fast-gathering darkness with a vicious sound, and struck the heavy sides and sloping front of the ice cave with a disconcerting "ping!"

"I don't hear Andy or his father firing!" called Tom, as he and the others returned the fire of the savage Indians. "I could tell their guns by the sharper reports. The Fogers carry repeating rifles, and they're fine ones, if they're anything like the one we took from Andy, Ned."

"That's right," agreed Tom's chum, "I don't believe Andy or his father dare fire. They're afraid to, and they're putting the poor ignorant natives up to it. Probably they hired them to try to drive us away."

This, as they afterward learned, was exactly the case.

The battle, if such it could be called, was kept up. There was about a hundred natives, all of whom had guns, and, though they were slow to load, there were enough weapons to keep up a constant fusilade. On their part, Tom and the others fired at first over the heads of the natives, for they did not want to kill any of the deluded men. Later, though, when they saw the rush keeping up, they fired at their legs, and disabled several of the Eskimos, the electric gun proving very effective.

It was now quite dark, and the firing slackened. From their position in the cave, Tom and the others could command the hole where the gold was, and, as they saw several natives sneaking up to it the young inventor and Ned, both of whom were good shots, aimed to have the bullets strike the ice close to where the Indians were.

This sort of shooting was enough, and the natives scurried away. Then Tom hit on the plan of playing the searchlight on the spot, and this effectually prevented an unseen attack. It seemed to discourage the enemy, too for they did not venture into that powerful glow of light.

"They won't do anything more until morning," declared Abe. "Then we'll have it hot an' heavy, though, I'm afeered. Well, we'll have t' make th' best of it!"

They took turns standing guard that night, but no attack was made. The fact of the Fogers coming back with the band of Indians told Tom, more plainly than words, how desperately his enemies would do battle with them. Anxiously they waited for the morning.

Several times in the night Mr. Parker was seen roaming about uneasily, though it was not his turn to be on guard. Finally Tom asked him what was the matter, and if he could not sleep.

"It isn't that," answered the scientist, "but I am worried about the ice. I can detect a slight but peculiar movement by means of some of my scientific instruments. I am alarmed about it. I fear something is going to happen."

But Tom was too worried about the outcome of the fight he knew would be renewed on the next day, to think much about the ice movement. He thought it would only be some scientific phenomena that would amount to little.

With the first streak of the late dawn, the gold-seekers were up, and partook of a hot breakfast, with strong coffee which Mr. Damon brewed. Tom took an observation from the mouth of the cave. The searchlight was still dimly glowing, and it did not disclose anything. Tom turned it off. He thought he saw a movement among the ranks of the enemy, who had camped just beyond the gold hole.

"I guess they're coming!" cried the lad. "Get ready for them!"

The adventurers caught up their guns, and hurried to the entrance of the cave. Mr. Parker lingered behind, and was observed to be narrowly scanning the walls of the cavern.

"Come on, Parker, my dear man!" begged Mr. Damon. "We are in grave danger, and we need your help. Bless my life insurance policy! but I never was in such a state as this."

"We may soon be in a worse one," was the answer of the gloomy scientist.

"What do you mean?" asked Mr. Damon, but he hurried on without waiting for a reply.

Suddenly, from without the cave came a series of fierce yells. It was the battle-cry of the Indians. At the same moment there sounded a fusillade of guns.

"The battle is beginning!" cried Tom Swift, grimly. He held his electric gun, though he had not used it very much in the previous attack, preferring to save it for a time of more need.

As the defenders of the cave reached the entrance they saw the body of natives rushing forward. They were almost at the gold hole, with Andy Foger and his father discreetly behind the first row of Eskimos, when, with a suddenness that was startling, there sounded throughout the whole valley a weird sound!

It was like the wailing of some giant—the sighing of some mighty wind. At the same time the air suddenly became dark, and then there came a violent snow squall, shutting out instantly the sight of the advancing natives. Tom and the others could not see five feet beyond the cave.

"This will delay the attack," murmured Ned, "They can't see to come at us."

Mr. Parker came running up from the interior of the cave. On his face there was a look of alarm.

"We must leave here at once!" he cried.

"Leave here?" repeated Tom. "Why must we? The enemy are out there! We'd run right into them!"

"It must be done!" insisted the scientist. "We must leave the cave at once!"

"What for?" cried Mr. Damon.

"Because the movement of the ice that I predicted, has begun. It is much more rapid than I supposed it would be. In a short time this cave and all the others will be crushed flat!"

"Crushed flat!" gasped Tom.

"Yes, the caves of ice are being destroyed! Hark! You can hear them snapping!"

They all listened. Above the roar of the storm could be made out the noise of crushing, grinding ice-sounds like cannon being fired, as the great masses of frozen crystal snapped like frail planks.

"The ice caves are being destroyed by an upheaval of nature!" went on Mr. Parker. "This one will soon go! The walls are bulging now! We must get out!"

"But the natives! They will kill us!" cried Mr. Damon. "Bless my soul! what a trying position to be in."

"I guess the natives are as bad off as we are," suggested Ned. "They're not firing, and I can hear cries of alarm, I think they're running away."

There was a lull in the snow flurry, and the white curtain seemed to lift for a moment. The gold-seekers had a glimpse of the natives in full retreat, with the Fogers—father and son—racing panic-stricken after them. Tom could also see a big cave, just beyond the gold hole, collapse and crumble to pieces like a house of cards.

"We have no time to lose!" Mr. Parker warned them. "The roof of this cave is slowly coming down. The sides are collapsing! We must get out!"

"Then wheel out the airship!" cried Tom. "We must save that! We needn't fear the natives, now!"

The young inventor hurried to the *Red Cloud* calling to Ned and the others. They hastened to his side. It was an easy matter to move the airship along on the wheels. It neared the opening of the cave. The rumbling, roaring, grinding sound of the ice increased.

"Why—why!" cried Tom in surprise and alarm, as the craft neared the mouth of the ice cavern, "we can't get it out—the opening is too small! Yet it came in easily enough!"

"The cave is collapsing—growing smaller every moment!" cried Mr. Parker. "We have only time to save our lives! Run out!"

"And leave the airship? Never!" yelled Tom.

"You must! You can't save that and your life!"

"Get axes and make the opening bigger!" suggested Ned, who, like his chum, could not bear to think of the destruction of the beautiful craft.

"No time! No time!" shouted Mr. Parker, frantically, "We must get out! Save what you can from the ship—the gold—some supplies—the guns—some food—save what you can!"

Then ensued a wild effort to get from the doomed craft what they could—what they would need if they were to save their lives in that cold and desolate country. Food, some blankets—their guns—as much of the gold as they could hastily gather together—their weapons and some ammunition—all this was carried from the cabin outside the cave. The entrance was rapidly growing smaller. The roof was already pressing down on the gas-bag.

Tom gave one last look at his fine craft. There were tears in his eyes. He started into the cabin for something he had forgotten. Mr. Parker grabbed him by the arm.

"Don't go in!" he cried hoarsely. "The cave will collapse in another instant!" He rushed with Tom out of the cavern, and not a moment too soon. The others were already outside.

Then with a rush and a roar, with a sound like a great explosion, with a rending, grinding and booming as the great pieces of ice collapsed one against the other, the big ice cave settled in, as does some great building when the walls are weakened!

Down crashed the roof of the ice cave! Down upon the *Red Cloud*, burying out of sight, forever, under thousands of tons of ice and snow, the craft which was the pride of Tom Swift's heart! It was the end of the airship!

Tom felt a moisture of tears in his eyes as he stood there in the midst of the snowstorm.

The Rescue—Conclusion

For a few moments after the collapse of the cave, and the destruction of the airship, on which they depended to take them from that desolate land, no one spoke. The calamity had been too terrible—they could hardly understand it.

The snow had ceased, and, over the frozen plain, in full retreat, could be seen the band of attacking Indians. They had fled in terror at the manifestation of Nature. And Nature, as if satisfied at the mischief she had wrought, called a halt to the movement of the ice. The roaring, grinding sounds ceased, and there were no more collapses of caves in that neighborhood.

"Well, we are up against it," spoke Tom, softly. "Poor old *Red Cloud*! There'll never be another airship like you!"

"We are lucky to have escaped with our lives," said Mr. Parker. "Another moment and it would have been too late. I was expecting something like this—I predicted it."

But his honor was an empty one—no one cared to dispute it with him.

"Bless my refrigerator! What's to be done!" exclaimed Mr. Damon.

"Start from here as soon as possible," decided Abe.

"Why, do you think the natives will come back?" asked Ned.

"No, but we have only a small supply of food, my lad, an' it's hard to git up here. We must hit th' trail fer civilization as soon as we kin!"

"Go back—how; without the airship?" asked Tom, blankly.

"Walk!" exclaimed the miner, grimly. "It's th' only way!"

They realized that. There was no hope of digging through that mass of fantastically piled ice to reach the airship, and, even if they could have done so, it would have been crushed beyond all hope of repair. Nor could they dig down for more food, though what they had hastily saved was little enough.

"Well, if we've got to go, we'd better start," suggested Tom, sadly. "Poor old *Red Cloud!*"

"Maybe we can get a little more gold," suggested Ned.

They walked over to the hole whence they had taken the yellow nuggets. The "pocket" was not to be seen. It was buried out of sight under tons of ice.

"We'll get no more gold here," decided Abe, "If we get safely out of th' valley, and t' the nearest white settlement, we'll be lucky."

"Bless my soul! Is it as bad as that!" cried Mr. Damon.

Abe nodded without speaking. There was nothing else to do. Sadly and silently they made up into packs the things they had saved, and started southward, guided by a small compass the miner had with him.

It was a melancholy party. Fortunately the weather had turned a little warmer or they might have been frozen to death. They tramped all that day, shaping their course to take them out of the valley on a side well away from where the hostile natives lived. At night they made rude shelters of snow and blocks of ice and ate cold victuals. The second day it grew colder, and they were slightly affected by snow-blindness, for they had lost their dark glasses in the cave.

Even the gold seemed too great a burden to carry, and they found they had more of it than at first they supposed. On the third day they were ready to give up, but Abe bravely urged them on. Toward the close of the fourth day, even the old miner was in despair, for the food they could carry was not such as to give strength and warmth, and they saw no game to shoot.

They were just getting ready to go into a cheerless camp for the night, when Tom, who was a little in advance, looked ahead.

"Ned, do I see something or is it only a vision?" he asked.

"What does it look like?" asked his chum.

"Like Eskimos on sleds."

"That's what it is," agreed Ned, after an observation. "Maybe it's the Fogers, or some of the savage Indians."

They halted in alarm, and got out their guns. The little party of natives kept coming on toward them.

Suddenly Abe uttered a cry, but it was one of joy and not fear.

"Hurrah!" he yelled, "It's all right—they're friendly natives! They're of the same tribe that helped me an' my partner! It's all right, boys, we're rescued now!"

And so it proved. A few minutes later the gold-seekers were on the sleds of the friendly Eskimos, some of whom remembered Abe, and the weary and hungry adventures were being rushed toward the native village as fast as the dogs could run. It was a hunting party that had come upon our friends just in time.

Little more remains to be told. Well cared for by the kind Eskimos, Tom and his friends soon recovered their spirits and strength. They arranged for dog teams to take them to Sitka, and paid their friends well for the service, not only in gold, but by presenting what was of more value, the guns they no longer needed. Tom, however, retained his electric rifle.

Three weeks after that they were on a steamer bound for civilization, having bidden their friends the Eskimos good-by.

"Homeward bound," remarked Tom, some time later, as they were in a train speeding across the continent. "It was a great trip, and the gold we got will more than repay us, even to building a new airship. Still, I can't help feeling sorry about the *Red Cloud*."

"I don't blame you," returned Ned. "Are you going to build another airship, Tom?"

"Not one like the *Red Cloud*, I think. But I have in mind plans for a sort of racing craft. I think I'll start it when I get back home."

How Tom's plans developed, and what sort of a craft he built will be related in the next volume of this series, to be called "Tom Swift and His Sky Racer; or, the Quickest Flight on Record." In that will be told how the young inventor foiled his enemies, and how he saved his father's life. Our friends arrived safely at Shopton in due season. They learned that the two Fogers had reached there shortly before them. Tom and his party decided not to prosecute them, and they did not learn the identity of the men who tried to rob Tom of the map.

"But I guess Andy won't go about boasting of his airship any more," said Ned, "nor of how he got our gold mine away from us. He'll sing mighty small for a while."

The store of gold brought from the North, proved quite valuable, though but for the unforeseen accidents our friends could have secured much more. Yet they were well satisfied. With his share Abe Abercrombie settled down out West, Mr. Damon gave most of his gold to his wife, Mr. Parker bought scientific instruments with his, Ned invested his in bank stock, and Tom Swift, after buying a beautiful gift for a certain pretty young lady, used part of the remainder to build his Sky Racer.

And now, for a time, we will take leave of Tom and his friends, and say good-by.

TOM SWIFT AND HIS SKY RACER
or The Quickest Flight on Record

TABLE OF CONTENTS:

THE PRIZE OFFER

"Is this Tom Swift, the inventor of several airships?"

The man who had rung the bell glanced at the youth who answered his summons.

"Yes, I'm Tom Swift," was the reply. "Did you wish to see me?"

"I do. I'm Mr. James Gunmore, secretary of the Eagle Park Aviation Association. I had some correspondence with you about a prize contest we are going to hold. I believe—"

"Oh, yes, I remember now," and the young inventor smiled pleasantly as he opened wider the door of his home. "Won't you come in? My father will be glad to see you. He is as much interested in airships as I am." And Tom led the way to the library, where the secretary of the aviation society was soon seated in a big, comfortable leather chair.

"I thought we could do better, and perhaps come to some decision more quickly, if I came to see you, than if we corresponded," went on Mr. Gunmore. "I hope I haven't disturbed you at any of your inventions," and the secretary smiled at the youth.

"No. I'm through for to-day," replied Tom. "I'm glad to see you. I thought at first it was my chum, Ned Newton. He generally runs over in the evening."

"Our society, as I wrote you, Mr. Swift, is planning to hold a very large and important aviation meet at Eagle Park, which is a suburb of Westville, New York State. We expect to have all the prominent 'bird-men' there, to compete for prizes, and your name was mentioned. I wrote to you, as you doubtless recall, asking if you did not care to enter."

"And I think I wrote you that my big aeroplane-dirigible, the *Red Cloud*, was destroyed in Alaska, during a recent trip we made to the caves of ice there, after gold," replied Tom.

"Yes, you did," admitted Mr. Gunmore, "and while our committee was very sorry to hear that, we hoped you might have some other air craft that you could enter at our meet. We want to make it as complete as possible, and we all feel that it would not be so unless we had a Swift aeroplane there."

"It's very kind of you to say so," remarked Tom, "but since my big craft was destroyed I really have nothing I could enter."

"Haven't you an aeroplane of any kind? I made this trip especially to get you to enter. Haven't you anything in which you could compete for the prizes? There are several to be offered, some for distance flights, some for altitude, and the largest, ten thousand dollars, for the speediest craft. Ten thousand dollars is the grand prize, to be awarded for the quickest flight on record."

"I surely would like to try for that," said Tim, "but the only craft I have is a small monoplane, the *Butterfly*, I call it, and while it is very speedy, there have been such advances made in aeroplane construction since I made mine that I fear I would be distanced if I raced in her. And I wouldn't like that."

"No," agreed Mr. Gunmore. "I suppose not. Still, I do wish we could induce you to enter. I don't mind telling you that we consider you a drawing-card. Can't we induce you, some way?"

"I'm afraid not. I haven't any machine which—"

"Look here!" exclaimed the secretary eagerly. "Why can't you build a special aeroplane to enter in the next meet? You'll have plenty of time, as it doesn't come off for three months yet. We are only making the preliminary arrangements. It is now June, and the meet is scheduled for early in September. Couldn't you build a new and speedy aeroplane in that time?"

Eagerly Mr. Gunmore waited for the answer. Tom Swift seemed to be considering it. There was an increased brightness to his eyes, and one could tell that he was thinking deeply. The secretary sought to clinch his argument.

"I believe, from what I have heard of your work in the past, that you could build an aeroplane which would win the ten-thousand-dollar prize," he went on. "I would be very glad if you did win it, and, so I think, would be the gentlemen associated with me in this enterprise. It would be fine to have a New York State youth win the grand prize. Come, Tom Swift, build a special craft, and enter the contest!"

As he paused for an answer footsteps were heard coming along the hall, and a moment later an aged gentleman opened the door of the library.

"Oh! Excuse me, Tom," he said, "I didn't know you had company." And he was about to withdraw.

"Don't go, father," said Tom. "You will be as much interested in this as I am. This is Mr. Gunmore, of the Eagle Park Aviation Association. This is my father, Mr. Gunmore."

"I've heard of you," spoke the secretary as he shook hands with the aged inventor. "You and your son have made, in aeronautics, a name to be proud of."

"And he wants us to go still farther, dad," broke in the youth. "Me wants me to build a specially speedy aeroplane, and race for ten thousand dollars."

"Hum!" mused Mr. Swift. "Well, are you going to do it, Tom? Seems to me you ought to take a rest. You haven't been back from your gold-hunting trip to Alaska long enough to more than catch your breath, and now—"

"Oh, he doesn't have to go in this right away," eagerly explained Mr. Gunmore. "There is plenty of time to make a new craft."

"Well, Tom can do as he likes about it," said his father. "Do you think you could build anything speedier than your *Butterfly*, son?"

"I think so, father. That is, if you'd help me. I have a plan partly thought out, but it will take some time to finish it. Still, I might get it done in time."

"I hope you'll try!" exclaimed the secretary. "May I ask whether it would be a monoplane or a biplane?"

"A monoplane, I think," answered Tom. "They are much more speedy than the double-deckers, and if I'm going to try for the ten thousand dollars I need the fastest machine I can build."

"We have the promise of one or two very fast monoplanes for the meet," went on Mr. Gunmore. "Would yours be of a new type?"

"I think it would," was the reply of the young inventor. "In fact, I am thinking of making a smaller monoplane than any that have yet been constructed, and yet one that will carry two persons. The hardest work will be to make the engine light enough and still have it sufficiently powerful to make over a hundred miles an hour, if necessary.

"A hundred miles an hour in a small monoplane! It isn't possible!" cried the secretary.

"I'll make better time than that," said Tom quietly, and with not a trace of boasting in his tones.

"Then you'll enter the meet?" asked Mr. Gunmore eagerly.

"Well, I'll think about it," promised Tom. "I'll let you know in a few days. Meanwhile, I'll be thinking out the details for my new craft. I have been going to build one ever since I got back, after having seen my *Red Cloud* crushed in the ice cave. Now I think I had better begin active work."

"I hope you will soon let me know," resumed the secretary. "I'm going to put you down as a possible contestant for the ten-thousand-dollar prize. That can do no harm, and I hope you win it. I trust—"

He paused suddenly, and listened. So did Tom Swift and his father, for they all distinctly heard stealthy footsteps under the open windows of the library.

"Some one is out there, listening," said Tom in low tones.

"Perhaps it's Eradicate Sampson," suggested Mr. Swift, referring to the eccentric colored man who was employed by the inventor and his son to help around the place. "Very likely it was Eradicate, Tom."

"I don't think so," was the lad's answer. "He went to the village a while ago, and said he wouldn't be back until late to-night. He had to get some medicine for his mule, Boomerang, who is sick. No, it wasn't Eradicate; but some one was under that window, trying to hear what we said."

As he spoke in guarded tones, Tom went softly to the casement and looked out. He could observe nothing, as the night was dark, and the new moon, which had been shining, was now dimmed by clouds.

"See anything?" asked Mr. Gunmore as he advanced to Tom's side.

"No," was the low answer. I can't hear anything now, either."

"I'll go speak to Mrs. Baggert, the housekeeper," volunteered Mr. Swift. "Perhaps it was she, or she may know something about it."

He started from the room, and as he went Tom noticed, with something of a start, that his father appeared older that night than he had ever looked before. There was a trace of pain on the face of the aged inventor, and his step was lagging.

"I guess dad needs a rest and doctoring up," thought the young inventor as he turned the electric chandelier off by a button on the wall, in order to darken the room, so that he might peer out to better advantage. "I think he's been working too hard on his wireless motor. I must get Dr. Gladby to come over and see dad. But now I want to find out who that was under this window."

Once more Tom looked out. The moon had emerged from behind a thin bank of clouds, and gave a little light.

"See anything?" asked Mr. Gunmore cautiously.

"No," whispered the youth, for it being a warm might, the windows were open top and bottom, a screen on the outside keeping out mosquitoes and other insects. "I can't see a thing," went on Tom, "but I'm sure—"

He paused suddenly. As he spoke there sounded a rustling in the shrubbery a little distance from the window.

"There's something!" exclaimed Mr. Gunmore.

"I see!" answered the young inventor.

Without another word he softly opened the screen, and then, stooping down to get under the lower sash (for the windows in the library ran all the way to the floor), Tom dropped out of the casement upon the thick grass.

As he did so he was aware of a further movement in the bushes. They were violently agitated, and a second later a dark object sprang from them and sprinted along the path.

"Here! Who are you? Hold on!" cried the young inventor.

But the figure never halted. Tom sprang forward, determined to see who it was, and, if possible, capture him.

"Hold on!" he cried again. There was no answer.

Tom was a good runner, and in a few seconds he had gained on the fugitive, who could just be seen in the dim light from the crescent moon.

"I've got you!" cried Tom.

But he was mistaken, for at that instant his foot caught on the outcropping root of a tree, and the young inventor went flat on his face.

"Just my luck!" he cried.

He was quickly on his feet again, and took after the fugitive. The latter glanced back, and, as it happened, Tom had a good look at his face. He almost came to a stop, so startled was he.

"Andy Foger!" he exclaimed as he recognized the bully who had always proved himself such an enemy of our hero. "Andy Foger sneaking under my windows to hear what I had to say about my new aeroplane! I wonder what his game can be? I'll soon find out!"

Tom was about to resume the chase, when he lost sight of the figure. A moment later he heard the puffing of an automobile, as some one cranked it up.

"It's too late!" exclaimed Tom. "There he goes in his car!" And knowing it would be useless to keep up the chase, the youth turned back toward his house.

Mr. Swift Is Ill

"Who was it?" asked Mr. Gunmore as Tom again entered the library. "A friend of yours?"

"Hardly a friend," replied Tom grimly. "It was a young fellow who has made lots of trouble for me in the past, and who, lately, with his father, tried to get ahead of me and some friends of mine in locating a gold claim in Alaska. I don't know what he's up to now, but certainly it wasn't any good. He's got nerve, sneaking up under our windows!"

"What do you think was his object?"

"It would he hard to say."

"Can't you find him to-morrow, and ask him?"

"There's not much satisfaction in that. The less I have to do with Andy Foger the better I'm satisfied. Well, perhaps it's just as well I fell, and couldn't catch him. There would have been a fight, and I don't want to worry dad any more than I can help. He hasn't been very well of late."

"No, he doesn't look very strong," agreed the secretary. "But I hope he doesn't get sick, and I hope no bad consequences result from the eavesdropping of this Foger fellow."

Tom started for the hall, to get a brush with which to remove some of the dust gathered in his chase after Andy. As he opened the library door to go out Mr. Swift came in again.

"I saw Mrs. Baggert, Tom," he said. "She wasn't out under the window, and, as you said, Eradicate isn't about. His mule is in the barn, so it couldn't have been the animal straying around."

"No, dad. It was Andy Foger."

"Andy Foger!"

"Yes. I couldn't catch him. But you'd better go lie down, father. It's getting late, and you look tired."

"I am tired, Tom, and I think I'll go to bed. Have you finished your arrangements with Mr. Gunmore?"

"Well, I guess we've gone as far as we can until I invent the new aeroplane," replied Tom, with a smile.

"Then you'll really enter the meet?" asked the secretary eagerly.

"I think I will," decided Tom. "The prize of ten thousand dollars is worth trying for, and besides that, I'll be glad to get to work again on a speedy craft. Yes, I'll enter the meet."

"Good!" exclaimed Mr. Gunmore, shaking hands with the young inventor. "I didn't have my trip for nothing, then. I'll go back in the morning and report to the committee that I've been successful. I am greatly obliged to you."

He left the Swift home, after refusing Tom's invitation to remain all night, and went to his hotel. Tom then insisted that his father retire.

As for the young inventor, he was not satisfied with the result of his attempt to catch Andy Foger. He had no idea why the bully was hiding under the library window, but Tom surmised that some mischief might be afoot.

"Sam Snedecker or Pete Bailey, the two cronies of Andy, may still be around here, trying to play some trick on me," mused Tom. "I think I'll take a look outside." And taking a stout cane from the umbrella rack, the youth sallied forth into the yard and extensive grounds surrounding his house.

While he is thus looking for possible intruders we will tell you a little more about him than has been possible since the call of the aviation secretary.

Tom Swift lived with his father, Barton Swift, in the town of Shopton, New York State. The young man had followed in the footsteps of his parent, and was already an inventor of note.

Their home was presided over by Mrs. Baggert, as housekeeper, since Mrs. Swift had been dead several years. In addition, there was Garret Jackson, an engineer, who aided Tom and his father, and Eradicate Sampson, an odd colored man, who, with his mule, Boomerang, worked about the place.

In the first volume of this series, entitled "Tom Swift and his Motor-Cycle," here was related how he came to possess that machine. A certain Mr. Wakefield Damon, an eccentric gentleman, who was always blessing himself, or something about him, owned the cycle, but he came to grief on it, and sold it to Tom very cheaply.

Tom had a number of adventures on the wheel, and, after having used the motor to save a valuable patent model from a gang of unscrupulous men, the lad acquired possession of a power boat, in which he made several trips, and took part in many exciting happenings.

Some time later, in company with John Sharp, an aeronaut, whom Tom had rescued from Lake Carlopa, after the airman had nearly lost his life in a burning balloon, the young inventor made a big airship, called the *Red Cloud*. With Mr. Damon, Tom made several trips in this craft, as set forth in the book, "Tom Swift and His Airship."

It was after this that Tom and his father built a submarine boat, and went under the ocean for sunken treasure, and, following that trip Tom built a speedy electric runabout, and by a remarkable run in that, with Mr. Damon, saved a bank from ruin, bringing gold in time to stave off a panic.

"Tom Swift and His Wireless Message" told of the young inventor's plan to save the castaways of Earthquake Island, and how he accomplished it by constructing a wireless plant from the remains of the wrecked airship *Whizzer*. After Tom got back from Earthquake Island he went with Mr. Barcoe Jenks, whom he met on the ill-fated bit of land, to discover the secret of the diamond makers. They found the mysterious men, but the trip was not entirely successful, for the mountain containing the cave where the diamonds were made was destroyed by a lightning shock, just as Mr. Parker, a celebrated scientist, who accompanied the party, said it would be.

But his adventure in seeking to discover the secret of making precious stones did not satisfy Tom Swift, and when he and his friends got back from the mountains they prepared to go to Alaska to search for gold in the caves of ice. They were almost defeated in their purpose by the actions of Andy Foger and his father, who in an under-hand manner, got possession of a valuable map, showing the location of the gold, and made a copy of the drawing.

Then, when Tom and his friends set off in the *Red Cloud*, as related in "Tom Swift in the Caves of Ice," the Fogers, in another airship, did likewise. But Tom and his party were first on the scene, and accomplished their purpose, though they had to fight the savage Indians. The airship was wrecked in a cave of ice, that collapsed on it, and the survivors had desperate work getting away from the frozen North.

Tom had been home all the following winter and spring, and he had done little more than work on some small inventions, when a new turn was given his thoughts and energies by a visit from Mr. Gunmore, as narrated in the first chapter of the present volume.

"Well, I guess no one is here," remarked the young inventor as he completed the circuit of the grounds and walked slowly back toward the house. "I think I scared Andy so that he won't come back right away. He had the laugh on me, though, when I stumbled and fell."

As Tom proceeded he heard some one approaching, around the path at the side of the house.

"Who's there?" he called quickly, taking a firmer grasp of his stick,

"It's me, Massa Swift," was the response. "I jest come back from town. I got some peppermint fo' mah mule, Boomerang, dat's what I got."

"Oh! It's you, is it, Rad?" asked the youth in easier tones.

"Dat's who it am, Did yo' t'ink it were some un else?"

"I did," replied Tom. "Andy Foger has been sneaking around. Keep your eyes open the rest of the night, Rad."

"I will, Massa Tom."

The youth went into the house, having left word with the engineer, Mr. Jackson, to be on the alert for anything suspicious.

"And now I guess I'll go to bed, and make an early start to-morrow morning, planning my new aeroplane," mused Tom. "I'm going to make the speediest craft of the air ever seen!"

As he started toward his room Tom Swift heard the voice of the housekeeper calling to him:

"Tom! Oh, Tom! Come here, quickly!"

"What's the matter?" he asked, in vague alarm.

"Something has happened to your father!" was the startling reply. "He's fallen down, and is Unconscious! Come quickly! Send for the doctor!"

Tom fairly ran toward his father's room.

THE PLANS DISAPPEAR

Mr. Swift was lying on the floor, where he had fallen, in front of his bed, as he was preparing to retire. There was no mark of injury upon him, and at first, as he knelt down at his father's side, Tom was at a loss to account for what had taken place.

"How did it happen? When was it?" he asked of Mrs. Baggert, as he held up his father's head, and noted that the aged man was breathing slightly.

"I don't know what happened, Tom," answered the housekeeper, "but I beard him fall, and ran upstairs, only to find him lying there, just like that. Then I called you. Hadn't you better have a doctor?"

"Yes; we'll need one at once. Send Eradicate Tell him to run—not to wait for his mule—Boomerang is too slow. Oh, no! The telephone, of course! Why didn't I think of that at first? Please telephone for Dr. Gladby, Mrs. Baggert. Ask him to come as soon as possible, and then tell Garret Jackson to step here. I'll have him help me get father into bed."

The housekeeper hastened to the instrument, and was soon in communication with the physician, who promised to call at once. The engineer was summoned from another part of the house, and then Eradicate was aroused.

Mrs. Baggert had the colored man help her get some kettles of hot water in readiness for possible use by the doctor. Mr. Jackson aided Tom to lift Mr. Swift up on the bed, and they got off some of his clothes.

"I'll try to see if I can revive him with a little aromatic spirits of ammonia," decided Tom, as he noticed that his father was still unconscious. He hastened to prepare the strong spirits, while he was conscious of a feeling of fear and alarm, mingled with sadness.

Suppose his father should die? Tom could not bear to think of that. He would be left all alone, and how much he would miss the companionship and comradeship of his father none but himself knew.

"Oh! but I mustn't think he's going to die!" exclaimed the youth, as he mixed the medicine.

Mr. Swift feebly opened his eyes after Tom and Mr. Jackson had succeeded in forcing some of the ammonia between his lips.

"Where am I? What happened?" asked the aged inventor faintly.

"We don't know, exactly," spoke Tom softly. "You are ill, father. I've sent for the doctor. He'll fix you up. He'll be here soon."

"Yes, I'm—I'm ill," murmured the aged man. "Something hurts me—here," and he put his hand over his heart.

Tom felt a nameless sense of fear. He wished now that he had insisted on his parent consulting a physician some time before, when Mr. Swift first complained of a minor ailment. Perhaps now it was too late.

"Oh! when will that doctor come?" murmured Tom impatiently.

Mrs. Baggert, who was nervously going in and out of the room, again went to the telephone.

"He's on his way," the housekeeper reported. "His wife said he just started out in his auto."

Dr. Gladby hurried into the room a little later, and cast a quick look at Mr. Swift, who had again lapsed into unconsciousness.

"Do you think he—think he's going to die?" faltered Tom. He was no longer the self-reliant young inventor. He could meet danger bravely when it threatened himself alone, but when his father was stricken he seemed to lose all courage.

"Die? Nonsense!" exclaimed the doctor heartily. "He's not dead yet, at all events, and while there's life there's hope. I'll soon have him out of this spell."

It was some little time, however, before Mr. Swift again opened his eyes, but he seemed to gain strength from the remedies which Dr. Gladby administered, and in about an hour the inventor could sit up.

"But you must be careful," cautioned the physician. "Don't overdo yourself. I'll be in again in the morning, and now I'll leave you some medicine, to be taken every two hours."

"Oh, I feel much better," said Mr. Swift, and his voice certainly seemed Stronger. "I can't imagine what happened. I came upstairs, after Tom had received a visit from the minister, and that's all I remember."

"The minister, father!" exclaimed Tom, in great amazement. "The minister wasn't here this evening! That was Mr. Gunmore, the aviation secretary. Don't you remember?"

"I don't remember any gentleman like that calling here to-night," Mr. Swift said blankly. "It was the minister, I'm sure, Tom."

"The minister was here last night, Mr. Swift," said the housekeeper.

"Was he? Why, it seems like to-night. And I came upstairs after talking to him, and then it all got black, and—and—"

"There, now; don't try to think," advised the doctor. "You'll be all right in the morning."

"But I can't remember anything about that aviation man," protested Mr. Swift. "I never used to be that way— forgetting things. I don't like it!"

"Oh, it's just because you're tired," declared the physician. "It will all come back to you in the morning. I'll stop in and see you then. Now try to go to sleep." And he left the room.

Tom followed him, Mrs. Baggert and Mr. Jackson remaining with the sick man.

"What is the matter with my father, Dr. Gladby?" asked Tom earnestly, as the doctor prepared to take his departure. "Is it anything serious?"

"Well," began the medical man, "I would not be doing my duty, Tom, if I did not tell you what it is. That is, it is comparatively serious, but it is curable, and I think we can bring him around. He has an affection of the heart, that, while it is common enough, is sometimes fatal.

"But I do not think it will be so in your father's case. He has a fine constitution, and this would never have happened had he not been run down from overwork. That is the principal trouble. What he needs is rest; and then, with the proper remedies, he will be as well as before."

"But that strange lapse of memory, doctor?"

"Oh, that is nothing. It is due to the fact that he has been using his brain too much. The brain protests, and refuses to work until rested. Your father has been working rather hard of late hasn't he?"

"Yes; on a new wireless motor."

"I thought so. Well, a good rest is what he needs, and then his mind and body will be in tune again. I'll be around in the morning."

Tom was somewhat relieved by the doctor's words, but not very much so, and he spent an anxious night, getting up every two hours to administer the medicine. Toward morning Mr. Swift fell into a heavy sleep, and did not awaken for some time.

"Oh, you're much better!" declared Dr. Gladby when he saw his patient that day.

"Yes, I feel better," admitted Mr Swift.

"And can't you remember about Mr. Gunmore calling?" asked Tom.

The aged inventor shook his head, with a puzzled air.

"I can't remember it at all," he said. "The minister is the last person I remember calling here."

Tom looked worried, but the physician said it was a common feature of the disease from which Mr. Swift suffered, and would doubtless pass away.

"And you don't remember how we talked about me building a speedy aeroplane and trying for the ten-thousand-dollar prize?" asked Tom.

"I can't remember a thing about it," said the inventor, with a puzzled shake of his head, "and I'm not going to try, at least not right away. But, Tom, if you're going to build a new aeroplane, I want to help you. I'll give you the benefit of my advice. I think my new form of motor can be used in it."

"Now! now! No inventions—at least not just yet!" objected the physician. "You must have a good rest first, Mr. Swift, and get strong. Then you and Tom can build as many airships as you like."

Mr. Swift felt so much better about three days later that he wanted to get right to work planning the airship that was to win the big prize, but the doctor would not hear of it. Tom, however, began to make rough sketches of what he had in mind changing them from time to time, He also worked on a type of motor, very light, and modeled after one his father had recently patented.

Then a new idea came to Tom in regard to the shape of his aeroplane, and he worked several days drawing the plans for it. It was a new idea in construction, and he believed it would give him the great speed he desired.

"But I'd like dad to see it," he said. "As soon as he's well enough I'll go over it with him."

That time came a week later, and with a complete set of the plans, embodying his latest ideas, Tom went into the library where his father was seated in an easy-chair. Dr. Gladby had said it would not now harm the aged inventor to do a little work. Tom spread the drawings out in front of his father, and began to explain them in detail.

"I really think you have something great there, Tom!" exclaimed Mr. Swift, at length. "It is a very small monoplane, to be sure, but I think with the new principle you have introduced it will work; but, if I were you, I'd shape those wing tips a little differently."

"No, they're better that way," said Tom pleasantly, for he did not often disagree with his father. "I'll show you from a little model I have made. I'll get it right away."

Anxious to demonstrate that he was right in his theory, Tom hurried from the library to get the model of which he had spoken. He left the roll of plans lying on a small table near where his father was seated.

"There, you see, dad," said the young inventor as he re-entered the library a few minutes later, "when you warp the wing tips in making a spiral ascent it throws your tail wings out of plumb, and so—"

Tom paused in some amazement, for Mr. Swift was lying back in his chair, with his eyes closed. The lad started in alarm, laid aside his model, and sprang to his father's side.

"He's had another of those heart attacks!" gasped Tom. He was just going to call Mrs. Baggert, when Mr. Swift opened his eyes. He looked at Tom, and the lad could see that they were bright, and did not show any signs of illness.

"Well, I declare!" exclaimed the inventor. "I must have dozed off, Tom, while you were gone. That's what I did. I fell asleep!"

"Oh!" said Tom, much relieved. "I was afraid you were ill again. Now, in this model, as you will see by the plans, it is necessary—"

He paused, and looked over at the table where he had left the drawings. They were not there!

"The plans, father!" Tom exclaimed. "The plans I left on the table! Where are they?"

"I haven't touched them," was the answer. "They were on that table, where you put them, when I closed my eyes for a little nap. I forgot all about them. Are you sure they're missing?"

"They're not here!" And Tom gazed wildly about the room. "Where can they have gone?"

"I wasn't out of my chair," said Mr. Swift, "I ought not to have gone to sleep, but—"

Tom fairly jumped toward the long library window, the same one from which he had leaped to pursue Andy Foger. The casement was open, and Tom noted that the screen was also unhooked, It had been closed when he went to get the model, he was sure of that.

"Look, dad! See!" he exclaimed, as he picked up from the floor a small piece of paper.

"What is it, Tom?"

"A sheet on which I did some figuring. It is no good, but it was in with the plans. It must have dropped out."

"Do you mean that some one has been in here and taken the plans of your new aeroplane, Tom?" gasped his father.

"That's just what I mean! They sneaked in here while you were dozing, took the plans, and jumped out of the window with them. On the way this paper fell out. It's the only clue we have. Stay here, dad. I'm going to have a look." And Tom jumped from the library window and ran down the path after the unknown thief.

ANXIOUS DAYS

Peering on all sides as he dashed along the gravel walk, hoping to catch a glimpse of the unknown intruder in the garden or shrubbery, Tom sprinted on at top speed. Now and then he paused to listen, but no sound came to him to tell of some one in retreat before him. There was only silence.

"Mighty queer," mused the youth. "Whoever it was, he couldn't have had more than a minute start of me—no, not even half a minute—and yet they've disappeared as completely as though the ground had opened and let them down; and the worst of it is, that they've taken my plans with them!"

He turned about and retraced his steps, making a careful search. He saw no one, until, turning a corner, a little later, he met Eradicate Sampson.

"You haven't seen any strangers around here just now, have you, Rad?" asked Tom anxiously.

"No, indeedy, I hasn't, Massa Tom. What fo' kind ob a stranger was him?"

"That's just what I don't know. Rad. But some one sneaked into the library lust now and took some of my plans while my father dozed off. I jumped out after him as soon as I could, but he has disappeared."

"Maybe it were th' man who done stowed hisself away on yo' airship, de time yo' all went after de diamonds," suggested the colored man.

"No, it couldn't have been him. If it was anybody, it was Andy Foger, or some of his crowd. You didn't see Andy, did you, Rad?"

"No, indeedy; but if I do, I suah will turn mah mule, Boomerang, loose on him, an' he won't take any mo' plans— not right off, Massa Tom."

"No, I guess not. Well, I must get back to dad, or he'll worry. Keep your eyes open, Rad, and if you see Andy Foger, or any one else, around here, let me know. Just sing out for all you're worth."

"Shall I call out, Massa Tom, ef I sees dat blessin' man?"

"You mean Mr. Damon?"

"Dat's de one. De gen'man what's allers a-blessin' ob hisself or his shoelaces, or suffin laik dat. Shall I sing out ef I sees him?"

"Well, no; not exactly, Rad. Just show Mr. Damon up to the house. I'd be glad to see him again, though I don't fancy he'll call. He's off on a little trip, and won't be back for a week. But watch out, Rad." And with that Tom turned toward the house, shaking his head over the puzzle of the missing plans.

"Did you find any one?" asked his father eagerly as the young inventor entered the library.

"No," was the gloomy answer. "There wasn't a sign of any one."

Tom went over to the window and looked about for clues. There was none that he could see, and a further examination of the ground under the window disclosed nothing. There was gravel beneath the casement, and this was not the best medium for retaining footprints. Nor were the gravel walks any better.

"Not a sign of any one," murmured Tom. "Are you sure you didn't hear any noise, dad, when you dozed off?"

"Not a sound, Tom. In fact, it's rather unusual for me to go to sleep like that, but I suppose it's because of my illness. But I couldn't have been asleep long—not more than two minutes."

"That's what I think. Yet in that time someone, who must have been on the watch, managed to get in here and take my plans for the new sky racer. I don't see how they got the wire screen open from the outside, though. It fastens with a strong hook."

"And was the screen open?" asked Mr. Swift

"Yes, it was unhooked. Either they pushed a wire in through the mesh, caught it under the hook, and pulled it up from the outside, or else the screen was opened from the inside."

"I don't believe they could get inside to open the screen without some of us seeing them," spoke the older inventor. "More likely, Tom, it wasn't hooked, and they found it an easy matter to simply pull it open."

"That's possible. I'll ask Mrs. Baggert if the screen was unhooked."

But the housekeeper could not be certain on that point, and so that part of the investigation amounted to nothing.

"It's too bad!" exclaimed Mr. Swift. "It's my fault, for dozing off that way."

"No, indeed, it isn't!" declared Tom stoutly.

"Is the loss a serious one?" asked his father. "Have you no copy of the plans?"

"Yes, I have a rough draft from which I made the completed drawings, and I can easily make another set. But that isn't what worries me—the mere loss of the plans."

"What is it, then, Tom?"

"The fact that whoever took them must know what they are the plans for a sky racer that is to take part in the big meet. I have worked it out on a new principle, and it is not yet patented. Whoever stole my plans can make the same kind of a sky racer that I intended to construct, and so stand as good a chance to win the prize of ten thousand dollars as I will."

"That certainly is too bad, Tom. I never thought of that. Do you suspect any one?"

"No one, unless it's Andy Foger. He's mean enough to do a thing like that, but I didn't think he'd have the nerve. However, I'll see if I can learn anything about him. He may have been sneaking around, and if he has my plans he'd ask nothing better than to make a sky racer and beat me."

"Oh, Tom, I'm so sorry!" exclaimed Mr. Swift "I—I feel very bad about it!"

"There, never mind!" spoke the lad, seeing that his father was looking ill again. "Don't think any more about it, dad. I'll get back those plans. Come, now. It's time for your medicine, and then you must lie down." For the aged inventor was looking tired and weak.

Wearily he let Tom lead him to his room, and after seeing that the invalid was comfortable Tom called up Dr. Gladby, to have him come and see Mr.

Swift. The doctor said his patient had been overdoing himself a little, and must rest more if he was to completely recover.

Learning that his father was no worse, Tom set off to find Andy Foger.

"I can't rest until I know whether or not he has my plans," he said to himself. "I don't want to make a speedy aeroplane, and find out at the last minute that Andy, or some of his cronies, have duplicated it."

But Tom got little satisfaction from Andy Foger. When that bully was accused of having been around Tom's house he denied it, and though the young inventor did not actually accuse him of taking the plans, he hinted at it. Andy muttered many indignant negatives, and called on some of his cronies to witness that at the time the plans were taken he and they were some distance from the Swift home.

So Tom was baffled; and though he did not believe the red-haired lad's denial, there was no way in which he could prove to the contrary.

"If he didn't take the plans, who did?" mused Tom.

As the young inventor turned away after cross-questioning Andy, the bully called out:

"You'll never win that ten thousand dollars!"

"What do you know about that?" demanded Tom quickly.

"Oh, I know," sneered Andy. "There'll be bigger and better aeroplanes in that meet than you can make, and you'll never win the prize."

"I suppose you heard about the affair by sneaking around under our windows, and listening," said Tom.

"Never mind how I know it, but I do," retorted the bully.

"Well, I'll tell you one thing," said Tom calmly. "If you come around again it won't be healthy for you. Look out for live wires, if you try to do the listening act any more, Andy!" And with that ominous warning Tom turned away.

"What do you suppose he means, Andy?" asked Pete Bailey, one of Andy's cronies.

"It means he's got electrical wires strung around his place," declared Sam Snedecker, "and that we'll be shocked if we go up there. I'm not going!"

"Me, either," added Pete, and Andy laughed uneasily.

Tom heard what they said, and in the next few days he made himself busy by putting some heavy wires in and about the grounds where they would show best. But the wires carried no current, and were only displayed to impress a sense of fear on Andy and his cronies, which purpose they served well.

But it was like locking the stable door after the horse had been stolen, for with all the precautions he could take Tom could not get back his plans, and he spent many anxious days seeking them. They seemed to have completely disappeared, however, and the young inventor decided there was nothing else to do but to draw new ones.

He set to work on them, and in the meanwhile tried to learn whether or not Andy had the missing plans. He sought this information by stealth, and was aided by his chum, Ned Newton. But all to no purpose. Not the slightest trace or clue was discovered.

BUILDING THE SKY RACER

"What will you do, if, after you have your little monoplane all constructed, and get ready to race, you find that some one else has one exactly like it at the meet?," asked Ned Newton one day, when he and Tom were out in the big workshop, talking things over. "What will you do, Tom?"

"I don't see that there is anything I can do. I'll go on to the meet, of course, and trust to some improvements I have since brought out, and to what I know about aeroplanes, to help me win the race. I'll know, too, who stole my plans."

"But it will be too late, then."

"Yes, too late, perhaps, to stop them from using the drawings, hot not too late to punish them for the theft. It's a great mystery, and I'll be on the anxious seat all the while. But it can't be helped."

"When are you going to start work on the sky racer?"

"Pretty soon, now. I've got another set of plans made, and I've fixed them so that if they are stolen it won't do any one any good."

"How's that?"

"I've put in a whole lot of wrong figures and measurements, and scores of lines and curves that mean nothing. I have marked the right figures and lines by a secret mark, and when I work on them I'll use only the proper ones. But any one else wouldn't know this. Oh, I'll fool 'em this time!"

"I hope you do. Well, when you get the machine done I'd like to ride in it. Will it carry two, as your *Butterfly* does?"

"Yes, only it will be much different; and, of course, it will go much faster. I'll give you a ride, all right, Ned. Well, now I must get busy and see what material I need for what I hope will prove to be the speediest aeroplane in the world."

"That's going some! I must be leaving now. Don't forget your promise. I saw Mary Nestor on my way over here. She was asking for you. She said you must be very busy, for she hadn't seen you in some time."

"Um!" was all Tom answered, but by the blush that mounted to his face it was evident that he was more interested in Mary Nestor than his mere exclamation indicated.

When Ned had gone Tom got out pencil and paper, and was busily engaged in making some intricate calculations. He drew odd little sketches on the margin of the sheet, and then wrote out a list of the things he would need to construct the new aeroplane.

This finished, he went to Mr. Jackson, the engineer, and asked him to get the various things together, and to have them put in the special shop where Tom did most of his work.

"I want to get the machine together as soon as I can," he remarked to the engineer, "for it will need to be given a good tryout before I enter in the race, and I may find that I'll have to make several changes in it."

Mr. Jackson promised to attend to the matter right away, and then Tom went in to talk to his father about the motor that was to whirl the propeller of the new air craft.

Mr. Swift had improved very much in the past few days, and though Dr. Gladby said he was far from being well, the physician declared there was no reason why he should not do some inventive work.

He and Tom were deep in an argument of gasoline motors, discussing the best manner of attaching the fins to the cylinders to make them air-cooled, when a voice sounded outside, the voice of Eradicate:

"Heah! Whar yo' goin'?" demanded the colored man. "Whar yo' goin'?"

"Somebody's out in the garden!" exclaimed Tom, jumping up suddenly.

"Perhaps it's the same person who took the plans!" suggested Mr. Swift.

"Hold on, dere!" yelled Eradicate again.

Then a voice replied:

"Bless my insurance policy! What's the matter? Have there been burglars around? Why all these precautions? Bless my steam heater! Don't you know me?"

"Mr. Damon!" cried Tom, a look of pleasure coming over his face. "Mr. Damon is coming!"

"So I should judge," responded Mr. Swift, with a smile. "I wonder why Eradicate didn't recognize him?"

They learned why a moment later, for on looking from the library window, Tom saw the colored man coming up the walk behind a well-dressed gentleman.

"Why, mah goodness! It's Mr. Damon!" exclaimed Eradicate. "I didn't know yo', sah, wif dem whiskers on! I didn't, fo' a fac'!"

"Bless my razor! I suppose it does make a difference," said the eccentric man. "Yes, my wife thought I'd look better, and more sedate, with a beard, so I grew one to please her. But I don't like it. A beard is too warm this kind of weather; eh, Tom?" And Mr. Damon waved his hand to the young inventor and his father, who stood in the low windows of the library. "Entirely too warm, bless my finger-nails, yes!"

"I agree with you!" exclaimed Tom. "Come in! We're glad to see you!"

"I called to see if you aren't going on another trip to the North Pole, or somewhere in the Arctic regions," went on Mr. Damon.

"Why?" inquired Tom.

"Why, then this heavy beard of mine would come in handy. It would keep my throat and chin warm." And Mr. Damon ran his hands through his luxuriant whiskers.

"No more northern trips right away," said Tom. "I'm about to build a speedy monoplane, to take part in the big meet at Eagle Park."

"Oh, yes, I heard about the meet," said Mr. Damon. "I'd like to be in that."

"Well, I'm building a machine that will carry two," went on Tom, "and if you think you can stand a speed of a hundred miles an hour, or better, I'll let you come with me. There are some races where a passenger is allowed."

"Have you got a razor?" asked Mr. Damon suddenly.

"What for?" inquired Mr. Swift, wondering what the eccentric man was going to do.

"Why, bless my shaving soap! I'm going to cut off my beard. If I go in a monoplane at a hundred miles an hour I don't want to make any more resistance to the wind than possible, and my whiskers would certainly hold back Tom's machine. Where's a razor? I'm going to shave at once. My wife won't mind when I tell her what it's for. Lend me a razor, please, Tom."

"Oh, there's plenty of time," explained the lad, with a laugh. "The race doesn't take place for over two months. But when it does, I think you would be better off without a beard."

"I know it," said Mr. Damon simply. "I'll shave before we enter the contest, Tom. But now tell me all about it."

Tom did so, relating the story of the theft of the plans. Mr. Damon was for having Andy arrested at once, but Mr. Swift and his son pointed out that they had no evidence against him.

"All we can do," said the young inventor, "is to keep watch on him, and see if he is building another aeroplane. He has all the facilities, and he may attempt to get ahead of me. If he enters a sky craft at the meet I'll be pretty sure that he has made it from my stolen plans."

"Bless my wing tips!" cried Mr. Damon. "But can't we do anything to stop him?"

"I'm afraid not," answered Tom; and then he showed Mr. Damon his re-drawn plans, and told in detail of how he intended to construct the new aeroplane.

The eccentric man remained as the guest of the Swift family that night, departing for his home the next day, and promising to be on hand as soon as Tom was ready to test his new craft, which would he in about a month.

As the days passed, Tom, with the help of his father, whose health was slightly better, and with the aid of Mr. Jackson, began work on the speedy little sky racer.

As you boys are all more or less familiar with aeroplanes, we will not devote much space to the description of the new one Tom Swift made. We can describe it in general terms, but there were some features of it which Tom kept a secret from all save his father.

Suffice it to say that Tom had decided to build a small air craft of the single-wing type, known as the monoplane. It was to be a cross between the Bleriot and the Antoinette, with the general features of both, but with many changes or improvements.

The wings were shaped somewhat like those of a humming-bird, which, as is well known, can, at times, vibrate its wings with such velocity that the most rapid camera lens cannot quite catch

And when it is known that a bullet in flight has been successfully photographed, the speed of the wings of the humming-bird can be better appreciated.

The writer has seen a friend, with a very rapid camera, which was used to snap automobiles in flight, attempt to take a picture of a humming-bird. He got the picture, all right, but the plate was blurred, showing that the wings had moved faster than the lens could throw them on the sensitive plate.

Not that Tom intended the wings of his monoplane to vibrate, but he adopted that style as being the best adapted to allow of rapid flight through the air; and the young inventor had determined that he would clip many minutes from the best record yet made.

The body of his craft, between the forward wings and the rear ones, where the rudders were located, was shaped like a cigar, with side wings somewhat like the fin keels of the ocean liner to prevent a rolling motion. In addition, Tom had an ingenious device to automatically adapt his monoplane to sudden currents of air that might overturn it, and this device was one of the points which he kept secret.

The motor, which was air-cooled, was located forward, and was just above the heads of the operator and the passenger who sat beside him. The single propeller, which was ten feet in diameter, gave a minimum thrust of one thousand pounds at two thousand revolutions per minute.

This was one feature wherein Tom's craft differed from others. The usual aeroplane propeller is eight feet in diameter, and gives from four to five hundred pounds thrust at about one thousand revolutions per minute, so it can be readily seen wherein Tom had an advantage.

"But I'm building this for speed," he said to Mr. Jackson, "and I'm going to get it! We'll make a hundred miles an hour without trouble."

"I believe you," replied the engineer. "The motor you and your father have made is a wonder for lightness and power."

In fact, the whole monoplane was so light and frail as to give one the idea of a rather large model, instead of a real craft, intended for service. But a careful inspection showed the great strength it had, for it was braced and guyed in a new way, and was as rigid as a steel-trussed bridge.

"What are you going to call her?" asked Mr. Jackson, about two weeks after they had started work on the craft, and when it had begun to assume shape and form.

"I'm going to name her the *Humming-Bird*," replied Tom. "She's little, but oh, my!"

"And I guess she'll bring home the prize," added the engineer.

And as the days went by, and Tom, his father and Mr. Jackson continued to work on the speedy craft, this hope grew in the heart of the young inventor. But he could not rid himself of worry as to the fate of the plans that had disappeared. Who had them? Was some one making a machine like his own from them? Tom wished he knew.

ANDY FOGER WILL CONTEST

One afternoon, as Tom was working away in the shop on his sky racer, adjusting one of the rear rudders, and pausing now and then to admire the trim little craft, he heard some one approaching. Looking out through a small observation peephole made for this purpose, he saw Mrs. Baggert hurrying toward the building.

"I wonder what's the matter?" he said aloud, for there was a look of worriment on the lady's face. Tom threw open the door. "What is it, Mrs. Baggert?" he called. "Some one up at the house who wants to see me?"

"No, it's your father!" panted the housekeeper, for she was quite stout. "He is very ill again, and I can't seem to get Dr. Gladby on the telephone. Central says he doesn't answer."

"My father worse!" cried Tom in alarm, dropping his tools and hurrying from the shop. "Where's Eradicate? Send him for the doctor. Perhaps the wires are broken. If he can't locate Dr. Gladby, get Dr. Kurtz. We must have some one. Here, Rad! Where are you?" he called, raising his voice.

"Heah I be!" answered the colored man, coming from the direction of the garden, which he had been weeding.

"Get cut your mule, and go for Dr. Gladby. If he isn't home, get Dr. Kurtz. Hurry, Rad!"

"I's mighty sorry, Massa Tom," answered the colored man, "but I cain't hurry, nohow."

"Why not?"

"Because Boomerang done gone lame, an' he won't run. I'll go mahse'f, but I cain't take dat air mule."

"Never mind. I'll go in the *Butterfly*," decided Tom quickly. "I'll run up to the house and see how dad is, and while I'm gone, Rad, you get out the *Butterfly*. I can make the trip in that. If Dr. Kurtz had a 'phone I could get him, but he lives over on the back road, where there isn't a line. Hurry, Rad!"

"Yes, sah, Massa Tom, I'll hurry!"

The colored man knew how to get the monoplane in shape for a flight, as he had often done it.

Tom found his father in no immediate danger, but Mr. Swift had had a slight recurrence of his heart trouble, and it was thought best to have a doctor. So Tom started off in his air craft, rising swiftly above the housetop, and sailed off toward the old-fashioned residence of Dr. Kurtz, a sturdy, elderly German physician, who sometimes attended Mr. Swift. Tom decided that as long as Dr. Gladby did not answer his 'phone, he could not be at home, and this, he learned later, was the case, the physician being in a distant town on a consultation.

"My, this *Butterfly* seems big and clumsy beside my *Humming-Bird*," mused Tom as he slid along through the air, now flying high and now low, merely for practice. "This machine can go, hut wait until I have my new one in the air! Then I'll show 'em what speed is!"

He was soon at the physician's house, and found him in.

"Won't you ride back with me in the monoplane?" asked Tom. "I'm anxious to have you see dad as soon as you can.

"Vot! Me drust mineself in one ob dem airships? I dinks not!" exclaimed Dr. Kurtz ponderously. "Vy, I would not efen ride in an outer-mobile, yet, so vy should I go in von contrivance vot is efen more dangerous? No, I gomes to your fader in der carriage, mit mine old Dobbin horse. Dot vill not drop me to der ground, or run me up a tree, yet! Vot?"

"Very well," said Tom, "only hurry, please."

The young inventor, in his airship, reached home some time before the slow-going doctor got there in his carriage. Mr. Swift was no worse, Tom was glad to find, though he was evidently quite ill.

"So, ve must take goot care of him," said the doctor, when he had examined the patient. "Dr. Gladby he has done much for him, und I can do little more. You must dake care of yourself, Herr Swift, or you vill—but den, vot is der use of being gloomy-minded? I am sure you vill go more easy, und not vork so much."

"I haven't worked much," replied the aged inventor. "I have only been helping my son on a new airship."

"Den dot must stop," insisted the doctor. "You must haf gomplete rest—dot's it—gomplete rest."

"We'll do just as you say, doctor," said Tom. "We'll give up the aeroplane matters, dad, and go away, you and I, where we can t see a blueprint or a pattern, or hear the sound of machinery. We'll cut it all out."

"Dot vould he goot," said Dr. Kurtz ponderously.

"No, I couldn't think of it," answered Mr. Swift. "I want you to go in that race, Tom—and win!"

"But I'll not do it, dad, if you're going to be ill."

"He is ill now," interrupted the doctor. "Very ill, Dom Swift."

"That settles it. I don't go in the race. You and I'll go away, dad—to California, or up in Canada. We'll travel for your health."

"No! no!" insisted the old inventor gently. "I will be all right. Most of the work on the monoplane is done now, isn't it, Tom?"

"Yes, dad."

"Then you go on, and finish it. You and Mr. Jackson can do it without me now. I'll take a rest, doctor, but I want my son to enter that race, and, what's more, I want him to win!"

"Vell, if you don't vork, dot is all I ask. I must forbid you to do any more. Mit Dom, dot is different. He is young und strong, und he can vork. But you—not, Herr Swift, or I doctor you no more." And the physician shook his big head.

"Very well. I'll agree to that if Tom will promise to enter the race," said the inventor.

"I will," said Tom.

The physician took his leave shortly after that, the medicine he gave to Mr. Swift somewhat relieving him. Then the young inventor, who felt in a little better spirits, went back to his workshop.

"Poor dad," he mused. "He thinks more of me and this aeroplane than he does of himself. Well, I will go in the race, and I'll—yes, I'll win!" And Tom looked very determined.

He was about to resume work on his craft when something about the way one of the forward planes was tilted attracted his attention.

"I never left it that way," mused Tom. "Some one has been in here. I wonder if it was Mr. Jackson?"

Tom stepped to the door and called for Eradicate. The colored man came from the direction of the garden, which he was still weeding.

"Has Mr. Jackson been around, Rad?" asked the lad.

"No, sah. I ain't seed him."

"Have you been in here, looking at the *Humming-Bird?*"

"No, Massa Tom. I nebber goes in dere, lessen as how yo' is dere. Dem's yo' orders."

"That's so, Rad. I might have known you wouldn't go in. But did you see any one enter the shop?"

"Not a pusson, sab."

"Have you been here all the while?"

"All but jes' a few minutes, when I went to de barn to put some liniment on Boomerang's So' foot."

"H'm! Some one might have slipped in here while I was away," mused Tom. "I ought to have locked the doors, but I was in a hurry. This thing is getting on my nerves. I wonder if it's Andy Foger, or some one else, who is after my secret?"

He made a hasty examination of the shop, but could discover nothing more wrong, except that one of the planes of the *Humming-Bird* had been shifted.

"It looks as if they were trying to see how it was fastened on, and how it worked," mused Tom. "But my plans haven't been touched, and no damage has been done. Only I don't like to think that people have been in here. They may have stolen some of my ideas. I must keep this place locked night and day after this."

Tom spent a busy week in making improvements on his craft. Mr. Swift was doing well, and after a consultation by Dr. Kurtz and Dr. Gladby it was decided to adopt a new style of treatment. In the meanwhile, Mr. Swift kept his promise, and did no work. He sat in his easy-chair, out in the garden, and dozed away, while Tom visited him frequently to see if he needed anything.

"Poor old dad!" mused the young inventor. "I hope he is well enough to come and see me try for the ten-thousand-dollar prize—and win it! I hope I do; but if some one builds, from my stolen plans, a machine on this model, I'll have my work cut out for me." And he gazed with pride on the *Humming-Bird*.

For the past two weeks Tom had seen nothing of Andy Foger. The red haired bully seemed to have dropped out of sight, and even his cronies, Sam Snedecker and Pete Bailey, did not know where he had gone.

"I hope he has gone for good," said Ned Newton, who lived near Andy. "He's an infernal nuisance. I wish he'd never come back to Shopton."

But Andy was destined to come back.

One day, when Tom was busy installing a wireless apparatus on his new aeroplane, he heard Eradicate hurrying up the path that led to the shop.

"I wonder if dad is worse?" thought Tom, that always being his first idea when he knew a summons was coming for him. Quickly be opened the door.

"Some one's comin' out to see you, Massa Tom," said the colored man.

"Who is it?" asked the lad, taking the precaution to put his precious plans out of sight.

"I dunno, sah; but yo' father knows him, an' he said fo' me to come out heah, ahead ob de gen'man, an' tell yo' he were comin'. He'll be right heah."

"Oh, well, if dad knows him, it's all right. Let him come, Rad."

"Yes, sah. Heah he comes." And the colored man pointed to a figure advancing down the gravel path. Tom watched the stranger curiously. There was something familiar about him, and Tom was sure he had met him before, yet he could not seem to place him.

"How are you, Tom Swift?" greeted the newcomer pleasantly. "I guess you've forgotten me, haven't you?" He held out his hand, which Tom took. "Don't know me, do you?" he went on.

"Well, I'm afraid I've forgotten your name," admitted the lad, just a bit embarrassed. "But your face is familiar, somehow, and yet it isn't"

"I've shaved off my mustache," went on the other. "That makes a difference. But you haven't forgotten John Sharp, the balloonist, whom you rescued from Lake Carlopa, and who helped you build the *Red Cloud*? You haven't forgotten John Sharp, have you, Tom?"

"Well, I should say not!" cried the lad heartily. "I'm real glad to see you. What are you doing around here? Come in. I've got something to show you," and he motioned to the shop where the *Humming-Bird* was housed.

"Oh, I know what it is," said the veteran balloonist.

"You do?"

"Yes. It's your new aeroplane. In fact, I came to see you about it."

"To see me about it?"

"Yes. I'm one of the committee of arrangements for the meet to be held at Eagle Park, where I understand you are going to contest. I came to see how near you were ready, and to get you to make a formal entry of your machine. Mr. Gunmore sent me."

"Oh, so you're in with them now, eh?" asked Tom. "Well, I'm glad to know I've got a friend on the committee. Yes, my machine is getting along very well. I'll soon be ready for a trial flight. Come in and look at it. I think it's a bird—a regular *Humming-Bird!*" And Tom laughed.

"It certainly is something new," admitted Mr. Sharp as his eyes took in the details of the trim little craft. "By the way, Shopton is going to be well represented at the meet."

"How is that? I thought I was the only one around here to enter an aeroplane."

"No. We have just received an entry from Andy Foger."

"From Andy Foger!" gasped Tom. "Is he going to try to win some of the prizes?"

"He's entered for the big one, the ten-thousand-dollar prize," replied the balloonist. "He has made formal application to be allowed to compete, and we have to accept any one who applies. Why, do you object to him, Tom?"

"Object to him? Mr. Sharp, let me tell you something. Some time ago a set of plans of my machine here were stolen from my house. I suspected Andy Foger of taking them, but I could get no proof. Now you say he is building a machine to compete for the big prize. Do you happen to know what style it is?"

"It's a small monoplane, something like the Antoinette, his application states, though he may change it later."

"Then he's stolen my ideas, and is making a craft like this!" exclaimed Tom, as he sank upon a bench, and gazed from the balloonist to the *Humming-Bird*, and hack to Mr. Sharp again. "Andy Foger is trying to beat me with my own machine!"

Seeking a Clue

John Sharp was more than surprised at the effect his piece of information had on Tom Swift. Though the young inventor had all along suspected Andy of having the missing plans, yet there had been no positive evidence on this point. That, coupled with the fact that the red-haired bully had not been seen in the vicinity of Shopton lately, had, in a measure, lulled Tom's suspicions to rest, but now his hope had been rudely shattered.

"Do you really think that's his game?" asked Mr. Sharp.

"I'm sure of it," replied the youth. "Though where he is building his aeroplane I can't imagine, for I haven't seen him in town. He's away."

"Are you sure of that?"

"Well, not absolutely sure," replied Tom. "It's the general rumor that he's out of town."

"Well, old General Rumor is sometimes a person not to be relied upon," remarked the balloonist grimly. "Now this is the way I size it up: Of course, all I know officially is that Andy Foger has sent in an entry for the big race for the ten-thousand-dollar prize which is offered by the Eagle Park Aviation Association. I'm a member of the arrangements committee, and so I know. I also know that you and several others are going to try for the prize. That's all I am absolutely sure of.

"Now, when you tell me about the missing plans, and you conclude that Andy is doing some underhanded work, I agree with you. But I go a step farther. I don't believe he's out of town at all."

"Why not?" exclaimed Tom.

"Because when he has an airship shed right in his own backyard, where, you tell me, he once made a craft in which he tried to beat you out in the trip to Alaska, when you think of that, doesn't it seem reasonable that he'd use that same building in which to make his new craft?"

"Yes, it does," admitted Tom slowly, "but then everybody says he's out of town."

"Well, what everybody says is generally not So. I think you'll find that Andy is keeping himself in seclusion, and that he's working secretly in his ship, building a machine with which to beat you."

"Do you, really?"

"I certainly do. Have you been around his place lately?"

"No. I've been too busy; and then I never have much to do with him."

"Then take my advice, and see if you can't get a look inside that shop. You may see something that will surprise you. If you find that Andy is infringing on your patented ideas, you can stop him by an injunction. You've got this model patented, I take it?"

"Oh, yes. I didn't have at the time the plans were stolen, but I've patented it since. I could get at him that way."

"Then take my advice, and do it. Get a look inside that shed, and you'll find Andy working secretly there, no matter if his cronies do think he's out of town."

"I believe I will," agreed Tom, and somehow he felt better now that he had decided on a plan of action. He and the balloonist talked over at some length just the best way to go about it, for the young inventor recalled the time when he and Ned Newton had endeavored to look into Andy's shed, with somewhat disastrous results to themselves; but Tom knew that the matter at stake justified a risk, and he was willing to take it.

"Well, now that's settled," said Mr. Sharp, "tell me more about yourself and your aeroplane. My! To think that the *Red Cloud* was destroyed! That was a fine craft."

"Indeed she was," agreed Tom. "I'm going to make another on similar lines, some day, but now all my time is occupied with the Humming Bird."

"She is a hummer, too," complimented Mr. Sharp. "But I almost forgot the real object of my trip here. There is no doubt about you going in the race, is there?"

"I fully expect to," replied Tom. "The only thing that will prevent me will be—"

"Don't say you're worried on account of what Andy Foger may do," interrupted Mr. Sharp.

"I'm not. I'll attend to Andy, all right. I was going to say that my father's illness might interfere. He's not well at all. I'm quite worried about him."

"Oh, I sincerely hope he'll be all right," remarked the balloonist. "We want you in this race. In fact, we're going to feature you, as they say about the actors and story-writers. The committee is planning to do considerable advertising on the strength of Tom Swift, the well-known young inventor, being a contestant for the ten-thousand-dollar prize."

"That's very nice, I'm sure," replied Tom, "and I'm going to do my best. Perhaps dad will take a turn for the better. He wants me to win as much as I want to myself. Well, we'll not worry about it, anyhow, until the time comes. I want to show you some new features of my. latest aeroplane."

"And I want to see them, Tom. Don't you think you're making a mistake, though, in equipping it with a wireless outfit?"

"Why so?"

"Well, because it will add to the weight, and you want such a small machine to be as light as possible."

"Yes, but you see I have a very light engine. That part my father helped me with. In fact, it is the lightest air-cooled motor made, for the amount of horsepower it develops, so I can afford to put on the extra weight of the wireless outfit. I may need to signal when I am flying along at a hundred miles an hour."

"That's so. Well, show me some of the other good points. You've certainly got a wonderful craft here."

Tom and Mr. Sharp spent some time going over the *Humming-Bird* and in talking over old times. The balloonist paid another visit to Mr. Swift, who was feeling pretty good, and who expressed his pleasure in seeing his old friend again.

"Can't you stay for a few days?" asked Tom, when Mr. Sharp was about to leave. "If you wait long enough you may be able to help me work up the clues against Andy Foger, and also witness a trial flight of the *Humming-Bird.*"

"I'd like to stay, but I can't," was the answer. "The committee will be anxious for me to get back with my report. Good luck to you. I'll see you at the time of the race, if not before."

Tom resolved to get right to work seeking clues against his old enemy, Andy, but the next day Mr. Swift was not so well, and Tom had to remain in the house. Then followed several days, during which time it was necessary to do some important work on his craft, and so a week passed without any information having been obtained.

In the meanwhile Tom had made some cautious inquiries, but had learned nothing about Andy. He had no chance to interview Pete or Sam, the two cronies, and he did not think it wise to make a bald request for information at the Foger home.

Ned Newton could not be of any aid to his friend, as he was kept busy in the bank night and day, working over a new set of books.

"I wonder how I can find out what I want to know?" mused Tom one afternoon, when he had done considerable work on the *Humming-Bird.* "I certainly ought to do it soon, so as to be able to stop Andy if he's infringing on my patents. Yet, I don't see how—"

His thoughts were interrupted by hearing a voice outside the shop, exclaiming:

"Bless my toothpick! I know the way, Eradicate, my good fellow. It isn't necessary for you to come. As long as Tom Swift is out there, I'll find him. Bless my horizontal rudder! I'm anxious to see what progress he's made. I'll find him, if he's about!"

"Yes, sah, he's right in dere," spoke the colored man. "He's workin' on dat Dragon Fly of his." Eradicate did not always get his names right.

"Mr. Damon!" exclaimed Tom in delight, at the sound of his friend's voice. "I believe he can help me get evidence against Andy Foger. I wonder I didn't think of it before! The very thing! I'll do it!"

The Empty Shed

"Bless my dark-lantern! Where are you, Tom?" called Mr. Damon as he entered the dim shed where the somewhat frail-appearing aeroplane loomed up in the semi-darkness, for it was afternoon, and rather cloudy. "Where are you?"

"Here!" called the young inventor. "I'm glad to see you! Come in!"

"Ah! there it is, eh?" exclaimed the odd man, as he looked at the aeroplane, for there had been much work done on it since he had last seen it. "Bless my parachute, Tom! But it looks as though you could blow it over."

"It's stronger than it seems," replied the lad. "But, Mr. Damon, I've got something very important to talk to you about."

Thereupon Tom told all about Mr. Sharp's visit, of Andy's entry in the big race, and of the suspicions of himself and the balloonist.

"And what is it you wish me to do?" asked Mr. Damon.

"Work up some clues against Andy Foger."

"Good! I'll do it! I'd like to get ahead of that bully and his father, who once tried to wreck the bank I'm interested in. I'll help you, Tom! I'll play detective! Let me see— what disguise shall I assume? I think I'll take the part of a tramp. Bless my ham sandwich! That will be the very thing. I'll get some ragged clothes, let my beard grow again—you see I shaved it off since my last visit—and I'll go around to the Foger place and ask for work. Then I can get inside the shed and look around. How's that for a plan?"

"It might be all right," agreed Tom, "only I don't believe you're cut out for the part of a tramp, Mr. Damon."

"Bless my fingernails! Why not?"

"Oh, well, it isn't very pleasant to go around in ragged clothes."

"Don't mind about me. I'll do it." And the odd gentleman seemed quite delighted at the idea. He and Tom talked it over at some length, and then adjourned to the house, where Mr. Swift, who had seemed to improve in the last few days, was told of the plan.

"Couldn't you go around after evidence just as you are?" asked the aged inventor. "I don't much care for this disguising business."

"Oh, it's very necessary," insisted Mr. Damon earnestly. "Bless my gizzard! but it's very necessary. Why, if I went around the Foger place as I am now, they'd know me in a minute, and I couldn't find out what I want to know."

"Well, if you keep on blessing yourself," said Tom, with a laugh, "they'll know you, no matter what disguise you put on, Mr. Damon."

"That's so," admitted the eccentric gentleman. "I must break myself of that habit. I will. Bless my topknot! I'll never do it any more. Bless my trousers buttons!"

"I'm afraid you'll never do it!" exclaimed Tom.

"It is rather hard," said Mr. Damon ruefully, as he realized what he had said. "But I'll do it. Bless—"

He paused a moment, looked at Tom and his father, and then burst into a laugh. The habit was more firmly fastened on him than he was aware.

For several hours Tom, his father and Mr. Damon discussed various methods of proceeding, and it was finally agreed that Mr. Damon should first try to learn what Andy was doing, if anything, without resorting to a disguise.

"Then, if that doesn't work, I'll become a tramp," was the decision of the odd character. "I'll wear the raggedest clothes I can find Bless—" But he stopped in time.

Mr. Damon took up his residence in the Swift household, as he had often done before, and for the next week he went and came as he pleased, sometimes being away all night.

"It's no use, though," declared Mr. Damon at the end of the week. "I can't get anywhere near that shed, nor even get a glimpse inside of it. I haven't been able to learn anything, either'. There are two gardeners on guard all the while, and several times when I've tried to go in the side gate, they've stopped me."

"Isn't there any news of Andy about town?" asked Tom. "I should think Sam or Pete would know where he is."

"Well, I didn't ask them, for they'd know right away why I was inquiring," said Mr. Damon, "but it seems to me as if there was something queer going on. If Andy Foger is working in that shed of his, he's keeping mighty quiet about it. Bless my—"

And once more he stopped in time. He was conquering the habit in a measure.

"Well, what do you propose to do next?" asked Tom.

"Disguise myself like a tramp, and go there looking for work," was the firm answer. "There are plenty of odd jobs on a big place such as the Foger family have. I'll find out what I want to know, you see."

It seemed useless to further combat this resolution, and, in a few days Mr. Damon presented a very different appearance. He had on a most ragged suit, there was a scrubby beard on his face, and he walked with a curious shuffle, caused by a pair of big, heavy shoes which he had donned, first having taken the precaution to make holes in them and get them muddy.

"Now I'm all ready," he said to Tom one day, when his disguise was complete. "I'm going over and try my luck."

He left the house by a side door, so that no one would see him, and started down the walk. As he did so a voice shouted:

"Hi, there! Git right out oh heah! Mistah Swift doan't allow no tramps heah, an' we ain't got no wuk fo' yo', an' there ain't no cold victuals. I does all de wuk, me an' mah mule Boomerang, an' we takes all de cold victuals, too! Git right along, now!"

"It's Eradicate. He doesn't know you," said Tom, with a chuckle.

"So much the better," whispered Mr. Damon. But the disguise proved almost too much of a success, for seeing the supposed tramp lingering near the house, Eradicate caught up a stout stick and rushed forward. He was about to strike the ragged man, when Tom called out:

"That's Mr. Damon, Rad!"

"Wh—what!" gasped the colored man; and when the situation had been explained to him, and the necessity for silence impressed upon him, he turned away, too surprised to utter a word. He sought consolation in the stable with his mule.

Just what methods Mr. Damon used he never disclosed, but one thing is certain: That night there came a cautious knock on the door of the Swift home, and Tom, answering it, beheld his odd friend.

"Well," he asked eagerly, "what luck?"

"Put on a suit of old clothes, and come with me," said Mr. Damon. "We'll look like two tramps, and then, if we're discovered, they won't know it was you."

"Have you found out anything?" asked Tom eagerly.

"Not yet; but I've got a key to one of the side doors of the shed, and we can get in as soon as it's late enough so that everybody there will be in bed."

"A key? How did you get it?" inquired the youth.

"Never mind," was the answer, with a chuckle. "That was because of my disguise; and I haven't blessed anything to-day. I'm going to, soon, though. I can feel it coming on. But hurry, Tom, or we may be too late."

"And you haven't had a look inside the shed?" asked the young inventor. "You don't know what's there?"

"No; but we soon will."

Eagerly Tom put on tome of the oldest and most ragged garments he could find, and then he and the odd gentleman set off toward the Foger home. They waited some time after getting in sight of it, because they saw a light in one of the windows. Then, when the house was dark, they stole cautiously forward toward the big, gloomy shed.

"On this side," directed Mr. Damon in a whisper. "The key I have opens this door."

"But we can't see when we get inside," objected Tom. "I should have brought a dark lantern."

"I have one of those pocket electric flashlights," said Mr. Damon. "Bless my candlestick! but I thought of that." And he chuckled gleefully.

Cautiously they advanced in the darkness. Mr. Damon fumbled at the lock of the door. The key grated as he turned it. The portal swung back, and Tom and his friend found themselves inside the shed which, of late, had been such an object of worry and conjecture to the young inventor. What would he find there?

"Flash the light," he called to Mr. Damon in a hoarse whisper.

The eccentric man drew it from his packet He pressed the spring switch, and in an instant a brilliant shaft of radiance shot out, cutting the intense blackness like a knife. Mr. Damon flashed it on all sides.

But to the amazement of Tom and his companion, it did not illuminate the broad white wings and stretches of canvas of an aeroplane It only shone on the bare walls of the shed, and on some piles of rubbish in the corners. Up and down, to right and left, shot the pencil of light. "There's—there's nothing here!" gasped Tom,

"I—I guess you're right!" agreed Mr. Damon "The shed is empty!"

"Then where is Andy Foger building his aeroplane?" asked Tom in a whisper; but Mr. Damon could not answer him.

A Trial Flight

For a few moments after their exclamations of surprise Tom and Mr. Damon did not know what else to say. They stared about in amazement, hardly able to believe that the shed could be empty. They had expected to see some form of aeroplane in it, and Tom was almost sure his eyes would meet a reproduction of his Humming Bird, made from the stolen plans.

"Can it be possible there's nothing here?" went on Tom, after a long pause. He could not seem to believe it

"Evidently not," answered Mr. Damon, as he advanced toward the center of the big building and flashed the light on all sides. "You can see for yourself."

"Or, rather, you can't see," spoke the youth. "It isn't here, that's sure. You can't stick an aeroplane, even as small a one as my Humming Bird, in a corner. No; it isn't here,"

"Well, we'll have to look further," went on Mr. Damon. "I think—"

But a sudden noise near the big main doors of the shed interrupted him.

"Come on!" exclaimed Tom in a whisper. "Some one's coining! They may see us! Let's get out!"

Mr. Damon released the pressure on the spring switch, and the light went out. After waiting a moment to let their eyes become accustomed to the darkness, he and Tom stole to the door by which they had entered. As they swung it cautiously open they again heard the noise near the main portals by which Andy had formerly taken in and out the *Anthony*, as he had named the aeroplane in which he and his father went to Alaska, where, like Tom's craft, it was wrecked.

"Some one is coming in!" whispered Tom.

Hardly had he spoken when a light shone in the direction of the sound. The illumination came from a big lantern of the ordinary kind, carried by some one who had just entered the shed.

"Can you see who it is?" whispered Mr. Damon, peering eagerly forward; too eagerly, for his foot struck against the wooden side wall with a loud hang.

"Who's there?" suddenly demanded the person carrying the lantern.

He raised it high above his head, in order to cast the gleams into all the distant corners. As he did so a ray of light fell upon his face. "Andy Foger!" gasped Tom in a hoarse whisper.

Andy must have heard, for he ran forward just as Tom and Mr. Damon slipped out.

"Hold on! Who are you?" came in the unmistakable tones of the red-haired bully.

"I don't think we're going to tell," chuckled Tom softly, as he and his friend sped off into the darkness. They were not followed, and as they looked back they could see a light bobbing about in the shed.

"He's looking for us!" exclaimed Mr. Damon with an inward laugh. "Bless my watch chain! But it's a good thing we got in ahead of him. Are you sure it was Andy himself?"

"Sure! I'd know his face anywhere. But I can't understand it. Where has he been? What is he doing? Where is he building his aeroplane? I thought he was out of town."

"He may have come back to-night," said Mr. Damon. "That's the only one of your questions I can answer. We'll have to wait about the rest, I'm sure he wasn't around the house today, though, for I was working at weeding the flower beds, in my disguise as a tramp, and if he was home I'd have seen him. He must have just come back, and he went out to his shed to get something. Well, we did the best we could."

"Indeed we did," agreed Tom, "and I'm ever so much obliged to you, Mr. Damon."

"And we'll try again, when we get more clues. Bless my shoelaces! but it's a relief to be able to talk as you like."

And forthwith the eccentric man began to call down so many blessings on himself and on his belongings, no less than on his friends, that Tom laughingly warned him that he had better save some for another time.

The two reached home safely, removed their "disguises," and told Mr. Swift of the result of their trip. He agreed with them that there was a mystery about Andy's aeroplane which was yet to be solved.

But Tom was glad to find that, at any rate, the craft was not being made in Shopton, and during the next two weeks he devoted all his time to finishing his own machine. Mr. Jackson was a valuable assistant, and Mr. Damon gave what aid he could.

"Well, I think I'll be ready for a trial flight in another week," said Tom one day, as he stepped back to get a view of the almost completed *Humming-Bird*.

"Shall you want a passenger?" asked Mr. Damon.

"Yes, I wish you would take a chance with me. I could use a bag of sand, not that I mean you are to be compared to that," added Tom quickly, "but I'd rather have a real person, in order to test the balancing apparatus. Yes, we'll make a trial trip together."

In the following few days Tom went carefully over the aeroplane, making some slight changes, strengthening it here and there, and testing the motor thoroughly. It seemed to work perfectly.

At length the day of the trial came, and the *Humming-Bird* was wheeled out of the shed. In spite of the fact that it was practically finished, there yet remained much to do on it. It was not painted or decorated, and looked rather crude. But what Tom wanted to know was how it would fly, what control he had over it, what speed it could make, and how it balanced. For it was, at best, very frail, and the least change in equilibrium might be fatal.

Before taking his place in the operator's seat Tom started the motor, and by means of a spring balance tested the thrust of the propellers. It was satisfactory, though he knew that when the engine had been run for some time, and had warmed up, it would do much better.

"All ready, I guess, Mr. Damon!" he called, and the odd gentleman took his place. Tom got up into his own seat, in front of several wheels and levers by which he operated the craft.

"Start the propeller!" he requested of Mr. Jackson, and soon the motor was spitting fire, while the big, fanlike blades were whirring around like wings of light. The engineer and Eradicate were holding back the *Humming-Bird*.

"Let her go!" cried Tom as he turned on more gasoline and further advanced the spark of the motor. The roar increased, the propeller looked like a solid circle of wood, and the trim little monoplane moved slowly across the rising ground, increasing its speed every second, until, like some graceful bird, it suddenly rose in the air as Tom tilted the wing tips, and soared splendidly aloft!

A Midnight Intruder

Tom Swift sent his wonderful little craft upward on a gentle slant. Higher and higher it rose above the ground. Now it topped the trees; now it was well over them.

On the earth below stood Mr. Swift, Mr. Jackson, Eradicate and Mrs. Baggert. They were the only witnesses of the trial flight, and as the aged inventor saw his son's latest design in aeroplanes circling in the air he gave a cheer of delight. It was too feeble for Tom to hear, but the lad, glancing down, saw his father waving his hand to him.

"Dear old dad!" thought Tom, waving in return. "I hope he's well enough to see me win the big prize."

Tom and Mr. Damon went skimming easily through the air, at no great speed, to be sure, for the young inventor did not want to put too sudden a strain on his motor.

"This is glorious!" cried the odd gentleman. "I never shall have enough of aeroplaning, Tom!"

"Nor I, either," added his companion. "But how do you like it? Don't you think it's an improvement on my *Butterfly*, Mr. Damon?"

"It certainly is. You're a wonder, Tom! Look out! What are you up to?" for the machine had suddenly swerved in a startling manner.

"Oh, that's just a new kind of spiral dip I was trying," answered Tom. "I couldn't do that with my other machine, for I couldn't turn sharp enough."

"Well, don't do it right away again," begged Mr. Damon, who had turned a little white, and whose breath was coming in gasps, even though he was used to hair-raising stunts in the frail craft of the air.

Tom did not take his machine far away, for he did not want to exhibit it to the public yet, and he preferred to remain in the vicinity of his home, in case of any accident. So he circled around, did figures of eight, went up and down on long slants, took sharp turns, and gave the craft a good tryout.

"Does it satisfy you?" asked Mr. Damon, when Tom had once more made the spiral dip, but not at high speed.

"In a way, yes," was the answer. "I see a chance for several changes and improvements. Of course, I know nothing about the speed yet, and that's something that I'm anxious about, for I built this with the idea of breaking all records, and nothing else. I know, now, that I can construct a craft that will successfully navigate the air; in fact, there are any number of people who can do that; but to construct a monoplane that will beat anything ever before made is a different thing. I don't yet know that I have done it."

"When will you?"

"Oh, when I make some changes, get the motor tuned up better, and let her out for all she's worth. I want to do a hundred miles an hour, at least. I'll arrange for a speedy flight in about two weeks more."

"Then I think I will stay home," said Mr. Damon.

"No; I'll need you," insisted Tom, laughing. "Now watch. I'm going to let her out just a little."

He did, with the result that they skimmed through the air so fast that Mr. Damon's breath became a mere series of gasps.

"We'll have to wear goggles and mouth protectors when we really go fast!" yelled Tom above the noise of the motor, as he slowed down and turned about for home.

"Go fast! Wasn't that fast?" asked Mr. Damon.

Tom shook his head.

"You wait, and you'll see," he announced.

They made a good landing, and Mr. Swift hastened up to congratulate his son.

"I knew you could do it, Tom!" he cried.

"I couldn't, though, if it hadn't been for that wonderful engine of yours, dad! How do you feel?"

"Pretty good. Oh! but that's a fine machine, Tom!"

"It certainly is," agreed Mr. Jackson.

"It will be when I have it in better trim," admitted the young inventor modestly.

"By golly!" cried Eradicate, who was grinning almost from ear to ear, "I's proud oh yo', Massa Tom, an' so will mah mule Boomerang be, when I tells him. Yes, sah, dat's what he will be—proud ob yo', Massa Tom!"

"Thanks, Rad."

"Well, some folks is satisfied with mighty little under 'em, when they go up in the air, that's my opinion," said Mrs. Baggert.

"Why, wouldn't you ride in this?" asked Tom of the buxom housekeeper.

"Not if you was to give me ten thousand dollars!" she cried firmly. "Oh, dear! I think the potatoes are burning!" And she rushed back into the house.

The next day Tom started to work overhauling the *Humming-Bird*, and making some changes. He altered the wing tips slightly, and adjusted the motor, until in a thrust test it developed nearly half again as much power as formerly.

"And I'll need it all," declared Tom as he thought of the number of contestants that had entered the great race.

For the Eagle Park meet was to be a large and important one, and the principal "bird-men" of the world were to have a part in it. Tom knew that he must do his very best, and he spared no efforts to make his monoplane come up to his ideal, which was a very exacting one.

"We'll have a real speed test to-morrow," Tom announced to Mr. Damon one night. "I'll see what the *Humming-Bird* can really do. You'll come, won't you?"

"Oh, I suppose so. Bless my insurance policy! I might as well take the same chance you do. But if you're going to have such a nerve-racking thing as that on the program, you'd better get to bed early and have plenty of sleep."

"Oh, I'm not tired. I think I'll go out this evening."

"Where?"

"Oh, just around town, to see some of the fellows." But if Tom was only going around town merely to see his male friends, why did he dress so carefully, put on a new necktie, and take several looks in the glass before he went out? We think you can guess, and also the girl's name.

The young inventor got in rather late, and after a visit to the aeroplane shed, to see that all was right there, he went to bed, first connecting up the burglar-alarm wires that guarded the doors and windows of the aerodrome.

How long he had been asleep Tom did not know, but he was suddenly awakened by hearing the buzzing of the alarm at the head of his bed. At first he took it for the droning and humming of the aeroplane motor, as he had a hazy notion, and a sort of dream, that he was in his craft.

Then, with a start, he realized what it was—the burglar alarm.

"Some one's in the shed!" he gasped.

Out of bed he leaped, drawing on his trousers and coat, and putting on a pair of slippers, with speed worthy of a fireman. He grabbed up a revolver and rushed from his room, pounding on the door of Mr. Jackson's apartment in passing.

"Some one in the shed, after the *Humming-Bird!*" shouted Tom. "Get a gun, and come down!"

TOM IS HURT

As Tom passed down the hall on his way to the side door, from which he could more quickly reach the aeroplane shed, he saw his father coming from his room.

"What's the matter? What is it?" asked Mr. Swift, and alarm showed on his pale face.

"It's nothing much, dad," said the youth, as quietly as he could, for he realized that to excite his father might have a bad effect on the invalid.

"Then why are you in such a hurry? Why have you that revolver? I know there is something wrong, Tom. I am going to help you!"

In his father's present weakened state Tom desired this least of all, so he said:

"Now, never mind, dad. I thought I heard a noise out in the yard, and I'm not going to take any chances. So I roused Mr. Jackson, and I'm going down to see what it is. Perhaps it may only be Eradicate's mule, Boomerang, kicking around, or it may be Rad himself, or some one after his chickens. Don't worry. Mr. Jackson and I can attend to it. You go back to bed, father."

Tom spoke with such assurance that Mr. Swift believed him, and retired to his room, just as the engineer, partly dressed, came hurrying out in response to Tom's summons. He had his rifle, and, bad the invalid inventor seen that, he surely would have worried more.

"Come on!" whispered Tom. "Don't make any noise. I don't want to excite my father."

"What was it?" asked the engineer.

"I don't know. Burglar alarm went off, that's all I can say until we get to the shed."

Together the two left the house softly, and soon were hurrying toward the aeroplane shed.

"Look!" exclaimed Mr. Jackson. "Didn't you see a light just then, Tom?"

"Where?"

"By the side window of the shed?"

"No, I didn't notice it! Oh, yes! There it is! Some one is in there! If it's Andy Foger, I'll have him arrested, sure!"

"Maybe we can't catch him."

"That's so. Andy is a pretty slippery customer. Say, Mr. Jackson, you go around and get Eradicate, and have him bring a club. We can't trust him with a gun. Tell him to get at the back door, and I'll wait for you to join me, and we'll go in the front door. Then we'll have 'em between two fires. They can't get away."

"How about the windows?"

"They're high up, and hard to open since I put the new catches on them. Whoever got in must have forced the lock of the door. There goes the light again!"

As Tom spoke there was seen the faint glimmer of a light. It moved slowly about the interior of the shed, and with a peculiar bobbing motion, which indicated that some one was carrying it.

"Go for Eradicate, and don't make any more noise than you can help in waking him up," whispered Tom, for they were now close to the shed, and might be heard.

Mr. Jackson slipped off in the darkness, and Tom drew nearer to the building that housed his *Humming-Bird*. There was one window lower than the others, and near it was a box, that Tom remembered having seen that afternoon. He planned to get up on that and look in, before making a raid to capture the intruder.

Tom raised himself up to the window. The light had been visible a moment before he placed the box in position, but an instant later it seemed to go out, and the place was in darkness.

"I wonder if they've gone away?" thought Tom. "I can't hear any noise."

He listened intently. It was dark and silent in the shop. Suddenly the light flashed up brighter than before, and the young inventor caught sight of a man walking around the new aeroplane, examining it carefully. He carried, as Tom could see, a large-sized electric flash-lamp, with a brilliant tungsten filament, which gave a powerful light.

As the youth watched, he saw the intruder place the light on a bench, in such a position that the rays fell full upon the *Humming-Bird*. Then, adjusting the spring switch so that the light would continue to glow, the man stepped back and drew something from an inner pocket.

"I wonder what he's up to?" mused Tom. "I wish Eradicate and Mr. Jackson would hurry back. Who can that fellow be, I wonder? I've never seen him before, as far as I know. I thought sure it was going to turn out to be Andy Foger!"

Tom turned around to look into the dark yard surrounding the shed. He was anxious to hear the approach of his two allies, but there was no sound of their footsteps.

As be turned back to watch the man he could not repress a cry of alarm, for what the intruder had drawn from his pocket was a small hatchet, and he was advancing with it toward the *Humming-Bird*!

"He's going to destroy my aeroplane!" gasped Tom, and he raised his revolver to fire.

He did not intend to shoot at the man, but only to fire to scare him, and thus hasten the coming of Mr. Jackson and the colored man. But there was no need of this, for an instant later the two came running up silently, Eradicate with a big club.

"Whar am he?" he asked in a hoarse whisper. "Let me git at him, Massa Tom!"

"Hush!" exclaimed the young inventor. "We have no time to lose! He's in there, getting ready to chop my aeroplane to bits! Go to the back door, Rad, and if he tries to come out don't let him get away."

"I won't!" declared the colored man emphatically, and he shook his club suggestively.

"Come on! We'll go in the front door," whispered Tom to the engineer. "I have the key. We'll catch him red-handed, and hand him over to the police."

Waiting a few seconds, to enable Eradicate to get to his place, Tom and the engineer stole softly toward the big double doors. Every moment the youth expected to hear the crash of the hatchet on his prize machine. He shivered in anticipation, but the blows did not fall.

Tom pushed open the door and stepped inside, followed by Mr. Jackson. As they did so they saw the man standing in front of the *Humming-Bird*. He again raised the little hatchet, which was like an Indian tomahawk, and poised it for an instant over the delicate framework and planes of the air craft. Then his arm began to descend.

"Stop!" yelled Tom, and at the same time he fired in the air.

The man turned as suddenly as though a bullet had struck him, and for a moment Tom was afraid lest he had hit him by accident; but an instant later the intruder grabbed up his flashlight, and holding it before him, so that its rays shone full on Tom and Mr. Jackson, while it left him in the shadow, sprang toward them, the hatchet still in his hand.

"Look out, Tom!" cried Mr. Jackson.

"Out of my way!" shouted the man.

Bravely Tom stood his ground. He wished now that he had a club instead of his revolver. The would-be vandal was almost upon him. Mr. Jackson clubbed his rifle and swung it at the fellow. The latter dodged, and came straight at Tom.

"Look out!" yelled the engineer again, but it was too late. There was the sound of a blow, and Tom went down like a log. Then the place was in darkness, and the sound of footsteps in rapid flight could be heard outside the shed.

The intruder, after wounding the young inventor, had made his escape.

MISS NESTOR CALLS

"What's de mattah? Shall I come in? Am anybody hurted?" yelled Eradicate Sampson as he pounded on the rear door of the aeroplane shed. "Let me in, Massa Tom!"

"All right! Wait a minute! I'm coming!" called Mr. Jackson. He tried to peer through the darkness, to where a huddled heap indicated the presence of Tom. Then he thought of the electric lights, which were run by a storage battery when the dynamo was shut down, and a moment later the engineer had switched on the incandescents, filling the big shed with radiance.

"Tom, are you badly hurt?" gasped Mr. jackson.

There was no answer, for Tom was unconscious.

"Let me in! Let me git at dat robber wif mah club!" cried the colored man eagerly.

Knowing that he would need help in carrying Tom to the house, Mr. Jackson hurried to the back door. He had a key to it, and it was quicker to open it than to send Eradicate away around the shed to the front portals.

"Whar am he?" gasped the faithful darky, as he took a firmer grasp of his club and looked around the place. "Let me git mah hands on him! I'll feed him t' Boomerang, when I gits froo wif him!"

"He's gone," said the engineer. "Help me look after Tom. I'm afraid he's badly hurt."

They hastened to the unconscious lad. On one side of his head was a bad cut, which was bleeding freely.

"Oh! he's daid! I know he's daid!" wailed Eradicate.

"Not a bit of it. He isn't dead, but he may die, if we don't get him into the house, and have a doctor here soon," said Mr. Jackson sternly. "Catch hold of him, Rad, and, mind, don't carry on, and get excited, and scare Mr. Swift. Just pretend it isn't very bad, or we'll have two patents on our hands instead of only Tom."

They managed to get the youth into the house, and, contrary to their fears, Mr. Swift was not nearly so nervous as they had expected. Calmly he took charge of matters, and even telephoned for Dr. Gladby himself, while Mr. Jackson and Eradicate undressed Tom and got him to bed. Mrs. Baggert busied herself heating water and getting things in readiness for the doctor, who had promised to come at once.

Tom was just regaining consciousness when the physician came in, having driven over at top speed.

"What—what happened? Did the Humming Bird fall?" asked Tom in a whisper, putting his hand to his head.

"No, something fell on you, I guess," said the doctor, who had been hurriedly told of the circumstances. "But don't worry, Tom. You'll be all right in a few days. You got a bad cut on the head, but the skull isn't fractured, I'm glad to say. Here, now, just drink this," and he gave Tom some medicine he had mixed in a glass.

The cut was soon dressed, and Tom felt much better, though weak and a trifle dizzy.

"Did he hit me with the hatchet?" he asked Mr. Jackson.

"I couldn't tell," was the engineer's reply, "it all happened so quickly. In another instant I'd have bowled him over, instead of him landing on you, but I just missed him. He either used the hatchet, or some blunt instrument."

"Well, don't talk about it now," urged the doctor. "I want Tom to get quiet and go to sleep. We'll be much better in the morning, but I must forbid any aeroplane flights." And he shook his finger at Tom in warning. "You'll have to lie quiet for several days," he added.

"All right," agreed the young inventor weakly, and then he dozed off, for the physician had given him a quieting medicine.

"Haven't you any idea who it was?" asked Dr. Gladby of Mr. Jackson, as he prepared to leave.

"Not the slightest. It was no one Tom or I had ever seen before. But whoever it was, he intended to destroy the *Humming-Bird*, that was evident!"

"The scoundrel! I'm glad you foiled him in time; but it's too bad about Tom. However, we'll soon have him all right again."

"I knows who done it!" broke in Eradicate, who was a sort of privileged character about the Swift home.

"Who?" asked Mr. Jackson.

"It were dat Andy Foger. Leastways, he send dat man heah t' make mincemeat oh de Hummin'-Bird. I's positib 'bout dat, so I am!" And Eradicate grinned triumphantly.

"Well, perhaps Andy did have a hand in it," admitted Mr. Swift, but we have no proof of it, I can't see what his object would be in wanting to destroy Tom's new craft."

"Pure meanness. Afraid that Tom will beat him in the race," suggested Mr. Jackson.

"It's too big a risk to take," went on the aged inventor. "I'm inclined to think it might be one of the gang of men who made the diamonds in the cave in the mountains. They might have sent a spy on East, and he might try to damage the aeroplane to be revenged for what Tom and Mr. Jenks did to them."

"It's possible," agreed the engineer. "Well, we'll wait until Tom can talk, and we'll go over it with him."

"Not until he is stronger, though," stipulated the physician as he went away. "Don't excite Tom for a few days."

The young inventor was much better the following day, and when Dr. Gladby called he said Tom could sit up for a little while. Two days later Tom was well enough to he talked to, and his father and Mr. Jackson went over all the details of the matter. Mr. Damon, who had returned home, came to see his friend as soon as he heard of his plight, and was also a member of the consulting party.

"Bless my dictionary!" exclaimed the eccentric man. "I wish I had been here to take a hand in it. But, Tom, do you believe it was one of the diamond-making gang?"

"I hardly think so," was the reply. "They would take some other means of revenge than by destroying my new aeroplane. I'm inclined to think it was some one who is in with Andy Foger."

"Then we'll hire detectives, and locate him and them," declared Mr. Damon, blessing several things in succession.

Tom, however, did not like that plan, and it was decided to do nothing right away. In another few days Tom was able to be up, though he was still a semi-invalid, not venturing out of the house.

It was one afternoon, when, rather tired of his confinement, he was wishing he could resume work on his air craft, that Mrs. Baggert came in, and said:

"Some one to see you, Tom."

"Is it Mr. Damon?"

"No, it's a lady. She—"

"Oh, Tom! How are you?" cried a girlish voice, and Mary Nestor walked into the room, holding out both hands to the young inventor. Tom, with a blush, arose hastily.

"No! no! Sit still!" commanded the girl. "Oh! I'm so sorry to hear about your accident! In fact, I only heard this morning. We've been away, mamma and I, and we just got back. Tell me all about it, that is, if you feel able. But don't exert yourself. Oh! I wish I had hold of that man!"

And Miss Nestor clenched her two pretty little hands and set her white, even teeth grimly together, as though she would do most desperate things indeed.

"I wish you did, too!" exclaimed Tom. "That is, so you could hold him until I had a chance at him. But I'm all right now. It was very good of you to call. How are you, and how are your folks?"

"Very well. But I came to hear about you. Tell me," and she looked anxiously at Tom, while Mrs. Baggert discreetly withdrew to the adjoining room, and made a great noise, rattling papers and moving chairs about.

Thereupon Tom told what had happened, while Mary Nestor listened interestedly and with expressions of fear at times.

"But if Andy had anything to do with it," concluded Tom, "I can't understand what his object is. Andy is acting very strangely lately. We can't locate him, nor find out where he is building his airship. That's what

I want to know; but Mr. Damon and I, after a lot of trouble, only found his aeroplane shed empty."

"And you want to find out where Andy Foger is building his aeroplane which he has entered in the big race?" asked Miss Nestor.

"That's what I'd like to know," declared Tom earnestly. "Only we can't seem to do it. No one knows."

"Why don't you write to Mr. Sharp, or some one of the aviation meet committee?" asked the girl simply. "They would know, for you say Andy made his formal entry with them, and the rules require him to tell from what city and State he will enter his craft. Write to the committee, Tom."

For a moment the young inventor stared at her. Then he banged his fist down on the arm of his chair.

"By Jove, Mary! That's the very thing!" he cried. "I wonder why I never thought of that, instead of fiddling around in disguises, and things like that? I wonder why I never thought of that plan?"

"Perhaps because it was so simple," she answered, with a pretty blush.

"I guess that's it," agreed Tom. "It takes a woman to jump across a bridge to a conclusion every time. I'll write to Mr. Sharp at once."

A Clash with Andy

Tom lost no time in writing to Mr. Sharp. He wondered more and more at his own neglect in not before having asked the balloonist, when the latter was in Shopton, where Andy was building his aeroplane. But, as it developed later, Mr. Sharp did not know at that time.

While waiting for a reply to his letter, Tom busied himself about his own craft, making several changes he had decided on. He also began to paint and decorate it, for he wanted to have the *Humming-Bird* present a neat appearance when she was officially entered in the great race.

Miss Nestor called on Tom again, and Mr. Damon was a frequent visitor. He agreed to accompany Tom to the aviation park when it was time for the race, and also to be a passenger in the ten-thousand-dollar contest.

"It must be perfectly wonderful to fly through the air," said Miss Nestor one day, when Tom and Mr. Damon had the *Humming-Bird* out on the testing ground, trying the engine, which had been keyed up to a higher pitch of speed. "I consider it perfectly marvelous, and I can't imagine how it must seem to skim along that way."

"Come and try it," urged Tom suddenly. "There's not a bit of danger. Really there isn't."

"Oh! I'd never dare do it!" replied the girl, with a gasp. "That machine is too swift by name and swift by nature for me."

"Why don't you take Miss Nestor on a grass-cutting flight, Tom?" suggested Mr. Damon. "Bless my lawn mower! but she wouldn't be frightened at that."

"Grass cutting?" repeated the girl. "What in the world does that mean?"

"It means skimming along a few feet up in the air," answered the young inventor, who had now fully recovered from the effects of the blow given him by the midnight intruder. In spite of many inquiries, no clues to his identity had been obtained.

"How high do you go when you 'cut grass,' as you call it?" asked Miss Nestor, and Tom thought he detected a note of eager curiosity in her voice.

"Not high at all," he said. "In fact, sometimes I do cut off the tops of tall daisies. Come, Mary! Won't you try that? I know you'll like it, and when you've been over the lawn a few times you'll be ready for a high flight. Come! there's no danger."

"I—I almost believe I will," she said hesitatingly. "Will you take me down when I want to come?"

"Of course," said Tom. "Get in, and we'll start."

The *Humming-Bird* was all ready for a trial flight, and Tom was glad of the chance to test it, especially with such a pretty passenger as was Miss Nestor.

"Bless my shoelaces!" cried Mr. Damon. "I can see where I am going to be cut out, Tom Swift. I'll not get many more rides with you now that Miss Nestor is taking to aeroplaning, you young rascal!" And he playfully shook his finger at Tom.

"Oh, I don't expect to get enthusiastic over it," said Miss Nestor, who, now that she had taken her place in one of the small seats under the engine, appeared as if she would be glad of the chance to change her mind. But she did not.

"Now, if you take me more than five feet up in the air, I'll never speak to you again, Tom Swift!" she exclaimed.

"Five feet it shall be, unless you yourself ask to go higher," was the youth's reply, as he winked at Mr. Damon. Well he knew the fascination of aeroplaning, and he was almost sure of what would happen. "You can take a tape measure along, and see for yourself," he added to his fair passenger. "The barograph will hardly register such a little height."

"Well, it's as high as I want to go," said the girl. "Oh!" with a scream, as Tom started the propeller. "Are we going?"

"In a moment," was his reply. He took his seat beside the girl. The motor was speeded up until it sounded like the roar of the ocean surf in a storm.

"Let her go!" cried Tom to Mr. Damon and Mr. Jackson, who were holding back the *Humming-Bird*. They gave her a slight shove to overcome the inertia, and the trim little craft darted across the ground at every increasing speed.

Miss Nestor caught her breath with a gasp, glanced at Tom, and noted how cool he was, and then her frantic grip of the uprights slightly relaxed.

"We'll go up a little way in a minute!" shouted Tom in her ear as they were speeding over the level ground.

He pulled a lever slightly, and the *Humming-Bird* rose a little in the air, but only for a short distance, not more than five feet, and Tom held her there, though he had to run the engine at a greater speed than would have been the case had he been in the sustaining upper currents. It was as if the *Humming-Bird* resented being held so closely to the earth.

Around in a big circle, back and forth went the craft, at no time being more than seven feet from the ground. Tom glanced at Miss Nestor. Her cheeks were unusually red, and there was a bright sparkle in her eyes.

"It's glorious!" she cried. "Do you—do you think there's any danger in going higher? I believe I'd like to go up a bit."

"I knew it!" cried Tom. "Up we go!" And he pulled the wind-bending plane lever toward him. Upward shot the craft, as if alive.

"Oh!" gasped Mary.

"Sit still! It's all right!" commanded Tom.

"It's glorious; glorious!" she cried. I'm not a bit afraid now!"

"I knew you wouldn't be," declared the young inventor, who had calculated on the fascination which the motion through the air, untrammeled and free, always produces. "Shall we go higher?"

"Yes!" cried Miss Nestor, and she gazed fearlessly down at the earth, which was falling away from beneath their feet. She was in the grip of the air, and it was a new and wonderful sensation.

Tom went up to a considerable distance, for, once a person loses his first fright, one hundred feet or one thousand feet elevation makes little difference to him. It was this way with Miss Nestor.

Now, indeed, could Tom demonstrate to her some of the fine points of navigation in the upper currents, and though he did no risky "stunts," he showed the girl what it means to do an ascending spiral, how to cut corners, how to twist around in the figure eight, and do other things. Tom did not try for the great speed of which he knew his craft was capable, for he knew there was some risk with Miss Nestor aboard. But he did nearly everything else, and when he sent the *Humming-Bird* down he had made another convert and devotee to the royal sport of aeroplaning.

"Oh! I never would dared believe I could do it!' exclaimed the girl, as with flushed cheeks and dancing eyes she dismounted from the seat. "Mamma and papa will never believe I did it!"

"Bring them over, and I'll take them for a flight," said Tom, with a laugh, as Mary departed.

Tom received an answer to his letter to Mr. Sharp that night.

"Andy Foger's entry blank states," wrote the balloonist, "that he is constructing his aeroplane in the village of Hampton, which is about fifty miles from your place. If there is anything further I can do for you, Tom, let me know. I will see you at the meet. Hope you win the prize."

"In Hampton, eh?" mused Tom. "So that's where Andy has been keeping himself all this while. His uncle lives there, and that's the reason for it. He wanted to keep it a secret from me, so he could use my stolen plans for his craft. But he shan't do it! I'll go to Hampton!"

"And I'll go with you!" declared Mr. Damon, who was with Tom when he got the note from the balloonist. "We'll get to the bottom of this mystery after a while, Tom."

Delaying a few days, to make the final changes in his aeroplane, Tom and Mr. Damon departed for Hampton one morning. They thought first of going in the *Butterfly*, but as they wanted to keep their mission as secret as possible, they decided to go by train, and arrive in the town quietly and unostentatiously. They got to Hampton late that afternoon.

"What's the first thing to be done?" asked Mr. Damon as they walked up from the station, where they were almost the only persons who alighted from the train.

"Go to the hotel," decided Tom. "There's only one, I was told, so there's not much choice."

Hampton was a quiet little country town of about five thousand inhabitants, and Tom soon learned the address of Mr. Bentley, Andy's uncle, from the hotel clerk.

"What business is Mr. Bentley in?" asked Tom, for he wanted to learn all he could without inquiring of persons who might question his motives.

"Oh, he's retired," said the clerk. "He lives on the interest of his money. But of late he's been erecting some sort of a building on his back lot, like a big shed, and folks are sort of wondering what he's doing in it. Keeps mighty secret about it. He's got a young fellow helping him."

"Has he got red hair?" asked Tom, while his heart beat strangely fast.

"Who? Mr. Bentley? No. His hair's black."

"I mean the young fellow."

"Oh! his? Yes, his is red. He's a nephew, or some relation to Mr. Bentley. I did hear his name, but I've forgotten it. Sandy, or Andy, or some such name as that."

This was near enough for Tom and Mr. Damon, and they did not want to risk asking any more questions. They turned away to go to their rooms, as the clerk was busy answering inquiries from some other guests. A little later, supper was served, and Tom, having finished, whispered to Mr. Damon to join him upstairs as soon as he was through.

"What are you going to do?" asked the eccentric man.

"We're going out and have a look at this new shed by moonlight," decided Tom. "I want to see what it's like, and, if possible, I want to get a peep inside. I'll soon be able to tell whether or not Andy is using my stolen plans."

"All right. I'm with you. Bless my bill of fare! But we seem to be doing a lot of mysterious work of late."

"Yes," agreed Tom. "But if you have to bless anything to-night, Mr. Damon, please whisper it. Andy, or some of his friends, may be about the shed, and as soon as they hear one of your blessings they'll know who's coming."

"Oh, I'll be careful," promised Mr. Damon.

"Andy will find out, sooner or later, that we are in town," went on Tom, "but we may be able to learn to-night what we want to know, and then we can tell how to act."

A little later, as if they were merely strolling about, Mr. Damon and Tom headed for Mr. Bentley's place, which was on the outskirts of the town. There was a full moon, and the night was just right for the kind of observation Tom wanted to make. There were few persons abroad, and the young inventor thought he would have no one spying on him.

They located the big house of Andy's uncle without trouble. Going down a side street, they had a glimpse of a shed, built of new boards, standing in the middle of a large lot. About the structure was a new, high wooden fence, but as Tom and his friend passed along it they saw that a gate in it was open.

"I'm going in!" whispered Tom.

"Will it be safe?" asked Mr. Damon.

"I don't care whether it will be or not. I've got to know what Andy is doing. Come on! We'll take a chance!"

Cautiously they entered the enclosure. The big shed was dark, and stood out conspicuously in the moonlight.

"There doesn't seem to be any one here," whispered Tom. "I wonder if we could get a look in the window?"

"It's worth trying, anyhow," agreed Mr. Damon. "I'm with you, Tom."

They drew nearer to the shed. Suddenly Tom stepped on a stick, which broke with a sharp report.

"Bless my spectacles!" cried Mr. Damon, half aloud.

There was silence for a moment, and then a voice cried out:

"Who's there? Hold on! Don't come any farther! It's dangerous!"

Tom and Mr. Damon stood still, and from behind the shed stepped Andy Foger and a man.

"Oh! it's you, is it, Tom Swift?" exclaimed the red-haired bully. "I thought you'd come sneaking around. Come on, Jake! We'll make them wish they'd stayed home!" And Andy made a rush for Tom.

THE GREAT TEST

"Bless my gizzard!" exclaimed Mr. Damon, who hardly knew what to do. "We'd better be getting out of here, Tom!"

"Not much!" exclaimed the young inventor. "I never ran from Andy Foger yet, and I'm not going to begin now."

He assumed an attitude of defense, and stood calmly awaiting the onslaught of the bully; but Andy knew better than to come to a personal argument with Tom, and so the red-haired lad halted some paces off. The man, who had followed young Foger, also stopped.

"What do you want around here, Tom Swift?" demanded Andy.

"You know very well what I want," said the young inventor, calmly. "I want to know what you did with the aeroplane plans you took from my house."

"I never took any!" declared Andy vigorously

"Well, there's no use discussing that," went on Tom. "What I came here to find out, and I don't mind telling you, is whether or not you are building a monoplane to compete against me, and building it on a model invented by me; and what's more, Andy Foger, I intend to find this out, too!"

Tom started toward the big shed, which loomed up in the moonlight.

"Stand back!" cried Andy, getting in Tom's way. "I can build any kind of an aeroplane I like, and you can't stop me!"

"We'll see about that," declared the young inventor, as he kept on. "I'm not going to allow my plans to be stolen, and a monoplane made after them, and do nothing about it."

"You keep away!" snarled Andy, and he grabbed Tom by the shoulder and struck him a blow in the chest. He must have been very much excited, or otherwise he never would have come to hostilities this way with Tom, whom he well knew could easily beat him.

The blow, together with the many things he had suffered at Andy's hands, was too much for our hero. He drew back his fist, and a moment later Andy Foger was stretched out on the grass. He lay there for a moment, and then rose up slowly to his knees, his face distorted with rage.

"You—you hit me!" he snarled.

"Not until you hit first," said Tom calmly.

"Bless my punching bag! That's so!" exclaimed Mr. Damon.

"You'll suffer for this!" whined Andy, getting to his feet, but taking care to retreat from Tom, who stood ready for him. "I'll get square with you for this! Jake, come on, and we'll get our guns!"

Andy turned and hurried back toward the shed, followed by the evil-looking man, who had apparently been undecided whether to attack Mr. Damon or Tom. Now the bully and his companion were in full retreat.

"We'll get our guns, and then we'll see whether they'll want to stay where they're not wanted!" went on Andy, threateningly.

"Bless my powderhorn! What had we better do?" asked Mr. Damon.

"I guess we'd better go back," said Tom calmly. "Not that I'm afraid of Andy. His talk about guns is all bluff; but I don't want to get into any more of a row, and he is just ugly and reckless enough to make trouble. I'm afraid we can't learn what we came to find out, though I'm more convinced than ever that Andy is using my plans to make his aeroplane."

"But what can you do?"

"I'll see Mr. Sharp, and send a protest to the aviation committee. I'll refuse to enter if Andy flies in a model of my *Humming-Bird*, and I'll try to prevent him from using it after he gets it on the ground. That is all I can do, it seems, lacking positive information. Come on, Mr. Damon. Let's get back to our hotel, and we'll start for home in the morning."

"I have a plan," whispered the odd man.

"What is it?" asked Tom, narrowly watching for the reappearance of Andy and the man.

"I'll stay here until they come, then I'll pretend to run away. They'll chase after me, and get all excited, and you can go up and look in the shed windows. Then you can join me later. How's that?"

"Too risky. They might fire at you by mistake. No. We'll both go. I've found out more than enough to confirm my suspicions."

They turned out of the lot which contained the shed, and walked toward the road, just as Andy and his crony came back.

"Huh! You'd better go!" taunted the bully.

Tom had a bitter feeling in his heart. It seemed as if he was defeated, and he did not like to retreat before Andy.

"You'd better not come back here again, either," went on Andy.

Tom and Mr. Damon did not reply, but kept on in silence. They returned to Shopton the next day.

"Well," remarked Tom, when he had gone out to look at his *Humming-Bird*, "I know one thing. Andy Foger may build a machine something like this, but I don't believe he can put in all the improvements I have, and certainly he can't equal that engine; eh, dad?"

"I hope not, Tom," replied his father, who seemed to be much improved in health.

"When are you going to try for speed?" asked Mr. Damon.

"To-morrow, if I can get it tuned up enough," replied Tom, "and I think I can. Yes, we'll have the great test tomorrow, and then I'll know whether I really have a chance for that ten thousand dollars."

Never before had Tom been so exacting in his requirements of his air craft as when, the next day, the *Humming-Bird* was wheeled out to the flight ground, and gotten ready for the test. The young inventor went over every bolt, brace, stay, guy wire and upright. He examined every square inch of the wings, the tips, planes and rudders. The levers, the steering wheel, the automatic equilibrium attachments and the balancing weights were looked at again and again.

As for the engine, had it been a delicate watch, Tom could not have scrutinized each valve, wheel, cam and spur gear more carefully. Then the gasoline tank was filled, the magneto was looked after, the oil reservoirs were cleaned out and freshly filled, and finally the lad remarked:

"Well, I guess I'm ready. Come along, Mr. Damon."

"Am I going with you in the test?"

"Surely. I've been counting on you. If you're to be with me in the race, you want to get a sample of what we can do. Take your place. Mr. Jackson, are you ready to time us?"

"All ready, Tom."

"And, dad, do you feel well enough to check back Mr. Jackson's results? I don't want any errors."

"Oh, yes, Tom. I can do it."

"Very well, then. Now this is my plan. I'm going to mount upward on an easy slant, and put her through a few stunts first, to warm up, and see that everything is all right. Then, when I give the signal, by dropping this small white ball, that means I'm ready for you to start to time me. Then I'll begin to try for the record. I'll go about the course in a big ellipse, and—well, we'll see what happens."

While Mr. Damon was in his seat the young inventor started the propeller, and noted the thrust developed. It was satisfactory, as measured on the scale, and then Tom took his place.

"Let her go!" he cried to Mr. Jackson and Eradicate, after he had listened to the song of the motor for a moment. The *Humming-Bird* flew across the course, and a moment later mounted into the air.

Tom quickly took her up to about two thousand feet, and there, finding the conditions to his liking, he began a few evolutions designed to severely test the craft's stability, and to learn whether the engine was working properly.

"How about it?" asked Mr. Damon anxiously.

"All right!" shouted Tom in his ear, for the motor was making a great racket. "I guess we'll make the trial next time we come around. Get ready to drop the signal ball."

Tom slowly brought the aeroplane around in a graceful curve. He sighted down, and saw the first tall white pole that marked the beginning of the course.

"Drop!" he called to Mr. Damon.

The white rubber ball went to the earth like a shot. Mr. Jackson and Mr. Swift saw it, and started their timing-watches. Tom opened the throttle and advanced the spark. The great test was on!

The *Humming-Bird* trembled and throbbed with the awful speed of the motor, like a thing alive. She seemed to rush forward as an eagle dropping down from a dizzy height upon some hapless prey.

"Faster yet!" murmured Tom. "We must go faster yet!"

The motor was warming up. Streaks of fire came from it. The exhaust of the explosions was a continuous roar. Faster and faster flew the frail craft.

Around and around the air course she circled. The wind appeared to be rushing beneath the planes and rudders with the velocity of a hurricane. Had it not been for the face protectors they wore, Tom and Mr. Damon could not have breathed. For ten minutes this fearful speed was kept up. Then Tom, knowing he had run the motor to the limit, slowed it down. Next he shut it off completely, and prepared to volplane back to earth. The silence after the terrific racket was almost startling. For a moment neither of the aviators spoke. Then Mr. Damon said:

"Do you think you did it, Tom?"

"I don't know. We'll soon find out. They'll have the record." And he motioned toward the earth, which they were rapidly nearing.

A Noise in the Night

"Well, did I make it? Make any kind of a record?" asked Tom eagerly, as he brought the trim little craft to a stop, after it had rolled along the ground on the bicycle wheels.

"What do you think you did?" asked Mr. Jackson, who had been busy figuring on a slip of paper.

"Did I get her up to ninety miles an hour?" inquired Tom eagerly. "If I did, I know when the motor wears down a bit smoother that I can make her hit a hundred in the race, easily. Did I touch ninety, Mr. Jackson?"

"Better than that, Tom! Better than that!" cried his father.

"Yes," joined in Mr. Jackson. "Allowing for the difference in our watches, Tom, your father and I figure that you did the course at the rate of one hundred and twelve miles an hour!"

"One hundred and twelve!" gasped the young inventor, hardly able to believe it.

"I made it a hundred and fifteen," said Mr. Swift, who was almost as pleased as was his son, "and Mr. Jackson made it one hundred and eleven; so we split the difference, so to speak. You certainly have a sky racer, Tom, my boy!"

"And I'll need it, too, dad, if I'm to compete with Andy Foger, who may have a machine almost like mine."

"But I thought you were going to object to him if he has," said Mr. Damon, who had hardly recovered from the speedy flight through space.

"Well, I was just providing for a contingency, in case my protest was overruled," remarked Tom. "But I'm glad the *Humming-Bird* did so well on her first trial. I know she'll do better the more I run her. Now we'll get her back in her 'nest,' and I'll look her over, when she cools down, and see if anything has worked loose."

But the trim little craft needed only slight adjustments after her tryout, for Tom had built her to stand up under a terrific strain.

"We'll soon be in shape for the big race," he announced, "and when I bring home that ten thousand dollars I'm going to abandon this sky-scraping business, except for occasional trips."

"What will you do to occupy your mind?" asked Mr. Damon.

"Oh, I'm going to travel," announced Tom. "Then there's my new electric rifle, which I have not perfected yet. I'll work on that after I win the big race."

For several days after the first real trial of his sky racer Tom was busy going over the *Humming-Bird*, making slight changes here and there. He was the sort of a lad who was satisfied with nothing short of the best, and though neither his father nor Mr. Jackson could see where there was room for improvement, Tom was so exacting that he sat up for several nights to perfect such little details as a better grip for the steering-lever, a quicker way of making the automatic equilibriumizer take its position, or an improved transmitter for the wireless apparatus.

That was a part of his monoplane of which Tom was justly proud, for though many aeroplanes to-day are equipped with the sending device, few can receive wireless messages in mid-air. But Tom had seen the advantage of this while making a trip in the ill-fated *Red Cloud* to the cave of the diamond makers, and he determined to have his new craft thus provided against emergencies. The wireless outfit of the *Humming-Bird* was a marvel of compactness.

Thus the days passed, with Tom very busy; so busy, in fact, that he hardly had time to call on Miss Nestor. As for Andy Foger, he heard no more from him, and the bully was not seen around Shopton. Tom concluded that he was at his uncle's place, working on his racing craft.

The young inventor sent a formal protest to the aviation committee, to be used in the event of Andy entering a craft which infringed on the *Humming-Bird*, and received word from Mr. Sharp that the interests of the young inventor would be protected. This satisfied Tom.

Still, at times, he could not help wondering how the first plans had so mysteriously disappeared, and he would have given a good deal to know just how Andy got possession of them, and how he knew enough to use them.

"He, or some one whom he hired, must have gotten into our house mighty quickly that day," mused Tom, "and then skipped out while dad fell into a little doze. It was a mighty queer thing, but it's lucky it was no worse."

The time was approaching for the big aviation meet. Tom's craft was in readiness, and had been given several other trials, developing more speed each time. Additional locks were put on the doors of the shed, and more burglar-alarm wires were strung, so that it was almost a physical impossibility to get into the *Humming-Bird*'s "nest" without arousing some one in the Swift household.

"And if they do, I guess we'll be ready for them," said Tom grimly. He had been unable to find out who it was that had attempted once before to damage the monoplane, but he suspected it was the ill-favored man who was working with Andy.

As for Mr. Swift, at times he seemed quite well, and again he required the services of a physician.

"You will have to be very careful of your father, Tom," said Dr. Gladby. "Any sudden shock or excitement may aggravate his malady, and in that case a serious operation will be necessary."

"Oh, we'll take good care of him," said the lad; but he could not help worrying, though he tried not to let his father see the strain which he was under.

It was some days after this, and lacking about a week until the meet was to open, when a peculiar thing happened. Tom had given his *Humming-Bird* a tryout one day, and had then begun to make arrangements for taking it apart and shipping it to Eagle Park. For he would not fly to the meet in it, for fear of some accident. So big cases had been provided.

"I'll take it apart in the morning," decided Tom, as he went to his room, after seeing to the burglar alarm, "and ship her off. Then Mr. Damon and I will go there, set her up, and get ready to win the race."

Tom had opened all the windows in his room, for it was very warm. In fact it was so warm that sleep was almost out of the question, and he got up to sit near the windows in the hope of feeling a breeze.

There it was more comfortable, and he was just dozing off, and beginning to think of getting back into bed, when he was aware of a peculiar sound in the air overhead.

"I wonder if that's a heavy wind starting up?" he mused. "Good luck, if it is! We need it." The noise increased, sounding more and more like wind, but Tom, looking out into the night, saw the leaves of the trees barely moving.

"If that's a breeze, it's taking its own time getting here," he went on.

The sound came nearer, and then Tom knew that it was not the noise of the wind in the trees. It was more like a roaring and rumbling,

"Can it be distant thunder?" Tom asked himself. "There is no sign of a storm." Once more he looked from the window. The night was calm and clear—the trees as still as if they were painted.

The sound was even more plain now, and Tom, who had sharp ears, at once decided that it was just over the house— directly overhead. An instant later he knew what it was.

"The motor of an aeroplane, or a dirigible balloon!" he exclaimed. "Some one is flying overhead!"

For an instant he feared lest the shed had been broken into, and his *Humming-Bird* taken, but a glance toward the place seemed to show that it was all right.

Then Tom hastily made his way to where a flight of stairs led to a little enclosed observatory on the roof.

"I'm going to see what sort of a craft it is making that noise," he said.

As he opened the trap door, and stepped out into the little observatory the sound was so plain as to startle him. He looked up quickly, and, directly overhead he saw a curious sight.

For, flying so low as to almost brush the lightning rod on the chimney of the Swift home, was a small aeroplane, and, as Tom looked up, he saw in a light that gleamed from it, two figures looking down on him.

A Mysterious Fire

For a few moments Tom did not know what to think. Not that the sight of aeroplanes in flight were any novelty to him, but to see one flying over his house in the dead of night was a little out of the ordinary. Then, as he realized that night-flights were becoming more common, Tom tried to make out the details of the craft.

"I wish I had brought the night glasses with me," he said aloud.

"Here they are," spoke a voice at his side, and so suddenly that Tom was startled. He looked down, and saw Mr. Jackson standing beside him.

"Did you hear the noise, too?" the lad asked the engineer.

"Yes. It woke me up. Then I heard you moving around, and I heard you come up here. I thought maybe it was a flight of meteors you'd come to see, and I knew the glasses would be handy, so I stopped for them. Take a look, Tom. It's an aeroplane; isn't it?"

"Yes, and not moving very fast, either. They seem to be circling around here."

The young inventor was peering through the binoculars, and, as soon as he had the mysterious craft in focus, he cried:

"Look, Mr. Jackson, it's a new kind of monoplane. I never saw one like it before. I wonder who could have invented that? It's something like a santos-Dumont and a Bleriot, with some features of Cornu's Helicopter. That's a queer machine."

"It certainly is," agreed the engineer, who was now sighting through the glasses. In spite of the darkness the binoculars brought out the peculiarities of the aeroplane with considerable distinctness.

"Can you make out who are in it?" asked Tom.

"No," answered Mr. Jackson. "You try."

But Tom had no better luck. There were two persons in the odd machine, which was slowly flying along, moving in a great circle, with the Swift house for its center.

"I wonder why they're hanging around here?" asked Tom, suspiciously.

"Perhaps they want to talk to you," suggested Mr. Jackson. "They may be fellow inventor—perhaps one of them is that Philadelphia man who had the *Whizzer*."

"No," replied the lad. "He would have sent me word if he intended calling on me. Those are strangers, I think. There they are, coming back again."

The mysterious aeroplane was once more circling toward the watchers on the roof. There was a movement on the steps, near which Tom was standing, and his father came up.

"Is anything the matter?" he asked anxiously.

"Only a queer craft circling around up here," was the reply. "Come and see, dad."

Mr. Swift ascended to the roof. The aeroplane was higher now, and those in her could not so easily be made out. Tom felt a vague sense of fear, as though he was being watched by the evil eyes of his enemies. More than once he looked over to the shed where his craft was housed, as though some danger might threaten it. But the shed of the *Humming-Bird* showed no signs of invaders.

Suddenly the mysterious aeroplane increased its speed. It circled about more quickly, and shot upward, as though to show the watchers of what it was capable. Then, with a quick swoop it darted downward, straight for the building where Tom's newest invention was housed.

"Look out! They'll hit something!" cried the young inventor, as though those in the aeroplane could hear him.

Then, just as though they had heeded his warning, the pilots of the mysterious craft shot her upward, after she had hovered for an instant over the big shed.

"That was a queer move," said Tom. "It looked as if they lost control of her for a moment."

"And they dropped something!" cried Mr. Jackson. "Look! something fell from the aeroplane on the roof of the shed."

"Some tool, likely," spoke Tom. "I'll get it in the morning, and see what sort of instruments they carry. I'd like to examine that machine, though."

The queer aeroplane was now shooting off in the darkness and Tom followed it with the glasses, wondering what its construction could be like. He was to have another sight of it sooner than he expected.

"Well, we may as well get back to bed," said Mr. Jackson. "I'm tired, and we've got lots to do to-morrow."

"Yes," agreed Tom. "It's cooler now. Come on, dad."

Tom fell into a light doze. He thought afterward he could not have slept more than half an hour when he heard a commotion out in the yard. For an instant he could not tell what it was, and then, as he grew wider awake he knew that it was the shouting of Eradicate Sampson, and the braying of Boomerang.

But what was Eradicate shouting?

"Fire! Fire! Fire!"

Tom leaped to his window.

"Wake up, Massa Tom! Wake up! De areoplane shed am on fire, an' de *Humming-Bird* will burn up! Hurry! Hurry!"

Tom looked out. Flames were shooting up from the roof of the shed where his precious craft was kept.

MR. SWIFT IS WORSE

Almost before the echoes of Eradicate's direful warning cry had died away, Tom was on his way out of the house, pausing only long enough to slip on a pair of shoes and his trousers. There was but one thought in his mind. If he could get the *Humming-Bird* safely out he would not care if the shed did burn, even though it contained many valuable tools and appliances.

"We must save my new aeroplane!" thought Tom, desperately. "I've got to save her!"

As he raced through the hall he caught up a portable chemical fire-extinguisher. Tom saw his father's door open, and Mr. Swift looked out.

"What is it?" he called anxiously.

"Fire!" answered the young inventor, almost before he thought of the doctor's warning that Mr. Swift must not be excited. Tom wished he could recall the word, but it was too late. Besides Eradicate, down in the yard was shouting at the top of his voice:

"Fire! Fire! Fire!"

"Where, Tom?" gasped Mr. Swift, and his son thought the aged inventor grew suddenly paler.

"Aeroplane shed," answered the lad. "But don't worry dad. It's only a small blaze. We'll get it out. You stay here. We'll attend to it—Mr. Jackson and Eradicate and I."

"No—I'm going to help!" exclaimed Mr. Swift, sturdily. "I'll be with you, Tom. Go on!"

The lad rushed down to the yard, closely followed by the engineer, who had caught up another extinguisher. Eradicate was rushing about, not knowing what to do, but still keeping up his shouting.

"It's on de roof! De roof am all blazin'!" he yelled.

"Quit your noise, and get to work!" cried Tom. "Get out a ladder, Rad, and raise it to the side of the shed. Then play this extinguisher on the blaze. Mr. Jackson, you help me run the *Humming-Bird* out. After she's safe we'll tackle the fire."

Tom cast a hurried look at the burning shed. The flames were shooting high up from the roof, now, and eating their way down. As he rushed toward the big doors, which he intended to open to enable him to run out his sky racer, he was wondering how the fire came to start so high up as the roof. He wondered if a meteor could have fallen and caused it.

As the doors, which were quickly unlocked by Tom, swung back, and as he and the engineer started to go in, they were met by choking fumes as if of some gas. They recoiled for the moment.

"What—what's that?" gasped Tom, coughing and sneezing.

"Some chemical—I—I don't know what kind," spluttered Mr. Jackson. "Have you any carboys of acid in there Tom, that might have exploded by the heat?"

"No; not a thing. Let's try again."

Once more they tried to go in, but were again driven back by the distressing fumes. The fire was eating down, now. There was a hole burned in the roof, and by the leaping tongues of flame Tom could see his aeroplane. It was almost in the path of the blaze.

"We must get her out!" he shouted. "I'm going in!"

But it was impossible, and the daring young inventor nearly succumbed to the choking odors. Mr. Jackson dragged him back.

"We can't go in!" he cried. "There has been some mysterious work here! Those fumes were put here to keep us from saving the machine. This fire has been set by some enemy! We can't go in!"

"But I am going!" declared Tom. "We'll try the back door."

They rushed to that, but again were driven out by the gases and vapors, which were mingled with the smoke. Disheartened, yet with a wild desire to do something to save his precious craft, Tom Swift drew back for a moment.

As he did so he heard a hiss, as Eradicate turned the chemical stream on the blaze. Tom looked up. The faithful colored man was on a ladder near the burning roof, acting well his part as a fireman.

"That's the stuff!" cried Tom. "Come on, Mr. Jackson. Maybe if we use the chemical extinguishers we can drive out those fumes!"

The engineer understood. He took up the extinguisher he had brought, and Tom got a second one from a nearby shed. Then Mr. Swift came out bearing another.

"You shouldn't have come, dad! We can attend to it!" cried Tom, fearing for the effect of the excitement on his invalid parent.

"Oh, I couldn't stay there and see the shed burn. Are you getting it under control? Why don't you run out the *Humming-Bird*?"

Tom did not mention the choking fumes. He passed up a full extinguisher to Eradicate, who had used all the chemical in his. Then Tom got another ladder, and soon three streams were being directed on the flames. They had eaten, a pretty big hole in the roof, but the chemicals were slowly telling on them.

As soon as he saw that Eradicate and Mr. Jackson could control the blaze, Tom descended to the ground, and ran once more to the big doors. He was determined to make another try to wheel out the aeroplane, for he saw from above that the flames were now on the side wall, and might reach the craft any minute. And it would not take much to inflict serious damage on the sky racer.

"I'll get her, fumes or no fumes!" murmured Tom, grimly. And, whether it was the effect of the chemical streams, or whether the choking odors were dissipated through the hole in the roof was not manifested, but, at any rate, Tom found that he could go in, though he coughed and gasped for breath.

He wheeled the aeroplane outside, for the *Humming-Bird* was almost as light as her namesake. A hurried glance by the gleam of the dying fire assured Tom that his craft was not damaged beyond a slight scorching of one of the wing tips.

"That was a narrow escape!" he murmured, as he wheeled the sky racer far away, out of any danger from sparks. Then he went back to help fight the fire, which was extinguished in about ten minutes more.

"It was a mighty queer blaze," said Mr. Jackson, "starting at the top that way. I wonder what caused it?"

"We'll investigate in the morning," decided Tom. "Now, dad, you must get back to your room." He turned to help his father in, but at that moment Mr. Swift, who was trying to say something, fell over in a dead faint.

"Quick! Help me carry him into the house!" cried Tom. "Then telephone for Dr. Gladby, Mr. Jackson."

The physician looked grave when, half an hour later, he examined his patient.

"Mr. Swift is very much worse," he said in a low voice. "The excitement of the fire has aggravated his ailment. I would like another doctor to see him, Tom."

"Another doctor?" Tom's voice showed his alarm.

"Yes, we must have a consultation. I think Dr. Kurtz will be a good one to call in. I should like his opinion before I decide what course to take."

"I'll send Eradicate for him at once," said the young inventor, and he went to give the colored man his instructions, while his heart was filled with a great fear for his father.

THE BROKEN BRIDGE

Dr. Kurtz looked as grave as did Dr. Gladby when he had made an examination of the patient. Mr. Swift was still in a semi-conscious condition, hardly breathing as he rested on the bed where they had placed him after the fire.

"Vell," said the German physician, after a long silence, "vot is your obinion, my dear Gladby?"

"I think an operation is necessary."

"Yes, dot is so; but you know vot kind of an operation alone vill safe him; eh, my dear Gladby?"

Dr. Gladby nodded.

"It will be a rare and delicate one," he said. "There is but one surgeon I know of who can do it."

"You mean Herr Hendrix?" asked Dr. Kurtz.

"Yes, Dr. Edward Hendrix, of Kirkville. If he can be induced to come I think there is a chance of saving Mr. Swift's life. I'll speak to Tom about it."

The two physicians, who had been consulting together, summoned the youth from another room, where, with Mrs. Baggert and Mr. Jackson he had been anxiously awaiting the verdict.

"What is it?" the young inventor asked Dr. Gladby.

The medical man told him to what conclusion he and his colleague had arrived, adding:

"We advise that Dr. Hendrix be sent for at once. But I need hardly tell you, Tom, that he is a noted specialist, and his services are in great demand. He is hard to get."

"I'll pay him any sum he asks!" burst out the youth. "I'll spend all my fortune—and I have made considerable money of late—I'll spend every cent to get my father well! Money need not stand in the way, Dr. Gladby."

"I knew that, Tom. Still Dr. Hendrix is a very busy man, and it is hard to induce him to come a long distance. It is over a hundred miles to Kirkville, and it is an out-of-the-way place. I never could understand why Dr. Hendrix settled there. But there he is, and if we want him he will have to come from there. The worst of it is that there are few trains, and only a single railroad line from there to Shopton."

"Then I'll telegraph," decided Tom. "I'll offer him his own price, and ask him to rush here as soon as he can."

"You had better let Dr. Kurtz and me attend to that part of it," suggested the physician. "Dr. Hendrix would hardly come on the request of some one whom he did not know. I'll prepare a telegram, briefly explaining the case. It is the sort of an operation Dr. Hendrix is much interested in, and I think he will come on that account, if for no other reason. I'll write out the message, and you can have Eradicate take it to the telegraph office."

"I'll take it myself!" exclaimed Tom, as he got ready to go out into the night with the urgent request. "Is there any immediate danger for my father?" he asked.

"No; not any immediate danger," replied Dr. Gladby. "But the operation is imperative if he is to live. It is his one and only chance."

Tom thought only of his father as he hurried on through the night. Even the prospect of the great race, so soon to take place, had no part in his mind.

"I'll not race until I'm sure dad is going to get better," he decided. With the message to the noted specialist Tom also sent one to Mr. Damon, telling him the news, and asking him to come to Shopton. Tom felt that the presence of the odd gentleman would help him, and Mr. Damon, who first intended to stay on at the Swift home until he and Tom departed for Eagle Park, had gone back to his own residence to attend to some business Tom knew he would come in the morning, and Mr. Damon did arrive on the first train.

"Bless my soul!" he exclaimed with ready sympathy, as he extended his hand to Tom. "What's all this?" The young inventor told him, beginning with the fire that had been the cause of the excitement which produced the change in Mr. Swift.

"But I have great hopes that the specialist will be able to cure him," said Tom, for, with the coming of daylight, his courage had returned to him. "Dr. Gladby and Dr. Kurtz depend a great deal on Dr. Hendrix," he said.

"Yes, he certainly is a wonderful man. I have heard a great deal about him. I have no doubt but what he will cure your father. But about the fire? How did it start?"

"I don't know, but now that I have a few hours to spare before the doctor can get here, I'm going to make an examination."

"Bless my penwiper, but I'll help you."

Tom went into the house, to inquire of Mrs. Baggert, for probably the tenth time that morning, how his father was doing. Mr. Swift was still in a semi-conscious condition, but he recognized Tom, when the youth stood at his bedside.

"Don't worry about me, son," said the brave old inventor, as he took Tom's hand. "I'll be all right. Go ahead and get ready for the race. I want you to win!"

Tears came into Tom's eyes. Would his father be well enough to allow him to take part in the big event? He feared not.

By daylight it was seen that quite a hole had been burned in the aeroplane shed. Tom and Mr. Damon, accompanied by Mr. Jackson, walked through the place.

"And you say the fire broke out right after you had seen the mysterious airship hovering over the house?" asked the eccentric man.

"Well, not exactly after," answered Tom, "but within an hour or so. Why do you ask?"

But Mr. Damon did not answer. Something on the floor of the shed, amid a pile of blackened and charred pieces of wood, attracted his attention. He stooped over and picked it up.

"Is this yours?" he asked Tom.

"No. What is it?"

The object looked like a small iron ball, with a tube about half an inch in diameter projecting slightly from it. Tom took it'.

"Why, it looks like an infernal machine or a dynamite bomb," he said. "I wonder where it came from? Guess I'd better drop it in a pail of water. Maybe Eradicate found it and brought it here. I never saw it before. Mr. Jackson, please hand me that pail of water. We'll soak this bomb."

"There is no need," said Mr. Damon, quietly. "It is harmless now. It has done its work. It was that which set fire to your shed, and which caused the stifling fumes."

"That?" cried Tom.

"Yes. This ball is hollow, and was filled with a chemical. It was dropped on the roof, and, after a certain time, the plug in the tube was eaten through, the chemicals ran out, set the roof ablaze, and, dripping down inside spread the choking odors that nearly prevented you from getting out your aeroplane."

"Are you sure of this?" asked the young inventor.

"Positive. I read about these bombs recently. A German invented them to be used in attacking a besieged city in case of war."

"But how did this one get on my shed roof?" asked Tom.

"It was dropped there by the mysterious airship!" exclaimed the odd man. "That was why the aeroplane moved about over your place. Those in it hoped that the fire would not break out until you were all asleep, and that the shed and the *Humming-Bird* would be destroyed before you came to the rescue. Some of your enemies are still after you, Tom."

"And it was Andy Foger, I'll wager!" he cried. "He was in that aircraft! Oh, I'll have a long score to settle with him!"

"Of course you can't be sure it was he," said Mr. Damon, "but I wouldn't be a bit surprised but what it was. Andy is capable of such a thing. He wanted to prevent you from taking part in the race."

"Well, he sha'n't!" cried Tom, and then he thought of his invalid father. They made a further examination of the shed, and discovered another empty bomb. Then Tom recalled having seen something drop from the mysterious aeroplane as it passed over the shed.

"It was these bombs," he said. "We certainly had a narrow escape! Oh, wait until I settle my score with Andy Foger!"

As there would be but little use for the aeroplane shed now, if Tom sent his craft off to the meet, it was decided to repair it temporarily only, until he returned.

Accordingly, a big tarpaulin was fastened over the hole in the roof. Then Tom put a new wing tip on in place of the one that had been scorched. He looked all over his sky racer, and decided that it was in fit condition for the coming meet.

"I'll begin to take it apart for shipment, as soon as I hear from the specialist that dad is well enough for me to go," he said.

It was a few hours after the discovery of the empty bomb that Tom saw Dr. Gladby coming along. The physician was urging his horse to top speed. Tom felt a vague fear in his heart.

"I've got a message from Dr. Hendrix, Tom," he said, as he stopped his carriage, and approached the lad.

"When can he come?" asked the young inventor, eagerly.

"He can't get here, Tom."

"Can't get here! Why not?"

"Because the railroad bridge has collapsed, and there is no way to come. He can't make any other connections to get here in time—in time to do your father any good, Tom. He has just sent me a telegram to that effect. Dr. Hendrix can't get here, and..." Dr. Gladby paused.

"Do you mean that my father may die if the operation is not performed?" asked Tom, in a low voice.

"Yes," was the answer.

"But can't Dr. Hendrix drive here in an auto?" asked the lad. "Surely there must be some way of getting over the river, even if the railroad bridge is down. Can't he cross in a boat and drive here?"

"He wouldn't be in time, Tom. Don't you understand, Dr. Hendrix must be here within four hours, if he is to save your father's life. He never could do it by driving or by coming on some other road, or in an auto. He can't make the proper connections. There is no way."

"Yes, there is!" cried Tom, suddenly. "I know a way!"

"How?" asked Dr. Gladby, thrilled by Tom's ringing tones. "How can you do it, Tom?"

"I'll go for Dr. Hendrix in my *Humming-Bird*."

"Going for him would do no good. He must be brought here."

"And so he shall be!" cried Tom. "I'll bring him here in my sky racer—if he has the nerve to stand the journey, and I think he has! I'll bring Dr. Hendrix here!" and Tom hurried away to prepare for the thrilling trip.

A Nervy Specialist

There was little time to lose. Every moment of delay meant so much less chance for the recovery of Mr. Swift. Even now the periods of consciousness were becoming shorter and farther apart. He seemed to be sinking.

Tom resolutely refused to think of the possibility of death, as he went in to bid his parent good-by before starting off on his trip through the air. Mr. Swift barely knew his son, and, with tears in his eyes, though he bravely tried to keep them back, the young inventor went out into the yard.

There stood the *Humming-Bird*, with Mr. Jackson, Mr. Damon and Eradicate working over her, to get her in perfect trim for the race before her—a race with death.

Fortunately there was little to be done to get the speedy craft ready. Tom had accomplished most of what was necessary, while waiting for word from Dr. Hendrix. Now about all that needed to be done was to see that there was plenty of gasoline and oil in the reservoirs.

"I'll give you a note to Dr. Hendrix," said Mr. Gladby, as Tom was fastening on his faceguard. "I—I trust you won't be disappointed, Tom. I hope he will consent to return with you."

"He's got to come," said the young inventor, simply, as if that was all there was to it.

"Do you think you can make the trip in time?" asked Mr. Damon. "It is a little less than a hundred miles in an airline, but you have to go and go back. Can the aeroplane do it?"

"I'd be ashamed of her if she couldn't," said Tom, with a grim tightening of his lips. "She's just got to do it; that's all! But I know she will," and he patted the big propeller and the motor's shining cylinders as though the machine was a thing alive, like a horse or a dog, who could understand him.

He climbed to his seat, the other one holding a bag of sand to maintain a good balance.

"Start her," ordered Tom, and Mr. Jackson twisted the propeller. The motor caught at once, and the air throbbed with the noise of the explosions. Tom listened to the tune of the machinery. It sang true.

"Two thousand pounds thrust!" called the engineer, as he looked at the scale.

"Let her go!" cried Tom, whose voice was hardly heard above the roar. The trim little aeroplane scudded over the ground, gathering speed at every revolution of the wheels. Then with a spring like that of some great bird launching itself in flight, she left the earth, and took to the air. Tom was off on his trip.

Those left behind sent up a cautious cheer, for they did not want to disturb Mr. Swift. They waved their hands to the young inventor, and he waved his in reply. Then he settled down for one of the swiftest flights he had ever undertaken.

Tom ascended until he struck a favorable current of air. There was a little wind blowing in the direction he wished to take, and that aided him. But even against a powerful head-wind the *Humming-Bird* could make progress.

The young inventor saw the ground slipping backward beneath him. Carefully he watched the various indicators, and listened intently to the sound of the cylinders' explosions. They came rapidly and regularly. The motor was working well.

Tom glanced at the barograph. It registered two thousand feet, and he decided to keep at about that height, as it gave him a good view, and he could see to steer, for a route had been hastily mapped out for him by his friends.

Over cities, towns, villages, scattered farmhouses; across stretches of forest; over rivers, above big stretches of open country he flew. Often he could see eager crowds below, gazing up at him. But he paid no heed. He was looking for a sight of a certain broad river, which was near Kirkville. Then he knew he would be close to his goal.

He had speeded up the motor to the limit, and there was nothing to do now, save to manage the planes, wing tips and rudders, and to see that the gasoline and oil were properly fed to the machine.

Faster and faster went the *Humming-Bird*, but Tom's thoughts were even faster. He was thinking of many things— of his father—of what he would do if Mr. Swift died—of the mysterious airship—of the stolen plans—of the fire in the shed—of the great race—and of Andy Foger.

He took little note of time, and when, in less than an hour he sighted the river that told him he was near to Kirkville, he was rather startled.

"You certainly did come right along, *Humming-Bird!*" he murmured proudly.

He descended several hundred feet, and, as he passed over the town, the people of which grew wildly excited, he looked about for the house of the noted specialist. He knew how to pick it out, for Dr. Gladby had described it to him, and Tom was glad to see, as he came within view of the residence, that it was surrounded by a large yard.

"I can land almost at his door," he said, and he did, volplaning to earth with an ease born of long practice.

To say that Dr. Hendrix was astonished when Tom dropped in on him in this manner, would not be exactly true. The specialist was not in the habit of receiving calls from youths in aeroplanes, but the fact was, that Dr. Hendrix was so absorbed in his work, and thought so constantly about it, that it took a great deal to startle him out of his usual calm.

"And so you came for me in your aeroplane?" he asked of Tom, as he gazed at the trim little craft. It is doubtful if he really saw it, however, as Dr. Hendrix was just then thinking of an operation he had performed a few hours before. "I'm sorry you had your trip for nothing," he went on. "I'd like very much to come to your father, but didn't you get my telegram, telling about the broken bridge? There is no way for me to get to Shopton in time."

"Yes, there is!" cried Tom, eagerly.

"How?"

"The same way I came—in the aeroplane! Dr. Hendrix you must go back with me! It's the only way to save my father's life. Come with me in the *Humming-Bird*. It's perfectly safe. I can make the trip in less than an hour. I can carry you and your instruments. Will you come? Won't you come to save my father's life?" Tom was fairly pleading now.

"A trip in an aeroplane," mused Dr. Hendrix "I've never taken such a thing. I—"

"Don't be afraid, there's really no danger," said Tom.

The physician seemed to reach a sudden conclusion. His eyes brightened. He walked over and looked at the little *Humming-Bird*. For the time being he forgot about his operations.

"I'll go with you!" he suddenly cried. "I'll go with you, Tom Swift! If you've got the nerve, so have I! and if my science and skill can save your father's life, he'll live to be an old man! Wait until I get my bag and I'll be with you!"

Tom's heart gave a bound of hope.

JUST IN TIME

While Dr. Hendrix was in his office, getting ready to make the thrilling trip through the air with Tom, the young inventor spent a few minutes going over his monoplane. The wonderful little craft had made her first big flight in excellent time, though Tom knew she could do better the farther she was flown. Not a stay had started, not a guy wire was loose. The motor had not overheated, and every bearing was as cool as though it had not taken part in thousands of revolutions.

"Oh, I can depend on you!" murmured Tom, as he looked to see that the propeller was tight on the shaft. He gave the bearing a slight adjustment to make sure of it.

He was at this when the specialist reappeared. Dr. Hendrix, after his first show of excitement, when he had made his decision to accompany Tom, had resumed his usual calm demeanor. Once again he was the grave surgeon, with his mind on the case before him.

"Well, is my auto ready?" he asked absentmindedly. Then, as he saw the little aeroplane, and Tom standing waiting beside it, he added: "Oh, I forgot for the moment that I was to make a trip through the air, instead of in my car. Well, Mr. Swift, are we all ready?"

"All ready," replied the young inventor. "We're going to make fast time, Dr. Hendrix. You'd better put this on," and Tom extended a face protector.

"What's it for?" The physician looked curiously at it.

"To keep the air from cutting your cheeks and lips. We are going to travel a hundred miles an hour this trip."

"A hundred miles an hour!" Dr. Hendrix spoke as though he would like to back out.

"Maybe more, if I can manage it," went on Tom, calmly, as he proceeded to remove the bag of sand from the place where the surgeon was to sit. Then he looked to the various equilibrium arrangements and the control levers. He was so cool about it, taking it all for granted, as if rising and flying through the air at a speed rivaling that of the fastest birds, was a matter of no moment, that Dr. Hendrix was impressed by the calm demeanor of the young inventor.

"Very well," said the surgeon with a shrug of his shoulders, "I guess I'm game, Tom Swift."

The doctor took the seat Tom pointed out to him, with his bag of instruments on his knees. He put on the face protector, and had, at the suggestion of our hero, donned a heavy coat.

"For it's cold in the upper regions," said Tom.

Several servants in the physician's household had gathered to see him depart in this novel fashion, and the chauffeur of the auto, in which the specialist usually made his calls, was also there.

"I'll give you a hand," said the chauffeur to the young inventor. "I was at an aviation meet once, and I know how it's done."

"Good," exclaimed Tom. "Then you can hold the machine, and shove when I give the word."

Tom started the propeller himself, and quickly jumped into his seat. The chauffeur held back the *Humming-Bird* until the young aviator had speeded up the motor.

"Let go!" cried the youthful inventor, and the man gave the little craft a shove. Across the rather uneven ground of the doctor's yard it ran, straight for a big iron barrier.

"Look out! We'll be into the fence!" shouted the surgeon. "We'll be killed!" He seemed about to leap off.

"Sit still!" cried Tom, and at that instant he tilted the elevation planes, and the craft shot upward, going over the fence like a circus horse taking a seven-barred gate.

"Oh!" exclaimed the physician in a curious voice. They were off on their trip to save the life of Mr. Swift.

What the sensations of the celebrated specialist were, Tom never learned. If he was afraid, his fright quickly gave place to wonder, and the wonder soon changed to delight as the machine rose higher and higher, acquired more speed, and soared in the air over the country that spread out in all directions from Kirkville.

"Magnificent! Magnificent!" murmured the doctor, and then Tom knew that the surgeon was in the grip of the air, and was one of the "bird-men."

Every moment the *Humming-Bird* increased her speed. They passed over the river near where men were working on the broken bridge. It was now no barrier to them. Tom, noting the barograph, and seeing that they were twenty-two hundred feet high, decided to keep at about that distance from the earth.

"How fast are we going?" cried Dr. Hendrix, into the ear of the young inventor.

"Just a little short of a hundred an hour!" Tom shouted back. "We'll hit a hundred and five before long."

His prediction proved true, and when about forty miles from Shopton that terrific speed had been attained. It seemed as if they were going to have a trip devoid of incident, and Tom was congratulating himself on the quick time made, when he ran into a contrary strata of air. Almost before he knew it the *Humming-Bird* gave a dangerous and sickening dive, and tilted at a terrifying angle.

"Are we going to turn turtle?" cried the doctor.

"I—I hope not!" gasped Tom. He could not understand why the equilibrium weights did not work, but he had no time then to investigate. Quickly he warped the wing tips and brought the craft up on an even keel.

He gave a sigh of relief as the aeroplane was once more shooting forward, and he was not mistaken when he thought he heard Dr. Hendrix murmur a prayer of thankfulness. Their escape had been a narrow one. Tom's nerve, and the coolness of the physician, had alone saved them from a fall to death.

But now, as if ashamed of her prank, the *Humming-Bird* went along even better than before. Tom was peering through the slight haze that hung over the earth, for a sight of Shopton. At length the spires of the churches came into view.

"There it is," he called, pointing downward. "We'll land in two minutes more."

"No time to spare," murmured the doctor, who knew the serious nature of the aged inventor's illness. "How long did it take us?"

"Fifty-one minutes," replied Tom, glancing at a small clock in front of him. Then he shut off the motor and volplaned to earth, to the no small astonishment of the surgeon. He made a perfect landing in the yard before the shed, leaped from his seat, and called:

"Come, Dr. Hendrix!"

The surgeon followed him. Dr. Gladby and Dr. Kurtz came to the door of the house. On their faces were grave looks. They greeted the celebrated surgeon eagerly.

"Well?" he asked quickly, and they knew what he meant.

"You are only just in time," said Dr. Gladby, softly, and Tom, following the doctors into the house, wondered if his trip with the specialist had been in vain.

"Will He Live?"

Soon there were busy scenes in the Swift home, as preparations were made for a serious operation on the aged inventor. Tom's father had sunk into deep unconsciousness, and was stretched out on the bed as though there was no more life in him. In fact, Tom, for the moment, feared that it was all over. But good old Dr. Kurtz, noting the look on the lad's face, said:

"Ach, Dom, doan't vorry! Maybe it vill yet all be vell, und der vater vill hear of der great race. Bluck up your courage, und doan't gif up. Der greatest surgeon in der vorld is here now, und if anybody gan safe your vater, Herr Hendriz gan. Dot vos a great drip you made—a great drip!"

Tom felt a little comforted and, after a sight of his father, and a silent prayer that God would spare his life for years to come, the young inventor went out in the yard. He wanted to be busy about something, for he knew, with the doctors, and a trained nurse who had been hastily summoned, there was no immediate need for him. He wanted to get his mind off the operation that would soon take place, and so he decided to look over his aeroplane.

Mr. Damon came out when Tom was going over the guy wires and braces, to see how they had stood the strain.

"Well, Tom, my lad," said the eccentric man, sadly, as he grasped our hero's hand, "it's too bad. But hope for the best. I'm sure your father will pull through. We will have to begin taking the *Humming-Bird* apart soon; won't we, if we're going to ship it to Eagle Park?" He wanted to take Tom's mind off his troubles.

"I don't know whether we will or not," was the answer, and Tom tried to speak unbrokenly, but there was a troublesome lump in his throat, and a mist of tears in his eyes that prevented him from seeing well. The Hamming-Bird, to him, looked as if she was in a fog.

"Nonsense! Of course we will!" cried Mr. Damon. "Why, bless my wishbone! Tom, you don't mean to say you're going to let that little shrimp Andy Foger walk away with that ten-thousand-dollar prize without giving him a fight for it; are you?"

This was just what Tom needed, and it seemed good to have Mr. Damon bless something again, even if it was only a wishbone.

"No!" exclaimed Tom, in ringing tones. "Andy Foger isn't going to beat me, and if I find out he is going to race with a machine made after my stolen plans, I'll make him wish he'd never taken them."

"But if the machine he had flying over here when he dropped that bomb on the shed roof, and set fire to it, is the one he's going to race with, it isn't like yours," suggested Mr. Damon, who was glad he had turned the conversation into a more cheerful channel.

"That's so," agreed the young inventor. "We'll, we'll have to wait and see." He was busy now, going over every detail of the *Humming-Bird*. Mr. Damon helped him, and they discovered the defect in the equilibrium weights, and remedied it.

"We can't afford to have an accident in the race," said Tom. He glanced toward the house, and wondered if the operation had begun yet. He could see the trained nurse hurrying here and there, Mrs. Baggert helping her.

Eradicate Sampson shuffled out from the stable where he kept his mule Boomerang. On the face of the honest colored man there was a dejected look.

"Am Massa Swift any better, Massa Tom?" he asked.

"We can't tell yet," was the answer.

"Well, if he doan't git well, den I'm goin' t' sell mah mule," went on the dirt-chaser, from which line of activity Eradicate had derived his name.

"Sell Boomerang! Bless my curry comb! what for?" asked Mr. Damon.

"'Case as how he wouldn't neber be any good fo' wuk any mo'," explained Eradicate. "He's got so attached t' dis place, an' all de folkes on it, dat he'd feel so sorry ef— ef—well, ef any ob 'em went away, dat I couldn't git no mo' wuk out ob him, no how. So ef Massa Swift doan't git well, den I an' Boomerang parts!"

"Well, we hope it won't happen," said Tom, greatly touched by the simple grief of Eradicate. The young inventor was silent a moment, and then he softly added: "I—I wonder when—when we'll know?"

"Soon now, I think," answered Mr. Damon, in a low voice.

Silently they waited about the aeroplane. Tom tried to busy himself, but he could not. He kept his eyes fastened on the house.

It seemed like several hours, but it was not more than one, ere the white-capped nurse came to the door and waved her hand to Tom. He sprang to his feet and rushed forward. What would be the message he was to receive?

He stood before the nurse, his heart madly beating. She looked gently at him.

"Will he—will he live?" Tom asked, pantingly.

"I think so," she answered gently. "The operation is over. It was a success, so far. Time alone will tell, now. Dr. Hendrix says you can see your father for lust a moment."

OFF TO THE MEET

Softly Tom tiptoed into the room where his father lay. At the bedside were the three doctors, and the nurse followed the young inventor in. Mrs. Baggert stood in the hall, and near her was Garret Jackson. The aged housekeeper had been weeping, but she smiled at Tom through her tears.

"I think he's going to get well," she whispered. She always looked on the bright side of things. Tom's heart felt better.

"You must only speak a few words to him," cautioned the specialist, who had performed such a rare and delicate operation, near the heart of the invalid. "He is very weak, Tom."

Mr. Swift opened his eyes as his son approached. He looked around feebly.

"Tom—are you there?" he asked in a whisper.

"Yes, dad," was the eager answer

"They tell me you—you made a great trip to get Dr. Hendrix—broken bridge—came through the air with him. Is that right?"

"Yes, dad. But don't tire yourself. You must get well and strong."

"I will, Tom. But tell me; did you go in—in the *Humming-Bird*?"

"Yes, dad."

"How did she work?"

"Fine. Over a hundred, and the motor wasn't at its best."

"That's good. Then you can go in the big race, and win."

"No, I don't believe I'll go, dad."

"Why not?" Mr. Swift spoke mort strongly

"I—because—well, I don't want to."

"Nonsense, Tom! I know; it's on my account. I know it is. But listen to me. I want you to go in! I want you to win that race! Never mind about me. I'm going to get well, and I'll recover all the more quickly if you win that race. Now promise me you'll go in it and—and—win!"

The invalid's strength was fast leaving him.

"I—I—," began Tom.

"Promise!" insisted the aged inventor, trying to rise. Dr. Hendrix made a hasty move toward the bed.

"Promise!" whispered the surgeon to Tom.

"I—I promise!" exclaimed Tom, and the aged inventor sank back with a smile of satisfaction on his pale face.

"Now you must go," said Dr. Gladby to Tom. "He has talked long enough. He must sleep now, and get up his strength."

"Will he get better?" asked Tom, anxiously.

"We can't say for sure," was the answer. "We have great hopes."

"I don't want to enter the race unless I know he is going to live," went on Tom, as Dr. Gladby followed him out of the room.

"No one can say for a certainty that he will recover," spoke the physician. "You will have to hope for the best, that is all, Tom. If I were you I'd go in the race. It will occupy your mind, and if you could send good news to your father it might help him in the fight for life he is making."

"But suppose—suppose something happens while I am away?" suggested the young inventor.

The doctor thought for a moment. Then he exclaimed:

"You have a wireless outfit on your craft; haven't you?"

"Yes."

"Then you can receive messages from here every hour if you wish. Garret Jackson, your engineer, can send them, and you can pick them up in mid-air if need be."

"So I can!" cried Tom. "I will go to the meet. I'll take the *Humming-Bird* apart at once, and ship it to Eagle Park. Unless Dr. Hendrix wants to go back in it," he added as an after thought.

"No," spoke Dr. Gladby, "Dr. Hendrix is going to remain here for a few days, in case of an emergency. By that time the bridge will have been repaired, and he can go back by train. I gather, from what he said, that though he liked the air trip, he will not care for another one."

"Very well," assented Tom, and Mr. Damon and he were kept busy, packing the *Humming-Bird* for shipment. Mr. Jackson helped them, and Eradicate and his mule Boomerang were called on occasionally when boxes or crates were to be taken to the railroad station.

In the meanwhile, Mr. Swift, if he did not improve any, at least held his own. This the doctors said was a sign of hope, and, though Tom was filled with anxiety, he tried to think that fate would be kind to him, and that his father would recover. Dr. Hendrix left, saying there was nothing more he could do, and that the rest depended on the local physicians, and on the nurse.

"Und ve vill do our duty!" ponderously exclaimed Dr. Kurtz. "You go off to dot bird race, Dom, und doan't vorry. Ve vill send der with-out-vire messages to you venever dere is anyt'ing to report. Go mit a light heart!"

How Tom wished he could, but it was out of the question. The last of the parts of the *Humming-Bird* had been sent away, and our hero forwarded a telegram to Mr. Sharp, of the arrangement committee, stating that he and Mr. Damon would soon follow. Then, having bidden his father a fond farewell, and after arranging with Mr. Jackson to send frequent wireless messages, Tom and the eccentric man left for the meet.

There was a wireless station at Eagle Park, and Tom had planned to receive the messages from home there until he could set up his own plant. He would have two outfits. One in the big tent where the *Humming-Bird* was to be put together, and another on the machine itself, so that when in the air, practicing, or even in the great race itself, there would be no break in the news that was to be flashed through space.

Tom and Mr. Damon arrived at Eagle Park on time, and Tom's first inquiry was for a message from home. There was one, Stating that Mr. Swift was fairly comfortable, and seemed to be doing well. With happiness in his heart, the young inventor then set about getting the parts of his craft from the station to the park, where he and Mr. Damon, with a trusty machinist whom Mr. Sharp had recommended, would assemble it. Tom arranged that in his absence the wireless operator on the grounds would take any message that came for him.

The *Humming-Bird*, in the big cases and boxes, had safely arrived, and these were soon in the tent which had been assigned to Tom. It was still several days until the opening of the meet, and the grounds presented a scene of confusion.

Workmen were putting up grand stands, tents and sheds were being erected, exhibitors were getting their machines in shape, and excited contestants of many nationalities were hurrying to and fro, inquiring about parts delayed in shipment, or worrying lest some of their pet ideas be stolen.

Tom and Mr. Damon, with Frank Forker, the young machinist, were soon busy in their big tent, which was a combined workshop and living quarters, for Tom had determined to stay right on the ground until the big race was over.

"I don't see anything of Andy Foger," remarked Mr. Damon, on the second day of their residence in the park. "There are lots of new entries arriving, but he doesn't seem to be on hand."

"There's time enough," replied Tom. "I am afraid he's hanging back until the last minute, and will spring his machine so late that I won't have time to lodge a protest. It would be just like him."

"Well, I'll be on the lookout for him. Have you heard from home to-day, Tom?"

"No. I'm expecting a message any minute." The young inventor glanced toward the wireless apparatus which had been set up in the tent. At that moment there came the peculiar sound which indicated a message coming through space, and down the receiving wires. "There's something now!" exclaimed Tom, as he hurried over and clamped the telephone receiver to his ear. He listened a moment.

"Good news!" he exclaimed. "Dad sat up a little to-day! I guess he's going to get well!" and he clicked back congratulations to his father and the others in Shopton.

Another day saw the *Humming-Bird* almost in shape again, and Tom was preparing for a tryout of the engine.

Mr. Damon had gone over to the committee headquarters to consult with Mr. Sharp about the steps necessary for Tom to take in case Andy did attempt to enter a craft that infringed on the ideas of the young inventor, and on his way back he saw a newly-erected tent. There was a young man standing in the entrance, at the sight of whom the eccentric man murmured:

"Bless my skate-strap! His face looks very familiar!"

The youth disappeared inside the tent suddenly, and, as Mr. Damon came opposite the canvas shelter, he started in surprise.

For, on a strip of muslin which was across the tent, painted in gay colors, were the words:

The Foger Aeroplane

"Bless my elevation rudder!" cried Mr. Damon. "Andy's here at last! I must tell Tom!"

THE GREAT RACE

"Well," remarked Mr. Sharp, when Tom and Mr. Damon had called on him, to state that Andy Foger's machine was now on the grounds, and demanding to be allowed to view it, to see if it was an infringement on the one entered by the young inventor, "I'll do the best I can for you. I'll lay the case before the committee. It will meet at once, and I'll let you know what they say."

"Understand," said Tom, "I don't want to interfere unless I am convinced that Andy is trying an underhand trick. My plans are missing, and I think he took them. If his machine is made after those plans, it is, obviously, a steal, and I want him ruled out of the meet."

"And so he shall be!" exclaimed Mr. Sharp. "Get the evidence against him, and we'll act quickly enough."

The committee met in about an hour, and considered the case. Meanwhile, Tom and Mr. Damon strolled past the tent with its flaring sign. There was a man on guard, but Andy was not in sight.

Then Tom was sent for, and Mr. Sharp told him what conclusion had been arrived at. It was this:

"Under the rules of the meet," said the balloonist, "we had to guarantee privacy to all the contestants until such time as they choose to exhibit their machines. That is, they need not bring them out until just before the races," he added. "This is not a handicap affair, and the speediest machine, or the one that goes to the greatest height, according to which class it enters, will win. In consequence we cannot force any contestant to declare what kind of a machine he will use until he gets ready.

"Some are going to use the familiar type of biplanes and, as you can see, there is no secret about them. They are trying them out now." This was so, for several machines of this type were either in the air, circling about, or were being run over the ground.

"But others," continued Mr. Sharp, "will not even take the committee into their confidence until just before the race. They want to keep their craft a secret. We can't compel them to do otherwise. I'm sorry, Tom, but the only thing I see for you to do is to wait until the last minute. Then, if you find Andy has infringed on your machine, lodge a protest— that is unless you can get evidence against him before that time."

Tom well knew the uselessness of the latter plan. He and Mr. Damon had tried several times to get a glimpse of the craft Andy had made, but without success. As to the other alternative—that of waiting until the last moment—Tom feared that, too, would be futile.

"For," he reasoned, "just before the race there will be a lot of confusion, officials will be here and there, scattered over the ground, they will be hard to find, and it will be almost useless to protest then. Andy will enter the race, and there is a possibility that he may win. Almost any one could with a machine like the *Humming-Bird*. It's the machine almost as much as the operator, in a case like this."

"But you can protest after the race," suggested Mr. Damon.

"That would be little good, in case Andy beat me. The public would say I was a sorehead, and jealous. No, I've either got to stop Andy before the race, or not at all. I will try to think of a plan."

Tom did think of several, but abandoned them one after the other. He tried to get a glimpse inside the tent where the Foger aeroplane Was housed, but it was too closely guarded. Andy himself was not much in evidence, and Tom only had fleeting glimpses of the bully.

Meanwhile he and Mt Damon, together with their machinist, were kept busy. As Tom's craft was fully protected by patents now, he had no hesitation in taking it out, and it was given several severe tests around the aerial course. It did even better than Tom expected of it, and he had great hopes.

Always, though, there were two things that worried him. One was his father's illness, and the other the uneasiness he felt as to what Andy Foger might do. As to the former, the wireless reports indicated that Mr. Swift was doing as well as could be expected, but his improvement was not rapid. Regarding the latter worry, Tom saw no way of getting rid of it.

"I've just got to wait, that's all," he thought.

The day before the opening of the meet, Tom and Mr. Damon had given the *Humming-Bird* a grueling tryout. They had taken her high up—so high that no prying eyes could time them, and there Tom had opened the motor for all the power in it. They had flashed through space at the rate of one hundred and twenty miles an hour.

"If we can only do that in the race, the ten thousand dollars is mine!" exulted Tom, as he slanted the nose of the aeroplane toward the earth.

The day of the race dawned clear and beautiful. Tom was up early, for there remained many little things to do to get his craft in final trim for the contest. Then, too, he wanted to be ready to act promptly as soon as Andy's machine was wheeled out, and he also wanted to get a message from home.

The wireless arrived soon after breakfast, and did not contain very cheering news.

"Your father not so well," Mr. Jackson sent. "Poor night, but doctor thinks day will show improvement. Don't worry."

"Don't worry! I wonder who could help it," mused poor Tom. "Well, I'll hope for the best," and he wired back to tell the engineer in Shopton to keep in touch with him, and to flash the messages to the *Humming-Bird* in the air, after the big race started.

"Now I'll go out and see if I can catch a glimpse of what that sneak Andy has to pit against me," said Tom.

The Foger tent was tightly closed, and Tom turned back to his own place, having arranged with a messenger to come and let him know as soon as Andy's craft was wheeled out.

All about was a scene of great activity. The grand stands were filled, and a big crowd stood about the field anxiously waiting for the first sight of the "bird-men" in their wonderful machines. Now and then the band blared out, and cheers arose as one after another the frail craft were wheeled to the starting place.

Men in queer leather costumes darted here and there-they were the aviators who were soon to risk life and limb for glory and gold. Most of them were nervously smoking cigarettes. The air was filled with guttural German or nasal French, while now and then the staccato Russian was heard, and occasionally the liquid tones of a Japanese. For men of many nations were competing for the prizes.

The majority of the machines were monoplanes and biplanes though one triplane was entered, and there were several "freaks" as the biplane and monoplane men called them—craft of the helicopter, or the wheel type. There was also one Witzig Liore Dutilleul biplane, with three planes behind.

Tom was familiar with most of these types, but occasionally he saw a new one that excited his curiosity. However, he was more interested in what Andy Foger would turn out. Andy's machine had not been tried, and Tom wondered how he dared risk flying in it, without at least a preliminary tryout. But Andy, and those with him, were evidently full of confidence.

News of the suspicions of Tom, and what he intended to do in case these suspicions proved true, had gotten around, and there was quite a crowd about his own tent, and another throng around that of Andy.

Tom and Mr. Damon had wheeled the *Humming-Bird* out of her canvas "nest.". There was a cheer as the crowd caught sight of the trim little craft. The young inventor, the eccentric man, and the machinist were busy going over every part.

Meanwhile the meet had been officially opened, and it was announced that the preliminary event would be some air evolutions at no great height, and for no particular prize. Several biplanes and monoplanes took part in this. It was very interesting, but the big ten-thousand-dollar race, over a distance of a hundred miles was the principal feature of the meet, and all waited anxiously for this.

The opening stunts passed off successfully, save that a German operator in a Bleriot came to grief, crashing down to the ground, wrecking his machine, and breaking an arm. But he only laughed at that, and coolly demanded another cigarette, as he crawled out of the tangle of wires, planes and the motor.

After this there was an exhibition flight by a French aviator in a Curtis biplane, who raced against one in a Baby Wright. It was a dead heat, according to the judges. Then came a flight for height; and while no records were broken, the crowd was well satisfied.

"Get ready for the hundred-mile ten-thousand-dollar-prize race!" shouted the announcer, through his megaphone.

Tom's heart gave a bound. There were seven entrants in this contest besides Tom and Andy Foger, and as announced by the starter they were as follows:

CONTESTANT	MACHINE
Von Bergen Wright	Biplane
Alameda Antoinette	Monoplane
PeriqueBleriot	Monoplane
Loi Tong Santos-Dumont	Monoplane
Wendell Curtis	Biplane
De Tromp Farman	Biplane
Lascalle Demoiselle	Monoplane
Andy Foger	
Tom Swift	Monoplane

"What is the style of the Foger machine?" yelled some one in the crowd, as the announcer lowered his megaphone.

"It has not been announced," was the reply. "It will at once be wheeled out though, in accordance with the conditions of the race."

There was a craning of necks, and an uneasy movement in the crowd, for Tom's story was now generally known.

"Get ready to make your protest," advised Mr. Damon to the young inventor. "I'll stay by the machine here until you come back. Bless my radiator! I hope you beat him!"

"I will, if it's possible!" murmured Tom, with a grim tightening of his lips.

There was a movement about Andy's tent, whence, for the last half hour had come spasmodic noises that indicated the trying-out of the motor. The flaps were pulled back and a curious machine was wheeled into view. Tom rushed over toward it, intent on getting the first view. Would it prove to be a copy of his speedy *Humming-Bird*?

Eagerly he looked, but a curious sight met his eyes. The machine was totally unlike any he had expected to see. It was large, and to his mind rather clumsy, but it looked powerful. Then, as he took in the details, he knew that it was the same one that had flown over his house that night — it was the one from which the fire bomb had been dropped.

He pushed his way through the crowd. He saw Andy standing near the curious biplane, which type of air craft it nearest resembled, though it had some monoplane features. On the side was painted the name:

Slugger

Andy caught sight of Tom Swift.

"I'm going to beat you!" the bully boasted, and I haven't a machine like yours, after all. You were wrong."

"So I see," stammered Tom, hardly knowing what to think. "What did you do with my plans then?"

"I never had them!"

Andy turned away, and began to assist the men he had hired to help him. Like all the others, his machine had two seats, for in this race each operator must carry a passenger.

Tom turned away, both glad and sorry,—glad that his rival was not to race him in a duplicate of the *Humming-Bird*, but sorry that he had as yet no track of the strangely missing plans.

"I wonder where they can be?" mused the young inventor.

Then came the firing of the preliminary gun. Tom rushed back to where Mr. Damon stood waiting for him.

There was a last lock at the *Humming-Bird*. She was fit to race any machine on the ground. Mr. Damon took his place. Tom started the propeller. The other contestants were in their seats with their passengers. Their assistants stood ready to shove them off. The explosions of so many motors in action were deafening.

"How much thrust?" cried Tom to his machinist.

"Twenty-two hundred pounds!"

"Good!"

The report of the starting-gun could not be heard. But the smoke of it leaped into the air. It was the signal to go.

Tom's voice would not have carried five feet. He waved his hands as a signal. His helper thrust the *Humming-Bird* forward. Over the smooth ground it rushed. Tom looked eagerly ahead. On a line with him were the other machines, including Andy Foger's Slugger.

Tom pulled a lever. He felt his craft soar upward. The other machines also pointed their noses into the air.

The big race for the ten-thousand-dollar prize was under way!

Won by a Length

Rising upward, on a steep slant, for he wanted to get into the upper currents as soon as possible, Tom looked down and off to his left and saw one machine going over the ground in curious leaps and bounds. It was the tiny Demoiselle—the smallest craft in the race, and its peculiar style of starting was always thus manifested.

"I don't believe he's going to make it," thought Tom.

He was right. In another moment the tiny craft, after rising a short distance, dove downward, and was wrecked. The young inventor saw the two men crawling out from the tangled planes and wings, apparently uninjured.

"One contestant less," thought Tom, grimly, though with pity in his heart for the unfortunates.

However, he must think of himself and his own craft now. He glanced at Mr. Damon sitting beside him. That odd gentleman, with never a thought of blessing anything now, unless he did it silently, was watching the lubricating system. This was a vital part of the craft, for if anything went wrong with it, and the bearings overheated, the race would have to be abandoned. So Tom was not trusting to any automatic arrangement, but had instituted, almost at the last moment, a duplicate hand-worked system, so that if one failed him he would have the other.

"A good start!" shouted Mr. Damon in his car.

Tom nodded, and glanced behind him. On a line with the *Humming-Bird*, and at about the same elevation, were the Bleriot monoplane and a Wright biplane. Below were the Santos-Dumont and the Antoinette.

"Where's the Slugger?" called Tom to his friend.

Mr. Damon motioned upward. There, in the air above Tom's machine, and slightly in advance, was Andy Foger's craft. He had gotten away in better shape than had the *Humming-Bird*.

For a moment Tom's heart misgave him. Then he turned on more power, and had the satisfaction of mounting upward and shooting onward until he was on even terms with Andy.

The bully gave one glance over toward his rival, and pulled a lever. The *Slugger* increased her speed, but Tom was not a second behind him.

There was a roaring noise in the rear, and up shot De Tromp in the Farman, and Loi Tong, the little Japanese, in the Santos-Dumont. Truly the race was going to he a hotly contested one. But the end was far off yet.

After the first jockeying for a start and position, the race settled down into what might be termed a "grind." The course was a large one, but so favorable was the atmosphere that day, and such was the location of Eagle Park in a great valley, that even on the far side of the great ellipse the contestants could be seen, dimly with the naked eye, but very plainly with glasses, with which many of the spectators were provided.

Around and around they went, at no very great height, for it was necessary to make out the signals set up by the race officials, so that the contestants would know when they were near the finish, that they might use the last atom of speed. So at varying heights the wonderful machines circled about the course.

The *Humming-Bird* was working well, and Tom felt a sense of pride as he saw the ground slipping away below him. He felt sure that he would win, even when Alameda, the Spaniard, in the Antoinette, came creeping up on him, and even when Andy Foger, with a burst of speed, placed himself and his passenger in the lead.

"I'll catch him!" muttered Tom, and he opened the throttle a trifle wider, and went after Andy, passing him with ease.

They had covered about thirty miles of the course, when the humming and crackling of the wireless apparatus told Tom that a message was coming. He snapped the receiver to his ear, adjusting the outer covering to shut out the racket of the motor, and listened.

"Well?" asked Mr. Damon, as Tom took off the receiver.

"Dad isn't quite so well," answered the lad. "Mr. Jackson says they have sent for Dr. Hendrix again. But dad is game. He sends me word to go on and win, and I'll do it, too, only—"

Tom paused, and choked back a sob. Then he prepared to get more speed out of his motor.

"Of course you will!" cried Mr. Damon. "Bless my—!"

But they encountered an adverse current of wind at that moment, and it required the attention of both of the aviators to manage the machine. It was soon on an even keel again, and once more was shooting forward around the course.

At times Tom would be in advance, and again he would have to give place to the Curtis, the Farman, or the Santos-Dumont, as these speedy machines, favored by a spurt from their motors, or by some current of air, shot ahead. But, in general, Tom maintained the lead, and among the spectators there began a series of guesses as to how much he would win by.

Tom glanced at the barograph. It registered a little over twelve hundred feet. He looked at the speed gage. He was doing a trifle better than a hundred miles an hour. He looked down at the signals. There was twenty miles yet to go. It was almost time for the spurt for which he had been holding back. Yet he would wait until five miles from the end, and then he felt that he could gain and maintain a lead.

"Andy seems to be doing well," said Mr, Damon.

"Yes, he has a good machine," conceded Tom.

Five miles more were reeled off. Then an other five. Another round of that distance and Tom would key his motor up to the highest pitch, and then the *Humming-Bird* would show what she could do. Eagerly Tom waited for the right signal.

Suddenly the wireless began buzzing again. Quickly the young inventor clamped the receiver to his ear. Mr. Damon saw him turn pale.

"Dr. Gladby says dad has a turn for the worse. There is little hope," translated Tom.

"Will you—are you going to quit?" asked Mr. Damon.

Tom shook his head.

"No!" he cried. "My father has become unconscious, so Mr. Jackson says, but his last words were to me: 'Tell Tom to win the race!' And I'm going to do it!"

Tom suddenly changed his plans. There was to be no waiting for the signal now. He would begin his final spurt, and if possible finish the hundred miles at his utmost speed, win the race and then hasten to his father's side.

With a menacing roar the motor of the *Humming-Bird* took up the additional power that Tom sent into her. She shot ahead like an eagle darting after his prey. Tom opened up a big gap between his machine and the one nearest him, which, at that moment, was the Antoinette, with the Spaniard driving her.

"Now to win!" cried Tom, grimly.

Surely no race was ever flown as was that one! Tom flashed through the air so quickly that his speed was almost incredible. The gage registered one hundred and thirty miles an hour!

Down below in the grand stands, and on the aviation field, there were yells of approval—of wonder—of fear. But Tom and Mr. Damon could not hear them. They only heard the powerful song of the motor.

Faster and faster flew the *Humming-Bird* Tom looked down, and saw the signal put up which meant that there were but three miles more to go. He felt that he could do it. He was half a lap ahead of them all now. But he saw Andy Foger's machine pulling away from the bunch.

"He's going to try to catch me!" exulted Tom.

Then something happened. The motor of the *Humming-Bird* suddenly slackened its speed, it missed explosions, and the trim little craft began to drop behind.

"What's the matter?" cried Mr. Damon.

"Three of the cylinders are out of business!" yelled Tom. "We're done for, I guess."

On came the other machines, Andy in the lead, then the Santos-Dumont, then the Farman, and lastly the Wright. They saw the plight of the *Humming-Bird* and determined to beat her. Tom cast a despairing look up at the motor. There was nothing to be done. He could not reach it In mid-air. He could only keep on, crippled as he was, and trust to luck.

Andy passed by his rival with an evil smile on his ugly face. Then the Antoinette flashed by. In turn all the others left Tom in the rear Toms heart was like lead. Mr. Damon gazed blankly forward. They were beaten. It did not seem possible.

There was but a single chance. If Tom shut off all power, coasted for a moment, and then, ere the propeller had ceased revolving, if he could start the motor on the spark, the silent cylinders might pick up, with the others, and begin again. He would try it. They could be no worse off than they were.

"A mile behind!" gasped Tom. "It's a long chance, but I'll take it."

He shut off the power. The motor was silent. the *Humming-Bird* began to fall. But ere she had gone down ten feet Tom suddenly switched on the batteries. There was a moment of silence, and then came the welcome roar that told of the rekindled motor. And such a roar as it was! Every cylinder was exploding as though none of them had ever stopped!

"We did it!" yelled Tom. Opening up at full speed, he sent the sky racer on the course to overtake and pass his rivals.

Slowly he crept on them. They looked back and saw him coming. They tried to put on more speed, but it was impossible. Andy Foger was in the lead. He was being slowly overhauled by the Santos-Dumont, with the queer tail-rudders.

"I'll get him!" muttered Tom. "I'll pass 'em all!"

And he did. With a wonderful burst of speed the little *Humming-Bird* overtook one after another of her larger rivals, and passed them. Then she crept up on Andy's Slugger.

In an instant more it was done, and, a good length in advance of the Foger craft, Tom shot over the finish line a winner, richer by ten thousand dollars, and, not only that, but he had picked up a mile that had been lost, and had snatched victory from almost certain defeat.

There was a succession of thundering cheers as he shut off the motor, and volplaned to earth, but he paid little attention to them. He brought his craft to a stop just as the wireless on it buzzed again.

He listened with a look of pain on his face.

"My father is dying," he said simply. "I must go to him. Mr. Damon, will you fill the tanks with oil and gasoline, while I send off a message?"

"Oil and gasoline," murmured the odd man, while hundreds pressed up to congratulate Tom Swift "What are you going to do?"

"I'm going to my father in the *Humming-Bird*, said Tom. "It's the only way I can see him alive," and he began to click off a message to Mr. Jackson, stating that he had won the race and was going to fly to Shopton, while Mr. Damon and several others replenished the fuel and oil of the aeroplane.

Tom Swift had won one race. Could he win the other?

HOME AGAIN—CONCLUSION

Mr. Sharp pushed his way through the crowd.

"The committee has the certified check ready for you, Tom," called the balloonist. "Will you come and get it?"

"Send it to me, please," answered the young inventor. "I must go to my father."

"Huh! I'd have beaten him in another round," boasted Andy Foger. No one paid any attention to him.

"Monsieur ezz plucky!" said the Frenchman, Perique. "I am honaired to shake his hand! He has broken all ze records!"

"Dot's der best machine I effer saw," spoke the Dutchman, De Tromp, ponderously. "Shake hands!"

"Ver' fine, ver' good!" came from the little Japanese, and all the contestants congratulated Tom warmly. Never before had a hundred miles been covered so speedily.

A man elbowed his way through the press of people.

"Is your machine fully protected by patents?" he inquired earnestly.

"It is," said Tom.

"Then, as a representative of the United States Government, I would like an option to purchase the exclusive right to use them," said the man. "Can you guarantee that no one else has any plans of them? It will mean a fortune to you."

Tom hesitated. He thought of the stolen plans. If he could only get possession of them! He glanced at Andy Foger, who was wheeling his machine hack into the tent. But there was no time now to have it out with the bully.

"I will see you again," said Tom to the government agent. "I must go to my father, who is dying. I can't answer you now."

The tanks were filled. Tom gave a hasty look to his machine, and, bidding his new friends fairwell, he and Mr. Damon took their places aboard the *Humming-Bird*. The little craft rose in the air, and soon they had left Eagle Park far behind. Eagerly Tom strained his eyes for a sight of his home town, though he knew it would be several hours ere he could hover over it.

Would he be in time? Would he be in time? That question came to him again and again.

For a time the *Humming-Bird* skimmed along as though she delighted in the rapid motion, in slipping through the air and sliding along on the billows of wind. Tom, with critical ears, listened to the hum of the motor, the puffing of the exhaust, the grinding of the gear wheels, and the clicking of the trips, as valve after valve opened or closed to admit the mixture of air and gasoline, or closed to give the compression necessary for the proper explosion.

"Is she working all right?" asked Mr. Damon, anxiously, and, such was the strain on him that he did not think to bless anything. "Is she all right, Tom, my lad?"

"I think so. I'm speeding her to the limit. Faster than I ever did before, but I guess she'll do. She was built to stand a strain, and she's got to do it now!"

Then there was silence again, as they slid along through the air like a coaster gliding down a steep descent.

"It was a great race, wasn't it?" asked Mr. Damon, as he shifted to an easier position in his seat. "A great race, Tom. I didn't think you'd do it, one spell there."

"Neither did I," came the answer, as the young inventor changed the spark lever. "But I made up my mind I wouldn't be beaten by Andy Foger, if I could help it. Though it was taking a risk to shut off the current the way I did."

"A risk?"

"Yes; it might not have started again," and Tom looked down at the earth below them, as if measuring the distance he would have fallen had not his sky racer kept on at the critical moment.

"And—and if the current hadn't come on again; eh, Tom? Would we—?" Mr. Damon did not finish, but Tom knew what he meant.

"It would have been all up with us," he said simply. "I might have volplaned back to earth, but at the speed we were going, and at the height, around a curve, we might have turned turtle."

"Bless my—!" began Mr. Damon, and then he stopped. The thought of Tom's trouble came to him, and he realized that his words might grate on the feelings of his companion.

On they rushed through the air with the *Humming-Bird* speeded up faster and faster as she warmed to her task. The machinery seemed to be working perfectly, and as Tom listened to the hum a look of pleasure replaced the look of anxiety on his face.

"Don't you think we'll make it?" asked Mr. Damon, after another pause, during which they passed over a large city, the inhabitants exhibiting much excitement as they sighted the airship over their heads.

"We've got to make it!" declared Tom between his clenched teeth.

Ne turned on a little more gasoline, and there was a spurt in their speed which made Mr. Damon grasp the upright braces near him with firm hands, and his face became a little paler

"It's all right," spoke Tom, reassuringly. "There's no danger."

But Tom almost reckoned without his host, for a few moments later, as he was trying to get more revolutions out of the propellers, he ran into an adverse current of air.

In an instant the *Humming-Bird* was tilted up almost on her "beams' ends," so to speak, and had it not been that the young inventor quickly warped the wing tips, to counteract the pressure on one side, there might have been a different end to this story.

"Bless my——!" began Mr. Damon, but he got no further, for he had to bend his body as Tom did, to equalize the pressure of the wind current.

"A little farther over!" yelled the lad. "A little farther over this way, Mr. Damon!"

"But if I come any more toward you I'll be out of my seat!" objected the eccentric man.

"If you don't you'll be out of the aeroplane!" cried Tom grimly, and his companion leaned over as far as he could until the young pilot had brought the craft to an even keel again.

Then Tom speeded up the motor, which he had partly shut down as they passed through the danger zone, and again they were racing through space.

They were nearing Shopton now, as the lad and Mr. Damon could tell by the familiar landmarks which loomed up in sight. Tom strained his eyes for the first view of his home.

Suddenly, as they were skimming along, there came a cessation of the hum and roar that told of the perfectly-working motor. It was an ominous silence.

"What's—what's wrong?" gasped Mr. Damon.

"Something's given way," answered Tom quickly. "I'm afraid the magneto isn't sparking as it ought to."

"Well, can't we volplane hack to earth?" asked the odd man, for he had become familiar with this feat when anything happened to the motor.

"We could," answered Tom, "but I'm not going to."

"Why not?"

"Because we're too far from Shopton—and dad! I'm going to keep on. I've got to—if I want to be there in time!"

"But if the motor doesn't work?"

"I'll make her work!"

Tom was desperately manipulating the various levers and handles connected with the electrical ignition system. He tried in vain to get the magneto to resume the giving out of sparks, and, failing in that, he switched on the batteries. But, to his horror, the dry cells had given out. There was no way of getting a spark unless the little electrical machine would work.

The propellers were still whirring around by their own momentum, and if Tom could switch in the magneto in time all might yet be well.

They had started to fall, but, by quickly bringing up the head plane tips, Tom sent his craft soaring upward again on a bank of air.

"Here!" he cried to Mr. Damon. "Take the steering-wheel and kept her on this level as long as you can."

"What are you going to do?"

"I've got to fix that magneto!"

"But if she dips down?"

"Throw up the head planes as I did. It's our only chance! I can't go down now, so far from Shopton!"

Mr. Damon reached over and took the wheel from Tom's hands. Then the young inventor, leaning forward, for the magneto was within easy reach, looked to see what the trouble was. He found it quickly. A wire had vibrated loose from a binding-post. In a second Tom had it in place again; and, ere the propellers had ceased revolving, he had turned the switch. The magneto took up the work in a flash. Once more the spark exploded the gasoline mixture, and the propellers sent the *Humming-Bird* swiftly ahead.

"We'll make it now!" declared Tom grimly.

"We're almost there," added Mr. Damon, as he relinquished the wheel to the young pilot. The craft had gone down some, but Tom sent her up again.

Nearer and nearer home they came, until at last the spires of the Shopton churches loomed into view. Then he was over the village. Now he was within sight of his own house.

Tom coasted down a bank of air, and brought the *Humming-Bird* up with a jerk of the ground brakes. Before the wheels had ceased turning he had leaped out.

"It's Massa Tom!" cried Eradicate, as he saw Tom alight.

The young inventor hurried into the house. He was met by the nurse, who held up a warning finger. Tom's heart almost stopped beating. He was aware that Dr. Gladby came from the room where Mr. Swift lay.

"Is he—is he—am I too late?" gulped Tom.

"Hush!" cautioned the nurse.

Tom reeled, and would have fallen had not the doctor caught him, for the lad was weak and wornout.

"He is going to get well!" were the joyful words he heard, as if in a dream, and then his strength suddenly came back to him. "The crisis is just passed, Tom," went on Dr. Gladby, "and your father will recover, and be stronger than ever. Your good news of winning was like a tonic to him. Now let me congratulate you on the race." Tom had flashed by wireless a brief message of his success.

"Dad's news is better than all the congratulations in the world," he said softly, as he grasped the doctor's hand.

　　＊ ＊ ＊ ＊ ＊ ＊

It was a week later. Mr. Swift improved rapidly once the course of the disease was permanently checked, and he was soon able to sit up. Tom was with him in the room, talking of the great race, and how he had won. He fingered the certified check for ten thousand dollars that had just come to him by mail.

"You certainly did wonderfully well," said the aged inventor, softly. "Wonderfully well, Tom. I'm proud of you."

"You may well be," added Mr. Damon. "Bless my shoelaces, but I thought Andy Foger had us there one spell; didn't you, Tom?"

"Indeed I did. But you helped me win, Mr. Damon."

"Nonsense!" exclaimed the odd man.

"Yes, you did. You helped me a lot."

"Well, are you going to keep after more air-prizes, Tom, or are you going to try for something else?" asked his father.

"I don't believe I'll go in any more aeroplane races right away," answered the young inventor. "For some time I've been wanting to complete and perfect my electric rifle. I think I'll begin work on that soon."

"And go hunting?" asked Mr. Damon.

"I think so," answered Tom, dreamily. "I don't know just where, though."

Where he went, and what he shot, will be told in the next volume of this series, to be called: "Tom Swift and His Electric Rifle; or, Daring Adventures in Elephant Land."

For a few moments after Tom's announcement no one spoke, then the young inventor said:

"It's too bad that first set of plans were stolen. If I had them I could make a good deal with the Government about my little aeroplane. But they don't want to take up with it as long as there is a chance of some foreign nation getting information about the secret parts, and my patents won't hold abroad. I wonder if there is any way of getting those plans away from Andy Foger? I don't understand why he hasn't used them before this. I thought sure he would make a craft like the *Humming-Bird* to race against me."

"What plans are those?" asked Mr. Swift.

"Why, don't you remember?" asked Tom. "The ones I showed you one day, in the library, when you fell asleep, and some one slipped in and stole them."

A curious look came over Mr. Swift's face. He passed his hand across his brow.

"I am beginning to remember something I have been trying to recall ever since I became ill," he said slowly. "It is coming back to me. Those plans—in the library—I fell asleep, but before I did so I hid those plans, Tom!"

"You hid those plans!" Tom fairly shouted the words.

"Yes, I remember feeling a drowsy feeling coming on, and I feared lest some one might see the drawings. I got up and put them under the window, in a little, hollow place in the foundation wall. Then I came back in through the window again, and went to sleep. Then, on account of my illness, just as I once before forgot something, and thought the minister had called, I lost all recollection of them. I hid those plans."

Tom leaped to his feet. He rushed to the place named by his father. Soon his triumphant shout told of his success. He came hurrying back into the house with a roll of papers in his hands.

And there were the long-missing plans! damp and stained by the weather, but all there. No enemy had them, and Tom's secret was safe.

"Now I can accept the Government offer!" he cried. And a few weeks later he made a most advantageous deal with the United States officials for his patents.

Dr. Gladby explained that Mr. Swift's queer action was due to his illness. He became liable to lapses of memory, and one happened just after he hid away the plans. Even the hiding of them was caused by the peculiar condition of his brain. He had opened the library window, slipped oat with the papers, and hastened in again, to fall asleep in his chair, during the short time Tom was gone.

"And Andy Foger never took them at all," remarked Mary Nestor, when Tom was telling her about it a few days afterward.

"No. I guess I must apologize to him." Which Tom did, but Andy did not receive it very graciously, especially as Tom accused him of trying to destroy the *Humming-Bird*.

Andy denied this and denied having anything to do with the mysterious fire, and, as there was no way to prove him guilty, Tom could not proceed against him. So the matter was dropped.

Mr. Swift continued to improve, and was soon himself again, and able to resume his inventive work. Tom received several offers to give exhibition flights at big aero meets, but refused, as he was busy on his new rifle. Mr. Damon helped him.

Andy Foger made several successful flights in his queer aeroplane, which turned out to be the product of a German genius who was supplied with money by Mr. Foger. Andy became very proud, and boasted that he and the German were going abroad to give flights in Europe.

"I'd be glad if he would," said Tom, when he heard of the plan. "He wouldn't bother me then."

With the money received from winning the big race, and from his contracts from the Government, Tom Swift was now in a fair way to become quite wealthy. He was destined to have many more adventures; yet, come what might, never would he forget the thrilling happenings that fell to his lot while flying for the ten-thousand dollar prize in his sky racer.

www.ingramcontent.com/pod-product-compliance
Lightning Source LLC
Chambersburg PA
CBHW021507240626
47154CB00002B/529